Chasing Savannah

Dria Andersen

Dedication

To my husband who was my sounding board, my cheerleader, my critique partner, and all the things I needed to finish this project. I appreciate every hour, every word of input and most of all, your unwavering support.

To my family who had to deal with mommy being on in another world for hours at a time. Thank you for your patience.

To my sister Tina, who reads everything I write and gives me honest feedback and encouragement, thank you mucho mucho. I appreciate your continued support and cheerleading!

Thank you to every fan who continues to stick with me while I tell the stories playing in my head. I appreciate each and every one of you.

Table of Contents

Chapter 1

Cursing never helped.

Never.

And yet, some filthy words escaped Savannah Landry's mouth as the tire iron she was using slipped and scraped across her knuckles for the fourth time. She very much wanted to toss the blasted thing across the street, but, her son would be getting out of school in a little over an hour and she needed to change the flat tire on the front of her ancient sedan.

She could afford to get a new car, but she loved Patrice, her nickname for the battered sedan. It would take more than a flat tire, some alarming sounds, and a few stains on the car seats to get her to change it. Besides, as a mother of an eight-year-old, stains and dirt were bound to happen. Patrice had a few more good years in her.

"Fuggin, stupid piece of crap," she hissed, as she strained to turn the lug nut on her flat tire.

She dropped the tire iron, wincing as it hit her driveway with an angry twang. She took a few seconds to rest her arm. The sound of a heavy truck got louder, and curiosity had her peeking over her shoulder. A big U-Haul rounded the corner, pulling into the yard of the house next door.

New neighbors?

She lifted the iron and turned back to the tire, unwilling to be caught staring. The doors opened and closed with a loud slam and curiosity got the better of her. She turned her head for a quick peek. A tall woman jumped from the cab of the truck, her long curly hair hanging down her back in a ponytail. She was a curvaceous woman. Her rounded face was beautiful, with thick brows arched over large eyes and full lips.

Savannah took a look at her own reflection in the car door. The image, though obscured by dust, gave her a clear picture of a frazzled woman. She blew out a breath at her makeup-less face. Her mahogany skin was clear and smooth, thank God. Her large dark eyes were her favorite feature, the long thick lashes courtesy of her father. She ran a finger down her rounded nose, and pursed her full lips. She considered herself pretty on most days, so she shrugged off her temporary doubt in her appearance and went back to the tire.

"Christ all mighty!" She ground out as she bore down on the tire iron trying to make the lug nut budge.

Someone chuckled over her shoulder. She turned and sucked in a breath at the wide chest at her eye level. A black t-shirt, hugging the muscles across his chest and arms, hung loose over a pair of jeans covering his squatting legs. Thick legs, long legs.

Good lord the man's body was incredible.

He cleared his throat and she finally made her way up to his eyes. Dark, nearly black eyes watched her with an interested hooded gaze. He tilted his head and a hint of gold glinted in his eyes before disappearing. She almost dropped the iron in shock as her nerve endings came alive.

Mine.

It was her only thought as her eyes perused every inch of his face. His brown skin was clear, only marred by a dusting of his incoming beard. He smiled and her eyes widened as perfect teeth peeked between his thick lips.

Shock had her mute. She'd never been struck by instant attraction to anyone, let alone a stranger. She mentally shook herself.

Jesus H.

"Would you like some help?" His deep voice set off every nerve ending in her body.

"I, yes, yes please. I'm having a hard time loosening the nuts." Her cheeks burned as she held out the tire iron to him and worked to get her reaction under control.

"I'm Derrick Lincoln, my best friend, Theo is moving in next to you."

Savannah did a mental fist pump that the beautiful woman was not attached to him in a romantic capacity, but pasted on a polite smile. There was no call in mauling the man on their first meeting. "I'm Savannah."

His gaze raked her kneeling figure and she was really glad she'd worn a padded tank under her flannel shirt. It was, thankfully, not yet sticking to her despite the heat of the afternoon. Her jean shorts were frayed at the hem, and probably showed a lot more leg than was polite. She slid out of his way to let him get close to the tire. He gave her a little smile and fit the tire iron onto the lug nut. She lost herself watching the way his shoulders flexed as he worked. He'd nearly finished loosening the lug nuts, so she rolled the spare tire closer and sat on it while he finished the last one.

"It's a good thing you have a full-sized spare," he commented as he twisted the tire iron.

"Yeah, my ex-husband was adamant about it. Now that we don't live together, he's afraid I'd ride on a donut until it literally fell off."

He laughed and spared her a glance. "Would you?"

She shrugged. "It's likely I would've eventually remembered to buy a new tire."

"So, you're not married?"

"That's what you got from that story? Not that I could possibly be a flaky airhead, but that I'm single?" She joked.

"A flaky airhead wouldn't know how to change their own tire, for one." He pulled off the old tire and rolled it to the side.

She got off the spare and slid it to him.

"For two, you look like you'd be worth any possible aggravation." He stared at her a moment until she lowered her gaze.

Certainly not because she wanted to, it was compulsion. Which meant only one thing… She slowly inhaled, and caught the scent of hot days, and the woodsy fragrance of a sun baked forest. He wasn't human. She moved closer, the wild smell of fur and cat drifted to her. She'd recognize that scent anywhere.

He was a shifter.

She didn't know how to process that just yet.

First, she needed a drink of water, a fan, something to cool the heat flushing her body. "So, you're helping your best friend move?"

"Yes, he and his wife and kids."

She smiled, her interest peaked. She turned and spied a handsome man lifting the truck gate, two young boys trailing behind him chattering. "Oh, they look the same age as my son."

She was excited. Jamie would finally have kids in the neighborhood to play with. Most of their neighbors were retirees, or new families. There weren't any kids over the age of two on their street. She would definitely make it a point to go over and introduce themselves to the new neighbors.

"You have a son?"

She didn't detect any disappointment in his tone. "Yes, an eight-year-old, I'm headed to pick him up from school."

"All done, then, in time to get you on your way." He stood, brushing his hands along his thighs.

Of course her eyes followed every stroke. He cleared his throat and she hastily lifted her gaze. Gold flickered in his pupils, and his teeth gripped his bottom lip as he smiled and offered her his hand. She grabbed it and stood, stepping back as she realized how much taller than her he was. It was a delightful surprise. At five ten, there weren't a lot of men taller than her. Well, none outside of the men her grandfather had been trying to set her up with.

She held out her hand and he engulfed it with his own. The touch of his roughened palm sent a jolt through her and she stepped closer. Sensations she hadn't felt in years tingled across her skin and brought a sigh to her lips.

She cleared her throat, hoping to disguise the sudden longing. "Thank you so much for your help. It would've taken me forever."

"You're very welcome." His eyes pulled her in.

She held onto his hand, not wanting him to go. Her phone beeped several times, breaking their trance. "That's my alarm. I have to go get my son."

"You need an alarm?" Amusement danced in his eyes.

"Flaky, remember." She shook the phone at him. "Thank you again." She jumped in the car and waved as she cranked it.

Patrice purred as she put her in gear and backed out of the driveway. Despite what her ex-husband thought of her, and it had been one of their issues, she was not flaky. She took her son's safety very seriously. Though her car's age and outer appearance suggested otherwise, she did not play about the maintenance on it. She was as picky with her mechanic as she was about her hairdresser. The two were the most important women in her life outside of her family.

Carlos sighed. His animal was restless, which didn't come as a surprise. It had been growing more so for months now. Jersey had become more stifling with each day. He sat at his desk and watched the traffic go past his office window, wiggling the tie at his throat loose, and closing his eyes to soothe his panther. Yes, Jersey was becoming confining with the local alpha distrusting and starting to resent Carlos and his budding prowl being on his land.

It wasn't his fault rogue panthers flocked to him. According to Derrick, his second in command, his animal called to those who needed a place to belong. He blew out a frustrated breath. His panther's power was causing a problem with the local alphas from New York, all the way to Connecticut. He probably had another six months before either of the Alphas called him in to challenge them. They didn't realize Carlos wasn't any happier in their territory than they were to have him there.

But, he'd made a promise to his stepfather to step into the CEO position of their family's multi-million dollar security company once he retired and he was a man of his word. Already, using his government contracts he'd expanded the company, pushing them from million dollar profits into billions. He'd moved them from a smaller city in New Jersey to New York City to keep up with the expansion. He kept his small prowl outside of Union City, but commuted to the city to work. He hadn't made it in their current location a whole year before rogue panthers started showing up at the apartment building he and Derrick owned and the Manhattan office.

He'd talked to his stepfather, Daniel, months ago about the local alphas' concerns and together they'd come up with a solution he prayed would work. Through some of Daniel's contacts, contacts most humans would be too scared to cultivate, Daniel had heard of a prowl on the west coast of Florida that was quietly searching for a strong alpha. It would be a win-win for them both. It appealed to his stepfather in that it would expand their business south, and for Carlos, it would get him out of the area.

From the moment he'd heard about it, his cat perked up, interested. He'd done his research and sent his sister and his prowl's liaison down to Tampa to start negotiations. He wondered after he and Daniel had talked about it, if relocating to Florida was the right move. His mother had barely escaped the state with her life, and the lives of her children, it was risky for him to go back.

But, his cat wouldn't rest.

Something about the place compelled him, pulled to him, so he would follow instincts he'd honed his entire life and make the move. His mother was obviously worried, but he wasn't, not quite yet.

His phone rang and he wondered if it was his sister checking in. He looked at the caller ID and saw the name *Beta*.

"How is it?" Not one for small talk, he skipped the greetings.

Derrick laughed. "Hello to you, Carlos."

Carlos snarled.

"You're so easy to rile."

"Only you push my buttons, Beta. Everyone else knows better." Carlos sighed and leaned back in his leather desk chair.

Derrick sighed. "Too true." He paused a moment. "The land welcomed us, Carlos."

Relief loosened the tension in his shoulders. "Is it ours?"

"It feels like home." Derrick told him, his tone reverent. "How long should I stay?"

"Theo's good at what he does. He's our liaison for a reason. He should be fine alone down there. I say a week to help him and Laura settle, then I need you back here to prep for us to leave. I'd be surprised if the alphas gave me that long."

Derrick cursed. "How many times do we have to tell them we don't want their shitty territories?"

"Well, with Theo not here to smooth over ruffled feathers, I want to be out of here sooner rather than later."

"Your brother-in-law is good at his job. By next week you'll get your call with the Felix here, and we'll be moving down in a month, two at the latest."

"Why are you always so confident?"

"Come on now, it's me."

"Cocky bastard." Carlos muttered.

"Speaking of cocky, your sister has a beautiful neighbor."

"Focus on the task at hand please." Carlos shook his head.

Derrick paused a moment. "Normally I wouldn't ignore an edict by you, but there's something about her."

"That's not what you're there for." Carlos growled, irritated.

"Yes, I know, Felix. But she's calling my cat."

The use of his title let him know how serious Derrick was. Carlos sucked in a harsh breath. "You've met your mate?"

A momentary stab of jealousy, of loss, struck him, but he squelched it. He knew the games he and Derrick played wouldn't last forever.

"She feels like ours."

"Yours and your cat's?" Carlos clarified.

"No, mine… and yours."

Carlos' eyes widened, and his heart started a rapid drum beat. Hope and fear churned in his stomach. His panther's attention was raised, the cat spiking his power. He took a deep breath to push down on the energy. Could it really be true? Besides having a woman to share and protect between them, to have a Tribond was a powerful, but rare thing.

"Are you sure?" He whispered, unable to keep the longing from his voice.

"Remember when we first met and I told you I saw my future with you. I'm that sure." His Beta's promise and strength of resolve traveled across the phone line.

Carlos clenched the phone. "Make sure security for Laura, Theo and the kids is in place and then bring your ass back to Jersey to help keep the tristate prowls off our back. The faster we can leave here, the better for all."

He hung up on his Beta and turned his chair to face the downtown landscape. A mate, not just a mate, but a Tribond. It was almost too much to wish for. He couldn't be sure until his animal scented the woman. His cat rumbled, pacing under his skin, anxious. It was almost as if the panther knew what was waiting for them in Florida. He really needed those negotiations to work. He would first establish territory for his new prowl, and then he'd see about this mate business.

Chapter 2

"I need you on your best behavior." Savannah admonished.

She ran a hand over her son's short cropped hair and down the soft skin of his cocoa colored cheeks. Savannah straightened his shirt. Jamie had been with his father last weekend, and the hours in the sun showed in the darkening of his skin, hiding the barely visible spots that covered his body from the neck down.

Those spots told her that her son would grow into a fully shifting panther. She was latent, meaning she couldn't shift and had no panther spirit, so she'd never had those spots growing up. That Jamie had them worried her, but was an immense source of pride. Being a latent shifter, the granddaughter of the Alpha no less, had always been used against her. Jamie proved that the genes in her family ran true.

Her eight-year-old shrugged and rolled his eyes. "It's just new neighbors, mom, no big deal."

"Nevertheless, she has two young boys your age, we don't want them to think we're crazy."

"To know," he corrected. All the same, he used a small bit of power to hide his spots completely.

She pulled his ear and laughed. "Let's go."

She glanced once more at herself in the foyer mirror, adjusting the peasant top she wore over jean shorts. The shirt fell off one shoulder, an effect she loved, as it showed off her smooth brown skin. She locked the door as they walked out and trod the few steps next door. She was holding chicken wings from a supermarket in one hand and rang the doorbell with the other.

The door opened and the hottie who'd helped her change her tire was there with a smile on his face. Her gaze devoured him, taking stock of his every feature for her dreams later that night. His dark skin gleamed under the porch light. He exuded power, from his chiseled jaw to his high, sharp cheekbones. His ears were small, the tips of them narrowing into a noticeable point. Another feature marking him as 'other'. He narrowed his almond shaped eyes on her and Jamie.

"It has to be my lucky day." He murmured.

"I'm Jamie, are you a panther?" Her son spoke first, and with zero filter.

Her mouth dropped open and she put her free hand over her son's mouth. "Excuse him. That was rude."

And yet…she really wanted the answer herself. His features and his scent gave him away, but her instincts were dulled a bit due to her being latent, so confirmation would be nice.

Derrick laughed and the sound brought every one of her cells to life, a rush of blood flushing her skin. He grabbed her son's extended hand.

A pulse of power filled the air and Derrick's eyes changed to gold. "I am, how did you know?"

Jamie shot his mother a look. Sheepishly, she removed her hand from his mouth.

"I can tell." He said in answer.

"Can you now?" Intrigued, Derrick sent her a look full of questions. She shrugged.

"Who's at the door?" The voice belonged to the woman she'd seen getting out of the U-Haul.

"Your gorgeous neighbor." Derrick answered.

Savannah's cheeks heated. "I'm sure the food in my hand is bringing the flattery out of your friend."

The woman laughed and extended her hand. "I'm Laura." Her hair was dark brown, with copper highlights and pulled back into a high ponytail. Her tawny skin was smooth, and unadorned with makeup. Gold, heavily lashed eyes watched Savannah with curiosity.

She handed the food to Derrick and grabbed Laura's hand. "I'm Savannah, this is my son Jamie, we live just next door. I know how stressful moving is, so I brought you something to welcome you to the hood."

Laura's eyes lit. "That's great! The boys are running around here somewhere, they're about the same age as your son. Come in."

Derrick stepped back, his eyes traveling down the length of her. Savannah passed him to enter the house, and the heat from his body seeped into her skin. She would need to be careful around him.

Two rambunctious boys darted from a hallway and into the living room. Their skin was golden, darker than their mother's, faded spots visible on their arms and legs in their shorts as they slid to a stop. Laura waved them over.

"These two monsters are Ian and Ross. Boys, this is our new neighbor Ms. Savannah and her son, Jamie."

The boys smiled and waved. "We can show you our new room if you want." They offered.

Jamie, usually reticent with strangers looked up at her with a smile on his face. "Can I, mom?"

"Sure, just remember your manners."

"Of course!"

She smiled as the three of them went down the hallway. She turned and followed Laura. Her neighbor led them into a large kitchen, Savannah's sandals slapping against the light gray tile that ran throughout the front room into the kitchen. There was an island in the middle, its granite the same color as the floor. Boxes covered most of the countertops, but the island was clear. Dark gray linen high-backed stools lined it and Laura offered her a seat. She put the chicken down on the counter.

"I have some paper plates around here somewhere," Laura mumbled, as she went through boxes.

"Please, don't worry about me. This is for you guys. I remember how exhausting the moving process can be. The last thing you want to worry about is dinner."

Laura leaned on the counter. "You're so right."

"That was very considerate of you." Derrick sat next to her.

His energy reached out to her, surrounded her. She shuddered, stopping herself from leaning into him. Power raised along her skin and her mouth parted in shock.

Another large man came into the kitchen and bussed a kiss across Laura's cheek. She turned and smiled, and Savannah sensed their connection.

"This is my husband, Theo."

He held out his hand and she clasped it in greeting. "I'm your neighbor, Savannah."

"It's great to meet you."

"So how does your son know about shifters?" Derrick's expression was anything but casual.

The tone in the kitchen became serious. "Well, there are a lot of shifter families here. Mine included."

Relief swept the kitchen and Laura smiled. "You're a shifter?"

"No, I'm latent, so I don't shift into a panther, but I do carry some of the traits. I married a human, so it hasn't been a problem."

Theo's eyebrows raised. "If that kid in there is your son, he isn't latent. He's playing like a cub."

"I'm aware, trust me." She laughed.

"Cubs are a lot to handle." Laura said, laughing herself.

"Are you a part of the local prowl, or any other kind of panther group?" Theo's question brought everyone to another stand still.

She wondered at the dynamics of that. But, since she didn't know these people, she deflected as she always did. "No, I haven't been to any kind of prowl meeting since I was thirteen and we moved out to Tampa."

Derrick hummed and watched her, his eyes glowing. "How does he hide his spots? You cover them with makeup?"

She recoiled. She'd never hidden who her son was. "He can hide them when he wants. My grandfather says it's a part of my latency that I passed to him. It's one of the reasons you can't tell what either of us are, but, we're not ashamed."

Derrick's face cleared, and Theo relaxed.

Laura jumped in to break up the tension. "So, how are the schools in the area, are they tolerant of shifters?"

"Yes, Jamie is in a shifter only school and it's wonderful. It's a private school, but I can put in a word for you."

"That would be great!" Laura clapped. "I was really worried about that. You hear so many stories about prejudice in the south."

She nodded. "It's actually not as bad as you would think. Shifters have lived down here for centuries, so the only people surprised when they came out were you Yankees."

Theo laughed. "I like how southerners talk about history as though it happened yesterday."

She took a mini bow and laughed.

The conversation turned to more mundane things, like local attractions and things to do. She hadn't planned on spending so much time there, but they were a great couple and she enjoyed talking with them. The whole time she sat there, she was a little flushed because Derrick kept eyeing her. There was definite interest in his eyes as he raked looks over her. Every time he spoke, her body reacted. She stood, needing to put space between them. Not quite running away, but it was a good facsimile.

"I don't want to take up a lot of your time this evening. You must be tired. I'm just next door if you need anything."

"Thanks so much." Laura gave her hug.

Derrick hopped up from his stool. "I'll walk them out."

Her breath hitched as he smiled down at her. She looked away. "Jamie!"

Her son scurried around the corner, his face sweaty. She rolled her eyes, imagining what three eight-year-olds had gotten into. She waved good night and walked to the front door.

Derrick opened the door and leaned on the jamb. "So, how long have you been divorced?"

"Six years."

He ghosted a touch down her arm. "No lingering feelings?" his voice was mild, but the porch light caught his eyes and she read the hunger in them.

Though his touch had been light, electricity raised the hair on her arm. The space in the center of her chest fluttered as her power awakened.

"None." She smiled and grabbed her son's hand, leaving.

His gaze was a living, breathing touch on her back, it followed her across the yard and over to her house. She turned and waved as she unlocked the door. He gave her a small salute and a smile that made her salivate. It had been a while since she'd felt the warmth that awakened her sex. Even longer since she'd experienced the flush of excitement and tingles that came with flirting.

Derrick stood in the open doorway and watched Theo's new neighbor until she closed her front door. Tension tightened his body, impatience and need warring within him.

"She'll be ours soon," he murmured to soothe his panther.

She was beautiful, and everything he'd seen in his vision. Her eyes were so dark and expressive, he'd enjoyed watching her every emotion flicker across them when they touched. He couldn't wait to get to know her. So far he found her smart, funny, and confident. He loved that. He'd watched her talking, entranced by her energy.

He'd been stunned when he spotted her kneeled over her car tire earlier today. Just like the first time he met Carlos, in

Savannah he saw home. A warm feeling of relief had overtaken him the very moment her eyes had met his. That warmth had quickly turned to scorching heat the moment the honeyed tone of her voice flowed over him.

He took a step onto the porch, compulsion driving him to her. He stopped and shook his head.

Carlos was right in that he didn't have time to pursue her. And yet, he stared into the darkening evening, unwilling to miss even a moment of her. Her scent still stirred on the air, and his panther was anxious to track it, and her. He reminded himself that he was one step closer to the family he wanted. He needed to focus.

Territory first, then the reward of a mate.

"Savannah." He whispered her name, allowing himself that small taste of her.

"Beta," Theo called behind him.

He gave one last look to Savannah's doorway and turned, walking back into the house. "Yeah?"

Theo studied him, his shrewd gaze roving Derrick's face.

"What?"

"Is she the one?" Theo nudged his head towards the door.

Derrick flexed his hands, thinking about the power that coursed through his body at her simple touch. "It's happening."

"It's not like you're not prepared. For as long as I've known you, you've been waiting for her. What does Carlos say?"

He gave his friend a droll look.

Theo laughed. "One of these days he'll believe you the first time around."

"I only have a week here, Theo, I need you to—"

"Say no more, Beta. I'll protect her like my own."

Derrick rolled his shoulders and let out a relieved breath. He trusted Theo with his life, and now the life of his mate. Impatience stirred. "I need these negotiations to go well."

"It's me you're talking to. When have I ever let you down?" Theo held out his arms.

He grunted. In the years that they'd served together, and the years it had taken them to establish their budding prowl, Theo had been there, every step of the way, helping him nudge Carlos along. His fast talking charm kept them out of trouble as they built their prowl. If there was anyone who he could count on to get them this territory, it was Theo.

He walked to the door and gave one last lingering look out of the side window towards Savannah's house. He didn't have the time now…but soon.

Chapter 3

It had been three weeks since Derrick had come into her life and subsequently left and Savannah was restless. He'd only been next door for a week, helping Laura and Theo get adjusted, but she missed him. Not that she'd been able to act on her attraction. Work had kept her from him the whole time he'd been in Tampa. The account that she'd been working on had only wrapped a couple days ago, so she'd been swamped and buried under swatches, paint samples and furniture choices while he'd been in town. It hadn't stopped him from making up reasons to come over, making his presence felt, though.

Her son was with his father this week, and without the distraction of Jamie, acute loneliness weighed her down. Normally, the days without her son were spent working, but with the account wrapped up, outside of a couple of meetings, there had been nothing to do. She'd cleaned her house from top to bottom, and had run out of chores. Last night, alone in her bed, she'd been forced to examine her life and the results were depressing. She needed a life outside of her work and Jamie. She'd probably missed her chance with Derrick, but, maybe she could pump her new friend for information. With that thought, she'd called Laura and a couple of her cousins last night to plan a girls' day. It would give Laura some other women to meet in the area and make her questioning less obvious.

She mixed together some mimosas, cut cheese and put out a charcuterie tray. She lit her oil diffuser and a couple of scented candles on the kitchen counter. Soon the smell of citrus filled the room and she smiled happily.

The doorbell rang as she was setting everything out on the kitchen island. She greeted Naomi and Charlotte as they came in the door. Out of all of her cousins, they were the closest in age and her favorites. She and Naomi were bonded by their shared latency.

Charlotte came in first, her willowy body in a black rock band T-shirt that barely reached the top of her thighs. She wore a pair of black boots that reached her knees and the two sizes too big army jacket she loved on top.

Savannah kissed Charlotte's cheek, fiddling with the hem of her cousin's shirt. "Is there anything under this?"

Naomi gave a soft snort as she came in the door. Charlotte's sister contrasted her in every way. Where Charlotte was tall and svelte, Naomi was short and curvy. She wore a long black flowing skirt that tangled at her ankles and an off the shoulder black top that hugged her voluptuous figure.

"She already called me a hater." Naomi leaned over and kissed Savannah's cheek.

"Because you are." Charlotte sang over her shoulder as she walked to the kitchen.

Savannah laughed and was about to close the door when she noticed Laura, in tight ripped jeans and an off the shoulder t-shirt, walking up the driveway, so she waited. Laura handed her a plate of brownies that were warm and smelled like heaven.

"Oh my God, I love brownies." She kissed Laura's cheek and moved aside so she could enter. "You look great."

"Thank you, baby." Laura looked around as she entered. "This is my second time in your house and I swear I can't get over the difference between our décor."

Savannah tried to see her house through a stranger's eyes. She'd picked the place expressly for the open floor plan. Hardwood floors stretched from the small entranceway throughout the house. Her formal living room had an overstuffed sectional with fluffy teal pillows she used to accent the otherwise gray room. She used different shades of gray throughout the whole house, loving the calming color.

"She has an art degree and a thriving interior design business, don't let her make you feel bad." Charlotte joked from the kitchen.

"That hater is my cousin Charlotte and the one helpfully filling glasses is Naomi." Savannah introduced the women to Laura.

The women all waved. They sat around the dining room table off of the kitchen.

"The flowers are a nice touch, cuz." Charlotte indicated the fresh cut daisies she had in the center of her rustic table.

"Thank you." Savannah had a clear glass pitcher of mimosa next to the flowers, the orange slices floating in it giving it a cheerful vibe. She poured drinks as they settled into the padded chairs to get to know each other.

"Savi tells me you guys moved here from Jersey?" Charlotte reached over to snag a brownie.

Laura nodded. "Yes, we heard good things about this area of Florida."

"Is it just you and your boys then?" Naomi asked.

"For now. My brother is moving down. He should be here sometime today."

Naomi leaned close to the table. "Do tell. You're gorgeous, so your brother has to be fine as hell."

Savannah choked on the drink she was sipping. She rolled her eyes and wiped off her mouth.

"I don't know about all that. He is a handful though, so venture at your own risk."

"Well, my kind of man." Naomi winked.

Charlotte pushed her sister's shoulders. "You don't need that type of trouble. Vanna on the other hand…"

Savannah held up her hands. "Leave me out of this."

"You're not dating?" Laura asked.

"Something like that. I've sworn off shifters." She took a giant drink from her glass hoping to avoid answering why.

"We don't talk about it." Naomi said in a stage whisper.

Savannah snorted. "You bitch."

Charlotte wagged her finger. "A nickel in Jamie's curse jar."

Charlotte and Naomi laughed.

"Derrick will be disappointed." Laura's eyes twinkled with humor.

Both cousins shot her a surprised look.

Naomi raised an eyebrow. "Derrick?"

"We're not talking about this." Savannah stuffed a brownie in Charlotte's mouth, when she opened it to say something.

"Was that why your first husband was human?" Laura leaned forward, her interest apparent.

Savannah wondered if possibly she was asking on behalf of Derrick. A girl could hope. "I married him because I loved him. I thought he loved me."

"Despite grandmother telling you different." Naomi said into her glass.

She glared. "He cheated on me with one of his co-workers."

Laura gasped. "What did you do?"

"Nothing at first. We'd been together six years, but after I had Jamie, I don't know. We just slowly slid into this place of disinterest. By the time Jamie was two, I couldn't fake it anymore."

"I still say we should've trashed his shit." Charlotte muttered.

"Here, here," Naomi added.

"It wasn't worth it. When I found out, at first, I didn't say anything. I just quietly took business classes during the day, went to all his fancy fundraisers and dinners and cultivated clients from the people he knew. I set up my business, got a small office in South Tampa with some of my trust fund, *then* I told him to kick rocks." She mushed Charlotte's face as her cousin pretended to gag.

Naomi laughed and slapped her sister's shoulder.

"He got some hot shot lawyer he knew to make sure I didn't get anything in the divorce." Savannah sighed. "He gleefully kicked me out of our fancy house I never liked and married the woman he was seeing behind my back. Now, six years later we can finally be in the same room without exchanging nasty words."

Laura sat with her mouth agape for a full minute before she responded. "I'm with Charlotte. At the very least you could've keyed his car."

Naomi barked out a laugh and gave Laura a high five. "Ha! I knew I liked this girl."

Laura's phone vibrated across the table as they laughed. She picked it up and squealed. "My brother's here!" She stood. "Come, you have to meet him."

She and Naomi stood, but Charlotte grabbed her sister's arm. "We'll wait here."

Savannah frowned. "Are you sure?"

"Yep. We're good." Charlotte smiled, and waved her off.

Laura waited for her at the door. "You're coming, right, Savannah?"

She nodded, her curiosity too much for her to resist. They rushed to Laura's house and barreled through the front door. Derrick was standing in the foyer, his brow quirking up as they came in. He wore a red, long sleeved Henley that clung to his wide chest, tucked into a pair of jeans that just... He smiled as she came through the door.

Lord. Why was he so fine?

"Welcome back." She smiled warmly at him.

"Sexy Savannah." He murmured.

She rolled her eyes.

"Did you miss me while I was gone?" He held his arms out for a hug and she couldn't resist.

She walked into his arms and burrowed her head into his chest. Was it bad that she'd only known him a week and actually did miss him while he was gone? He smelled so good. Cedar, musk and a tangy citrus smell that warmed her from the inside out. Her body was flush with his and damned if it didn't take her a few minutes to remember her vow to avoid shifters and why it would be inappropriate to jump the man in her new friend's living room. Power raised under her skin, the nerves tingling as though she'd touched a live wire and she stepped back. She'd thought she imagined that when he was in town last. It was not a fluke, it seemed.

"Come, I'm sure Laura brought you over to meet her brother." He pulled back, anticipation darkening his eyes to onyx.

She nodded, walking in front of him. They rounded the corner into the kitchen and her breath stalled. A man she assumed was Laura's brother, stood at the island counter. He was beautiful, and all she could see was his profile. His hair was short, but long enough to see the curls that would cover his head if he let them grow. His shoulders were wide, but the rest of him tapered into a lithe grace that screamed panther. The vee neck t-shirt he wore clung to the muscles of his arms and his faded jeans were fitted enough for her know his thighs would be equally muscular.

A jolt went through her body. A lightning strike of recognition pierced her soul. Shocked, she could only stare. The same recognition had overtaken her body when she'd first met with Derrick, and to now feel it from another man, to have them both under the same roof. She just stared, unable to do anything more. Alpha poured off the guy. His power reached to her and ignited the small amount that had been dormant within her for her whole life.

She frowned.

Her power had never been that strong before. This wasn't a warm tide, like what happened in her grandfathers' presence, or even the sparks Derrick pulled from her. This power roiled in the center of her body, bringing goosebumps along her arms. She stood still and took a deep breath, trying to calm her riotous body. Her skin tingled, and she squeezed her thighs together. She'd never had these feelings with her ex-husband and here she was, hot from just a glance at this man.

Derrick came up behind her and touched her shoulder and her knees nearly buckled. The air in the room thickened and she swallowed. Two men her body craved…she knew what it meant.

She bit her lip, almost unable to move from the spot she was in. Laura's brother finally turned and she held her breath.

His eyes were gold, and tilted at the corners, testament to the wild cat so close under his skin. His full lips moved up into a smile that kept him from being perfect. His canines were longer than normal humans, probably also due to his dual nature, and his bottom teeth slightly crooked. It did nothing to detract from his chiseled good looks. She sucked in a breath. Behind her, Derrick chuckled and she shook her head. She wasn't ready for what the two of them could unleash within her body.

"Carlos, this is my friend, Savannah." Laura grinned.

Savi forced her cheeks up into a semblance of a smile. Carlos walked closer and extended his hand. She stared at it. Derrick still had his hand on her shoulder, she knew if she touched them both…

Derrick moved closer, crowding her back and Carlos smiled at her. Her body shuddered, and behind her, Derrick released a growl that told her he knew what was happening as well. Carlos stepped closer, his hand still out. Did she have the courage? Laura's face bunched in confusion and a forced cough, from somewhere in the kitchen, shook her from her stupor.

She extended a shaking hand and held her breath. Sure enough, the moment Carlos touched her it was as though a hurricane swept through her body. Wind whipped nerve endings into a frenzy and power washed through her, from Carlos to her, and up into Derrick's hand on her shoulder. A whimper escaped her throat and Carlos' eyes lit, his cat surfacing, his satisfied smile all tooth and predator. She should've been apprehensive, maybe even scared, but blood rushed to her hips, making her warm. She fought hard not to lift her chin and expose her neck to this man. She straightened her shoulders, breaking contact with first Derrick, then taking her hand out of Carlos' larger one, leaving her body bereft from their power.

She cleared her throat. "Um, I have to go."

She had to get home and make some phone calls. Carlos was an alpha, and his moving to town could only mean bad things for her family.

Chapter 4

Savannah raced home. Her cousins were standing at the window when she opened the door. They turned their expectant faces to her.

Naomi met her at the door. "What happened?"

"Her brother's an alpha."

"Little a, or big A?" Charlotte asked, peeking out of the window near the front door.

"Big ass A, like, a Felix."

Everything about Carlos broadcasted that he was strong enough to run his own panther prowl as Alpha. From the power he emitted, to his quiet confidence, he embodied the title of Felix. She paced the living room trying to figure out her next move. She could call her older cousins who were higher up in the hierarchy than Charlotte. They would possibly get word back to her grandfather without her seemingly involved.

"Is there like a prowl contact list for this type of thing, Charlotte?" She held her hands wide.

"What's his name?" Naomi asked.

"Carlos, I didn't get a last name."

The tension left Charlotte and she dropped the curtain. "Oh, ok."

"What does that mean?" Naomi asked.

"There has been talk of a turnover in the prowl," Charlotte said slowly.

Naomi slapped her sister's shoulder. "What? And you didn't tell us?"

"Ow! I been told you bitches to start coming to prowl meetings again. Maybe if you did, you would know stuff."

"So grandfather is going to give up the Felix position?" Naomi scrunched her face in confusion.

Charlotte shrugged. "Possibly."

Savannah growled at her cousin. "Let me see what I can find out. I'm going to call my mom."

Charlotte frowned. "You've gone to more prowl meetings than Aunt Karen, what could she know?"

"She's right, Savi," Naomi agreed.

Savannah pulled out her phone. "Maybe one of the aunts have said something to her."

Charlotte snorted and crossed her arms. "Doubtful."

The phone rang twice before her mom picked it up. She didn't bother to put it on speaker since she knew both her cousins would hear the conversation. Though she and Naomi were latent, they still had some of the shifter traits, like heightened senses, hearing being one of them. Though, they weren't anywhere near as powerful as a full shifter.

"Hi, sweetheart. What's going on?" Her mother's voice was always cheerful. Karen spent her days in her flower shop happily perched on the fringes of most people's happy events.

"So, look, mom, I called you because I don't know what to do."

"What's happened, is it something with Jamie, is Greg giving you a hard time?"

"No, mom. Listen, my neighbor next door, remember I told you about her?"

"Oh, yeah, the one with the twin boys, sure, what happened?"

"Her brother is visiting."

"Okay?"

"He's an alpha."

Her mother was silent. Savannah looked to her cousins, both of whom shrugged.

"Well, what do I do? Do I call grandfather?" She prodded.

Karen sighed. "I would suggest you stay out of the affairs of men, darling."

Naomi held her hand over her mouth to prevent her laughter, while Charlotte pretended to gag.

She rolled her eyes at their antics. "Mom, seriously, it's the twenty first century."

"Honey, you stopped going to meetings and gatherings, it's not your place to worry about the inner workings of the prowl. Leave it to your grandfather, he probably already knows."

Charlotte gave her an 'I told you so' look and Savannah flipped her the bird. "You think?"

"Well, I don't know because I stay out of their business."

Naomi gave up trying to contain her giggles. The conversation was going nowhere.

"I love you, goodbye, mom."

"I love you too, pumpkin." Her mother laughed as she hung up.

She chewed on the nail of her thumb, debating her next call. "Do you guys think I should warn grandfather?"

"Aunt Karen told you to stay in a woman's place." Charlotte said deadpan.

Naomi busted out in another fit of giggles.

"You two are ridiculous." She said as she dialed their grandfather's number.

It took three calls before he answered the phone. "Why are you blowing up my phone, child?"

"We gave you that phone so you would be available, grandfather. I was scared."

"For what reason? You know where I am if I'm not answering." His voice was distracted, telling her that Jeremiah was still tending to his farm, even as he spoke with her.

"The phone is so we can reach you in the field." She grumbled.

"How am I to answer the phone when I'm doing field work?"

"Grandfather!" She growled and decided to skip the speech on why a seventy-year-old man should not be doing field work, no matter how strong his panther was. "There's an alpha in town."

He hummed. "I'm aware."

She let out the breath she was holding and refused to look at Charlotte. Her cousin's smug look was still visible from the corner of her eye.

"What does this mean for you, for the prowl?"

"It means, we'll finally have someone strong enough to protect our prowl, and the territory we've held by sheer determination."

"What will happen to you?"

"If the land welcomes him, then I will step down."

"No fighting?" Naomi spoke up.

"I'm not afraid to fight," he scoffed. "But I've been Felix long enough to recognize what we need."

"So, what will happen?" Savannah chewed her lip.

"Far be it for me to tell you to stay out of alpha affairs, but…" he paused.

She let out an exasperated breath ignoring her cousins' laughter. "Fine, I'll stay out of it."

He chuckled. "This alpha, perhaps?"

"No." She shut him down. "I'm good on marriage, and I don't need my grandfather setting me up on dates."

"You married someone not for you." He reminded her.

"Granddad."

She didn't want to get into the lecture on her marriage, especially with Naomi and Charlotte's suddenly rapt attention focused on her. Besides, she got Jamie in the deal, she would not regret it, no matter how brief.

"For latent women, I have the most stubborn granddaughters." He commented.

"Love you too, old man." She hung up and looked at her cousins.

Savannah was a little worried, still. He'd said no violence, but who could really tell what a new alpha would do to their prowl. "So?"

They both shrugged. There was a knock on the door and the three of them scrambled to the front window. It was Derrick. Savannah gave her cousins a wide-eyed glance.

"Who is that?" Naomi whispered.

"Derrick," she hissed. And rushed for the door.

He stood there, his aura dripping sex. She cleared her suddenly dry throat. "Hey."

"Hi." He spared a quick glance behind her. "We're all going out to eat to celebrate our arrival, would you like to come? Your friends are invited too."

She stared at him for a long moment, debating. It must have been longer than she realized because a coin hit the side of her head and shook her from her thoughts. Derrick cleared his throat and covered a laugh as it bounced away.

She groaned in embarrassment. "Yes, sure. Just give me a moment to change clothes."

He smiled. "Take your time."

She closed the door as he walked away and spun around, glaring at her cousins. "What is wrong with you bitches?"

"You were the one standing there looking dumb. We helped you out. You're welcome." Naomi crossed her arms over her chest.

"Should I tell them the local Felix is my grandfather?"

Charlotte narrowed her eyes. "I say feel them out first. See what kind of person Carlos is. You heard grandfather. If the land welcomes him, he'll be the new Alpha. You can do a little snooping and let us know what you find out."

"Who is 'us'?" Savannah put her hands on her hip.

"The cousins, duh. We're still enforcers for the prowl. Forewarned is forearmed." Charlotte put a hand in her sister's face as Naomi mimicked her word for word.

She debated Charlotte's proposal. Her cousin was right, it couldn't hurt to know what kind of person Carlos was and maybe what kind of alpha he would be. No, she didn't go to prowl meetings, but her son was a full shifter and he would be a part of the prowl. She should know what he would be getting into. Should she ask outright and demand to know what they were going to do? Maybe nothing so bold, but she could feel them out, see what kind of man Carlos was.

"I'll see what I can find out, Char."

"Since I don't go to prowl meetings, it doesn't concern me. What does concern me is why you didn't jump that guy's bones last time he was here." Naomi waggled her eyebrows.

"I can't with you, Naomi."

"She's not wrong though, Vanna. He's fine as hell. If he looked at me the way he stared at you, I'd climb him like the tall tree he is."

Naomi laughed and bumped fists with her sister.

"You too, Char?" She threw her hands up.

"Well, we're going to leave so you can get dressed." Naomi dragged her sister out the door.

"Don't dress like a mom and embarrass us." Charlotte threw over her shoulder.

Savannah closed the door in her smirking face and leaned back against it. Dinner, with two men who'd awakened both her body and the power she'd long suppressed. Easy as could be, right?

Chapter 5

Carlos skimmed a finger across the condensation gathering on his beer glass. They'd chosen a seafood restaurant on the water, a little over a thirty-minute drive from his sister's house, and had he'd known it would take so long, he may have reconsidered. Trapped in Laura's minivan with the scent of his mate permeating the air, he'd been tempted to jump out of the car while it was moving.

Jesus, but she was beautiful.

He didn't know what was more attractive, her dark eyes, the way the light caught the smooth skin of her exposed shoulders, or her smile as she laughed with his sister.

All of it made him want to reach for her.

Her forehead had reached his nose when he stood in front of her at Laura's house. She was a tall woman, another thing about her he liked. Beautifully proportioned, the simple dress she wore clung to her curves, the dark blue color making her mahogany skin gleam. He wanted to run his hands and trace every line of her body. He ached to rub along her skin and marvel in their different hues. Her darker skin would no doubt glow next to his lighter brown. He adjusted in his chair.

How Derrick spent a week with her without taking her against the nearest wall was a small miracle as far as he was concerned. Clearly his Beta was more disciplined than he. Just the touch of her hand when he'd met her, had sent his body into a tailspin. He didn't quite get how Derrick had been so sure about the female when he'd talked about her, but one look at Savannah had his cat beating against his skull to get at their mate.

He breathed out.

Ours.

There was no doubt their mating would be a Tribond. He'd fought alongside Derrick in the Army Rangers for eight years, the two of them were closer than brothers. That they would get to share a mate was a gift to him. One he wanted to take his sweet time unwrapping. They'd shared women over the years, but because Tribonds were so rare, he thought that would end when either of them met their mate. He knew of no pack or prowl north in the tristate area that had a Tribond, not even back some generations.

He flexed his fingers, reliving the power the three of them had raised just by touching. If he'd had any further doubt about their Tribond, that would've sealed it for him. The contact had staggered him, both his cat and Derrick's rumbling through their connection. Soon, he'd have that same closeness with Savannah. He couldn't wait.

"You're staring." Derrick leaned over and whispered.

"Can you blame me?" He whispered back.

Derrick sipped from his beer. "No, no I cannot, but you don't want to scare our mate there, Alpha."

Carlos sighed and shifted his glance slightly over to his sister, though he still watched Savannah from the corner of his eye. Laura was animated, recounting something she'd done the other day, and the smile on Savannah's face made him as hard as an iron spike.

He groaned. How in the hell would he make it back in the car with her?

Derrick choked out a laugh and all eyes swiveled to them. He slapped his Beta on the back.

"What?"

"You're speaking aloud." Derrick whispered.

His face burned. "How loud?"

Theo cleared his throat on the other side of the table and raised an eyebrow.

Gods, he had to get better control. He excused himself from the table citing a bathroom break. He instead turned and headed outside. The heat was something he would need to get used to. It was October and still, outside felt like he was steaming in a bag.

Derrick joined him a moment later. "Do you see why I was so anxious to get back?"

"How in the hell did you do it? No way could I have met her and went back to New Jersey."

Derrick shrugged. "I know what we need to accomplish. I want this transition to go as smoothly as possible, if for nothing else than to make sure Savannah stays safe."

He nodded, he definitely understood that. When Derrick divulged to him that he believed they'd be in a Tribond, he'd been rightfully skeptical. Still, he'd planned and organized, pushing as much resources around as they needed to secure the land and the building where he would house his prowl. He wanted everything in place, on the off chance that Derrick had been right. Now seeing her, feeling his cat's need for her...

He wanted to leave the dinner and head straight for his office. There was so much more that needed to be done.

"When are we meeting with the other alpha?"

"Tomorrow afternoon."

He nodded. "Whatever it takes, Derrick. I want this area stable, safe for our mate and our new prowl."

"Did you ever think we would get here?" Derrick rolled his neck to loosen the tension riding him.

"As I recall you'd been urging me to establish a prowl from the day we met." He said dryly.

Derrick laughed. "I saw my future with you, I can't help you're slow to pick up."

Carlos laughed. "Shit, man, a mate."

"A damn fine one too."

Carlos growled, the sound carrying in the night. Heads turned from those on the patio.

"Keep calm a few more days and then we can actively go on the hunt." His Beta soothed.

He smiled, anticipating the dance with Savannah. "Do you think she likes shifters?"

"Oh, that's right, I didn't tell you. Our mate is latent."

His cat jerked from his reins momentarily, fur rippled along his arms. "Is that right?" How did he not notice?

He nodded. "Said she hasn't been to a prowl meeting in years, but she'll know what she is to us."

That was good news. "Explains her hasty exit this afternoon."

"That and she had company."

"What kind of company?" he growled, jealousy a quick response.

"Two females, one a cat, family from the scent." Derrick shrugged.

Interesting. "So, she'll definitely know what's up."

"Doesn't mean she'll be an easy win," Derrick cautioned.

Carlos scoffed. "You think our cats want easy?"

"You know how much I love a good chase." Derrick bared his teeth, his eyes changing back and forth to his panther.

Carlos smiled, him and his cat anticipating the hunt for their mate. Now all he had to do was get through dinner without touching her.

***

Derrick wouldn't say she ran, necessarily. Did she escape the confines of the van in a hasty manner?

Yes.

Nearly an hour later, they pulled back into the yard after dinner and Savannah had hauled ass out of Laura's van the moment it went into park. He'd sat next to her on the ride home and honestly, it had been a near thing, him keeping his hands to himself. Her scent was heady and his panther wanted to wallow in it. He followed her the few steps next door to her house. She didn't even notice him behind her. One part of his ego liked that they had her so rattled. The security expert in him frowned. She needed to be a lot more conscious of her surroundings.

Savi's hands shook as she dug through her purse. Though he'd warned Carlos to quit staring, he'd spent the whole dinner watching her, cataloguing the little mannerisms she used when speaking. It gave him pleasure to watch her. The car ride back had been torture, no doubt, but worth it. She'd sat against the window and he'd watched the passing street lights play against her skin. Her arousal had clouded the air in the car, and while it had been akin to torture, he enjoyed every moment.

"You cannot be in a Tribond." She muttered to herself, as she pulled out her keys. "You can use your vibrator and that will be that."

His keen hearing caught it all, from six feet away. His cat sprung forward and a snarl rumbled his chest. He would get no sleep tonight, knowing what she'd be busy doing. "Need help?"

She dropped her keys and whipped around, her eyes wide, and mouth parted in shock. "Jesus, you scared me." She held a hand to her chest.

Derrick laughed and bent over to get her keys. Their eyes met as she straightened, and lust tore through him, the heat in her eyes roasting him. She quickly averted her eyes, unable to hold his gaze. He let out a hungry growl. He handed over her keys, brushing a lingering touch over her fingers.

She cleared her throat. "Did you want something?"

He stepped closer and chuckled. "What are you offering, little one?"

She opened and closed her mouth, her pupils dilating, her chest rising as she took a deep breath.

"Your porch light was off. I just wanted to be sure you got into the house ok." He offered to break the silence.

She nodded. "Thank you." She turned and dropped them again, groaning, her hands shaking.

She stooped to get them and stepped back into his chest. His body went up several hundred degrees and he grabbed her waist to keep her from falling.

"Lord have mercy," she whispered.

He laughed outright, enjoying her flustered face. He grabbed the keys from her and opened her front door and stepped back, holding out her keys.

"Good night." He whispered.

"Good night," was her breathless reply as she rushed in and shut the door.

"Lock the door, babe." He said through the oak door. He smiled when he heard the lock snick into place.

Carlos met him at his truck, his arms folded over his chest as he leaned against the front of the hood. "Tell me again why I can't charge in and take our mate."

Derrick adjusted his cock, painfully hard and grunted. "Because we have to stabilize this prowl."

"A little taste, Beta." Carlos begged, a mock pout on his face.

Derrick groaned and leaned on the truck next to his alpha. Carlos may be joking, but he was more than tempted to go knock on her door and charm his way inside.

"I don't think a little taste will work with our mate, Alpha. She's fucking beautiful, and perfect, and I know once either of us tastes her…"

Carlos groaned. "It will be a dream." He said finishing Derrick's sentence.

Derrick stood next to his best friend and willed his body under control. He wanted nothing more than to go next door after Savannah, but he didn't want to rush her. It was okay, he could be patient. As it had been with Carlos, before he'd convinced him to become Felix of their pride, he'd wear his mate down just the same. Soon he'd have the family he wanted, and he didn't intend to fuck it up. He pushed his body off the truck and handed Carlos the keys.

"Let's get home, we have an alpha to meet tomorrow and a prowl to stabilize. I want our mate sooner rather than later."

"Damn right." Carlos growled and headed to the driver's side.

They drove the fifteen minutes away from Savannah's neighborhood to the apartment building they'd bought near downtown to be prowl housing. It had two separate towers. While they'd been in Jersey, the contractors they'd hired had finished refurbishing the first tower which would be used as their main living space and family housing. The other was for the single panthers and still being worked on. The prowl they'd established in Jersey would be trickling down to Florida as soon as they finished the deal with the new alpha and he wanted the building ready for them to move in.

The Felix put in the code to open the front gate and drove around the perimeter of both towers to check out everything. Derrick knew Carlos would still do a round on foot to check out security and be sure his scent markings held. Derrick headed to his apartment on the fifth floor once they'd pulled into the garage. The two-bedroom was temporary. They refurbed the seventh floor to be a penthouse suite, one that would be their permanent residence once they'd fully mated.

His panther chaffed at being down here when he should be upstairs assuring their mate would be comfortable. There wasn't anything he could do for now, so he pushed down on his cat, promising him they would take care of their mate soon.

Chapter 6

It was only twenty miles outside of the city, but the drive to meet the Felix of the West Florida panther prowl was a long one. Between the traffic and Carlos' tension, it seemed longer. Theo navigated the back roads with ease. Soon they were turning into a heavily forested area cordoned off with a barbed wire fence. They were waved into a guarded gate and Derrick had to admit, he was impressed. The forest soon gave way to neatly manicured lawns with houses set a little ways off the main road. Some of the beautiful brick structures were bunched together closer than others.

As far as prowl territory went it was story book, and his heart expanded. Memories of his childhood prowl land threatened to swamp him. He'd once lived in place much like this one. He could picture cubs playing in the fields plotted for farming that were interspaced on the land. His family had a smaller prowl, so their territory hadn't been as extensive as the one they were currently driving through. Still, the parallels were enough to stall his breath.

Carlos turned back to him and raised a brow.

He exhaled, and wiped his hands on his pants. "I'm good."

Carlos nodded and turned back to the front. Theo drove slowly through the winding dirt roads between the houses to get to the Felix's house. The white farmhouse at the end of the road was big, two stories, with a porch wrapped around the entire bottom floor. Steely faced women surrounded it. Two of them, identical, and obviously alpha, stood on the wide porch of the main house, their hair windswept, the jeans and t-shirt something it seemed they threw on quickly after shifting. Carlos and Derrick stepped out of the truck, keeping their body language open, non-threatening. There were multiple dirt paths that led to the front of the house as well as to the forest surrounding it. It indicated to him that the panthers met at the Felix's often. It boded well, in that it meant communication was open in the prowl.

The Alpha stepped out, his power strong despite his age, his brown face weathered from hours in the sun. The male was brawny, his t-shirt faded, but clinging to muscles humans wouldn't have at his age. His second in command stood next to him, his power equally strong. The slender male in pressed khakis and a button down shirt, a direct opposite to the rough and tumble alpha, but his elegant grace every bit a powerful feline.

It peaked his curiosity and made his panther wary. An alpha this strong, willing to give up his territory? It didn't make sense to him. The women made no move to intercept him or Carlos as they started walking towards the house. They kept a wary eye on them, though. Derrick, Carlos and Theo stopped a few feet from the porch, making no move to enter. He knew entering without an invitation would send the wrong message.

Perhaps a week ago, he'd have had no problem arrogantly going in, asserting their power. Today? Today he had a mate to think about. He wanted this turnover done as neat and peaceful as possible. Nervous energy buzzed along his skin. He tamped down his impatience. Soon he would have territory and a large prowl, two things he'd fervently wished for. The security of both would go a long way to soothing years old wounds.

Theo smiled at everyone. "Felix Carlos, Derrick, this is Felix Jeremiah and his Beta, Harper of the Watson prowl. Brielle and Brianne, the charming ladies on either side of them are his granddaughters and two of the strongest females I've ever ran across. It's no surprise Felix Jeremiah has been able to hold on to territory this size."

One of the women snorted. "A charming one, that one is."

"Makes me think you're a smart enough Alpha to send him down to pave the way for you." Harper commented.

"That was the idea." Carlos tucked his hands in the pocket of his jeans.

The Alpha eyed Carlos a moment more, seeming to read him. "Well, come on in then, let's see if smart's all you got."

Derrick snickered and followed him up onto the porch.

The cool air of the ac swept over them as they entered. But the feel of the place in comparison, was warm. There was obvious love and warmth through their prowl. The house was well taken care of, the vaulted ceilings giving the home a grand feel. The Alpha shuffled them into a sitting room and invited them to sit.

"There are a lot of women in this prowl." Derrick commented.

Felix Jeramiah nodded. "We had nine daughters who in turn had few sons."

"Is that why you were looking outside for a Felix to take over?" Carlos watched Jeremiah's face for any deception.

"Partly." Jeremiah waved his hand at the pictures lining their walls. "A few of my granddaughters are latent, because their mamas married humans. The ones who did mate shifters, didn't mate men strong enough to take over. Not that I'm disparaging or knocking my family. It's just time to bring in new blood."

Carlos nodded. Derrick could understand the sentiment. Sometimes prowls could get too insular and breed themselves out of the alpha gene. Though, from the power that buzzed across his skin as they crossed onto the land, he didn't think it was the case with this prowl.

"Have you been having issues?" Carlos asked.

"The prowl to the south of us is trying to push for more land. They're becoming peskier as Jeremiah ages." Harper commented.

"Your power reverberated the moment you stepped onto this land. Your Beta's power is also loud and clear, you would bring a lot to our prowl." Brianne or Brielle added, he wasn't introduced to them individually, so he wasn't sure which one spoke.

"But you're a new Felix." Jeremiah rubbed his chin.

Carlos nodded. "I am, and a reluctant one."

Jeremiah tilted his head as he considered him. "Your power calls, son. I imagine you've had shifters following you your whole life."

Derrick laughed and Carlos shot him a look. He'd been telling his best friend that for years. It was partly the reason they'd been run out of New Jersey. Everywhere Carlos went, a group of loner shifters showed up.

"What of your father?" Harper asked.

Carlos fisted his hand and looked away. "I didn't grow up with my father. My mother re-married a human, he raised me. I was hoping you would remain here and guide me." He turned back, meeting Jeremiah's eyes as he made the request.

It was no small ask and Derrick saw first the surprise, then respect that crossed both the Alpha and his Beta before they covered it. He breathed easier.

"It says a lot of a man who knows when he needs help. You are as Theo presented. That makes me more inclined to believe the promises he's given to us."

"I know your mate wants to remain in the house she loves. I have no problem with that, and would frankly love having you here as Elders." Carlos hastened to reassure them all.

Carlos had no need to banish the Felix and his family off the prowl land. He, Derrick and Theo had spoken for long hours before they even started the process. Having a more experienced alpha would go a long way to making their changeover easier on all involved. Showing the old prowl that Carlos respected their Alpha and took council from him would go a long way to soothing ruffled feathers.

"It would be my honor. Besides, the women here take a little bit of finessing. You'll need help there, if you're to completely win them over." Jeremiah laid a hand over his heart.

The women at his back scoffed.

"You won't get any push back from the males, but the alpha gene runs true through the women in this family." Harper advised with a smile.

"Why haven't either of them stepped up to run the prowl?" Carlos asked.

Derrick was genuinely curious. The power emanating from the women at his back packed heat and strength.

"They've kept outside prowls from encroaching, and have brokered, both peace and territory from those north of us. Make no mistake, they could if they had a mind to. But at the end of the day, the prowls in this area are old-fashioned." Jeremiah supplied.

"Without a male leading, they would get pushback from the council on everything. As it is, council meetings take way longer than they should." Harper groused.

The old man got a calculating gleam to his eye. "Not for nothing, but marrying into this family would carry a lot of weight."

Carlos smiled. "I've met our mate."

Just hearing Carlos say it had his panther rolling through his body. He was anxious to begin pursuit of Savannah.

"Our, a Tribond?" Jeremiah narrowed his eyes.

"Yes. It's rare where we come from so, I feel especially blessed." Carlos laid a hand on Derrick's shoulder.

"Not so much for this prowl." Harper sat back in the chair in which he sat, a satisfied smile on his face.

They didn't have to say anymore. Since they were in a Tribond, then chances are, Savannah was indirectly tied to the prowl. He went back over the little bit of information she'd given them weeks ago at Theo's house. Interesting.

"We have three in our prowl alone." Jeremiah stated.

Now that would explain how an aging alpha with a prowl full of women was able to keep hold of the amount of territory they ran.

"That's a lot of power."

A smile ghosted across the Alpha's lips. "Indeed it is. Who is your mate, if you don't mind me asking?"

"We haven't, I haven't made even the first move. I wanted this to be done before I approached her," Carlos explained.

"Sensible," Jeremiah murmured. "And another point in your favor."

"Her name is Savannah." Derrick offered.

"Landry," Theo filled in.

Jeremiah and his Beta shared a look. One of the women behind them cleared their throat.

"Do you know her?" Carlos asked.

He nodded. "If you're talking about the same Savannah, then yes, I do." He smiled and stood, ending the meeting. "I'll give you a few days to get settled, but you'll want to have the ceremony to change over the prowl soon. I want no indication of power changing hands until it's done. I plan to spend my retirement here, in peace with my mates, and my fields."

He waved his hands to get them to stand and escorted them to the door. "Come by tomorrow. I can show you around, let you meet the enforcers and others in the hierarchy."

"You have my word." Carlos promised.

They shook hands and left.

Derrick was quiet as he navigated the dirt roads to leave the alpha's property.

"He definitely knows Savannah." Theo commented from the back seat.

"That he does." Carlos agreed. "We'll find out how, soon enough."

"What do you think?" Theo leaned forward and rested his arms on their seat.

"I think he's being truthful." Derrick commented.

"There was no discernable hostility while we were on the land. The women in the meeting were strong, but neither of them gave us push back. There will be a bit of jostling throughout the hierarchy." Carlos smiled in anticipation. "We'll have to find a way to let them fight it out without it becoming contentious."

"Could be fun to do a tournament, let both sides get their animals out while we work out the hierarchy." Derrick suggested.

Theo laughed. "Yeah, that could be fun actually."

"We will thrive here." His Beta announced, his voice rang with conviction.

"I felt the same welcome from them as the land gave me when we crossed the state line." Carlos rubbed his hands together excited.

Derrick grunted. "It will be an adjustment, but well worth it."

"We're home." Theo said, moving back.

Carlos sighed. "We are."

His panther moved through his body underlining his best friend's words. They'd found a place to call home and it felt damn good.

Chapter 7

Once again Savannah stood on Laura's doorstep, food in hand. She had a mission, one she'd executed poorly the other night, let Charlotte tell. Not that she could blame her cousin. She really hadn't gotten much information out of Carlos, or Derrick. This morning she would do better. She planned to use coffee and donuts from her favorite café to bribe her new friend into giving her information.

Theo answered the door in jogging pants and a tank top, his hair wet and slicked back from his face. Tattoos she'd never noticed before covered his muscular arms down to a few inches before his wrist. She realized she'd never seen him without a long sleeved shirt.

He raised an eyebrow. His green eyes sparkled with curiosity. "You've got negotiation all over your face this morning, Ms. Landry."

She held up the donuts and waved them under his nose. "I come for information, hopefully that doesn't require much negotiation."

"The donuts help," he said with a twinkle in his eye.

He moved back to allow her entrance into the house. Laura shuffled into the kitchen, her curly hair all over the place, a fuzzy robe with dancing t-rexes, loosely tied.

"How in the world is your hair so nice, so early in the morning?" she groused.

Savi shook her head from side to side and laughed as her straightened hair tousled, then settled back into place. "Umm, black women sleep in a scarf for a reason. Keeps our hair from becoming the nest you got on top of your head."

"Luckily you brought coffee or I would be offended." Laura grabbed a cup and brushed a kiss across her cheek.

"I also brought donuts." She wiggled the bag.

"Hmm, sounds like a bribe." Laura sipped out of her cup.

"I came to get the tea on your brother."

Laura's eyebrows shot up and she choked on her coffee. Theo laughed and patted her back.

"This should be good." He leaned forward on the counter and grabbed the second cup.

She put the donuts on their kitchen island. "It's nothing like that."

She'd fantasized and dreamt about both men over the past two nights, but they didn't need to know that.

"Well, what's it like then?" Laura sat on a stool next to her.

"I just want to know if he's here to stay. I know he's an Alpha, but is he a Felix?"

Theo nodded.

"Well, I talked to my grandfather last night and—"

It was Theo's turn to choke. Coffee spilled down the front of his shirt. "So Felix Jeremiah is your grandfather, then?"

"You know my grandfathers?"

"Grandfathers?" Laura inquired.

"My grandparents are in a Tribond," she said off hand. If Theo knew her grandparents, then he would have information about the prowls merging.

"I've been here three months, back and forth for negotiations, why haven't I seen you on prowl land?"

"I don't…" she waved a hand. "That's not important."

"I know it's early in the morning, but I'm lost." Laura grumbled.

"So, you don't participate in prowl gatherings?" Theo narrowed his eyes, speculation all over his face.

She sighed, she would give them information if it meant they would return the exchange. "I'm latent, remember? My father is human, and my mother isn't a person that likes the politics of prowl life, so I haven't been to a meeting or gathering since I was fourteen."

There were other reasons, not ones that necessarily concerned them, so she left it at that. They needn't know the prophecies surrounding her and her life if she stayed a part of her family's prowl.

Theo tilted his head. "But your son isn't latent."

"We established that when we met. Granddad told me he has another year before I need to start preparing him to shift."

"He should already be going to gatherings," Theo said gently. "It'll help him feel close to the prowl, and help strengthen the prowl link he'll need for his first shift."

Savannah sighed at the assumption, but answered his unspoken question. "I'm aware. I've gotten the lectures from grandfather. Just because I don't go, doesn't mean he doesn't. Grandpa Harper comes and gets him. He spends a lot of time on prowl land. I visit my grandparents, I just don't go to meetings or gatherings."

Nor did she spend more than a couple of hours at her grandparents' house on the off chance one of her cousins would come and start shit with her. It happened often enough that her internal clock always knew when it was time to leave.

Theo nodded, respect coloring his gaze.

"I don't play about my baby, Theo." She reassured him.

"I see that." He took another sip of his coffee.

"Your ex is human, right? How did he take it when you told him?" Laura asked.

"About Jamie? Greg knew it was a chance before we married, he doesn't say anything one way or the other."

"So, your questions?" Theo steered the conversation back.

"Grandad says he has a deal with Carlos to turn over the territory without a challenge?"

Theo nodded. "I negotiated it myself."

Relief coursed through her. She slapped a hand down on the countertop. "And Carlos agreed?"

Theo smiled and waggled his brows. "I take it since you're asking me, you've been told to stay out of the Felix's business."

Laura laughed.

Savannah growled in frustration.

Laura laughed again and shrugged. "It's the same thing I was told, you're getting way more information that I've gotten about the whole thing." She shot her husband a scathing look.

"I tried to talk to grandpa Harper this morning and he kept changing the subject. Is it a merger, a change over, when is it all happening?"

Theo held up his hand to stem the tide of her questions. "We're merging the prowls and Carlos is taking over as Felix. Will you attend the changeover ceremony?"

She shook her head. "Grandpa Harper will come get Jamie, that's why he called this morning. I imagine it will be a big to do, changing over Alphas."

"You should go."

She shook her head again. "That's not for me."

"Why not?" Laura perked up. "Wait, Naomi said you all don't talk about it."

"It's a long story, one I don't like reliving, so..."

It was a lot to explain to people she'd only known for months, so she clamped her lips shut.

"Fair enough." He reached into the donut bag and grabbed two. "Well, I thank you for the donuts, but I've got work to do, and you ladies will not be getting any additional information out of me."

He circled the island to get to his wife. He leaned down and gave Laura a kiss that scorched her just sitting next to them. Theo rubbed his cheek against the top of Laura's hair and left the kitchen.

Savi turned to Laura once she heard a door close. "What's your brother like? I know my grandparents told me not to worry, but I can't help it."

Laura touched her hand. "Carlos is a great Felix. He really wants this transition to go smoothly. He has a daughter, she's with our parents until Carlos gets everything settled here. Trust me, Carlos would never endanger that little girl."

"And Derrick?"

Laura gave her a sly look. "Derrick is our Beta. He and Carlos are really close, you know."

Savannah hummed, but motioned her to continue.

"I heard rumors that they share their women." Laura whispered.

Her cheeks burned, but she kept her face straight. "But what is he like?"

Laura pouted. "Fine, if you wanna be like that." She pushed a hand in her hair. "He's awesome. We sort of adopted him into our family when he and Carlos left the army. My parents love him, the kids adore him. You couldn't ask for a better Beta."

Savannah nodded, too chicken to ask more pointed questions. "Well, I have to go pick up Jamie from his father, thank you for the info, and I feel much better."

"Hmph, so you're not going to share?"

"What? I just want to know what's in store for my family." Savannah shrugged.

Laura stood with her and gave her a hug. "You should really reconsider coming to the changeover. It would be nice to have you there, and you can see for yourself."

She shrugged. "I'll think about it."

Maybe.

Maybe she'd think about renewing her link with the prowl. It had been some years and a heck of a lot of tears. While she was mostly tolerated by her cousins higher up in the hierarchy, those still fighting for a spot regularly used their challenge to her to show off their prowess. Her grandmother said it was because they sensed her innate power, but she didn't care what it was. Between the fighting and what the prowl's Seer had told her when she was younger, she'd stayed away. She didn't know if she wanted to put herself through that again.

Chapter 8

Carlos closed his eyes and stood still. Power reached to him, the land embracing him, and his panther lavished in it. He felt rooted, the wildness of his panther tamed by the winds blowing through the trees. That same breeze amplified his power, filling his body until he felt drunk. Magic raised the hair on his arm and his Beta growled next to him.

It was as if he stood still enough he could feel the footsteps of every animal on the land. Did it translate to the prowl? When the power fully transferred, would he be able to find the members of his prowl so long as they were on the land?

"It's a heady power."

Jeremiah came up, and the aging Felix's heat was like a fur blanket at Carlos' back.

Jeremiah gripped his shoulder. His hands were wrinkled, and calloused from what was probably years of fieldwork. "You're what this territory needs. Though my granddaughters have the strength, the land never responded to them in that way."

A lump gathered in Carlos' throat, emotions swamping him. He didn't know it could be this way. It was no wonder the tristate prowls wanted him from their land. No one would willingly give up this type of power. He turned to Felix Jeremiah, trying to puzzle out why he would do so.

"It's time." Jeremiah answered his unspoken question. "The responsibility of a good Felix is to do what's best for the land and the magic that flows through the prowl."

It humbled him. Though he'd found himself a reluctant Alpha, he wanted to be a good one for those under him. He was happy Jeremiah agreed to stay on and advise him. They continued their walk through the land, with Harper and Jeremiah explaining the reach of their territory. Both men moved unhurriedly, the ground underfoot seeming to sigh as they passed. They went over county lines and where their territory intersected with the other packs and prides that made Tampa their home.

He was impressed. The prowl held a lot of territory, stretching all the way northwest into the state and farther east than he'd expected. It was a lot of land to cover. A lot of responsibility. His small group had only consisted of twenty enforcers and their family. With the merging it would bring their number up to ninety. He worried about the politics of handling a prowl of that size. The weight of it settled on his shoulders, but his panther seemed to take it in stride. Jeremiah explained the network of safe houses they had set up in the area for panthers who got stuck too far from home.

He'd been a city cat his whole life. It hadn't occurred to him the logistics of running a prowl in a place where there were enough woods to roam free. His cats had had to practice stealth, only able to run free at state parks under the cover of darkness. This would be new…freeing. He couldn't help the smile that curled his lips.

Derrick, Theo, Harper and Rebecca trailed behind them, Rebecca and Harper holding hands. Carlos glanced back at them.

He cleared his throat. "How is it in a Tribond?"

At first he thought the Alpha wouldn't answer. He walked on, hands in his pocket. He broke the silence a moment later.

"It's the best thing to ever happen to me. You know the pull of our animal as Alpha, the constant war to stay in control. The two of them balance that out. The power between the three of us reaches levels not even your imagination can conjure. The power exchange to the prowl will grow tenfold under it."

He wasn't concerned about the power. He fumbled to find another way to ask what he wanted to know.

Jeremiah chuckled. "You're worried about sharing?"

Carlos turned and looked back at his best friend talking with the other Beta. He and Derrick had been through things most would buckle under.

"No."

That would never be a problem between him and Derrick. It would be a privilege to share a mate between them, each of them caring for and protecting her.

"It's not the sharing. I'm more concerned with how our mate will deal with two strong males."

His panther was aggressive, its power overwhelming even for him and he shared his body with it. He could be overbearing, at least according to his sisters, he didn't know how his mate would deal with that from him, and Derrick.

Jeremiah hummed. "If your mate is who you say she is, don't be too concerned."

"So you do know her?"

"Very well." Felix Jeremiah didn't elaborate. He instead changed the subject. "You'll have a problem with the Miami prowl. Our seer has foreseen it."

He hummed, not sure if he'd take the word of a seer he'd never met. Especially since he'd never really consulted one before. His prowl was young, comprised of mostly loner panthers looking for a place to settle. They hadn't yet melded into a cohesive unit, but they were getting there. They hadn't attracted any Seers, so he didn't know much about them, or whether their advice would be something he actively sought out.

But still, it couldn't be a coincidence that with his arrival, trouble would visit. "Miami specifically?" He looked up as they came upon a house.

Jeremiah smiled and pat him on the back. "I'll let her tell you herself."

Carlos had to wonder if he was easily readable or if Jeremiah could read minds. The Felix ushered them all in. The woman who greeted them was a lot younger than he'd expected. She was Hispanic, her skin browned from what looked like many hours in the sun. Her beautiful face was open, her curiosity and excitement easy to discern. She grabbed his hand as they were introduced.

She smiled widely. "I'm Joelle. You will bring a lot to this prowl." She moved to Derrick and gripped his hand. "A strong Beta, you've seen your future and are making steps to ensure it comes to fruition."

Carlos rolled his eyes as Derrick shot him a smug look. "Don't encourage him, please. He's already hard to deal with."

They all laughed. The seer waved at them to sit. She went to the kitchen and brought a tray with glasses and a pitcher of tea. She was clearly expecting them. She set the tray on the coffee table and served them.

"Your Beta got you to where fate wanted you to be."

He took a sip of the cold tea and promptly choked.

Theo snickered next to him. "I probably should've warned you about sweet tea."

He glared at his brother in law and put the glass down on a coaster, vowing to avoid the rest. Derrick sipped happily from his glass.

"This is heaven." His Beta settled back on the sofa and crossed his ankle over his knee.

It was diabetes in a glass, but he would keep his opinions to himself. Carlos rolled his eyes and addressed the seer. "Tell me about the Miami prowl."

Joelle looked to Felix Jeremiah for guidance.

He waved away her concern. "He needs to know before the changeover. It's to be his prowl, he should know what he's signing up for."

She nodded. "The Felix has been giving us push back for a while, nothing outside of the norm. Every Alpha tries to expand their territory. Especially one with no mate or heirs to keep him content. With the way I see it, he could start escalating soon."

Carlos sat forward on the edge of the sofa. "What has changed?"

"Something makes taking this territory personal for him." She said, averting his eyes.

Carlos got a sinking feeling. "Are you sure it's Miami?"

Her eyes filled with compassion and knowledge of why it mattered to him. "It's definitely south of us. It's a pretty specific motive."

"When will he come?" He asked quietly.

"He seeks to take back what he feels is rightfully his." She tucked her hair behind her ear, again looking away.

"This territory has never been his." Harper growled.

The Seer looked at Carlos. "It's not only land he wants."

"He's nothing to me. He has never been a part of my life." It was as his mother feared. He'd hoped to avoid any involvement with his biological father, but it seemed there was no help for it.

"All the same." She shrugged.

"How does it play?" Derrick asked.

She sighed. "I assume he'll lose face trying to claim a son who wants nothing to do with him. Pride demands he take the next best thing."

"Our land." Jeremiah murmured.

"How do we stop him?" Derrick asked.

A growl rumbled his chest as his panther riled. "Like we've done every other obstacle in our life, Beta."

Theo sighed. "We fight."

Jeremiah's hand formed a steeple. "We're no strangers to fight, ourselves."

Carlos turned to Felix Jeremiah. "I'm sorry your retirement won't be as peaceful as you wanted."

"He won't fight fairly." Joelle warned. "Gather your prowl, keep them tightly together until your Tribond is secure. Once that power is running throughout the prowl, there's nothing he can do."

Jeremiah nodded. "The Miami Felix is your father then?"

He shook his head. "Daniel Ayala is my father. Outside of a few stories from my mother, I know nothing about Yasim."

"What happened, if you don't mind my asking?" Harper asked.

Carlos stretched his legs out in front of him. "I never got the complete story from my mother or my older sister. It's painful for them both."

He thought about what his mother had told him before he headed down. She was afraid he'd run into his father in the local council meeting, so she wanted to make sure he was prepared. He knew she'd left out a lot of details, but she'd told him more than she'd ever did about the subject. And though it happened over thirty years ago, she still had tears in her eyes.

"My mother mated him, and from what she tells me, things were fine. He was Beta to a cruel Alpha in a disjointed prowl. Yasim pulled together a few panthers and they challenged their way up the hierarchy. He beat the Alpha, and took over the prowl. She said he changed then. She would never say in what way. Just that while better than the other Alpha, he was not without his cruelties. She withstood a lot with my sister Yasmeen, but she said once she was pregnant with me something whispered to her that her son would never be safe there. She said something to him that must've struck a nerve. He beat her, and had his enforcers drop her off in the middle of the swamp with nothing but the clothes on their back."

Rebecca gasped.

"Daniel found her wandering, dehydrated and clutching my sister's hand." He shook his head. "My father took care of both Yasmeen and me as though we were his. My mother was very upset about me coming here and possibly running into him."

He turned to the seer. "Does he know I'm here?"

She shook her head. "I don't know when he finds out, but he will eventually and it will start a sort of escalation."

"When will he come?" He asked again.

She closed her eyes and breathed deep. "It will be a while before he realizes the power that entered the state is you."

Harper spoke up. "Right now, I suspect he'll send out spies to find out what's happening. To see how our prowl holds up to your power. He's unaware we're blending together."

"Then we need the ceremony done." Carlos said. "I can't begin to work on the Tribond until I know our prowls are together and not infighting."

"You'll have a fight on your hands with your mate." Rebecca cautioned.

Carlos looked to her in surprise. "You think?"

"I know." She told him.

Harper nodded, and Rebecca sighed. "We'll help in whatever way we can. But Savi has her own mind and her own way of doing things. It will make her a great Alpha female, but will give you hell."

Jeremiah snorted. "She'll challenge your panther at every turn."

Joelle gave him a commiserating look. "The Miami Felix will unfortunately not help with that."

Carlos was confused as to how well they knew Savannah, but he didn't have time to explore it. He needed to get his enforcers moved down, and settled before his father caught wind of him in the state. Once the prowl was his, he would focus on moving everyone else.

"Tomorrow evening then," Jeremiah proposed.

"My prowl is small, and they are ready to move down, but I want my enforcers here immediately."

Jeremiah acquiesced. "Of course, but, about your enforcers..."

"We thought having a tournament would help settle hierarchy quickly and with minimal bloodshed." Derrick proffered.

"It will give the prowls a chance to know each other in between matches." Rebecca's shoulders slumped in relief and she laid a hand on the shoulder of her mate.

Joelle gave Carlos a dazed look, growing respect lighting her eyes.

"It could work," Harper mused.

"It would be fun, a way to celebrate the blending of the prowls." Theo added helpfully.

"We'll arrange it for the day after the turnover." Rebecca clapped. "I'll talk to the butcher, and double our order, get the grills going, I'm excited."

"Perfect." Carlos stood. "Though I would say the day after to give my enforcers a day of rest after they travel."

"Then I'd better get to work." Jeremiah said standing. He held his hand out to Carlos. "I'm looking forward to this."

They left Joelle's house with business settled and a growing sense of purpose. He'd expected to have to deal with his father, but outright war with him wasn't on the agenda.

"We came down to avoid a war," Theo said lazily getting into the truck.

Carlos grunted. "A prowl of soldiers is no stranger to war."

Chapter 9

"Mom, this shirt is too tight." Jamie walked out of his bedroom pulling on the collar of his white dress shirt.

She sighed and held up a finger as her phone rang. Her son hated dressing in anything other than a t-shirt and basketball shorts. She expected he'd complain about wearing the dress shirt and white linen pants. She had a white v neck t-shirt that she would have him put on right as his grandfather arrived. He'd be grateful to not have to wear the dress shirt and forget to complain about the pants. It was a dance all moms did with their children she knew, still, she shot him an irritated glare.

"Yes." She answered the phone.

"Honey, I can't make it to come get Jamie. There's so much to be done here. Can you bring him?" Her grandfather Harper sounded winded.

"He doesn't have to come, Grandpa. I can bring him by when there's not so much going on." She didn't want to step foot on prowl land with a changeover ceremony going on. It was too tempting.

"No!" Jamie rushed over and put his hands together in a pleading gesture.

"I know how you feel sweetheart, but please bring him. I don't want to disappoint my boy. You can leave before the ceremony starts."

She grumbled. "Damn it, I mean, dang it."

"Five cents in the jar." Jamie sang.

She growled.

"Savannah, he needs to feel the new prowl link." Her grandfather's voice was adamant.

"Fine. We'll be there."

"Yes!" Jamie pumped his fist.

She ended the call and then realized what she'd agreed to. God. She scrambled to get dressed, digging in her closet for something white. Her grandmother would kill her if she showed up in any other color. All ceremonies were performed and attended in white. She didn't attend any ceremonies, but, luckily she'd gone to an all-white party with Naomi some months back. She had a cute skater dress, but the front was a little club-y. Her grandfathers would both probably say something, but she didn't have anything else.

She slapped on some makeup, cursing herself the whole time. She should just drop Jamie off, no need for her to stay. Yet, she lined her eyes carefully, wanting to look her best. Darn it, she was going to the ceremony. There was no use in pretending otherwise. Her son danced in and out of the bathroom, excited she was going with him. He kept up a steady stream of chatter as she put on the finishing touches. She packed a bag with a change of clothes for them both, because there was only so long they could wear white in the country.

It only took her forty five minutes to get to their place. She navigated the dark dirt road by rote, her mind churning with what she'd decided to do. She sighed. Surely attending the ceremony wouldn't bring down the end of days. Some of her cousins were hanging out on the porch as she parked, their quiet chatter ending as she reached the front step. She waved and walked right into house. There were more cousins milling around, all of them her immediate family, and she was happy she'd come. She gave out hugs and kisses, having not seen this many of her cousins gathered at once since Thanksgiving last year.

Her grandmother came from upstairs and spotted her. "You came!" Rebecca rushed over and gave her a hug. She wore a simple sheath dress, the color making her dark skin glow. "Do you think there is enough cleavage showing in that dress?"

She tugged up on the bodice of her dress, shooting her guffawing cousins a glare. "It was all I had to wear."

"Well, never mind then. I'm just glad you're here."

She looked around the living room, nostalgia overwhelming her. "Will the new Alpha take this over?"

She was a little sad thinking about it, she'd grown up in the house, visiting her grandparents. She ran her fingers over the pictures her grandmother had scattered across the room. It was Rebecca's grandkids in various school portraits. She had a giant album underneath the coffee table that held years and years of pictures. If she had more time, she'd open it and laugh with her cousins as they always did when they got together.

"No, they have their own prowl house set up in town." Rebecca tossed over her shoulder as she flitted off to do something else.

That made her happy to hear. "How will that work?" she murmured more to herself than to Rebecca's retreating form.

"You ask a lot of questions for someone who doesn't care." Her grandfather Harper looked handsome in his white linen pants and pressed, button down shirt. As always he was immaculate, his manner precise and competent. He hugged her as he came into the living room.

"I'm just curious, granddad."

"We will merge our prowls, and your grandfather and I will step aside and take our place as elders." He patted the top of Jamie's head and her son tiptoed to rub his head under his great-grandfather's chin.

"Won't that be strange having the old Alpha around?" She crossed her arms over her chest.

"The young man is powerful, trust me, the panthers will have no problem following him. His power calls to all around him." Harper reassured her.

"I'm happy and will enjoy retirement with my mates." Jeremiah stepped into the room, his power preceding him. Her cousins straightened in his presence, their joking coming to a halt.

She hugged her other grandad, soaking in his smell. He always smelled of mint, the dark musk of his panther and a wild scent she associated with him and his fields. Her latent power swelled a little, as it always did when she was near him. Not enough to alarm anyone, and bring undue attention to her. Certainly not enough to hold her own within the prowl. She quickly squashed the bitter thought. Her grandfather was dressed in white pants with a silk sash. His chest was bare, and she couldn't believe he was seventy years old. It did not reflect in his build.

Rebecca stood in the hallway outside of the living room and clapped her hands to get everyone's attention. "It's time." She announced.

Her grandmother gave Jeremiah one last kiss, their foreheads meeting as they murmured to each other. Grandpa Harper joined them, his arms going around them both. Jeremiah rubbed his chin against the top of his mates' heads, their power swelling, overtaking the room.

Savannah let out a shuddering breath, tears clogging her throat. Her grandparents' love was palpable. Her cousins all paused and watched as the three of them exchanged affection.

Rebecca sighed and wiped her face. She stepped back from her mates and cleared her throat. Jeremiah cupped her chin and stared into his mate's eyes before turning to his family. He gave one long whistle and everyone in the house followed him out the door. Some of her cousins glared at her as she joined the group. One in particular shoved past her to take up a spot in front of her. She sighed, and started her mental countdown. She needed to be away from everyone in another hour, or surely she'd have to fight someone.

She and her family walked in a group towards the clearing where they held all their ceremonies and family cook outs. Murmuring from the already gathered crowd traveled in the night air, the prowl's excitement palpable. They walked to the meeting circle and there stood Carlos, strong and proud in loose white pants and a sash, to match her grandfather. His curly hair was tamed, and slicked down, showing off his high cheekbones and strong chin. His chest was chiseled, tapering into washboard abs that made her mouth water. She longed to run her fingers across his stomach, to touch his skin. Her power swelled again, and she frowned. Both her grandfathers turned to her and smiled, satisfaction gleaming in their eyes. Why, she didn't know, but they were up to something, no doubt. She didn't want any parts of it. She slowed her steps to hide behind her cousins towards the back to keep their grandfathers' attention away from her.

Once they entered the circle with the other prowl members, her aunts turned and magic swelled as they closed the circle. Close to seventy members of the prowl formed a circle and sat on benches ringing the fighting area, leaving only the alphas standing.

Carlos' eyes followed her as she sat next to Charlotte. Her body heated, and flushed and she looked away to escape his piercing gaze.

"Biiitch," Charlotte whispered and bumped her shoulder.

"Don't even." She hissed.

A beautiful woman she didn't recognize stood and started chanting. Her aunts and grandmother followed suit, the remaining prowl members catching the melody and joining. Soon, the circle's power flared and her heart started thumping with excitement.

Her grandfather Jeremiah started moving his feet in a complicated pattern, circling Carlos. After three revolutions Carlos' feet took up the rhythm, his graceful movements mesmerizing. They started mock fighting, their swings still near enough for tension to coat the circle. Her heart raced, fear for her grandfather coming to the forefront. Power raised, the strength of it stealing her breath, weighing on her body. Carlos' skin was covered in sweat as he picked up speed, showing off his Alpha power.

Despite his age, Jeremiah's panther was still strong, and his power moved through the circle, reminding the prowl of why he'd led them for so long. Their feet moved, kicking up dust, their hands moving in a fast pattern as they circled each other, ducking and dodging punches and kicks. Jeremiah threw punches and Carlos' parried them with quick movements.

Jeremiah kicked, and Carlos dodged, their elegant movements keeping the gathered panthers spellbound. Power built to a feverish pitch, and the chanting slowed, softened until the crowd leaned forward to catch the ancient words. Carlos raised his leg, kicking towards Jeremiah's chest, pausing less than a hairs breadth away. She sucked in a surprised breath, afraid he'd actually struck her grandfather. Jeremiah stood still, the two of them locking eyes, their breathing sawing in and out of their chest, the sound of it overpowering the chanting.

All movement stopped, the chanting quieted and Jeremiah lifted his chin, exposing his neck. Roars filled the circle as Carlos leaned over Jeremiah's neck. They stepped apart a moment later and Jeremiah raised Carlos' arm and presented him to the prowl. Whistles and cheers lifted and magic flowed around, raising goosebumps on her arms.

Jeremiah removed his sash and presented it to Carlos, who accepted it with a bow. Power flowed from her grandfather to Carlos, and then outward to the circle. The magic pressed against her. Carlos turned to her, and her head buzzed, pressure building. His eyes glowed as he watched her, the light in his gaze trapping her, raising power in her body until her ears popped. A rush of warmth, and togetherness flooded her body until she choked up. Carlos had intentionally added her to the prowl link. She lowered her head as tears gathered in her eyes. She wiped her face and once the ceremony was done, kissed her son and escaped during the chaos of the congratulations. She'd promised Jamie that they would spend the night, so she hastened to her grandparent's house.

She couldn't be a part of this, it was too much, brought back too many memories. She raced to her car to get the small bag she'd packed and was fumbling in her purse for the keys when her power flared, and smoldering heat warmed her back. She refused turn around.

"Elder Jeremiah is your grandfather." Carlos' growl tightened her body.

She sighed, finally finding her keys and unlocking the door. She turned to face them. "Yes."

Carlos' canines flashed in the moonlight, his smile predatory. "Okay then."

Derrick tilted his head, his eyes flashing gold before he too smiled. "So, it begins."

"What?" She looked between them.

"You're leaving?" Carlos asked.

Shit. If she stayed, what would they do? She could easily lie and come back, right? Derrick stared, and her core clenched in need.

No way would she tell them she was staying.

"Yeah, I just, I wasn't supposed to be here. I was just making sure Jamie was here to merge with the new prowl link." She ran a nervous hand over her hair.

Carlos nodded. "And you, did you feel the new link?"

She looked away, her heart aching to be a normal part of the prowl. "Yeah, I shouldn't have been there for that."

They both stared, their eyes amber, claws out, and their animals close to the surface. Derrick opened his mouth to say something, but Carlos grabbed his arm.

"Good night then, we don't want to hold you up," Carlos purred.

She blew out a sigh of relief and jumped in the car.

Derrick watched their mate drive off and turned to the Felix. "What was that about?"

"Our mate is running scared, Beta, allow her her momentary sanctuary."

He was confused, with his animal so close to the surface he wanted their mate, and watching her drive off was angering his panther.

Carlos turned to him and rubbed his cheek against the side of his face. His cat reached for its Alpha and basked in his calming presence.

"Two more days and we go on the hunt." Carlos promised.

"Two days." He said aloud, but it was meant for his cat. The animal swiped his insides, an angry swat that told him what he thought about the plan.

"Right, let's go back to our new prowl members and reassure them."

Derrick nodded, his gaze going back to the now deserted road his mate used to escape. "Yeah, let's put on a good show."

He'd allow her a respite for now. His mate didn't know it yet, but his panther was a patient hunter. He'd bide his time, and enjoy every minute of it.

Chapter 10

Baking made Savannah feel better. It always did. Which would explain why she was elbow deep in dough, listening to her son rattle on about how much fun he had last night. Jamie always enjoyed what he called 'prowl time'. He loved running around in the country free of his mother's rules. He was happy she would let him spend the whole weekend here after the prowl change over. Her grandmother was out prepping for another gathering, so she currently had the kitchen to herself.

Thoughts of last night chased themselves around in her head. She'd left early and selfishly, she could admit. But feeling the prowl link after so many years out was…she sighed.

It was a wonderful feeling.

But it was not for her. For the safety of her family, she would continue her self-imposed isolation. She thought about Lydia and the looks she'd shot her all night. It was best she stay away. If ever there was a reminder, her cousin was it. Lydia's mom had been kicked out of the prowl, for reasons unknown to most. Speculation pinned it on Savannah and her own absence. Gossip moved as it did, and no amount of denial from her had stopped the talk. So now, her cousin Lydia hated her.

She tuned back in as Jamie mentioned the new Felix. "How is he?"

Asking a kid was low, but her son was very observant. He didn't miss details, and she envied him a little with how well he used his instincts.

"I like him. Marcella says he's a great dad."

So he'd brought his daughter down. Laura had mentioned that he would only do so if he thought it was safe. That was a good sign. She punched down into the dough turning it over, humming for him to go on.

"After the ceremony the whole prowl was calling to the moon, you should've felt it, mom." Jamie sighed and rested his chin on his hand. "They even let us run with them after. I like Felix Carlos."

She turned to him, intrigued by the wistful tone. "What's that tone to your voice?"

He shrugged. "I kind of wished we lived with the prowl. The link feels so awesome when we're around the others."

She lowered her head and shaped the cinnamon rolls unsure of how to even answer that.

"So, anyway. Grandpa Harper said there will be a tournament today."

She stopped. "What tournament?"

That explained why her grandparents were all so busy today. It also explained why Rebecca had asked for so many baked goods. She'd been distracted and all too happy to bake away her feelings to get clarification.

"Well, because they're blending prowls, Grandpa Jeremiah says they have to see who is stronger and form a new heir, hera, hi-arch..."

"Hierarchy?" She supplied, resting a hand on her hip, giving her son her full attention.

"Yeah, that. So they're going to battle, but Derrick says probably minimal bloodshed." Jamie finished stirring the icing and was now dipping his spoon in the bowl and eating it.

She snatched the bowl, because who wanted an eight year old on a sugar high? "Minimal bloodshed?"

He shrugged and walked to the sink with his spoon. "Grandpa Harper said it's a great idea and he respects the new Felix for thinking of it."

She growled and wiped her hands on a towel. She snatched her cellphone from the counter and dialed her grandfather's number. It took several rings before he picked up.

"What's this about a tournament?"

"It will fun, you should come since you're already on property." Jeremiah answered.

"Grandfather, it doesn't sound appropriate for an eight-year-old." She growled.

"An eight-year-old panther cub," Jeremiah reminded her. He sounded neither chagrined nor alarmed by her tone. "It's more than appropriate."

She sighed. "He said there would be minimal bloodshed, I don't want my son to see something violent."

Her grandfather snorted. "It's no more violent than a boxing or wrestling match, or the skirmishes you got into as a child."

She ignored the not so subtle jab and drummed her fingers against the cabinet over her head. "I don't know."

"I'm no longer Felix, so I can't order you, but as the cub's grandfather, he will be here."

She growled and her grandfather answered with his own growl. His power, even over the phone, inundated her, especially strong since Carlos had renewed her prowl link.

"Fine," she said through clenched teeth.

"Come see for yourself, Vanna, if at any point you feel it's too violent, there are plenty other things happening. You've been in enough challenges to know it won't get too violent. We're doing it so the two prowls will get to know each other. There's food, and games for the kids."

She thought it through, even though he wasn't really giving her a choice. "Fine."

"Perfect," she heard the smile in his voice and couldn't help but feel as though she'd fallen for something.

***

Carlos roamed the empty field where they were having the prowl gathering. Picnic tables were set up near the grills, there were games set up for the cubs, and panthers from both prowls pitched in to get food prepared and decorations set. He crossed his arms over his chest and surveyed the area. Pride filled him, the magic of the territory flowed through him and he was once again happy he'd made the move.

Dried leaves crunched on the ground behind him a moment before a soft touch rested on his shoulder.

"Fela," he murmured in greeting, recognizing her scent.

She circled him until she hovered at his peripheral and smiled, "not any longer." She sighed and there was relief, not regret in the sound. "What do you think so far?"

"I think you guys have outdone yourself. The excitement is palpable through the prowl link." He turned to face her.

She laughed, "That is an understatement."

He smiled. She was right. The link was buzzing, enough to make a one giddy.

"So, my granddaughter..."

He tensed and she pat his shoulder.

"Don't worry, I ain't here to warn you off."

As if she could. He kept that thought to himself.

"Her grandfathers are happy about the mating, but they don't know Savannah the way I do. They don't understand how deep rooted her…fear of being a part of this prowl is."

He turned to her then, and took in her worried expression. "Do you know the cause of it?"

She shook her head. "She used to spend her every spare moment here. She loves this prowl, no matter how hard she fights to show it. One evening she was happy at a gathering, dancing and playing with the others her age, and the next morning, she left with her mother, angry."

"Did something happen?"

"Clearly, but what? Even after all these years, I've been unable to find out."

"And no one will talk?"

She shook her head and rubbed her arms. "I suspect it had something to do with the seer we used to have."

"In what way?"

She shrugged her shoulders. "My mates will tell me nothing, save, Jeremiah's sister was no longer our seer, and unwelcome on our lands. Her children chose to stay, but she and her mate left, banished."

He frowned.

She sighed and shook off her melancholy, "you'll have a fight on your hands. She thinks she's not strong enough as a latent to be in our prowl, good luck convincing her she's strong enough to be alpha female."

He nodded. "I'm no stranger to fighting."

"If you give her too much leeway, she'll run, and she'll keep running. You'll need to be sneaky." She warned. She kissed his cheek. "Let me go supervise, I don't know how well you city cats can cook."

He laughed and she winked and walked off. She was a beautiful woman, he could well imagine his mate at her age. He surveyed the grounds, satisfied with the progress. The two groups were so far getting along. He'd settled most of the incoming prowl in the buildings he'd bought. Some of the prowl members, though there were a small number of them, preferred the country and with the help of the old Fela, they were being settled into empty houses. He was satisfied, deeply, with the way things were going. After the tournaments tonight, once the hierarchy was settled, he could work on his mate. He looked forward to it.

***

Savannah wondered for about the tenth time, what she was doing in her grandmother's kitchen, chopping up vegetables. She should've left. She could've easily made up a work excuse and left. It wasn't as though she didn't trust her family with her son. If her grandparents said Jamie wouldn't see anything, then more than likely he wouldn't.

Still.

She'd stayed, and now stood next to Charlotte chopping lettuce. Most of her cousins expressed shock at seeing her, some even gave her hostile looks. Though, 'some' was an exaggeration. One cousin was leading the pack, her disapproving gaze following Savannah across the kitchen as she went about her work.

Charlotte bumped her shoulder. "Ignore her."

"What is her problem?" The knife bit through the lettuce, slamming with a thud into the cutting board. Savannah blew out a frustrated breath.

"She's a bitch, duh." Charlotte rolled her eyes.

Savannah peered over her shoulder. Lydia was still staring, whispering to her clique. She sighed and turned back to her task. The chatter throughout the house ebbed and flowed, the volume swinging from loud laughter, to whispers of gossip. She loved the sound, and focused on it instead of her cousin. The women from the new prowl intermingled with the old one, the women getting to know each other. Earlier, Laura had introduced her to her older sister Yasmeen as well as Carlos' daughter Marcella. She was beautiful, and Jamie had talked about her all morning as though they were long lost brother and sister.

There were not a lot of ladies in the prowl that came with Carlos, according to the gossip she was gleaning, so her cousins were excited. The new prowl brought new blood in and a chance to mate closer to home.

The back of her neck tingled as though she could feel Lydia's stare. She dismissed her cousin, she had every right to be there.

She tensed as Lydia sniffed behind her. She kept chopping, it was no use allowing Lydia to see her discomfort.

"You've been around here a lot, have you decided to come crawling back? We don't need any more weak latents in the prowl," Lydia sneered.

Savannah took her time turning. "That's funny, because here you are, a whole panther and still weak as hell, yet they let you stay."

"Just barely." Charlotte crossed her arms over her chest next to her as she turned to face their cousin.

The kitchen quieted.

"She has a reason to worry, I guess," Brielle chimed in from her position at the stove, "even without a panther Savi is likely to kick her ass."

The women laughed and went back to work.

Lydia leaned over into Savannah's space. "I'm willing to take that bet."

"We can handle this right now, cuz. Just say the word." Savannah stared Lydia down.

Her cousin sniffed and flipped her hair. "You're not worth it."

Charlotte snorted. "You don't want your ass kicked in front of all these new people, you mean?"

Savannah laughed, rolled her eyes and turned her back on Lydia. She wasn't afraid to fight. She'd been latent her whole life, fighting was a part of that. Panthers would go after anyone they perceived weaker. She'd made plenty examples of other prowl members growing up. Even after she'd stopped going to meetings, she would occasionally be challenged. She had no problems accepting the challenges.

If anything, saying no to a fight was her problem, as her grandfather not so subtly reminded her this morning.

She wanted her son to have his place in the prowl, and she'd fight anyone to make it happen. Lydia could kiss her ass. She growled and dropped the knife, her nerves jangled, though nothing physical had happened.

"I need a minute, Char."

Charlotte's gaze roved her face and she nodded. "I'll handle this, take a break."

She blew out a relieved breath and walked out into the heat of the day, nearly no different from the stifling heat in the kitchen. She pressed a hand to her wet brow and walked to the porch railing. Her skin heated, and goosebumps prickled along her arms.

She was being watched.

Nothing about the sensation was alarming, which meant it was one of two people. Derrick or Carlos. She didn't know which, but she would not look around to see. She knew enough about predators to know that acknowledging him would make his panther excited. Still, her skin flushed and a restless feeling overtook her body. She paused at the rocking chair her grandmother kept outside and sat, her knees weakening. The weight of his stare was a physical caress. The bushes surrounding her grandparents' house shuffled.

Whether in human or panther form, he was stalking her like prey.

She would not get excited, though some primal part of her wanted to stand and preen for him. She suppressed it. When after a moment he didn't get a response, he sauntered from the woods and approached her. His steps measured, his narrowed eyes holding her captive. Derrick was gorgeous, his body honed and muscular, his dark skin gleaming in the sunlight. His hair was close cropped to his skull, a fresh lineup on the edges framing his face. His five o'clock shadow had grown since she'd last seen him. A short beard framed his chin and gave him a rugged look that stole her breath. He strode from the woods, barefoot with no shirt on and jeans slung low.

The jeans were a little big, so she could only assume he'd grabbed the first pair of pants he'd found lying around. The woods were filled with baskets where wandering panthers would find clothes for when they shifted back.

Her mouth dried as he approached the porch, his movements as graceful as the animal beneath his skin. He leaned over her, planting his hands on the arms of the chair, caging her in.

"Savannah."

That was all he said. Just her name. His voice, deep and gravelly, filled places in her she'd just recently been aware were empty.

"Derrick," she said after trying to swallow.

His eyes traced her face, his canny gaze cataloguing her every expression. As he studied her mouth, his tongue swept over his bottom lip. "You didn't want to play with me?"

She let out a rough exhalation. Lord, she wanted to play with him. He ran his cheek against hers in a greeting she'd not had in years. She closed her eyes and basked in his touch.

"I'm busy helping with the cooking, I can't go playing in the woods with you."

He hummed and leaned into her neck. His breath on her skin raised goosebumps. "You smell fantastic."

"That's the hungry predator talking, I smell like food." she whispered as he nuzzled against her skin.

"In more ways than one, little one." The hair of his beard scraped against the sensitive skin of her neck and her nipples tightened, her core clenching. He pulled back, his onyx eyes scrutinized her.

She couldn't keep eye contact, so she looked over his shoulder. She kept her hands gripped in her lap, knowing she'd run them over his body if she let them go. Power unfurled within her as he rubbed his head under her chin, his Beta power surging in response. He hummed again, this time satisfaction was laced within the sound. Longing sped her heartbeat and she exhaled a ragged breath. She wanted him like nothing else she'd ever wanted. But she knew the cost. Knew what her body was telling her. Had it simply been Derrick, it may have been different, her fate, possibly averted, but the beginning strings of a Tribond were tethering her to both men so just choosing one was out of the question. Grief welled up and she closed her eyes.

His head lifted, confusion bunching his eyebrows. His panther bled into his eyes, and it was the animal's wary gaze that appraised her. He lifted his hand, his fingers tracing her face.

"What's wrong, kitten?" he whispered.

She shook her head knowing if she opened her mouth, tears would be close behind her words. He rubbed his face against the side of hers and she sighed.

"There's going to be dancing tonight." He used a sing song voice that made her smile, despite her mood. "Will you dance with me, gorgeous?"

She cleared her throat and nodded.

He smiled, his straight white teeth showing the hungry predator lurking beneath his human façade. "I'll leave you to your grandmother's rule, but I'll see you later tonight."

Derrick backed away and she nodded. She considered leaving before then, but discarded the thought before it fully formed.

He leaned back in suddenly, his face once again serious. "Are you thinking of escape, Savannah?"

Her eyes widened, guilt rising. She scoffed, forcing nonchalance into her tone. "After all the work I've done, I'm not leaving until I'm too full walk."

He smiled and her power spiked again. She wondered if it was because Carlos had included her in the prowl link.

"See you later then." He leaned down and kissed her softly on the lips.

She blinked in surprise at his boldness. She watched him leave, the muscles on his back flexing, those jeans giving her a peek of his ass.

"Savi," her grandmother's voice startled her and she realized she'd still been staring at the spot he'd disappeared.

"Yes, Grandmother?" She turned towards the front door.

Rebecca stood with her shoulder against the jamb and stared for a moment. "Why are you fighting it so hard, love?"

Savannah sighed, pushing up out of the chair. "Prowl life isn't for me. Didn't you hear the little demonstration Lydia put on for everyone in the kitchen?"

Rebecca scoffed, "Lydia don't know her place."

"Well, she seems to want to keep me in mine. You know what will happen if I got involved with the Felix. She won't be the only one with something to say about it."

Her grandmother sighed.

"I know what you think, Grandma."

"I've said nothing, Savannah. I know you feel your power awakening. You left the prowl before you could learn what that meant."

Savi flinched.

Rebecca narrowed her eyes. "Ah, so you do know what it means, and you still plan to fight."

"I'm not made for a prowl, nor a Tribond, and we both know it."

"The only thing I know is that I tire of you repeating that same mess about prowl life. But I guess you have to tell yourself something to excuse you giving up a mating bond. I wish you good luck with that, granddaughter, but to your mates I wish even better luck. Now, get back in here and come help ready this food to be carted to the clearing. I for one am happy to have such strong backed men coming into this prowl."

"Good lord, grandmother." She laughed following Rebecca back into the house.

Chapter 11

Derrick stood in the middle of the gathered circle, eying their head enforcer. Simon was a little worse for wear after having to battle for his position. He smiled as he thought of the hierarchy matches. Some of the men in their group had been sorely surprised to learn they could not in fact beat all the women from the Tampa prowl. There was a moment there when he thought he'd have to fight for the Beta position, but Simon had held onto his position, thus keeping him from having to battle for Beta. Still, they'd give the crowd a demonstration of why he was Beta.

He'd given Simon time after his last match to catch his breath before starting their official fight. They both bowed and took up defensive positions. They paced around, circling each other, familiar sparring partners. Simon smiled before opening aggressively, trying to kick Derrick. As his foot rose, Derrick shifted his weight to avoid the blow. He slapped Simon's leg higher, throwing off the man's balance. He straightened and slapped his palm down on Simon's exposed chest, slamming him to the ground. Before Simon could roll, Derrick's panther ripped from his skin and snapped at Simon's neck.

Jumping back, Simon quickly yielded, shock across his face at the speed of Derrick's change. Hell, he too was surprised. His cat had never reacted to a sparring match with Simon in such an aggressive manner. His panther turned toward the audience and roared. Half the spectators shifted under the weight of the Beta power. He just as smoothly returned to his human form, firmly establishing his position.

He held his hand out to help Simon stand, "Sorry about that, he snapped out of my control for a moment."

"This territory has welcomed you well. I've never seen you move that quickly, it shocked the shit out of me. Your power is growing, Beta." Simon clasped his outstretched hand.

Derrick laughed. "Next time we spar, you won't be tired from hierarchy matches, we'll see how it goes then.

Simon snorted and stood, lifting his chin in submission. "I look forward to it."

He grabbed his enforcer on the back of the neck and brought their foreheads together. The mantle of Beta settled over Derrick's shoulders, tightening his bond with the prowl that had come with them from New Jersey, as well as the new prowl. He stepped back from Simon and rolled his shoulders, reveling in the power.

He groaned at his shredded clothes left at his feet. Someone handed him a pair of jeans and a shirt. He gave them a thankful nod and left the circle, needing to expend the energy still running through his body. He hastily slipped on the clothes, and decided to walk the perimeter of the clearing, not that he needed to. Felix Jeremiah ran a tight prowl, and their prowls blended damn near seamlessly.

He nodded as a woman walked from the woods, her eyes glowing in the night, her cat close to the surface.

"Beta." She inclined her head in greeting and went back to her watch.

Yeah, so walking the perimeter was definitely not needed. It gave him a sense of pride to do it, though, knowing the land was theirs and their small prowl had expanded. Safety and security was important to him, especially now that he had a mate. The small prowl he'd grown up in hadn't stood a chance against the supremacists who'd targeted them. He wouldn't let that happen again.

He had nagged Carlos into starting their prowl and he'd pushed to make them as strong as possible. In a prowl full of ex-military, it hadn't been hard. A natural hierarchy had formed, the men and women grateful for a place their cat was comfortable. He understood the sentiment. He wanted a place where his children could grow up, secure and safe and he'd finally found it.

He thought to Savi and his panther paced his subconscious. Usually he could calm the cat, keep it furled within him, but with the tournament going, and the way the energy buzzed through their new prowl, his cat was impossible to curtail. He gave thought to shedding his clothes and exploring their new territory more. But, if he shifted again, his cat would make a beeline for their mate, and that was a fact.

He'd been checking out the territory earlier when he'd come up on Savannah standing on the porch alone. His cat had watched her for long moments, trying to entice its mate into the woods to play, before he let Derrick shift back into his human form.

He gave a quiet snort.

As though he would keep them from their mate. His cat swiped at him, and he had to laugh, aware that yes, he was currently keeping them from their mate. He bade his cat patience. He was playing a long game. Savannah seemed reluctant and he aimed to find out why. Her sadness had reached out to him when he'd saw her on her grandmother's porch and he didn't understand it. It had beckoned him closer.

Just thinking of her had his feet turning to look for her. He didn't know where she was, and yet, when he looked up from his introspection, he spotted her dancing with her cousins around the large bonfire that had been built.

His senses had unerringly found her without conscious thought. The firelight danced across her, the tight jeans she wore damn near painting a map of her curves. He hardened. She was so beautiful he ached with need for her. A snarl rumbled his chest and he stalked toward her. He looked up to see Carlos doing the same. His Alpha nodded at him as they surrounded their mate. Her cousins shuffled out of the way, giving them a clear path to Savannah.

She turned, her eyes widening as Derrick grabbed her waist, bringing her closer. His hips moved with hers, and her breath hitched. His cat circled his body, heightening his magic. Their steps synched as though they'd danced together their whole lives. Carlos' growl surrounded them as he sidled up to their mate. As soon as the Felix's hands touched her shoulders, power raised down the prowl link. Derrick threw his head back and called to the moon. Answering calls went up around the bonfire, upping the power level. He brought his head down and stared at Savannah. Her mouth was open, her breath coming out in short pants.

He craved her.

Derrick pulled her into his shaft, grinding his hips into her along with the beat of the music. The three of them moved together, their hips gyrating, the heat between the three of them rivaling that of the fire. Savannah threw her arms up and her head back in abandon. Their mate must have had a few drinks, because her face was flushed. As much as he wanted to take their dancing further, he wouldn't take advantage of that.

He and Carlos exchanged looks, their bond deepening as they danced with their mate. Power raised along the prowl link and everyone around them started dancing. The children had long since been put to bed and it was just adults. As they danced, there were no inhibitions, no worries and he was drunk off the scent of his mate and their budding bond. He leaned in and kissed her in front of the prowl. It made their intentions known to all who saw them. It wouldn't take long for the gossip to spread. Especially not with the amount of power that the three of them touching generated.

He pulled from the kiss and spun her, nudging Savannah into Carlos' arms. Carlos devoured her mouth, pulling their mate closer to him. Derrick scraped his teeth along the back of her neck, aching for the day he'd leave his mark. Power inched higher, energy pushing through the prowl link in a way that made some shift. Others released their cats enough to yowl their approval. Derrick's panther pushed against him, trying to force its way out. He only let him off his leash enough to revel in the alpha power.

Savi pulled back from the kiss, her eyes unfocused. Her hand went to her mouth, her fingers skimming her lips. Savannah's magic rose, and melded with him and the Felix's power. It was amazing how powerful their connection was already. Her mewl of need had hunger, sharp and insistent, bombarding him and he watched as Carlos kissed her again. Derrick spun her around when they parted, needing to taste her once more. Their tongues dueled, and she gripped his shoulders, coming to her toes. He was seconds from begging.

She pulled back and touched her lips. "I need…I have to go." She whispered.

Derrick's chest was heaving, his breath sawing in and out of his lungs as he fought his cat. He put his forehead against hers. "Do what you have to do, kitten, but be real careful with the way you leave this clearing."

She nodded and sighed, rubbing her cheek along his. The affectionate gesture ratcheted up his need for her.

"I won't run, I know it will only rile up your panthers more."

That was the understatement of the year. If she left the clearing at anything but a sedate walk his cat would chase her down and Lord help them all. He leaned down and kissed her softly.

"We would enjoy the chase, nevertheless." Carlos' voice was barely human behind her.

Derrick glanced at his co-mate, the Felix's eyes were glowing, the panther staring back at him. Savannah's eyes widened and she walked from them, keeping her steps slow. Carlos growled, the sound carrying despite the music, speeding their mate's steps. He stepped up to Carlos as he spun to go after their mate and put a calming hand on his chest.

"She's scared about something." Derrick could barely get the words out, his panther was near feral with need.

Carlos was no better. The Alpha was agitated, pacing in front of him as they watched their mate disappear into the darkness.

Derrick's panther rose in response. "Reign in it, Felix. With a bit of patience she'll be ours." Carlos had given him the same speech the night before, and Derrick didn't miss the irony of that. "The prowl is settled, the hierarchy laid out. There's nothing stopping us from going after our mate tomorrow."

Carlos nodded, and walked in the opposite direction of Savannah. Derrick wiped a hand down his face and battled to subdue his panther. He wasn't worried.

Horny?

Yes. Anxious, absolutely, but worried? Not in the least. He would have his mate.

***

Carlos' head was full of thoughts of his mate the next morning. His Beta had been the only thing between his cat and Savannah. He'd never had an issue with patience. His time in the Special Forces had honed it even. But, waiting for Savannah, was fast becoming unbearable.

"Papa, just so you know, I met my new mother yesterday." His daughter interrupted his thoughts.

Carlos choked on the cereal he was eating, spilling milk from the bowl onto the small table in his kitchen. His daughter's small hands slapped at his back and he grabbed napkins to pick up the mess.

"Excuse me?" He managed the strangled question.

"Jamie's mom is gonna be my mom." Ella's tone was so matter of fact he could only stare.

Thick lashes surrounded her serious brown eyes. She blinked at him, nonplussed by his reaction.

"What makes you say that?" He asked cautiously.

She shrugged, her dark eyes watching his for a reaction. She tilted her head and he noticed that one of the two ponytails he'd wrestled into her head this morning was crooked. The curly puffs were neat, though, and that was all that mattered.

"I just know it." She lifted her arm and shoveled cereal into her mouth as though she hadn't just dropped a bomb.

He stared at his daughter unable to even formulate anything to say to that. His phone rang, saving him from having to comment.

"Yeah."

"Felix, there was a breach last night." A female voice reported.

He didn't know who was on duty, he hadn't yet learned everyone's name. "What happened?"

"So far we only have an unrecognizable scent on the border of our prowl land."

"Anywhere near the prowl?"

"No, Felix, but I'll keep you posted." She promised.

"Thank you." He hung up to find his daughter staring at him. He sighed. Perhaps he'd brought her down too soon. She would've been happy at her grandmother's, but he selfishly would've missed her.

"What's wrong, Papa?" She asked.

"Nothing, bunny. Wanna go see TiTi Yasmeen?" He texted his sister and let her know what was happening.

"Yes!" She jumped up and headed to her room.

She came back a few moments later with an arm full of dolls. He winced at the amount. He and Derrick may have gone overboard when they'd taken her to the toy store when she arrived. He knew he'd get a lecture from his sister about spoiling her.

"Amelia hasn't seen the new dolls you guys bought me." She smiled.

He stood at the knock on the door and rushed to answer it. It was one of his enforcers. His third in command looked over his shoulder and greeted Ella.

"Hey, bunny, I'm your escort."

"Simon! TiTi is just down the hall, I can walk by myself." She insisted.

Simon gave her a mock pout. "Oh, so I'm not good enough to be your bodyguard?"

"Papa!" She growled, gave him a scowl and walked out the door.

He could only sigh as Simon smiled and shrugged. His daughter was a handful. But, he was happy for every second with her. He'd pulled a lot of strings and greased a lot of palms to take custody of Marcella after his unit had rescued her. Her entire family had been killed and there had been no way he was leaving the little girl to get lost in a system that barely handled the humans they had in their custody. He shook that from his mind and pulled out his phone.

"What's going on?" Derrick answered on the first ring.

"Come over, we had a breach on prowl land." He ordered.

"Did you call the Seer?"

He hummed. It hadn't occurred to him. "Do you trust her?"

"I do. What do you always say?"

He groaned. "Everything that can be of use, use." He sighed. "I'll call the seer and find out what she knows."

"Roger." Derrick hung up.

The Seer was a foreign concept, and it felt strange to even talk about it. He had no experience with seers, and depending on one he barely met had him reticent. But he would use what he had at his disposal. She answered quickly.

"It's begun."

He cursed, no need pretending he didn't know what she meant. "Any suggestions?"

She sighed in frustration. "Nothing new has come to me, but it's starting and will escalate. Just keep your mate safe."

He growled and hung up.

Derrick entered minutes later. "What do we know?"

"Shit. Just a breach for the moment, but the seer thinks it will escalate."

"Not surprising, anyone would be curious enough to want to know the source of power. We raised a lot last night with our mate. They probably came to investigate."

Derrick pulled out a chair to sit, when his phone rang again.

"Felix, a woman was attacked." He recognized Brielle's voice.

"On prowl land?" Shock had him standing.

"Near one of the safe houses," came the answer.

He cursed. "Send me the address, we're on our way."

"Speaking of escalating." Derrick murmured.

His phone beeped with the address and he and Derrick headed out.

Chapter 12

Groggy and horny was not exactly the way Savannah wanted to face her grandparents this morning. But, no one slept in, in Rebecca's house. No matter the bacchanal that had taken place the night prior. There were church services to attend, and prayers to be sent up. She yawned as she cracked another egg into the mixing bowl, making breakfast as per Rebecca's orders. She should've stayed with one of her cousins last night, but she'd ran from the clearing, her instinct to hide at her grandparents' house.

Power raised the hair along her arms as she thought about last night. She sighed in longing. The two of them together was a temptation that took everything in her to fight. She wanted them, desperately. It was an awful choice for anyone to have to make. To choose between the safety of their family, and a love that would transcend anything she'd ever known.

She looked up as her grandfather came into the room. Jeremiah's gaze raked over her grandmother, his eyes devouring Rebecca as though they hadn't spent the last fifty years together. She wanted that. Jeremiah cuddled into Rebecca's neck and her grandmother giggled. She sighed and blinked the mist from her eyes and started beating the eggs.

Rebecca handed Jeremiah his morning coffee and waved for him to sit at the kitchen table.

"Granddaughter, there was a mighty spike in power last night."

"Don't, granddad. Not today, please." Not while her body still throbbed with magic and power.

She couldn't handle the conversation. He hummed and sat at the big oak table with his coffee cup. Someone came into the house and leaned over and spoke with Jeremiah in low tones.

Her granddad's face got hard and he nodded. The panther left and Jeremiah settled back into his seat. He gave a low whistle and inclined his head to one of her cousins standing guard at the window of the living room. There was always someone in her grandparents' home keeping watch. It was something she'd grown up with.

Rebecca turned and stared at Jeremiah, her grandfather's eyebrows raising. She wasn't sure what they communicated between each other but curiosity had her huffing out an impatient breath.

"What was that about?"

Jeremiah turned his dark gaze to her. His power saturated the space between them, stopping just short of comfortable. "You cannot straddle the fence, Vanna. Either you want to be a part of this prowl and thus know what's going on within it, or you can be out."

She growled and both her grandparents raised a brow in chastisement. Grandpa Harper came into the kitchen as she lowered her gaze. His face was serious. He kissed her grandmother, the heat between them no less than what was between Rebecca and Jeremiah.

"Do you need me to help?" Rebecca placed a hand on Harper's chest as she handed him a cup of coffee.

"I should be able to handle it, I'll let you two know what I find out." He rubbed his chin along the top of Rebecca's hair, his eyes closed.

Rebecca sighed, as she clutched her mate tight. She back away and Harper kissed her again.

He left and she was more confused than ever. Harper was a retired doctor and one of the prowl's healers, so that meant someone was hurt. She wondered who, but she'd bite her tongue off before she asked her grandparents another question.

"Good morning!" Jamie came into the front door already dirty.

How long he'd been up playing, she didn't even bother asking. She knew he was safe on prowl land so instead she bade him to wash his hands and face before breakfast. All through the meal her grandmother kept looking to the door. Afterwards, Savannah washed dishes and told Jamie to get packed. There was school in the morning so she wanted to get back into the city. She used Rebecca's distraction to get out of Sunday services. Jamie groaned but did what she said. She waited until she got in the car and called her cousin Charlotte to possibly get the tea.

Charlotte answered, clearly still sleeping. "You can't be serious, Vanna."

"Something is going on in the prowl, how are you still sleeping?" Charlotte wasn't high enough in the hierarchy to know too much, but her cousin always had her ways of getting information.

"Girl, after all the drinking and debauchery from last night, why are you even awake?" Charlotte complained.

"There was no debauchery on my end, madam. I called to get the tea. Roll off whatever woman you picked up last night and get with it. Something has happened."

Charlotte snorted. "Well, I have no clue. I wouldn't be awake if you hadn't called."

"Grandpa Harper was sent out, so someone could be hurt." She was speculating aloud. She peeked into the backseat. Jamie was engrossed in his tablet and not paying attention to her.

"I'll see what I can find out." Charlotte hung up.

Technically grandpa Jeremiah was right. She shouldn't care what happened within the prowl since she was so hell bent on not being a part of it. But, her son would be, and that was the story she was sticking with. She needed to know what was happening in order to ensure her son was safe. She would continue to fight for his spot until he could fight for himself.

Yeah.

That was why she was so invested. She'd stick with that.

***

Carlos stepped down from his truck and took in the chaos surrounding the small cabin. There were panthers, in both their cat form, and some in their human form. The yard was trashed, flowers and clothes strewn across the carefully manicured lawn. It was the only house within at least five miles of wilderness. Not visible from neither the highway, nor the closest road, it was not a place someone would stumble across. Harper met him at the front door as he and Derrick walked to the house. He clasped the elder panther's hand.

"She's pretty banged and bruised. She was out alone, in panther form, when she was attacked. Says she didn't see anything that can help." Harper walked them into the small cabin.

A woman in a robe with bandages covering her neck and shoulder, was sitting on a chair at a small dining room table in the kitchen. Her face was bruised, her lip swollen and cut.

"It will take her a little bit for the bruising to go away. We tried coaxing her into her panther form to heal faster, but right now she's refusing," Harper said softly.

He nodded and walked over to her. His panther raised, and the woman responded by lifting her chin and lowering her gaze. He pushed down on his anger at her injuries and stooped to reach her. He let his panther off the leash a little. The woman reached up and rubbed her head under his chin. He smoothed his chin over her hair and let out a reassuring chuff. Her shuddering sigh relaxed her body and her panther reached up to his. Their magic brushed each other's as the Alpha panther offered her comfort. She closed her eyes, her breathing easier and less panicked than when he'd arrived.

He waited until she opened her eyes. "Did they say anything?"

She pulled her robe closed. "They wanted to know who the power that moved through the land was. I simply said our Felix and he called me a liar and kept hitting me."

Derrick growled behind him and she flinched. "We'll get someone here to see you home. Would you prefer they stay with you?"

She lowered her gaze. "Yes, Beta."

"Done." Derrick walked from the cabin, taking some of the anger with him.

Carlos gave her a final nuzzle and left as well.

"This safe house is one of our more easily accessible ones. Anyone could have known about it." Harper said.

"It doesn't sit well with me for a lone woman to be attacked and questioned. What ran him off?"

"She said they smelled the patrol coming." An enforcer walked up, her jeans and combat boots dusty. Her black t-shirt was soaked with perspiration, more than likely from their chase.

"And?" He stared at the woman, seeing her own frustration.

She shrugged. "We lost him. We followed his scent from the prowl land to here. I sent off others to follow his trail as far as we could. We lost them at the river."

Carlos growled and pushed down on his panther, knowing the cat wanted to go on the hunt.

"There's nothing we can do about it now, save keep an eye on our women," Derrick commented.

"Restricting their movement won't go over well," Harper said.

He groaned because he knew if he asked any of his sisters to stay in their homes they would physically fight him.

"No one goes out alone," he ordered. "Not even the males." He pushed the order down his link, enforced with his power. "Pairs of two for now until we catch these guys. I have a feeling this is them gathering information."

Derrick nodded. "What kind of prowl are they, that this is the way they send out to get information. Wouldn't they want to be subtle?"

"If it's who we suspect it is, from what my mother told me, their prowl link can't be healthy. Not with two insane alphas back to back." Carlos looked around at the destruction.

Harper grunted. "I'm off, let me know if you need anything else."

"I have healers that came with us, I'd be happy if you got them together and acclimated them to the prowl."

Harper looked surprised. "How many?"

"There are four of them." Derrick supplied.

"Wow, that's a lot." Harper looked astonished.

"We all came from armed forces, we're used to fighting. Granted most of the security work we do is by computer, or small person security jobs, but my mother said the prowl attracts what it needs. We're always in need of healers." Carlos shrugged.

"I'll be happy for the help," Harper said. "Now, I can really retire. We've only two ourselves, I'll get with them all and establish how we'll work together."

They waved him off and stood there for a moment. He looked to the enforcer still standing there. "Escort the woman home and make sure someone stays with her."

"Of course, Felix."

Derrick turned to him as they got in the truck. "How bad do you think this will get?"

Carlos sighed. "We'll handle it, no matter how bad it gets."

Derrick nodded and they pulled off.

Chapter 13

Worry coated the walls of his office, and had his knee bouncing as he tapped his foot. He tried calling his mate for the third time, cursing as her phone went to voicemail. It was late, or rather early morning, it didn't shock him that she didn't answer, but still…he worried. Since yesterday morning there had been three other women attacked. He sent down his rule for them to move in pairs, but two of them were attacked in a pair. Derrick had set up a communication chain so they responded faster to the assaults, but it still wasn't fast enough to catch the attackers.

He was pissed and his panther was riled. He'd called a prowl meeting for this sunrise, but he knew Savannah wouldn't attend. He wanted her safe, where he could keep an eye on her, and he was racking his brain for an excuse to get her in the prowl house he'd set up. The women in the country had banded together, and so far were secure. It was the women here, in the city, which, despite her protest included his mate.

He should've claimed her.

He should've let his panther take over and claim its mate. That way she'd be here, safe in his care. She was reluctant to mate for reasons he'd yet to determine, and getting her to stay in his building was a big ask. Her grandmother had told him allowing her too much freedom would have her running from them, and he saw that. His mate scurried away from them every chance she got.

Slow was not the way to go.

He picked up the desk phone and tried her number again. It went to voice mail and he growled and hung up. He fought the urge to swipe his arm across his desk in frustration. His panther was on a hair trigger. Derrick walked in and stood over his desk.

"Did you figure out a way to get her in the building?"

Carlos groaned. "She's not answering her phone, but yes, I figured a way to get her here."

"Well, it's one in the morning, that's probably why she's not answering."

He gave his Beta a droll look and Derrick smiled. Derrick picked up a glass paperweight Ella had bought him for Father's day last year and toyed with it in nervousness.

"Just saying." Derrick gently put the weight back on the desk and tucked his hands in his pockets. "I'm just gonna go pick her up. If you don't reach her by the time I get there, I'll finesse something. I don't like her out from under our protection."

Carlos nodded. He picked up his desk phone and dialed her number. His cellphone vibrated across his desk. He blew out a relieved breath when he saw Savannah's name.

"What's wrong?" Savannah's voice was thick with sleep, the sexy timbre running down his spine.

He nearly crushed the phone in his grip. Her emotions transmitted across their tentative bond. She was worried, and tired. His cat stretched and reached for her.

"There is a prowl emergency and I called a meeting for sunrise. Would you mind coming over and watching Ella?" He held his breath hoping his made up excuse would work.

She was quiet on the other end, shifting around in bed. "Laura's right next door. If you want to bring her here, I can watch them all."

Her voice was stronger, and the sheets rustled. He imagined she was getting out of bed, and his cat, already riled, went a little crazy. What did she wear to bed? His cock hardened and he ran a hand over his face to wipe out those wayward thoughts.

"Laura's here already, and I would feel better knowing you and the kids were safe here in our building."

Her grandfather had warned him that she was still an alpha. Telling her to do anything was a sure way to get cussed out, so he'd ask instead of ordering her to come over.

"What's wrong, what's happened?" Her worry was evident.

"A few women in the prowl have been attacked since yesterday."

She gasped. "Oh no."

"I know you don't do prowl meetings, but I wanted to ask you if you'd watch the kids."

"It's no problem. I'll get dressed now."

Getting dressed. He sucked in a sharp breath, need spearing through him. Now he really wanted to know what she slept in. He cleared his throat.

"Derrick got worried, so he's coming over to pick you and Jamie up."

"Ok. We'll be ready."

She didn't argue, he smiled at the victory.

"How are you feeling? I can't imagine having to deal with all this as a new Alpha, is there anything I can do to help?"

Did she even realize she was falling into the role of Alpha female? "No, but I appreciate the offer."

She gasped again. "Oh God, my family, was it…"

"They're fine. Right now, it seems centered on the prowl here in the city."

She breathed out a sigh of relief. "Okay, then I should still call my grandmother and check on them."

"Whatever you need, love."

Her breath hitched and she cleared her throat. Had the pet name caught her off guard? She would soon be used to to it. He was no longer hiding what he wanted from her.

"Ok, I'll see you soon." She hung up before he pushed his luck further.

He shot over a text to let Derrick know she was expecting him.

***

Derrick rode the street to Savannah's house slowly, his window down. He took deep inhales, taking in the early morning smells, sifting through for scents that didn't belong. He was two houses down from her house when he smelled a foreign shifter. He knew there were lone shifters in and around Tampa, but he knew for a fact that there were none in Savannah's neighborhood. He had made sure before he allowed Theo and Laura to move in next door.

His lips peeled back as he snarled. Theo had marked the neighborhood thoroughly before he'd moved in with his family. Any lone shifter knew the place was protected. It would be foolish for any to wander through here. A growl rumbled his chest. He was glad he came over instead of waiting. He pulled into her driveway and got out of the truck, turning in a circle. Satisfied that the scent was not stronger in her yard, he went and knocked on the door.

She answered, her hair tied in a scarf, her breasts unbound in a tank top and very short, soft cotton shorts. His reaction was immediate, visceral.

She held up the phone. "I just talked to Felix, give me few more minutes and I'll be ready."

He walked her back from the door, his hand spanning her waist. Her body was lush under his hand and he had to push his cat down as it jumped for control. He pulled her into his arms, craving her touch. He took a deep inhale at the crook of her neck. His panther damn near purred, and power danced along his skin. She wrapped her arms around his neck and sighed, her power rising to meet his. The sleepy sound burrowed into his heart.

She rubbed her cheek along his chin and the submissive gesture rocketed his body temperature. He closed the door behind him with his foot and breathed her in.

"What are you doing answering the door wearing this, kitten?"

She snorted. "I knew it was you." She stepped back, her gaze roaming his face. "Are you guys okay?"

Her sincerity touched him. "Yeah, we'll have a meeting, soothe some of the prowl's fears and try and find out who's behind the attacks."

She shivered and crossed her arms over her chest.

"Can you pack for a couple of days at the prowl house?"

Fear filled her eyes, the scent of it rising in the room. "A couple of days? Do you think I'm in danger?"

He thought about the foreign scent in her neighborhood and the possibility of them coming after her. He shrugged, "just in case."

She narrowed her eyes. "Will I have my own room there?"

"Whatever you're comfortable with," he answered quickly, not wanting to give her a reason to change her mind.

If he had his way, she'd be sleep with him, but telling her that didn't seem prudent.

She studied him a bit longer and then sighed. "Okay. Let me get some stuff together."

He smiled and watched the pulse speed at her neck. He choked back a growl as his cat tried to force him to claim her. He knew they had to play it carefully with their mate, but he was done playing fair. Stubbornness be damned, he wanted Savannah and he would push past whatever hang-ups she had about dating shifters. She walked away to pack and he watched her ass in the small shorts as she walked down the hallway towards her bedroom. Lord have mercy, that woman was fine as fuck.

He adjusted the bulge in his jeans and walked into her kitchen, pulling out his cellphone. The Felix answered on the first ring.

"There's an unknown shifter in her neighborhood."

"I want her here." Carlos growled.

"Agreed, and I'm done waiting to claim her." Derrick turned to keep an eye out for her so she wouldn't overhear.

"Bring our mate home and when the meeting is over, we'll work on that." Carlos' voice was deep, the panther riding him. "I'll send someone over to check out the neighborhood."

He hung up as Savannah trod up the hallway towards him. She carried a large duffle bag. "You're gonna have to carry the eight year old, he's not budging."

He smiled. He liked the cub, and looked forward to being there for Jamie and watching him grow into the alpha he knew the kid was. He leaned down and kissed her lightly, pleased with her bemused expression. Every time he kissed her it was just as sweet as the first time. He forced himself back.

"I'll get him now. Don't go outside without me." He ordered.

He rushed from the kitchen before he took more than the small kiss he did.

Chapter 14

Why did such a small kiss affect her? Maybe she was still half asleep. Yeah, that's why her body still buzzed nearly thirty minutes after Derrick had kissed her. The night had turned navy, the stars slowly dimming as the new day beckoned. She watched the city go by as Derrick drove through the quiet streets on their way to the prowl house.

It was a strange night that was for sure. Carlos had called her love, and Derrick kissed her again. Her hands shook as she brushed them down her pants. She wanted them both. She breathed out a hard breath. Her grandparents were the perfect example of how well a Tribond could work, so she knew it was possible and how happy the couples were. Hell, just the thought of having them both made her hot. It just wasn't for her. She was latent, dating a shifter that high in the hierarchy was out for her. Especially an Alpha. The women in the prowl would challenge her at every meeting, besides that, she couldn't ignore the prophecy.

Her aunt...she sighed, it was years ago. She shook her head and banished the thoughts.

They pulled into a garage entrance of the condo building. She didn't know what she was expecting, this elegant building was not it. Derrick gave her a longing look, sighed and exited the truck. He came around the side and opened her door before opening the back and reaching for her son. She stepped down out of the front seat and grabbed their bag. She turned and watched as Derrick carefully extracted her sleeping son from the back seat. Jamie shuffled a little before settling his head across Derrick's shoulder and she melted. It made her think about him in a domestic capacity and it was dangerous thinking.

Derrick held out his hand and she grabbed it without hesitation. She looked down at their joined hands and wished things were simple.

Jamie's head popped up and he gave her a groggy look. "Where are we going?"

"We're going to stay with the prowl for a couple days." She gave him a reassuring smile.

"Yes!" he whispered and lay his head back down.

She couldn't help but smile. Jamie was nothing if not predictable. He loved spending time with the prowl. Guilt tried to wiggle in but she squashed it. She never deprived Jamie when it came to the prowl, doing the best she could with the cards fate had dealt her.

She thought about what Carlos had told her as they trekked through the parking garage. "Do you think I could be in any danger?"

Derrick turned to her for a moment and she was blasted by the longing in his eyes. "Don't worry, we'll keep you and Jamie safe."

She nodded, she had no doubt that he'd try his hardest to keep them safe. She squeezed his hand. There were people milling around as they reached the entrance of the building. She tried to ignore the looks of his prowl mates as they passed. She didn't recognize any of the faces, so they had to be members that had come down with Carlos.

Derrick loaded them into the elevator and up to the third floor. Curiosity had her glancing around the hallway as he led them to an apartment. A part of her was redecorating in her mind. It was a good distraction from the way Derrick made her feel. She followed him inside and her eyes widened at the large apartment. Carlos' walls were chocolate, the dark hardwood floors matching. His sofa and love chairs were various shades of taupe, a large rug pulled together the living room. His windows, floor to ceiling covered one wall and with the curtains open, the city lights from downtown were twinkling in the early morning sky and kept the room from feeling dark.

"I'll take Jamie into Ella's room, they are all hunkered down in there." He told her, lifting her hand and brushing a kiss across her knuckles.

She nodded absently, as she glanced around the place. Laura was pacing in the living room area, her husband on the couch with a worried look on his face. Savannah immediately went to her friend and hugged her.

"Are you okay?"

Laura's breath shuddered out, her eyes red from what could only be crying. "My friend was attacked."

"I'm so sorry, Laura. Don't worry about the boys, I'll take care of them while the prowl deals with this." She assured her.

Laura gripped her tight, rubbing her cheek against Savannah's. Savi frowned as her power raised, and her friend relaxed. It was odd, and something that had never happened to her.

She shrugged away the foreign feeling and stepped back, keeping a hold of Laura's hands. "Where's Felix?"

No sooner than she asked the question, the heat of his power warmed her back. He settled his hands on her shoulder and nuzzled against the back of her neck. She shuddered as need swamped her body. Her power raised as it always seemed to do in his presence, but instead of suppressing it, she closed her eyes and reveled in it for just a moment. Just five minutes ago she reminded herself that she didn't do shifters, but with him touching her, she pushed that worry aside.

Carlos inhaled deeply, barely stilling his hips to keep from grinding his hard-on into her back. He wanted to kiss her, hell, he wanted more than that. Like his Beta, he too was tired of waiting for their mate. Her scent filled him and his cat roamed his body in complete happiness.

"Thank you for watching the kids." He murmured against her skin, knowing he was taking liberties.

"No problem, though I'm sure you have enough enforcers to leave with them." She turned around and raised a brow.

He smiled. He'd wondered how long it would take her to see through his ruse. "Yes, I could have, but the kids would prefer you."

"And you wanted me under guard." She narrowed her eyes.

"When you say it like that it sounds manipulative." He pulled her closer. He considered it a small victory when she didn't move back.

"Perhaps because it was," she said, running her hands down his arms.

He leaned over and nuzzled under her chin. His panther purred, power running down his arm and over her. She tilted her head to the side and that gave him better access and was a good sign as far as he was concerned. He couldn't resist a little bite. Nothing to break the skin, just a little nibble. He licked the spot to mark her skin with his scent.

Gods, he wanted this woman.

He wrapped an arm around her waist, splaying his fingers across her back. He pushed her into his groin, letting out his breath in a hard sigh.

"I want you," he whispered in her ear. He nipped her earlobe. "I'm sorry the timing is so bad, but can we talk when I get back?"

He moved down her neck and nipped her on the shoulder. She nodded and her scent deepened, arousal scenting the air.

His sister touched his arm. "We need to go, Felix."

He hated the fear and anger swirling in Laura's eyes. But one of the last women attacked was her friend. She was rightfully angry. Especially to find out that his father could possibly be behind the attacks. Though he and Laura had different fathers, it didn't affect their relationship. The two of them couldn't be closer. She was latent, but she'd followed him when he decided to start his own prowl. She could've easily made a life for herself in the human world. Instead she used her huge intelligence and law degree to help him and Derrick build their prowl into a prosperous one.

He nodded, gave one last lingering kiss to Savi's neck and released her. It was hard, but they had a prowl meeting and he needed to get his head into it. They needed to figure out how to keep the females in his new prowl safe.

Savannah surprised him by going up on her toes and hugging him tight. "Be safe." She whispered.

He was touched and curious at how intuitive she was. He nodded, leaning to drop a light kiss to her lips. Derrick had entered the living room behind her. The Beta grabbed her and pulled her up into a hug. They whispered to each other and he didn't bother trying to decipher what they were saying. He was happy she responded well to Derrick. It would make their Tribond happier, stronger. He prayed he'd find the words to get past her worries about mating. Seeing her in Derrick's arms triggered his need like nothing else could have.

He stepped closer to them, touching her shoulders, raising power as the three of them touched. Her energy soothed his, and in turn trickled down the prowl link. Laura let out a shuddering sigh and turned into her husband's chest. His prowl needed this link, needed their Tribond and he would do whatever he needed to do to secure his mating.

"We'll talk when we get back, ok?" Derrick whispered into her ear.

Her head jerked in agreement, panic intertwining in her scent. He sighed. It would take a lot.

"Keep the kids in the building, if possible. I don't know how long the meeting will last."

She whipped around to him, "are you worried about their safety?"

Derrick kept his arms around her waist, keeping their connection intact.

Laura touched his back. "We'll wait for you downstairs"

His gaze didn't stray from Savannah. "I don't want to alarm you, but I would rather be safe than sorry. It's why I asked you to stay here. I'll have someone positioned at the gate, so no one should be able to get onto the property."

He wanted to tell her everything. It was her right as Alpha female to know what was happening in the prowl. But...until he could get past her reluctance to mate, he wasn't sure how much to tell. Should he tell her what the seer said, especially after what her grandparents told him about her experience with the last seer? He wasn't sure how she would react.

"I don't have a lot of time to explain." Carlos leaned down and nuzzled her neck. "You won't be in the building alone. There is help downstairs if something happens."

She sighed and looked away. He caught Derrick's eye, not having to use words to tell his Beta how hard it was to leave their mate. Derrick nuzzled on the other side of her neck. She let out a snarl that held a hint of power, a growl escaped both he and his Beta.

"I can't think with you guys doing that," she whispered.

"Fuck." Derrick let out a harsh breath, his arms coming around her waist, brushing against his stomach.

He watched his best friend's teeth scrape against her neck and it took everything in Carlos not to sink his teeth into Savannah. "We'll explain everything when we get back. Just please keep yourself and the kids safe." He forced his mind back to their conversation.

Her arm slid up to cup his face, as she moved her hips, grinding them back into him and then into Derrick. They both let out harsh breaths. He bit down on her neck barely restraining himself from sinking his teeth into her.

"My God, how is this possible?" she whispered.

His phone buzzed at his hip. He released her fragrant skin reluctantly. "We'll sit and talk when we get back, ok?"

She hummed and kissed his neck. He shuddered, his panther damn near ripping through him to get to her. "You said that already."

Derrick didn't want to let go of Savannah, never mind actually leave her. He spun her around and kissed her lips, intending for it to be short, chaste. But Savi went up on her toes and sighed, her mouth opening. He took it for an invitation and devoured her. The kiss was hot, her moans sending his cat into a frenzy. She pulled back and licked her lips. He growled, the sound rattling his spine.

Her smile was mischievous. She knew what she did to him. "Be careful."

Carlos turned her around and took his kiss and it took everything in Derrick to hold his cat back. His head started pounding, a hint that a premonition was coming in. He closed his eyes and let the images come. They flashed, each one giving him a hint of what would happen in the next few hours. He opened his eyes and knew what had to be done.

He needed to start the bond with their mate and it needed to be done before they entered the prowl meeting. It was urgent that they did so. The seer had been right in that he had a small trace of psychic power passed down to him. He'd used it to guide his life, and he never put aside any visions he had. Those same visions that told him Carlos was his future when he met him, was urging him to put some type of claim on Savannah. It would be important for them to go into the meeting with their mating bond started.

He looked to Carlos to convey that. When Carlos lifted from their mate's kiss, his eyes were glazed with lust. Derrick let his canines drop to broadcast his intention. The Felix's eyes burned with need and in an unspoken agreement he leaned down to their mate and Derrick followed his lead.

He allowed the Alpha first bite before he nipped Savi just hard enough to break skin and leave a mark. He lapped at the small drop of blood, not enough for a mating bond, but enough to initiate a claim on her and show the panthers in the prowl their intentions. All the same, the beginning tugs of what they could have, snapped into place and power raised down their prowl link. It flooded his body and his cat turned in circles. Fur sprouted along his arm and disappeared as his panther celebrated. Her lust, confusion and worry bombarded him, but so did a tide of calm. It soothed his cat, even as the panther prowled his body begging for a chance to come out. With her being latent, he wondered if she would understand the mark.

She jerked back with a gasp and shoved away from them both. "Did you two really just bite me without permission?"

"I'm sorry, that was really rude. I got carried away." He rushed to placate her.

Her dark eyes narrowed in suspicion. "Do you usually mark women before you ask them out?"

So she didn't quite understand what was happening. He had a feeling if she had, there would've been hell to pay.

He leaned down and nibbled along her lips. "I've never so much as rubbed my scent on any woman, never mind a woman I wasn't dating." He assured her.

Carlos rubbed his cheek against the top of her head. "From the moment I saw you, other women ceased to exist."

Her eyes softened and her sigh pushed air across his lips before she kissed him softly. "That was so sweet." She whispered.

He used his fangs to cut into his tongue a little. Grabbing her head, he kissed her, slipping his tongue into her mouth, feeding her a small drop of his blood. He was pushing his luck, he knew, but he wanted a connection with her, even if it would only last a few days. Power surged, his dick hardened and he growled low in his throat.

He spun her around and Carlos did the same. The bond tightened, and he felt the cats up and down the link, proof that the link with the Felix was initiated. Derrick rubbed his head along the top of hers, reveling in her scent and in the tentative bond formed between the three of them. If not nurtured, the bond would fade in a few days, he planned to be bonded to their mate before it faded.

"Try to get some more sleep." Carlos told her. "You can use my bed if you want."

Derrick pushed down on his cat before he snatched Savannah and took her to that bed. Her eyes were dazed, her lips wet from their kisses. Her arousal spiked, scenting the air and Derrick forced himself to move back. His cat wanted to bond them, now. He was in agreement, anything that ended with him inside his mate as she clawed his back, he was up for. It wouldn't happen until they talked and explained everything to her, so he needed to back up just a little further. Especially if she continued to lick her lips with that lust filled gaze.

"I don't think sleeping in your bed is a good idea," she whispered.

Carlos rubbed against her neck and smiled. "Your choice," he said and let her go. "The guest room is next to Ella's."

Derrick said nothing as she passed him and headed down the hallway towards the bedrooms.

"I need you to drag me out of here, Beta, or I'm headed in there to fuck our mate." Carlos growled, his voice deep with his panther.

Shit, if the Felix was counting on him, they were screwed. Luckily, Carlos' phone rang again. He sighed.

"I'm coming." Carlos barked into the phone and stuffed it back into his pocket.

Derrick gave one last lingering look to the direction in which his mate had disappeared. Yeah, they would be having that talk when they returned.

Chapter 15

A thick layer of tension blanketed Derrick's senses as soon as he got out of the truck on prowl land. He looked at Carlos and his lips tightened in a grim look. Carlos rounded the truck and stood next to him. They eyed the cars scattered at the meeting place.

"With the Tribond initiated, I can feel the prowl's bond more." He told Carlos.

The Alpha grunted. "Makes sense. The tighter we're bound together, the more you'll feel what I do. Let's get this over with."

Carlos whistled, a series of warbles that let the prowl know he'd arrived. The whistles of his enforcers answering that call sounded out in the night as Carlos walked over to the Alpha mound. He held his hand up for silence. After a moment, the cats settled and everyone turned their attention to him.

"Three women were attacked on prowl land in the past week."

The crowd grumbled and Derrick watched them, looking for any telltale signs of guilt. Carlos continued his speech, encouraging the prowl to be aware of everything happening around them.

"One of the women was attacked at a pack safe house while she was cleaning the place, which no one should know about. That means, someone is selling out the prowl's secrets." Carlos' power settled over the crowd.

As the Beta, Derrick took his job seriously. Though Simon as third in command was head enforcer, Derrick was in charge of their security. He watched the crowd, wondering if anyone would step forward and admit guilt. Carlos turned and looked at him and Simon. He nodded, conveying to the Felix that he was already looking for signs.

"We think perhaps a prowl to the south of us, the Miami one, is behind the attacks." Carlos continued. "Until we know for sure, I want us all to stay in pairs."

"And not just the women?" Brielle spoke.

The crowd held its breath and Carlos smiled. "Everyone, enforcer."

Brielle nodded and stepped back into her place among the other enforcers.

The prowl moved around, their nervousness broadcasting, the extra power flowing through the link making them restless and jumpy. He knew until the bond between them and Savannah was completed they would be a little unsettled. Two women stepped forward, along with one guy who had stealthily tried to undermine him and his place as Beta. They wanted to get to Carlos, and he'd yet to figure out why.

He growled, he should've dealt with them before they left New Jersey. They were one of the last members to join their prowl before they'd left. He'd wanted to kick them out, but Carlos had argued to give them a chance. The Felix had wanted stronger males to make up for their lack, so he'd let it go. Seeing the calculation on their faces as they stepped forward, Derrick cursed his decision anew. He would be harsher in the future about accepting new members.

"Do you have information to offer?" He stepped in front of them, blocking their path to Carlos. He didn't bother disguising his contempt for the male.

Ryan stepped forward. "I propose an alliance with the southern panthers to bring peace. It's not a good idea for a newly blended prowl to invite trouble."

The Felix stepped down from the mound and snarled. "What do you know of the Miami prowl?"

"We were approached by a liaison from their alpha." Ryan stammered.

Derrick stepped closer. "And why exactly did they feel comfortable enough to talk to you when they've attacked everyone else they approached?"

Ryan lowered his head. "I don't know, but maybe if we can have a truce between us, the attack on the women would stop."

Carlos moved Derrick aside and stepped right into Ryan's face. "Or maybe it will give the other Alpha an in to take over our budding prowl. The strength of the women here is rightly coveted."

Whistles and hisses went up around the circle at their Felix's praise.

"Felix, he spared us when my brother stepped up. Surely we can find a way." One of Ryan's sister's, Callie, spoke.

Yasmeen stepped forward. "You don't know anything about that prowl. Their Alpha threw away his mate, what makes you think he'll respect the women in this prowl?"

"How do you know the Miami prowl isn't simply bluffing?" Derrick asked.

The three siblings looked between each other, then back down to the ground.

Callie spoke again. "Maybe if the Felix mates into the southern prowl it will be more amicable."

Yasmeen snarled, and stepped closer to Callie. "So you're too weak of a cat to smell the scent of my brother's mate on him?"

The other stronger females lined up behind Yasmeen.

Ryan's head popped up. "Since when do you have a mate? Who is she?"

"She is the old Felix's granddaughter." Carlos' voice sent a shiver of warning throughout the prowl link.

"She's latent!" Someone shouted from the back of the gathering.

Grumbling started around the mound. One of Savannah's many cousins growled and stepped forward.

"Would anyone like to challenge me again and see how strong a latent female can be?"

Excited chatter raised around the group and Carlos raised his hand for silence.

Ryan's sister Mallory spoke up, her eyes conniving. "The mating is not complete, so it can still be undone."

Brielle and Brianne both pushed to the front of the females and growled loudly into Mallory's face.

"Watch your words, girl, you're talking about our kin." Brianne pointed her finger into Mallory's chest.

Brielle lifted her lips showing her canines. "I don't know how you do things in the city, but here, we don't play about that."

A loud yowl accompanied the woman's words, the females agreeing.

Carlos looked to Derrick, very happy that his second in command had them start the Tribond before they left their mate. He knew that if her scent had not been intertwined with theirs, the female could've possibly swayed more people to their side. Especially since Savannah was latent. Not everyone would want a latent female over the prowl. Anger had him clenching his fists. It was already going to be hard enough to convince his mate that they were meant to be together. She would know how hard it was for a latent panther to become Alpha female, and gossip around the prowl would fill her in on the rest.

Carlos lifted his hand again for silence.

"Our mate will not be put aside and the next person to suggest otherwise will be put in their place." Derrick growled next to him.

Carlos nodded. "I won't set aside a fated Tribond to play politics to an Alpha who has no care for his own prowl." He turned his back on the siblings and caught the eye of Jeremiah.

The old Felix and his mate were along the side of the crowd with the other elders. Jeremiah nodded to him in approval.

He jumped back up onto the alpha mound. "We're actively finishing the prowl building renovations and it will be ready for those of you who want to live in the prowl house. For now, though, I want all single females in the building, and the Beta will make a roster for patrolling the mating housing. Laura will coordinate to get people into finished apartments, and we will all work together to get rid of the threat." His gaze roamed over the crowd, conveying his concern.

He looked over to Ryan and his sisters and knew his Beta had been right to protest their joining the prowl. He should've listened.

"Be careful as you go about your business. And keep a special eye out for traitors." He pushed down his alpha power, and the trio paled and exposed their necks.

He ignored them as the rage of the alpha flowed through him and down the prowl link. He threw back his head and yowled, calling his cat forward. He knew the best way to calm the prowl and bring closeness was a run. His cat's power rushed over him and he shifted into a panther. The prowl followed his lead and changed along with him. Looking around, the prowl shifted and pushed the weaker members and the latents in the middle of the group as they set off for a run.

Chapter 16

Savannah rolled her neck and slid the scarf off her hair as she entered the kitchen. The kids were all chattering in the living room, giving up the pretense of whispering. They now giggled loudly, debating what movies they'd watch.

"What do you jerks want for breakfast?" She shouted into the living room.

More giggling, along with shouts of eggs and pancakes.

She rolled her eyes. She'd barely gotten any sleep, so pancakes were not in their future. She opened the refrigerator giving a happy exhale of air at the tube of croissants on the shelf. Easy enough. She yawned and grabbed the eggs and...turkey bacon.

Ugh.

She shut the door with her hip and set everything down on the counter. She found the coffee and sent up a prayer of thanks. How many hours of sleep had she accomplished? She looked at the oven clock and shook her head. It was eight a.m., so barely three hours. Carlos and Derrick had been on her mind as she attempted to go back to sleep. Just thinking about them heated her body. She cinched her robe tighter and shuddered as the silky fabric slid across her legs.

They were two very sexy men. A woman would be crazy not to consider being with them. She'd told herself last night when Derrick picked her up that she wouldn't get involved with them, but when Carlos leaned down over her...she sighed. How was she supposed to refuse? She touched her neck where they'd bitten her. It was a small scratch, certainly not big enough to be a mating bite, but still, for a moment she reveled in it. It was only after she'd went back to Carlos' guest bed and lay up well into the morning thinking about the implications, that she'd gotten a little scared.

Her grandfathers would be beyond happy, it would keep the alpha position in their family. And as far as they were concerned, any one of his granddaughters would be strong enough to lead the prowl. They just didn't know what she knew. Did she want them? Yes, she wanted them with a desperation that was scary. Would she put her family in danger to be with them?

No.

That was a simple answer. She shook herself out of her thoughts and finished the kids' breakfast. She'd managed to keep thoughts of Carlos and Derrick out of her head as they all ate and discussed their options for a movie marathon. She was cleaning the kitchen when she sensed Carlos enter the apartment. She turned to greet him as he entered the kitchen and paused at the exhaustion on his face.

"Ready to sleep?"

He shook his head and walked closer, crowding her until her back met the counter. "I still have a few things to do before I can sleep. I just needed to see you."

She frowned in concern, and cupped his face. "Well, I can't offer you any help with prowl business, but I can make you some coffee and breakfast, if you want."

He leaned down and nuzzled her neck. "Coffee would be great."

He snuggled into her back as she fixed his coffee and she soaked up his presence. She needed to get distance, some clarity. She needed to remind herself that she couldn't handle an Alpha, that a shifter was too much, but the way he felt against her…

She sighed and fought to keep from moaning. "Did you make any decisions about the attacks?"

She wanted to kick herself for asking. She wasn't getting involved with the prowl, she reminded herself.

He hummed. "It's partners for the time being, and I have the single females moving into the prowl house. I asked everyone to be on the lookout for anyone on our land who doesn't belong."

"That's hard with a new prowl coming in." She commented, loading the coffee machine.

"Very true. Someone sold us out, because one of the last attacks was at a safe house no one outside of the prowl should know about."

She turned. "Really? You'll need to do some kind of gag order." She slapped a hand across her mouth. "I'm sorry, that's not my place."

He said nothing, just rubbed his hands down her sides. She turned back to his coffee and fiddled with the cup while she waited on the machine to finish. She'd taken off her head scarf, but her hair was still pinned and wrapped around her head.

She smiled as he took out the pins one by one until her hair fell down to her shoulder in a silky waterfall. Her press out had taken three hours, and this man was running his fingers through it, mussing it. She easily forgave him because it felt great to have his hands on her. She sighed in pleasure as he leaned in and smelled her hair. She liked how touchy feely he was. Having been away from the prowl for a while, she'd forgotten the simple pleasure of touch.

He continued nuzzling her neck as she made his coffee. She felt closer to him for some reason, like she could actually feel his exhaustion, worry and a hint of angry frustration. Her mind strayed to the scratch on her neck. She wished she'd paid better attention to her grandmother as she talked about her mating. Since she didn't see it in the cards for her, she'd brushed off the talk. Now, she wondered if the small bite they'd given her earlier meant anything.

She turned and smiled at him. "Sit for a moment before you fall down." She pushed down on his shoulders into a chair at the small café table and set the coffee in front of him. "You can't even try a nap?"

He shook his head and took a small sip. "I need to make some calls first, I want to check in with some of the allies I've built to see if they can send some people down if need be."

"You should talk to Brianne about that. I believe she'd have a full list of truces the prowl has with the other packs and clans in the area."

He eyed her over his coffee cup. "You know a lot about what goes on in the prowl."

"Well," she hedged. "I try to keep up, you know since Jamie will be joining."

He gave her a small smile, his gaze raking over her body as he brought up the hot coffee to his mouth. He set down his cup and crooked his finger. "Come here."

His voice was soft, but the weight of his command settled over her. She took a step closer and he pulled her into his lap.

"Sit here with me for just a moment, beautiful."

She sat in his lap and stroked his hair, unable to stop from touching him. He was a beautiful man. His chiseled features and full lips made him the stuff of fantasies. She could easily imagine him leaving a bevy of women in his wake. She knew if she acted on the heat between the three of them, she would be it for him. Somehow that made her more scared.

He closed his eyes and sighed. His body relaxed under her, and some of the stress left his body. She frowned a bit in confusion at the sensation. He finished his coffee and they sat in silence.

"Better?" she asked after a moment.

He cupped her chin and kissed her, his lips demanding, hungry. It didn't even occur to her to stop him. She tangled her fingers in his hair and sucked on his tongue, her whole body coming alive under his kiss. She tasted his coffee and underneath was a taste she would forever associate with him. God, she wanted him.

He pulled back from the kiss. "Yes, thank you, babe. I'm hoping to be done in a few hours."

She gave him a dazed nod. "You want me to take the kids out so you can sleep? We were going to do a movie marathon."

His gaze traced her face a moment before he spoke. "I plan to come back here and lay in your lap and sleep, even if it's in the noisy room with the kids."

She smiled and gave in to the pleasure of kissing him again. He sighed, a contented sound, as she lifted from his lap. His gaze lingered over her body in a heated stare, before he stood and left, waving to the kids on the way out. She stayed in the kitchen, distracted for long moments. She sighed, and knew what she could do. One person would understand how she felt.

Rebecca answered and they made small talk for a while. Her grandmother raved about the new Felix, happy to have her mates home and safe.

"I'll be glad when all the turmoil is over, though. It leaves the prowl unsettled, it does."

"Is that what's happening?" Her heart skipped a little in fear in hearing there were already issues.

Chasing Savannah

The Seer's words played through her head. She was a lot more involved in the prowl than she let on. Could that be why they were having the problems? Did she need to step back more?

"The whelp from the south thinks he can push onto our lands as though this family hasn't held it down for centuries." Rebecca scoffed.

Guilt rushed through her, was her nearness to the prowl causing the trouble?

"But, prowl gossip is not why you called, especially since you don't attend meetings."

"Grandmother."

Rebecca continued her lecture as though she'd not spoken. "That's on your mother and your father. I don't know why your mother insisted on raising you as though you were full human."

"May as well be," she muttered.

Rebecca growled. "Savannah, don't start. Latent or not, you are a panther, and eventually you will find out the hard way. Keep suppressing your nature if you want to, you're going to make yourself sick."

She sighed, having heard this from her grandmother since she was thirteen and stopped going to prowl meetings. Rebecca fussed that a panther needed touch from the prowl members, even though she was latent. When she had Jamie, she'd started back regularly going to visit her grandparents, wanting to make sure her son knew his roots. It turned out for the best since he wouldn't be latent.

"I'm not only latent, but I'm a weak latent." She reminded her grandmother.

Rebecca snorted. "I never could tell who told you that bullshit. I wish I knew, I'd whip their ass. There's no way a 'weak' latent could come through all the challenges you've gone through in this prowl."

Savannah laughed, even as a tear fell. She wiped it away hastily. "Never mind that, grandma. I called to ask you a question."

"About what?"

"Your Tribond."

"Is that right?" Her grandmother's tone changed, her curiosity palpable. For a second nerves flared and she nearly changed her mind.

"I'm waiting on your question, my love." Rebecca broke the silence. "Is perhaps the nature you work so hard to suppress, asserting itself?"

She squirmed and huffed out an aggravated breath.

"So your grandfather was right."

"About what?" She asked sharply.

"Tone, young woman," her grandma growled.

"I apologize. What was grandfather right about?"

"Nothing that's my business, so I'll not repeat it. But, I will say this, what I have with your grandfathers is everything. I can't explain our happy because there are no words. If you find yourself in a Tribond, granddaughter of mine, understand that there is no love like it. But you can't go in with doubts, there's no room for that."

She sighed. "I don't know if this is a good idea, and yet I can't stop myself from wanting to be with them. What if I can't even mate with them? What if the bond doesn't hold because I'm latent? And even if I could, the prowl would be up in arms about a latent Alpha female."

"I won't lie to you, Savi, it will be an uphill battle gaining the trust of the panthers because you're latent, especially with the amount of latents we've had born lately. But, I know of no stronger reason, than to be with your mates. Would you want them to choose another?"

A growl left Savannah's throat. A sound, she'd never made before.

"Exactly." Was Rebecca's smug reply.

"I'll just bring more trouble to a prowl, clearly having trouble already." She whispered, self-pity threatening to swamp her.

Her grandmother said a few inventive curse words. "Get your stuff together, young lady or you're going to miss your blessings."

She hung up and left Savannah with her mouth wide open. Was her grandmother right? Her grandparents' bond was tangible, visible to anyone who observed them. Hell, most of the mate bonds were that way. She would be stupid to give it up. She looked at the kids giggling on the floor in front of the big TV and sighed. She'd do anything to keep them safe. The prowl was already having issues, she couldn't in good conscious add more.

Chapter 17

Carlos hung up the phone and scrubbed a hand down his face. He'd reached out to the allies he'd built up north and received promises of help if it came down to it. He'd worked hard for those allies as he built his small prowl and having the added weight of a larger one had made their conversation infinitely easier than it used to be. Before, they were smaller, certainly no threat to anyone. Now with the two prowls blended, the panthers on both sides strong, they could easily become a force to be reckoned with.

He'd talked with Brianne as Savannah had suggested and got the name of the local allies the prowl had built. They would have the backup they needed if it came to that, though, Brianne had given him strong words about looking to allies.

He smiled.

That Savannah came from women so strong made him happy, his mate would have no problem with the aggressiveness of his cat. He'd worried for years that he would have a hard time finding a mate. He knew it would take a strong woman to handle his cat, but strong women did not tend to be submissive, and his cat demanded it. What alpha female would allow him to dominate her, Felix of a prowl or not? He had no desire to fight with a mate for dominance every night in their bed.

It made everything about Savannah stand out in sharp contrast. He knew she would be strong enough, yet, her being latent would make her soft in places that would soothe his cat. Already with their tentative bond in place she settled him. Just being in her presence calmed his cat, and relaxed his body. He couldn't wait to complete the bond.

He looked up as power entered the floor. The ding of the elevator sounded on the quiet floor a moment later. He lifted his nose and inhaled, relaxing as he recognized the scent. Whistles rang out as the former Alpha announced himself and his mate. Jeremiah and Harper knocked and walked into his office. He waved them into the chairs in front of his desk. Curiosity must've beckoned Derrick from his office down the hall, because his Beta stood at the doorway. He rested his shoulder on the jamb and crossed his arms over his chest.

"We felt the beginnings of the bond flow down the prowl link." Jeremiah commented, crossing his leg over his knee.

Harper nodded and looked between him and Derrick. "She won't be an easy win."

Carlos grunted. "An understatement."

Her grandfathers both laughed. Jeremiah was serious a moment later. "That's part of the reason we're here. You should know, my sister is the reason Savi left the prowl."

Harper sighed next to him.

"I kicked Antoinette out of the prowl years ago. She was our old seer."

Carlos sat back in his chair and put his hands behind his head. "What happened?"

"She'd been giving out false prophecies."

Harper scoffed. "She was using the apprentices under her. Claiming their prophecies as her own. With a twist of course."

His panther stirred. He already was wary of using a seer. "This new Seer?"

"I'm embarrassed to say, I didn't notice what my sister was doing. Joelle is how we found out. We haven't had any issues with her since she's taken over." Jeremiah scratched his hair.

"In our defense, Antoinette used just enough of the truth to make her prophecies come true to a certain degree." Harper added.

"How does it affect Savannah?" He leaned forward.

The two elders looked at each other before turning to him. Jeremiah spoke. "We didn't get the exact story. Joelle wasn't sure what Antoinette told Savi." Jeremiah sighed. "My sister wouldn't tell us, and there were no means I could stomach to get her to tell us."

Harper gripped his co-mate's shoulder.

"Something she said to my granddaughter ran her off. Antoinette disappeared once we banished her, and Joelle said it didn't matter what her exact words were, but that if we pushed Savi, she would be locked into the false prophecy. She said eventually Savannah would come back to the prowl as she was supposed to. When Jamie was born, she started working for the cub's place in the prowl and I thought she'd finally come around which gave me more faith in Joelle's vision."

Carlos cursed and turned his chair. He pulled his panther under control and faced the men. "So you still don't know what Savannah's hang up is?"

"Other seers wanted to go to Savannah and read her, to maybe mitigate the damage, but I—"

"We." Harper interjected.

Jeremiah nodded. "We didn't think it was a good idea. She was so young. We instead tried other ways to guide her back into the prowl."

"She wouldn't have trusted anything a new Seer had to say anyway." Carlos murmured.

Harper nodded. "Exactly. You already know her."

He nodded. What he knew of his mate, he knew she wouldn't have wanted to hear from another seer. "So it was something about her place in the prowl?"

"We think so, because Savannah insists that she wouldn't be strong enough to hold a place in the prowl. As it was, she and Naomi were in constant fights with the other kids. I think she was tired of it." Jeremiah sighed.

Harper held up a hand. "Our granddaughter has since said several times that she would not mate with an alpha, any alpha. So we think that was part of it too."

He scoffed. His mate was more than strong enough to hold a place in their prowl. Without the help of a panther, she already held her son's place. Hell, the fact that her son, only twenty five percent panther, fully manifested said a lot about her strength.

"What do you think can be done?" Derrick spoke from the door.

Harper sighed and shrugged. "Joelle came to us and told us that Savannah would be alpha female. We've done what we could to...help her along in that direction."

Jeremiah grunted. "There is only so much we can do without pushing her away. Of course that didn't stop us from trying to set her up with the stronger alphas in the area. You're the first ones she's reacted to, half of the battle is already won. She and Naomi are going to have to take their positions in the prowl eventually. It starts with Savannah, so I wish you both luck."

Carlos looked at Derrick and his Beta raised an eyebrow. "Thank you, for bringing this to me." He stood and held out his hands to both elders.

They shook hands and left. Derrick shook their hands as they passed him and closed the door behind him.

"What do you think?"

He groaned. "It can't hurt, Beta."

"You sure about that? I don't want to push her away." Derrick slumped in the chair, his exhaustion all over his face.

"You want to wait…how long?"

Derrick grunted and changed the subject. "We checked the whole territory and there were some unfamiliar scents lingering in some areas, but they were long gone."

Carlos rubbed his eyes in exhaustion. "Ok, are the women settled?"

"Yes, they are in the building, some of the country prowl along with them. It's like a sorority house in here."

"Please say that where they can hear you, I'd love to see what happens."

Derrick smiled. "Anyways. I talked to the contractor. They'll be done in the next two weeks with both buildings so we can move everyone in."

"Fine. Go get some rest then."

Derrick stood. "What are the chances I can go up to your apartment and convince our mate to lay between us?"

"Worst she could say is no, right?" Carlos shut down his computer and stood. He looked forward to sleeping cuddled up with their mate.

Derrick smiled wistfully. "I don't want to overwhelm her just yet. I'll be in my apartment if you need me."

"We need to finish the bond soon. The sooner the better, Beta. If nothing else, sleeping in the same apartment as her will help your panther settle."

"I guess nothing beats a try." Derrick sighed and ran a hand down his face. "I've been waiting my entire life to spoil my mate."

Carlos laughed and walked around the desk to meet him at the door. They walked to the elevator. He slapped his Beta's back as the elevator doors closed. "What makes you think our mate is going to let us spoil her?"

Derrick smiled and shook his head. "Yeah, we'll need to work on that."

They entered the apartment together, the sound of the giggling kids filling Derrick's heart.

Derrick grabbed Ella as she ran up to him. "Hi, my darling girl."

She preened. "Beta, are you staying?"

He kissed her on the cheek, inhaling her innocent scent. He loved the little girl, and had from the moment he and Carlos had rescued her.

"I'm going to try and convince Savi to cuddle me to sleep, think it will work?" He whispered in her ear.

She giggled and grabbed his cheeks. "She's my new mom, you know? I can put in a good word." She whispered.

He laughed and set her down on the floor. His mate stood and wiped her hands down her shorts. He watched as she greeted Carlos, his heart hammering. He adjusted his hard-on as they whispered to each other. She looked up and the lust in her eyes scorched him. He greeted the boys and waited on his mate to come to him.

Her son, the kid he would be overjoyed to claim, that his cat had already claimed, came over and hugged him. "Hi, Beta."

Derrick lifted him and nuzzled against his cheek in greeting. "Hey, kiddo."

The young cub in Jamie was strong, nearing the time for his first shift. He was amazed that although Jamie had only a quarter panther, it was strong enough to manifest. It spoke of his mother's strength and that of her family. It made him anxious for the day he and Savi had their own.

"Glad you're back." Jamie said, as Derrick put him back down.

He waved at Carlos' nephews and watched silently as his mate walked over to him.

"You're staying here?" She asked quietly as she came over.

He watched her face for signs of discomfort. "If that's alright with you." He traced a thumb across her cheek.

She grabbed his hand and rubbed her cheek against it. "The kids will probably be pretty loud."

She was so beautiful she took his breath away. "I don't mind, so long as I can lay next to you."

She sighed, her eyes dewy. "That's the same thing Felix said.

"If you're not comfortable, I can leave, love."

The indecision was on her face. Her emotions running the gamut from fear to acceptance. He watched it all. She finally sighed and turned her face into his hand and kissed his palm.

"I don't mind."

He kissed her lightly, mindful of the kids. "I'll just shower and make a pallet here in the living room." He'd give her space. Just being in the same apartment with her was enough for him.

She nodded and stepped back. "I'll make it for you."

He smiled and walked into the hallway bathroom. There was a towel and clothes on the sink, probably courtesy of his co-mate. He showered quickly, exhausted and eager to spend any type of time with Savannah. By the time he came out, there were blankets, pillows and giggling kids scattered across the floor.

The Felix was already laid out next to their mate, to his surprise. He assumed Carlos would lay in bed with Savannah. His mate looked up and smiled, waving him over. His panther circled his body, and relaxed the moment he sat next to Savannah. He adjusted the pillow and laid out, his hand snaking out across her stomach. The Felix adjusted his arm lower so they were both comfortable and despite the noise of the kids, he was asleep in minutes. Content for the first time in a long time.

Chapter 18

Carlos kept his eyes closed, using his senses to figure out where the hell he was. He smelled his mate, and his panther was pushing to come out. He took a slow breath, and nearly growled when he realized he was laying on top of Savi, his head nuzzled into her neck. His Beta was curled into the other side of her. Derrick's arm was across his back. It was quiet around them, so he assumed the kids were not in the living room.

He peeked and saw they were alone. He moved to get a look at his mate, her deep breathing telling him she was still asleep. He moved Derrick's hand from his back for more room and his Beta peeked his head up groggily. He waved him back down and Derrick curled back into her side.

Carlos studied Savannah, amazed at her beauty and the fact that she was his, theirs, he self-corrected. Unable to stop himself he nuzzled into her neck licking at the bite he'd left earlier. She moaned, and wiggled her hips and damn if he could stop his own hips from jerking, the reflex to bury his hardness into her warm body a compulsion.

He nibbled along her jaw line and she sighed, he loved the little sound. He skimmed the side of her body, snaking his hand under her shirt. Her skin was silky against his fingertips. He cupped her breast, swiping a thumb against her beading nipple. She mewled, her arms reaching to wrap around his neck. He ached to replace his fingers with his tongue.

She arched her back, her mouth opening on a sigh. He leaned down and rubbed his head against her stomach, pushing up her shirt. He licked along the skin of her belly, wanting, no, needing the taste of her on his tongue. Her body stiffened when she seemed to realize it wasn't a dream. Derrick growled next to him and kissed across her shoulders, his Beta's teeth scraping across her skin. Her eyes widened, the fog of sleep clearing within seconds. He lifted his head from her stomach and dropped her shirt. He moved to her mouth, nibbling on her bottom lip.

She sighed again and her arms circled Carlos' neck. "Hey," her raspy voice raked over him.

He pushed into her center and her gasp pleased him.

"The children are in the next room," she whispered.

"And if they weren't?" Derrick rasped beside her, his nails scraping against her legs.

Her eyes widened, uncertainty mixed in with her lust. She didn't answer. He kissed her, a possessive need to make a mark on her. The scent of her lust washed over him.

"Where are the children?" He asked.

"In Ella's room." She answered huskily.

He cocked his head and listened for them, satisfied when he could hear the commentary from whatever they were watching. He moved again, a little twist of his hips that sped the heart beat at her throat. Her shudder shook Carlos' body. Her nipples pebbled beneath him, a temptation he'd no longer resist. He lifted her shirt, and nuzzled his cheek against the skin of her stomach. He trailed slow kisses up until he reached her breast. Her breath caught, her body going still as she froze, waiting to see what he'd do. He opened his mouth and blew out a breath over her nipple. She released a sigh, her body going pliant beneath him.

"You can be quiet, right, darling?" Derrick whispered against the skin of her neck.

She whimpered in response. Carlos smiled and watched her as he licked across her nipple, a long wet stroke. She writhed beneath him.

"Yes, or no, sweetheart. How quiet can you be when you're coming?" He asked a moment before sucking the bud into his mouth.

Derrick's hands moved between them, maneuvering up the leg of her shorts. He lifted his hips and moved to the side of Savannah, giving his best friend better access. He took a deep pull on her breast, biting down on the tip. Her legs widened and she arched.

"She's so wet, Carlos." Derrick murmured.

He growled in hunger and scraped his teeth against the side of her breast. She grabbed his head and guided him back to her nipple. He rubbed his shaft against the side of her leg, desperately wanting to bury his cock into her wet heat.

"Oh God," she whispered.

"Tell me what you want, kitten?" Derrick licked a path up her neck to her mouth.

She turned her head and kissed him. One hand held Carlos in place over her breast, and the other gripped Derrick's chin. He watched them kiss, longing for what they could be if she'd let it happen. She broke from the kiss and threw her head back gasping. He twirled his tongue around her nipple, sucking it into the heat of his mouth and she lifted her hips.

"Please." She whimpered.

"Let's show her what she could have with us." He ordered his Beta.

He used one hand to toy with the tip of her other breast, renewing his assault on the nipple in his mouth. His other hand slid beneath the waist band of her shorts. He met Derrick's hand over her warm, wet entrance. He added a finger to the two Derrick had working in and out of her sex. She moaned, and her nails scored the back of his neck.

"Tsk, tsk, kitten. Gotta be quieter than that." Derrick admonished.

Carlos pulled his finger from her heat and separated the lips of sex. He pinched the tight bud of her clit and studied her face, needing to see the moment she exploded. Her mouth opened on a silent scream as Derrick pumped his finger in and out of her.

"Shit, you're so hot." Derrick closed his eyes, his face pinched in desire.

Her body stiffened and her hand left his neck to cover her mouth. She smothered her own keening cry as she climaxed. Pleasure suffused her face and his cock throbbed. He moved her hand and devoured her mouth, swallowing her mewls as they brought her down from her orgasm.

Derrick took his hands out of her shorts and brought his fingers up to taste their mate. Carlos sighed and promised himself that he would taste her soon. He moved from her lips and kissed down her neck, petting her sex until she stopped squirming beneath them. She sighed, and stared between her two mates, dazed.

He sat up, jostled his bulge to the side and climbed off their mate. She sat up and adjusted her tank top. His mouth watered just watching the way the fabric scraped across her breast.

"We need to talk." Derrick turned her to face him. "But first..." He grabbed the back of her head and pulled her into a kiss.

She moaned, the sound torn from her, her chest heaving as he ended the kiss.

"Good afternoon." Derrick said. "You taste amazing and I can't wait to eat you."

She sucked in a breath, her lips parting.

Derrick sat up and moved to the armchair across from her. She ran a hand over her hair and took a few deep breaths.

Derrick stared at her until she lowered her eyes. "We want to talk to you about the mating."

Her eyes widened and she licked her lips nervously. "What do you mean?"

They both stared, not letting her get away with her pretense.

She stood and started to pace. "I can't, there's no way I can keep up with you guys. I'm not strong enough to be Alpha female."

Carlos growled. Her grandfathers said she would say that. It pissed him off all the same.

She shrugged. "I'm latent, Felix, no way the women will accept that."

He wanted to disagree with her, but having just had this same argument at the prowl meeting this morning, he couldn't dispute her worry. "Savi you know how this works, our panthers wouldn't pick a woman who couldn't handle the lifestyle, who wasn't strong enough to stand toe to toe with our cats."

She waved aside his words. "I've seen enough Tribonds to know how they work, that's not…that's partially my concern. I haven't been to prowl meetings, I'm not prepared for this. I don't….this isn't a good idea, Carlos."

"My cat doesn't give a shit," Derrick said.

She turned to him, regret in her eyes. "Be that as it may, I won't saddle you with a mate that could weaken your position as Felix."

Carlos growled again. "I suggest you stop calling my mate weak, even if you're talking about yourself."

She looked at him, her eyes tortured. "I live in this body Carlos, I know what I am."

Derrick held out a hand to stop Carlos from arguing with her. "You're not ready."

She shook her head. "I don't know that I would ever be ready."

"Fair enough,"

"The hell!" His panther swiped at his insides, the alpha power flaring in the room.

Derrick shrugged. "We'll give you time to think about it."

"No." It was an automatic answer, one his panther was in full agreement with. His cat raked against him, making him wince.

Derrick turned to him. "We can't force her, Felix, we can give her time to get used to it."

"Was it not you just this morning ready to chase her down?"

Derrick held his hands out in a helpless gesture.

"You're not hearing me," she whispered, her pain clearly broadcasting across their connection, tentative as it was. She cleared her throat and sat down. "My aunt was the prowl Seer."

"Exactly…was, so nothing she said matters between us." Carlos growled.

A bit of hope flashed, before fear took over and then disappeared behind a blank face. "Nevertheless, she was the Seer at the time. She saw things, things I don't want to talk about, don't want to rehash, but they all lead to the same thing. I can't be Alpha female." A tear slipped from her eye. "I lose track of that when either of you touch me."

Carlos moved, unable to take it. He gathered her in his arms, feeling her resolve, her stubbornness. He thought about her grandparents' words earlier in the day. They knew she would fight the mating, and now she just confirmed to him that it had to do with the old seer.

He sighed. "I'll back off, baby." At least until he could find a better way to convince her.

She shuddered, the scent of her arousal swirling around them, mingled with smell of her sex. He growled, fur rippled down his arm as he lost control of his panther. He backed away. "I need…"

He left the room, certain his cat would burst from his skin if he stayed close to their mate.

Derrick watched his Alpha leave, taking some, but not all of the tension with him. Savannah sighed and turned her back on him. He went up behind her and stopped within a hair of touching her.

"I'm sorry, Derrick." She whispered.

He leaned closer and inhaled the scent of her hair. He clenched his hands at his sides to keep from touching her. Now that he knew how she tasted, he'd have a harder time keeping away.

"You understand that nothing will stop us from trying to claim you."

Her shoulders stiffened. "I'll leave."

He sighed and pulled her into his chest. She stubbornly refused to turn and face him. He swallowed his chuckle. Her grandfathers were certainly right about how hard they would have to work.

"Do what you feel you must, kitten, it won't make a difference. Our cats have as good as claimed you." He moved her hair from her neck and laid a small kiss. "But I will work on our mate, and keep him from pressuring you."

She lowered her head and exposed the back of her neck further, instinctively giving him submission. He swallowed a growl, and cautioned his panther patience. Soon, he'd be able to make his mark on her there.

He took a deep breath. "It's going to be hard work keeping our mate from raining down alpha on you. Don't I get a reward for that?"

She whipped around, her eyebrows lowered in vexation. "He can't make me do anything I don't want to do."

He wiped the smug look off his face and gave her his best innocent expression. "You're right, but, nothing will stop him from trying to sway you into changing your mind. I could be persuaded to reign the Felix in."

She growled, her burgeoning power flaring and his lips twitched as he fought a smile. Not strong enough, his ass.

"One itty bitty kiss is all I ask in payment." He slid his arm around her waist and brought her into his chest.

She leaned back and narrowed her eyes in suspicion. "You're trying to hustle me."

"I'm trying to cheer up my mate." He countered her accusation.

"I'm not..." she sighed not bothering to argue the statement, which to his mind, was a step in the right direction.

"Now, one little kiss to keep the scary Alpha away, is that so much?"

She stared at him, and he gave her a small smile. "Don't think I didn't notice you excluding the Beta from this negotiation. Will this kiss keep you from trying?"

He feigned shock. "Sweetheart, I will respect your wishes."

Not quite an agreement, he hoped she didn't call him on it. He gave her a fake pout. She smiled, then looked down, her expression serious once more.

"I don't want to mess up, Derrick. I can't do that to you both, or the prowl, you don't understand what's at stake."

He grabbed her chin. "You let us worry about that, love. One little kiss?" His growl was all hungry animal. "Just a small one," he whispered.

She came up on her toes and tentatively touched his lips with her soft ones. He sighed in relief, his breath mingling with hers. He licked at the seam of her lips, moaning in triumph when she opened her mouth. His tongue swept into her mouth and his cat purred at Savannah's taste. Their kiss heated and she gripped his shirt in her hands. He ate at her mouth, wanting her unable to think of nothing, save him.

Yes, he would back away and keep their mate back as much as he could, but he would make sure she knew what she was missing out on.

"Mom," Jamie called from the other room and Savannah stiffened and tried to back away.

He held her in his arms a moment more. "I'll convince the Felix to give you space."

She nodded in thanks. "I need to..." She inclined her head towards the kids' room.

"Of course," he said, backing away. Allowing her to go tend to their son.

He watched her leave, his body hard to the point of pain, but his mind even more determined. Nothing had been easy about getting the family of his dreams. Convincing Carlos to take the position as Felix of their fledgling prowl had been an uphill battle. He'd nagged him at every turn, and finally they had their own prowl and territory to go with it. Now that he'd found their mate, and knew they would be in a Tribond, he would work just as hard to convince her that they all belonged together.

His mate didn't yet know that there were seers in his own family and he'd seen his future. He had from the first moment he'd met Carlos. And his future was with them. Yes, he'd keep the Felix from going alpha on her, but he'd be more subtle in his persuasion. She'd be in a mating before she saw it coming. He left the apartment and took the elevator down to the ground level.

They were in the middle of the city, so though they had a huge privacy fence covering what little of a yard they had, he knew the Felix wouldn't have much space to release his anger. He found Carlos pacing around the pool, still in his human form. Points for him, he thought for sure he would find the Alpha shifted.

Carlos' head lifted as he scented him. "I want our mate."

"Me too, Alpha, but we can't rush her."

Carlos lifted his head and released a frustrated growl. Derrick waited out his anger.

"The old Felix said she would be stubborn." He reminded him.

Carlos hissed and rounded the pool, invading Derrick's space. He was in his face, his eyes yellow, and his panther right under the surface. "I want to know what the Seer told her."

Carlos' voice was a growl that traveled down Derrick's spine. It reminded him that his best friend had rightly been made the Felix of their prowl. His power settled over him, full alpha.

"It doesn't matter what she was told, the damage is done." Derrick said. But Carlos was right, and Derrick planned to get to the bottom of it. "Now we have to find a way to convince our mate she belongs with us."

Carlos turned his back and his breathing was harsh as he battled his cat. It was times like this when Derrick could appreciate what Carlos dealt with as an alpha. His animal was stronger, more powerful, and more aggressive than them all. Controlling a beast with that much power took work. He watched his friend pull his power back, the angst that was being pushed down the prowl link loosening. He imagined many cats in the building breathed a little easier.

Carlos turned around and his eyes were back to their normal hazel color. His voice was still raspy with his panther. "You still smell like her."

He smiled, "I told her I could convince you to back off if she gave me a kiss."

A surprise bark of laughter left Carlos. "And that worked?"

His smile turned cocky, "it's a gift."

Carlos grabbed his shoulder and brought him into his chest for a hug. Their cats reached for each other, reveling in the touch of its prowl mate.

"Fuck, Derrick. I need her."

"I know, Alpha. I eventually wore you down, I can do the same for our mate."

Carlos laughed and backed away. "Yeah, you got a gift."

"What can I say?"

Chapter 19

Steam blew into her face as she lifted the top off the pot on the stove. She was making dinner, her hands still shaking from her conversation with Carlos and Derrick. The way Carlos had left the apartment, she wasn't sure if she should still be here. She should've taken Jamie and went home. Who knew what mood he would be in when he came back?

They wanted to claim her.

She blew out a breath. According to Derrick they were going to do what they could to convince her. She should be scared, instead, her nipples were beaded, and she was damn close to panting over the stove. Just replaying that scene on the living room floor had her squeezing her legs tighter together. Derrick and Carlos worked seamlessly together as they teased her sex, driving her careening into an orgasm. There had been nothing she could do, but hold on tight as the flood of sensations consumed her.

She tensed as the front door clicked, announcing Carlos' arrival. Though, she didn't need the sound, she could feel him enter the apartment. She didn't know what to expect, he'd left upset, his panther right near the surface. She glanced at the kids and wondered if she should send them to Ella's room to give the two of them time to talk. They were sitting at the table discussing their Halloween costumes.

Carlos came up behind her and kissed the top of her head, calmer than when he'd left an hour ago. "It smells good, what are you making?"

"Chicken Chow Mein."

"You know how to make Chinese food?"

She laughed, "Well, my version of Chinese food."

He kissed her neck, and snuggled her in closer to his chest. "I'm sorry about earlier," he murmured against her skin.

"I understand." She put the lid back on the wok.

"Do you now?" He chuckled and released her. He walked over and kissed the top of both kids head before leaving the kitchen.

His footsteps traveled the length of the hallway and paused. His growl reached the kitchen. She and the kids tensed.

She turned off the burner and turned to the kids. "Hey guys, give dinner like ten minutes to cool and then we can eat. But go into Ella's room while I talk to Carlos for a moment."

Her son watched her, a look that told her despite his human progeny she would have to deal with a panther cub soon. She made a mental note to talk to his father and her grandfather. Carlos prowled into the room. That could only be the word for it. She felt like prey as he held her duffle bag and watched her from the living room.

"Kids, your room, please." His command whipped through the room.

Her son looked to her and she nodded and gave him what she hoped looked like a reassuring smile. The whole time, Carlos' gaze never strayed from her.

"You're packed, why?"

She wiped her hands on her shorts. "Well, with the way you left, I didn't think you'd want me here when you got back."

He snarled, his eyes switching to his panther. It was fascinating to see. She lowered her gaze, knowing the submissive gesture would appease his cat.

He dropped her bag and stepped closer. "I want you here, where I can be sure you and my cubs are safe."

Her eyes jerked back up. "Your cubs?" She whispered. Then she registered what he said. "You don't think we'll be safe at home?"

"Until I can stop these attacks, I want you under my roof."

She held up her hands to stop him from getting closer. She knew if he touched her, he'd be able to talk her into all sorts of things. "I can go to grandfather, we'd be safe there."

Hurt flashed across his face a moment before his eyes flashed again with the panther. "I can keep my mate safe here."

"Carlos," she sighed. "I'm not, I can't be your mate. We've talked about this."

He stepped closer, his arms caging her against the sink. Calculation changed the expression on his face, and she understood how a rabbit in the field felt.

"Savannah." He leaned over and licked the spot on her neck where he'd bitten her. "I don't think my cat could take it if someone else was protecting you other than me or Derrick. Please stay. Just another night, I'll make sure your house is safe for you to go home tomorrow."

Her body melted, her resolve scattering as he grabbed the skin of her neck between his teeth.

"Carlos," she whispered. "That's not fair."

His hand slid under her shirt and his claws, oh God… claws trailed the skin of her back, the bite of danger throwing her body into heat. Her lids fluttered shut, as his warm, calloused palm pressed against her spine, pulling her closer until their hips aligned.

"Say yes, kitten, I promised the Beta I'd behave and I will." He moved his hips side to side, rubbing his shaft into her center.

She reached between them and grabbed his cock. He hissed, and froze, his gaze turning watchful, waiting on her next move.

"This is you behaving?"

His breath left his body in a shuddering gasp as she squeezed.

"I'm going to stay, but it's because I don't want to drive an hour from my grandfather's land back here to take Jamie to school. Not because you might do amazing things with your dick." Now, if she could remind her body of that.

He nipped her bottom lip. "Whatever you need to tell yourself, darling."

He gripped her hand, pumping it over his cock, once, twice, his eyes closing, his beautiful face pinched with desire. He opened his eyes and she felt struck by lightning, frozen in place.

"You're sleeping in my bed tonight."

"I don't think that's a good idea," she whispered, releasing his dick.

He chuckled, and leaned over her neck. "It's cute how you think you have a say in this."

She growled, her chest tightening, power raising the hair on her arms. Who did he think he was talking to? "I have a say in anything that goes on with me."

"You, my mate, will soon find that when it comes to you, my panther and I can be very…insistent." He scraped his canines down her neck.

She shuddered, her womb clenching in lust. She cleared her throat. "I don't do anything I don't want to do, but sure, try your hardest."

She didn't know what made her say it, but she regretted it the moment it left her lips. Challenging an alpha, any alpha, would have consequences. The way Carlos' eyes lit, the satisfaction rolling off him, she knew she'd made a misstep. He laughed and leaned back over her neck.

He pulled the lobe of her ear into his mouth. "Tell me again why you don't think you're strong enough for us?"

She sucked in a surprised breath and turned her back to him, damn him.

"Kids, dinner!" he called, the amusement in his voice irritating her.

"We're not done with this conversation." She hissed over her shoulder.

"I welcome the debate, my mate." He purred.

She pasted on a smile as the kids rushed into the kitchen.

"Mom makes the best Chow Mein," Jamie gushed as he sat.

"I'm looking forward to it," Carlos said taking a seat at the table with the kids.

He was so good with the children. He and Jamie talked as though they'd known each other their whole lives. She watched him over the rim of her wine glass as he regaled her son with a story from his Ranger days. Carlos was smart enough to know that she'd not give either of them the time of day if her son didn't like them. Though to be fair, he was just as attentive with his daughter.

The petty part of her didn't want to acknowledge how well he would fit into her and Jamie's life. She could easily picture nights with the five of them at the dinner table discussing their day. She took a deep gulp of wine.

It wasn't to be, and daydreaming was for suckers.

She put down her glass and focused on eating. She needed to get a grip. She looked up as her skin tightened. The heat of Carlos' gaze flushed her body. He leaned back in his chair and stared, his face daring her to take what she wanted.

Damn him.

Carlos' body buzzed with anticipation. His panther was on the hunt and his mate their current target. He'd watched her throughout dinner. The kids' chatter flowed over them, while tension between the two adults built. He offered to do the dishes so she could put the kids to bed. He needed the time and space to control himself. He tensed a moment as she came around the corner to the kitchen as he wiped down the counters. Her scent, fresh from the shower, wafted over to him and he gripped the counter top.

"I'm sleeping in the guest room." She announced and walked back out.

He grinned. He didn't care where she slept, he would be wherever she was. He shut down the apartment, locking the door and turning out the lights. He took a quick shower to give her time to settle. By the time he came out, the guest room was dark.

Savannah wasn't sleep, with his heightened senses, her heartbeat was easy to discern. He went to the door and watched her. Her eyes were shut tight as she pretended to sleep. Silly woman.

He climbed under the covers behind her. She sighed, not surprised, but her wariness was apparent.

"I'm not here to argue, love, I just want to be in bed with my mate." He rubbed his cheek against the top of her head.

"Carlos, you can't keep calling me your mate."

He snuggled in behind her. "You smell amazing," he said, instead of arguing.

He wrapped his arms around her, pressing against her stomach, to push her back into his hips.

"You can't just seduce me into being your mate."

He hummed, nibbling on the back of her neck, ignoring her statement. "I can't wait to bite you here."

She'd find out soon enough that he usually got what he wanted, and by the time he was done she'd surely want him as much as he wanted her.

"Carlos." She protested.

"Do you know what the bites mean?" He asked, running his tongue across her skin.

She shook her head.

He was glad she couldn't see his smug smile. "Derrick and I will each bite you."

His teeth gripped the back of her neck and her body trembled, her breath hissing out in a hard pant. His panther pushed against his skin. He was moments from biting down.

He released her skin. "The bite in the back, is in the same spot a cat in the wild would grab their cub to carry them around. It symbolizes our promise to nurture and take care of you." He traced the front of her neck along her trachea. "We bite here, to show dominance, and exact your promise to submit to your mates. Do you know the amount of trust needed between mates to allow a bite so dangerous?"

He wanted to push the issue, but his mate's heart was pounding, her arousal scenting the space between them. He stuck out his tongue, tasting her need in the air. He groaned and hugged her closer.

"Now, rest. You have work in the morning." He turned her chin towards him. "Goodnight," he whispered, sealing their lips together.

She pulled back. "You're not going to..."

"Push, no. I told you I wouldn't. I promised our mate I'd behave, remember?"

He kissed her again and settled behind her, smiling at her disgruntled tone. There just might be something to Derrick's way. He'd wear his mate down, no matter how long it took.

Chapter 20

Derrick prowled around his target, his gaze steady on her as she worked in her garden. As if sensing him, she looked up and smiled. He growled and walked back to the basket of clothes he'd spotted on his way over. Fully dressed, he stepped out from the side of her house.

Joelle waved and bent back over her vegetables. "Can you bring my some water while you're over there?"

He unwound the garden hose and lugged it to her, after turning on the water. She gave him a grateful nod and sprayed the dry dirt on a seemingly empty row. He crossed his arms over his chest and watched in silence for a few moments.

"I know what you're looking for, but I can't give you an exact answer for what Savannah was told."

Derrick sighed. "I want you to go see her. It's time."

The seer nodded. "I think you're right about that."

"What was Antoinette's purpose?"

The spray of water stopped and Joelle looked up at him in surprise. "No one has ever asked me that."

"Well?"

She restarted the spray. "She wanted control of this prowl. Being Seer gave her that. I saw Savi as alpha female and a stronger prowl under her. If Toni's brother were no longer Felix, her power over the prowl was gone."

It was a good of motive as any. Anger brought his power flooding his body. "Do you have any idea where she could've gone?"

"I was so young," she said as way of apology.

He nodded. It didn't hurt to try. He would find Antoinette on his own. It was time she was found and made to answer for what she'd done.

"I'll leave you to it then."

Joelle waved him away and went back to her work.

Derrick drove back into town, their conversation playing in his head. He would have to talk to the old Felix and find out if his sister had any contacts in the area. By the time he got back to the apartment building, he spotted his mate and the kids in the garage, loading into Savannah's car.

He knocked on the driver's window and waved at the kids as Savi lowered the glass.

"Can I help you?" She gave him an impish smile.

"Where are you guys going?"

"Costumes!" Marcella answered from the backseat.

"Wants some help?" He leaned into the window, rubbing his cheek against Savannah's.

She sighed and rubbed the top of his head. "Are you sure?"

He tilted her chin up. "Am I sure I want to spend time with my mate and children?"

"Derrick," her soft entreaty brushed his lips. "We talked about this."

He dropped a small kiss to her lips. "I don't remember any conversation like that."

"Come with us, Beta." Jamie said.

Derrick raised his eyebrows and kissed her again. "Our kids want me go."

Her gaze studied him for a quiet moment, her eyes broadcasting her inner struggle. She blew out an impatient breath. "Fine."

He smiled and crossed to the passenger seat of the car. He groaned as he squeezed into the seat, pushing back as far as he could without crushing Mari behind him. She slid an amused glance over him before taking off. He pulled out his phone.

Going shopping with our mate.

Putting our plan in affect? Was Carlos' reply.

You know it.

A thumbs up emoji came next.

Savannah jerked to a stop at a redlight and he grunted in irritation.

Also, our mate need a new car.

Lol. already on it.

He put his phone in his pocket and focused on his mate. He and Carlos had come up with the plan to seduce their mate, one at a time. Today was his turn. He put a hand on Savannah's leg, running a soft caress down to her knee. She whipped her head to him. He gave her his most charming smile before turning to watch the scenery. The muscle under his hand relaxed as he made no further moves. He kept his smile to himself.

He helped her get the kids out of the car and held their hands as they headed for the party supply store. It was crowded, which made him nervous, but he spotted Simon coming into the store a few people behind them. He relaxed and sidled closer to his mate.

He put an arm around her shoulder. "Any clue what we're getting?"

She snorted. "Nope, my only hope is that whatever they find, this store has it in their size."

"Fair enough." He nuzzled into her neck. "You smell good."

"Don't start," she murmured.

"I haven't done anything." Not yet anyways.

"Seducing me is not going to work."

He nibbled the skin under her ear. "Didn't I promise to behave?"

Her breath hitched, and she tucked her body closer to his. "This is you behaving?"

He trailed his fingers across shoulder towards her chest. "Compared to what I really want to do, oh absolutely."

Jamie called her name, breaking up the sensual fog built around them. She turned and pressed her finger into Derrick's chest. "Whatever you and Carlos are planning, it won't work."

He wrapped an arm around her waist and pulled her closer. "Didn't anyone ever tell you about daring a shifter?"

She snorted and pushed out of his arms. He smiled at her retreating figure. Yeah, today would be fun.

Princess…zombie.

Carlos sighed and stared at the piece of charcoal in his hand. "I'm supposed to do what now?"

A tiny growl. "Papa, it's easy. Just make my dress look dirty and bloody, duh."

Dark eyes stared at him in exasperation, the tip of her fingers red from the fake blood spilled all along her dress and on the kitchen table. It was Halloween and Ella was irritated at his lack of understanding. Fortunately for him, Savannah had taken her shopping days earlier for her costume. Unfortunately, she'd changed her mind about being a fairy princess.

"Why does the princess have to be a zombie?"

"Papa." She stomped her foot.

He sighed. "Fine."

He spent the next twenty minutes transforming a perfectly decent princess costume into one that mimicked the walking dead. She held her hand up, haughtiness transforming her face from the placid child she'd used to be, to tell him…

"My mom will do the makeup part."

She left the kitchen to go gather her stuff and all he could do was shake his head. His sisters had told him her burgeoning attitude was a good thing, in that it signified her being secure in her place in his life. For a child who'd gone through the amount of trauma Marcella had at such a young age, it was a great sign.

He'd rescued her as a toddler, from a prowl ravaged by supremacists. When they were done, the small prowl's numbers had dwindled to the little girl huddled in the clothes dryer where her mother had hidden her. His unit had come up on the small cougar prowl's land, entirely by accident while on a training excursion. The carnage had sickened him. He'd taken one look at Marcella's fear filled, dark eyes and promised to keep her safe.

It had taken him and Derrick countless hours and too many pages of red tape to count before they were given custody of the young cub. He left the army within that year and started the prowl Derrick had been bugging him to start. Now, he had a place where his daughter was secure and he was anxious to put down roots.

Marcella had decided that Savannah would be her mother, and no amount of talking had changed the little girl's mind. Not that he'd tried especially hard. As far as he was concerned, Savannah would be his mate.

That meant Ella was technically right.

He stood and smiled, anticipation at seeing his mate making him happy. She'd left the house two mornings ago as if the hounds of hell were on her heels. He gave yesterday to Derrick, knowing his Beta would use every ounce of charm he had on their mate. Tonight was his turn. They'd decided that splitting up would keep her off guard. According to Derrick it was working.

He couldn't wait to see her.

He locked the door and he and Ella headed to her house. Her whole street was decorated, the cul-de-sac where her house was, more so. There was a table set up with a giant cauldron and music blaring. There were a lot of cars parked up and down the street in front of her house.

Ella squealed in the back seat in excitement. "It's a party! This will be so exciting, Papa."

They walked into the house and was greeted by a chorus of hellos from his siblings and their children, along with nods and waves from other members of their prowl. More proof his mate was falling into the role of alpha female. A good portion of the prowl was gathered at her house, and not just her cousins. Some of the men and women who had come down with him were sitting around the living room talking and mingling with the Tampa group.

It looked impromptu, though food trays were spread on the table in the dining room. He found Savannah at the kitchen counter painting her son's face. She looked up at him and smiled and his heart contracted.

"It's a lot bigger to do than I expected." She smiled sheepishly.

"It's great. Anything I can do to help?" he offered.

She shook her head and put her paint brushes down. She held out her arms to Ella and the little girl rushed to hug her.

"Savi, I didn't want Papa to mess up my zombie face so can you do it?" Ella's look of adoration was probably the same look on his own face.

Savannah kissed Ella's nose. "Of course, baby girl. Let me finish Jamie's then it's your turn."

Carlos laughed at Jamie's black and white striped suit. "Are you supposed to be Beetlejuice?"

Jamie smiled and shrugged. "Mom's a dork and it's one of our favorite movies."

"Hey, what does me, being a dork, have to do with anything?" She pulled his nose before going back to painting his face.

"I'm going outside with the males until you guys are ready."

She nodded and waved him away. "We're leaving when it gets dark."

He rounded the kitchen island and pulled her into his chest. "Before I forget." He kissed her, a soft coaxing until her mouth opened. Their tongues dueled and his body heated. He pulled back, satisfied with the bemused look on her face. More satisfied that Savannah didn't fight his public claiming.

"Hello, love." He whispered.

"Hi." She said softly.

"I'll walk with you and the kids, 'kay?"

She nodded and he smiled, kissing her forehead and leaving. Derrick's way was definitely working. He found his brothers-in-law, and some of his enforcers outside drinking beer and sitting around a cauldron of candy. They passed him a soda and he chatted about prowl business with them. The kids trickled out as their costumes were finished and they ran around the cul-de-sac playing.

He was out there nearly an hour before dusk settled and the scent of his mate reached him. He turned as she walked out of her garage in a pair of tight jeans that just...

He breathed out and put a chokehold on his panther as it reared up. She wore a t-shirt that read 'This girl bites back' with fangs on the front. Lord, did he want to test that theory. Theo bumped his elbow into him and shook him out of the fantasy reel playing in his head. The raised voices reached him next. A tall slender woman stalked out of the back door and walked off in a huff.

Savannah growled, her face tight in anger. He turned to follow the woman with his gaze, curious as to who she was. His mate cleared her throat and he turned back. Savannah stood in front of him, her head cocked expectantly.

"I'm sorry, did you say something?"

She snorted. "Let's go."

"Who was that?" He asked, glancing back towards the woman as she got into her car.

"My cousin Lydia. Your kiss didn't go over well." She blew out an exasperated breath and shook her head.

"I didn't mean to cause you any trouble." Not that he cared what anyone thought of him kissing his mate.

"Don't worry about it," She said over her shoulder as she walked away to catch up with the other moms.

He let her walk in front of him, just so he could watch her ass in those jeans. The view had such a payoff. He turned his head and whistled. The two enforcers he had watching her house sidled from around the corner, following behind at a discreet distance. He wanted the time with his mate, but was ever aware of the danger still hovering over the prowl.

There hadn't been any other attacks in the past two days, but until he knew for sure who was behind them, he wasn't taking any chances. He caught up to Savannah, reaching down to grab her hand. They walked that way in silence a little while, watching the kids go from house to house. His sisters and her cousins were chatting a few feet in front of them. He pulled on her hand to slow her down so they could have a little privacy.

He broke the silence. "Did you sleep well, last night?"

She rolled her eyes and blew out a breath. "You and Derrick are certainly not helping my sleep pattern."

He laughed and lifted her hand, laying a kiss on her knuckles.

"You're especially cruel for the stunt you pulled the other night."

"Who me?" He put a hand to his chest. "I did what you asked and left you alone to sleep."

"You made sure to rile me up first." She accused.

"You had only to take what you wanted." He reminded her.

"First of all, who in the world falls asleep that fast."

He smiled at her disgruntled tone. "You could've left the bed and slept on the sofa."

"Umm, your arm had been tight around me and you complained every time I tried to move."

He grabbed her around the waist and walked behind her, "what's the matter, sleeping next to my hot body too much for you?"

She laughed, and he loved the sound. "You're ridiculous."

He grabbed her hand again and walked next to her. "I'm sticking to my promise."

"Hmph," she said.

"I liked waking up next to you."

She smiled shyly and changed the subject. "Have you had any other attacks? No one was really talking about it at the house."

He sighed. "It's been quiet the past two days, which makes me wary. Derrick and I have started patrolling the territory along with the enforcers. It's good, because I'm getting more familiar with the area. The sooner we catch them the better. The pairs order is already starting to chaff some people."

"Yeah, Charlotte said you tried to limit it to the women at first." She gave him a sideways glance.

He grimaced. "Yes, your cousins can be quite explicit when saying no."

Even after Brielle had asked for clarification, her cousins had cornered him after the prowl meeting and let him know in no uncertain terms what they thought about the order.

She laughed outright. "Let that be a lesson to you, Felix."

"Trust me, I've learned my lesson on that."

"How are you finding the prowl otherwise?"

He considered his answer, happy to be discussing the prowl like this with her. He wanted to share his vision and get her input.

"I'm new to the whole Alpha role. Having a bigger prowl is daunting, but your family has been amazing…welcoming."

She nodded. "I'm glad."

"Will you tell me some of your misgivings about the mating, love?"

She grimaced. "You mean, you need to ask even after that display a little bit ago?"

He shrugged and held his breath as she went quiet. After a minute, he didn't think she'd answer.

"Latents have to fight…like, a lot. We have to show we're strong enough to even be in the prowl, let alone have a place in the hierarchy. I was challenged at every meeting I attended, from as far back as I can remember. It gets exhausting."

"Even with your cousins?"

"Especially after the Seer, my aunt, spread that I didn't know my place." She sighed. "Aunt Toni constantly pitted my cousins against me. Even now, anytime someone wants to move up the hierarchy, they find a way to challenge me."

He rubbed the back of his neck. They didn't have many latents in the group that had come down with him. He made a mental note to make sure that wasn't going on in his prowl.

"I bring that up, only to say that I don't want to spend the rest of my life constantly fighting as the alpha female. That's not her job. The Fela's job is to nurture the prowl, I can't do that if I'm fighting every meeting."

He looked away and squelched his irritation. She had a valid point. She knew the prowl better than he did at the moment. Who was he to argue her experience?

"I hear your concerns, but I have to be honest, Savannah. I'm willing to fight the whole prowl myself to have you." He sighed.

She chuckled and rubbed a hand down his back. "And we both know that's not how panthers work. Now, let's change the subject. What are your plans for Thanksgiving?"

He stared at her for long moments debating whether or not he wanted to press the subject. Her eyes beseeched him to let it go, and he couldn't tell her no. He smiled and allowed the subject to change, but in his mind...

He planned.

Chapter 21

Savannah drummed her fingers along the steering wheel and bit her lip. She had one eye on the red light, and one ear on the conversation taking place in her earpiece. She hated early morning conference calls, but it was the only time that fit into her client's schedule. She turned her head and smiled at Ella and Jamie in the backseat quietly going over their candy haul from last night. She was on her way to drop them off to school. The little girl had begged her dad to let her spend the night with them. It was cute, the way her and Jamie had bonded.

She didn't blame Ella. She hadn't wanted the fun from last night to end either. Last night with Carlos was nice. When he wasn't in alpha mode he was easy to talk with. She learned a lot about him, and had to admit, she was attracted to him.

They talked the whole lap they'd taken around the neighborhood and even when they'd come back to the impromptu party at her house with his family. He'd left her with a kiss on the lips that fueled her fantasies as she slept. He was planning a slow seduction, she was sure of it, and damn it, it was working.

She thought back on the other night she'd stayed over to his house. He'd teased her about it last night. She smiled. She couldn't believe he'd been true to his word and not tried anything with her. He'd given her a kiss and settled into a spoon position, sleep within a few minutes. He was right, she could've tried to leave the bed, but she'd wanted to be there. She may as well admit it.

She sighed, she didn't know why she was fighting so hard. Maybe she could talk to the current seer and find out if something had changed. Perhaps her fate didn't have to be what Antoinette had said. She was smart enough to figure out a way to cement her place as Fela.

The light turned green and she pulled out into the intersection. She looked up in the rearview at the kids and smiled. It turned into a frown as she noticed the same black car that had been behind her the past three stoplights. Carlos' words about their safety crossed her mind and she bit her lip.

Could be a coincidence, Tampa wasn't that big.

Besides, there were only so many routes to their school. She slowed down to see if the car would pass. It didn't and she was only slightly relieved when it pulled off as she pulled into the school parking lot and got in the carline. She blew kisses at the kids and merged back into traffic headed towards her office. She finished her conference call and took the earpiece out.

She didn't have any pressing work now that the meeting was done, so she wasn't in a rush. She turned into the gas station and her heart started thumping when the black car following her earlier, pulled into the gas station but didn't get out of the car. Hands shaking, she replaced the pump and canceled her transaction. She slid into her car and drove off.

She kept her eyes on her rearview mirror and noticed the car was directly behind her. Was it the people responsible for the attacks on the other women? Were they waiting to corner her someplace less crowded?

She looked up and the car was still behind her. Her hands were shaking on the steering wheel. She fumbled through her purse for her phone praying she didn't run herself off the road. She called Carlos.

"Yeah, babe."

She took a deep breath working to keep the panic from her voice. "There's someone following me."

"Are you sure?" His voice sharpened.

"Yes, I'm sure." She peered in the mirror and he was still there.

"Come home to me then. I don't want you to lead him to your house."

Oh God. Her breath left her mouth on a shudder. What if he already knew where she lived?

"Come home, baby, we'll handle it."

The strength of his voice reassured her. She sped up, going through a yellow light, her breath hitching when the car behind her ran the red light.

"Oh God," she whispered.

She flew to the prowl house praying the whole way there. She had to stop at the guard gate before being allowed into the parking garage. The guard came out and waved her in. She was so relieved. She checked her mirror, her eyes widening when the car following her was waved in as well.

That meant...he worked for Carlos.

How dare he?

She parked her car and stomped over to the elevator. She fumed all the way up to his office. She bypassed his assistant, ignoring her as she tried to stop Savi's entrance.

"How dare you!" She shouted.

She sucked in a breath as she saw his enforcers gathered around the office, some faces she recognized since they were her cousins. She didn't care. She passed them, her body trembling with adrenaline.

"How dare you?" she said again, between gritted teeth.

Carlos stood and came from around his side of his desk and met her in the front. "Savannah."

"Uh-oh," someone whispered.

She whipped around, fury shaking her hands. "Get the fuck out. All of you." She turned back to Carlos and shoved his chest, fuming when he didn't move an inch. "You have some nerve."

He raised an eyebrow saying nothing. The room was silent as everyone except Carlos and Derrick cleared out.

She took a deep breath, reigning in her temper, fighting the power running up and down her skin. It was a foreign power, and it was hard to control. "How dare you have me followed? Do you not trust me with your daughter? I was scared as hell thinking someone was following me to kill me, when this whole time it was you. How long have you been following me?"

He continued to stare and her anger ratcheted up another notch. She stabbed her finger at his chest. "Answer me!"

He stared, his eyes changing, his panther fighting with him to come forward. She should've been alarmed, but her heart was still drumming, adrenaline and anger flooding her body.

She continued her rant, ignoring the snarls rumbling his chest. "You put us all in danger by not telling me. What if I had called the police? What if I had gotten us hurt or killed trying to avoid him? He ran a red light behind me, what if he had run into someone? You have no excuse for scaring me like that."

She cursed the tears flowing down her face. She hadn't been this mad in years. She's spent a good portion of her marriage with a condescending husband who didn't trust her to do anything. Greg thought her flighty and incapable of complex thought. He constantly 'checked on her' and came behind her making sure things were done to his liking. She wouldn't put herself in that position again.

She knew it was wrong to bring that residual resentment into her argument with Carlos, but it was baggage she hadn't realized she was carrying. On top of that, some kind of power was surging in her body, making her fury hard to contain. She covered her eyes and took deep breaths to calm herself.

He stepped forward and grabbed her wrists, uncovering her eyes. "I'm sorry, you're right. I got intel from one of my enforcers and panicked, it was instinct to protect my mate and children, but I still should've called you. I've been on edge and I did the first thing that came to mind."

She took another shuddering breath, her heart finally slowing. She couldn't tell if he was being truthful or not, but the apology deflated her anger. The silence of the room wrapped around her and she realized what she'd done. How she'd talked to him in front of his enforcers...

She'd even put her hands on him.

No wonder his eyes were changing, his panther had to be riled.

Her face drained of blood. "Oh my God, I can't believe I just did that."

Carlos inclined his head, a cat like gesture that really showed her how close his panther was to the surface. What had she been thinking? She hadn't been thinking, and now, she could only wait to see what the Felix would do.

Savannah's eyes were wide with panic a moment before she doused it. Meanwhile, his cat prowled his body, on edge and ready to claim its mate. Alpha power infused his body, and the teeth in his mouth grew longer. The fact that their mate had come in and controlled a room full of dangerous cats, was riling his panther. Savannah hadn't even flinched as she stared them down. Her power and anger was not challenged, the enforcers didn't look to him before they left.

Hell, he'd felt her power from the elevator. The meeting he was holding had paused as her power filled the whole floor. She was getting stronger, and he didn't think she realized it. He'd felt a hint of it the other night when the two of them argued.

He hid a triumphant smile. "You have every right to be upset with me, especially if you thought the children were in danger."

He stepped closer, letting his panther a little off the leash. Answering power flared from her and Derrick growled softly behind her. She whipped her head around to his friend. The Beta's cat was right on the surface, his eyes flashing.

Distracting them both, he tugged gently on her arm. "I'm sorry for worrying you."

She nodded absently, running a shaking hand across her face.

He closed the distance between them. "I couldn't be prouder and more turned on by the way you entered the room, though. Now that you've come here and exerted your power and influence, I know you can handle both of your mates."

She gaped at him. Panic flared in her eyes and she looked between the two of them, taking a step back.

"Tsk Tsk, no use in hiding now, mate." Still, he let her have a little distance, not wanting to push just yet. "No backing down. You've already shown the strength. That was your worry, no? That you couldn't handle the two of us. And yet you walked in here, with your righteous anger and cleared a room full of my enforcers."

"That's not...I didn't mean, that was unacceptable, I apologize."

Derrick came up behind her and gripped her waist. "Don't apologize, baby, he deserved it for scaring you. You have every right as our mate to check either one of us."

She shook her head. "But I shouldn't have talked to you like that in front of everyone."

"Why not?" Derrick asked as he trailed a finger down her neck.

She sighed in pleasure and Carlos flexed his fingers in a fist, eager to touch her, but he knew he had to tread carefully. His mate was pissed still, even if she'd gotten better control of it. Her anger burned steady along the edge of their tentative connection. Derrick splayed his hand across her stomach and smiled over her shoulder.

Just a little longer, Carlos implored his panther. "I apologize, love." He moved closer with his hands up in placation. "But my point still stands. You're our mate, and you couldn't have found a better way to prove it than you did just now." He lowered his voice. "You know what that means?"

Her eyes widened, her breath quickened, though he couldn't tell if it was from the circles Derrick was tracing on her stomach or her apprehension of what she'd done.

"We'll take this slow, right?" Derrick murmured nipping a trail down her neck.

Carlos leaned over her, crowding her space. Her body quivered. He spared no glance at Derrick, knowing seeing the Beta kissing her would snap his control and lose him her rapt attention.

He kissed the corner of her mouth. "We can start with dinner. Surely that's not so threatening?"

"Just dinner?" Her lips moved against his as she asked.

He ghosted another kiss across her lips. "That's up to you."

He wouldn't lie outright, because if he had his way, he would be talking her into a lot more then dinner.

She nodded. "When?"

"You're taking Jamie to his father's this weekend, right? What are you doing Friday night?" He nipped her bottom lip.

Her eyes closed. "I promised Ella we could have a girls' night."

He groaned, his daughter was cock blocking and she didn't even know. "Saturday?" He pushed, trailing his finger down the front of her shirt.

"Okay." She acquiesced.

He suppressed his growl of joy. He smiled at his co-mate, giving him a fist bump over her shoulder. "Now that that's settled. On our date, we'll discuss your tone when speaking to your Alpha."

"I was mad!" She protested.

Carlos nodded. "Yes, you were, and perhaps this first time I'll let you go without punishment."

Her scent deepened, her arousal thick in the air. It seemed his mate liked his dominance, though he was pretty sure she'd never admit it aloud.

"What kind of punishment?" She whispered.

Derrick growled and answered for him, "The kind that ends with you splayed, ass up, over any one of these surfaces."

Her shuddering breath shook her breasts and he damn near snatched her from Derrick's arms to make good on that promise. She shook her head, dispelling the thrall he had over her.

"I have to go, I need to call and confirm with Greg."

He kissed her, delving his tongue into her mouth. Just hearing her speak about another male, so important to her, made him and his cat jealous. Derrick turned her around when he was done and did the same. She moaned and he stepped back. He was seconds from taking the choice from her. She pulled out of Derrick's arms and shook her head again, her gaze bouncing between them before she turned and left his office.

He and the Beta were silent as they watched her leave, taking her power with her. The office felt cold without it. They both turned to each other and sighed in relief.

"Risky move letting her see her tail." Derrick exhaled the breath he'd been holding.

"It paid off, didn't it? Didn't she storm in here with her Fela power surrounding her, demanding respect?"

"Fucking right. Are you as hard as I from the display of her power?"

Carlos laughed, running a hand through his hair. "I nearly lost it there with my panther for a moment." He blew out a breath. "If everything goes according to plan, we'll be able to finally have her this weekend."

"I can't wait." Derrick murmured. "Is it just me, or is her power getting stronger?"

He crossed his arms over his chest. "I noticed it the other night. She's definitely getting stronger. I'll ask her grandfather about it first before I bring it to her attention."

"A few more nights and she's ours."

He looked at the door one final time before turning back to Derrick. "I'm sending the Seer over to talk to her. Perhaps she can allay some of her fears."

"Smart. I'm…taking a shower first, then getting back to work," Derrick said leaving.

Carlos walked to the window of his office, looking down at the street below. He saw Savannah's car leave the garage and turn towards her house. Two minutes later, her tail left the garage and followed. Their orders were to be invisible this time, so hopefully his smart mate wouldn't see them.

He'd apologized to her, but until he knew who was attacking the women in his prowl, there was no way he'd let her go anywhere without security.

He smiled and turned back to his desk. He had work of his own to do, hopefully thoughts of Savannah wouldn't make that impossible.

Chapter 22

Savannah would admit to being a little scared as her cousin studied her closet with a critical eye.

"I don't have all day, Naomi, just pick something." She finally growled.

"Hey, you asked for my help, let me work my magic." Naomi groused.

She groaned and flopped back onto her bed. "This is crazy, I'm crazy for doing this, right?"

Naomi hummed, ignoring her.

What made her think she could just date two alpha men who claimed to be her mates? She knew they would play for keeps. It wasn't just dating to them, it was just a necessary step to the inevitable.

She growled. "This is stupid, I don't know why I agreed to this."

"Well, you've agreed and that's that." Naomi murmured as she dug around in her walk-in closet. "I've seen them, they're hot, and you'd be stupid not to agree."

"It's just a date, right?"

Naomi snorted but said nothing.

Her phone rang, it was her cousin Charlotte's ringtone, a song from their favorite movie. "Yeah?"

"She agreed to meet with you, but it has to be today." Charlotte didn't bother with a greeting.

"Today?" She sucked in a shocked breath.

Charlotte scoffed. "What are you doing now?"

"Naomi's helping me find an outfit for tonight."

"For tonight?"

"Long story that ends with me agreeing to a date with Carlos and Derrick." She rushed out.

"Well, then." Charlotte said. She could almost see the curious expression that would be on her cousin's face. "We're on our way over."

"What? Are you serious? Right now, Char?"

"I think it's perfect really. Don't you want to know before you go out with them?"

She did have a point. "Ok, we'll be ready." She ended the call and sat up. "That was Char."

Naomi came out of the closet with a couple of dresses slung over her arm. "I heard, the Seer is coming over."

"What do you think?"

"It's not a bad idea, Savi. I mean, Aunt Toni was mad biased. Granddad kicked her out of the prowl. Perhaps some of the stuff she'd told us isn't true." Naomi joined her on the bed. "Plus, Charlotte said they call Joelle into the enforcer meetings now. They have to really trust her after what happened with Aunt Toni. Maybe she's the real deal?"

"You think?"

"We'll only know if we ask."

Savannah exhaled a shaky, nervous breath. "And if she confirms that it's us who brings down the prowl?"

Naomi shrugged, her eyes misting a little. "We already gave up the prowl, what would be different?" She whispered.

"I'll lose my mates." She shivered, it was the first time she'd admitted it aloud.

She knew they were her mates, but she'd go to her grave denying it if it kept her family safe, and out of trouble. Naomi rolled over and gave her a bear hug. They both held on for longer than normal, taking comfort in the touch.

Naomi cleared her throat. "Enough of that, let's at least make sure you're hot if this is the only date you get to have with your mates."

She nodded and they went back to her closet.

Thirty minutes later they were talking out hair options when the doorbell rang. They gave each other nervous looks and rushed to the living room. She gave one final look to Naomi, who was wringing her hands and opened the door. Charlotte came in first, a baseball cap pulled low on her face, a crop top and tight jeans. She gave Savannah a hug, rubbing her cheek against hers in a prowl greeting, which brought a little bit of Savannah's power alive. She frowned, it had been happening more often, which was confusing. As far as she knew, nothing had changed with her. She thought about that small bite Carlos and Derrick had given her days ago. It wasn't enough for a mating bite, but could being around them heighten her power?

The Seer came in behind her. A petite woman, her caramel hair was down around her shoulders in a riot of big curls. She wore a black knit tank top and blue jean bellbottoms. Her makeup was understated, and gave a glow to her copper skin. Savannah held out her hand for a shake and the woman smiled.

"You don't remember me, do you?"

She shook her head, "I'm sorry."

"Don't worry about it. I'm Joelle. I was apprentice to your aunt Antoinette." Joelle studied her.

Savannah's smile froze on her face.

Joelle patted her hand. "Don't…I promise you, it's not like what you're thinking." She rubbed her cheek along Savannah's.

Savannah cleared her throat and walked them into the kitchen. She waved them into the stools around her kitchen island and turned to the range. She busied herself making tea, her hands shaking as she set the kettle onto the stove.

Joelle sat at the kitchen island and looked around. "You have a beautiful home."

Savannah looked around to keep from staring at Joelle. The soothing gray theme she had throughout the house, carried into the kitchen. Her cabinets were all painted in *'smoke'* a color Jamie had rolled his eyes at when she'd picked it. Subway tiles filled in the space between the counter tops and ceiling, the white color stark against the gray. She'd brought in color by making the cabinet doors glass and having all the dishes inside bright red and yellow. She cleared her throat and gave up stalling.

Savannah turned and gave Joelle a smile. "Thank you."

She passed them all cups and stood, awkward as they waited on the kettle to finish. The teakettle whistled and she made a show of fixing tea.

Joelle didn't take a sip, she simply warmed her hands on the mug. "Let's just get rid of some of this tension. Were you aware that your aunt was kicked out of the prowl?"

Both she and Naomi shot looks to their cousin Charlotte and nodded.

Naomi cleared her throat. "It doesn't change what she'd done. I still wouldn't have come back."

She agreed with her cousin. The fights still continued after Toni left, so obviously her aunt leaving wasn't enough to change anything.

"Why was she banished?" Savannah asked, crossing her arms over her chest.

Joelle sighed. "I went to your grandfather and told him I thought she was lying about having visions."

Her knees weakened and she grabbed the edge of the counter. Both Naomi and Charlotte gasped.

"Are you serious?" She asked between numb lips.

Joelle nodded. "When my mother joined the prowl, I was a few years older than you were when you left. It took Antoinette months before she gave into my mother's request to mentor me. I had already started showing my seer powers and both the Felix and my mother thought it best I learn to control them. I studied under Antoinette and she used me. She gave the Felix visions from me as her own. I didn't find anything strange about it, since apprentices weren't allowed to give out prophecies. It took me until I was eighteen to figure it out she was changing the wording on my visions." Joelle sighed and finally took a sip of her tea. "I was so brainwashed that even after I knew, it took me a while to get the courage to speak up about it. I want to apologize to you. To you both. I wish, more than anything, that I had spoken up before. You were so young…"

Savannah waved her hand and shook her head, unable to speak. Naomi put her head on the table and her cousin's shoulders shook.

Joelle's eyes met hers, entreaty glistening in them. "I need you to understand, anything your aunt told you was probably false."

She really had to sit then. She grabbed a stool and sat limply into it. "I don't understand."

"Antoinette didn't have any power. She'd been faking it for years. I think, using those who apprenticed under her."

She felt nauseous, and couldn't breathe. Naomi sobbed next to her sister and Charlotte held her in her chest.

"I don't know what she said to you, and I'm sorry it took me so long to say anything." Joelle reached her hand and put it over's Savannah's.

"She told us we would be the downfall of the prowl." Naomi hiccupped.

Savannah pulled her hand back and gripped her cup. "And when that didn't stop us from coming to meetings, she made sure someone challenged us every time we stepped foot on prowl land. She said letting latents into the hierarchy would make the prowl sterile, and she'd do everything in her power to stop it from happening."

"That's..." Joelle covered her mouth and a tear spilled over. "None of that is true."

"Oh my God." Charlotte gasped.

Joelle took several deep breaths. "I'd known she was twisting my prophecies to fit her ambitions, but I never imagined..." She turned to Naomi, and put a hand on her back. "Same with you?"

Naomi nodded. "We left immediately. What twelve year old wants to hear that they'll bring down their prowl and their family will suffer?"

"Lord above." Joelle whispered. She got up from the chair and left the room. She walked into the living room and looked out the window.

Savannah stood and went to her cousins. They all embraced. "Did you know why Aunt Toni had been expelled?" She asked Charlotte.

Charlotte had tears in her eyes. "I swear I didn't. I just knew she was gone. I believed what you guys did, that your staying would endanger us all."

"That bitch," Naomi hissed.

"I hate her." Savannah whispered, grief and anger taking turns, making her both feverish and sick to her stomach. Power raised in her and she didn't know what to do or think about it.

Joelle turned back to them and walked back, wiping her hands along her jeans. "Sorry is not enough, not for what I imagined you've felt all these years. I should've insisted on seeing you when Antoinette left. Your grandparents were pretty adamant that saying something to you would make it worst. Visions I had after, confirmed it, so I let it go on all these years."

Savannah retook her seat.

"It's not much but everything that has happened, has led you both to this point. You're so very important to the prowl." Joelle gripped the edge of the island.

Savi lifted her chin. "What does that mean?"

Joelle turned her eyes to her and took deep breaths. "You're going to be Alpha female and Naomi the Zeta."

"We haven't had a Zeta in all the time I've been in the pride hierarchy," Charlotte's face was bunched in confusion. "What does that mean, what does a Zeta do?"

"I don't have any power." Naomi insisted.

"Yet," Joelle said. "Zetas stabilize a prowl. Their power lies in their ability to drain any toxic emotions. The connection in a prowl goes through the Felix, he connects us together, a Zeta boosts those connections, and brings us all closer together."

Naomi gave Savannah a stunned look. She could only shrug. She was busy digesting that she would be alpha female.

"I'm latent." she said aloud.

Joelle shrugged and turned her attention back to Savannah. "I told your aunt that you would be Fela. I saw it from the first moment I saw you."

"What?" She blinked in surprise. How young was she when Joelle first saw her?

"At the time, I was still learning to control my visions, to see them through to completion, so I didn't have the full scope. Antoinette said that having a latent alpha female would tear the prowl apart. I didn't know any better." She shrugged again. "You'll be Alpha female and your Tribond will bring untold power to this prowl. From the visions I've been having, your mates won't have it any other way."

"Did they put you up to this?" She whispered. "Why haven't you told me this before?"

"I swear they didn't, but we both know you wouldn't have believed me had I just shown up. The Felix asked me to see you and read you, but he didn't put me 'up' to anything. When you asked Charlotte to meet with me, I knew the time was right. All the visions I've been having lately have warned me that it was time to tell you."

"I'm latent," she repeated.

"Yes, but you are powerful, or will be once your mates unlock it. You're already stronger than the last time I saw you."

The kitchen went silent as they all took in the seer's words.

"Did you tell our grandparents?" Naomi asked.

Joelle nodded. "I told them everything."

"Why didn't they say anything before this?" Savannah was lost. She couldn't imagine her grandfathers knowing she would be alpha female and not doing everything in their power to make it happen.

Except…

Her grandparents were constantly trying to set her up with an alpha. She sighed. They knew and instead of coming to her directly, they were trying to push her into her position.

"Sneaky bastards." She put her finger to her lip. "But, why not bring Naomi back into the prowl? No way would granddad give up a Zeta."

Joelle cleared her throat. "Your tribond is supposed to bring in enough power to trigger the Zeta. It doesn't happen without you."

Savannah's eyebrows winged up. "I…"

"Wow," Naomi whispered.

Charlotte laughed after a moment the sound startling them all. "You're about to make some bitches mad."

Naomi gave a watery laugh, and she let out a shaky breath.

"My family?" She turned back to the seer.

"There will be turmoil in the prowl for a while, but it's not for you to take on your own. Your mates are supposed to help you."

"And children?" Naomi whispered.

"I have never seen anything about the prowl going sterile. If the amount of power coming to our prowl is anything like I've seen, our cubs will have no problem keeping our place in this world."

"Oh my God, I think I'm going to faint." Savannah hissed, so stunned. She sobered. "Why should we believe you?"

"Fela." Joelle sighed. "You don't have to believe me. Your fate will unfold as it should with no input for me. Whether your mates have to work for six months instead of two, you are theirs and no amount of running will stop that."

She looked down at her hardwood floors seeing nothing and then looked up at her cousins and smiled. She realized that there was nothing stopping her from being with her mates.

"Oh, God. I have mates."

"You have hot mates," Charlotte corrected.

Yes, she had hot mates, and a date with them in a few hours' time. A weight lifted from her chest and heat flooded her body. She could be with her mates.

Chapter 23

He'd resorted to pacing. Him, big bad, Beta Panther was pacing the living room in his Alpha's home, anxious to pick up their mate. It was a first date, something panthers as a rule didn't do. Maybe that's why he was nervous.

Convincing Savannah to mate with them was nerve-wrecking for him. He had to remember that so far, he'd gotten everything he set out to get. They'd doubled the size of their prowl, thereby giving them greater safety. All that was left was convincing their mate that she belonged with them.

"Do you have everything ready?" He asked the Felix, not for the first time.

"Will you chill, please?" Carlos walked from his bedroom. "I washed and changed the sheets, but it's no guarantee we'll even sit on that bed, much less have sex with our mate on it."

Derrick shrugged, a burning certainty telling him that their mate would be theirs, soon. "Are we picking her up or meeting her someplace?"

"We're going to pick her up. I got a list of shifter run restaurants from one of her cousins. We can go there and not be bothered."

He nodded. While they lived out among humans, some of their customs left the humans confused, judging. They wanted to avoid that, on their first date with their mate. He was excited. Carlos grabbed the keys and they headed downstairs.

It took them twenty minutes to reach Savannah's house. Carlos turned off the truck and they both sat in the quiet darkness.

"What's with you, your buzzing nerves are driving me nuts." Carlos put a hand on Derrick's shoulder.

"You know how long I've wanted this, Carlos." He wiped a hand over his face.

"I do, and we've worked hard to get here. I promise, we'll have our family. We're doing this your way because I love you and want this for us just as much."

"I know, and now we can share that love through Savi and this land and these people. It's a lot to deal with suddenly. I thought I understood what I was missing, but having our own territory…"

Carlos nodded. "It's all I've thought about since we got here."

Derrick sighed and shook out his hands to release his nervous energy. "Let's go."

They got out the truck and walked up to her doorstep together. Carlos rang the doorbell and he fiddled with the buttons on his suit jacket until she answered.

She opened the door and Derrick's cat sprang to attention. She looked amazing. She wore a pair of red pants that were wide legged, but fit her waist, emphasizing her curves. The off the shoulder blouse was white and he was nearly certain she wore no bra beneath it. He breathed out, would they make it to the restaurant? She sighed and her nipples beaded, poking out of her blouse.

Derrick stepped forward, his every intention to push her into her house and ravish her. She put a hand to his chest to stop him, before trailing it down to the front of his pants.

"You can wait." She whispered, as she tiptoed and kissed his cheek.

His body trembled, could he wait? Her scent wafted to him, a dark honey fragrance that gave away her arousal. Waiting seemed harder with his every inhale. She smiled at him, before turning around and grabbing her keys off a small table at the door. She closed and locked the door, her hands trembling.

Her hair was slicked back into a ponytail, her sleek hair bouncing as she turned back to them. "Are you going to say anything?"

"You look...phenomenal." Derrick managed past the lump in his throat.

If possible, she smiled bigger. He tilted his head, his cat wary and curious. Something about her had changed. She seemed, lighter, eager, as she grabbed both their arms. He looked over at Carlos who had the same bewildered look on his face.

"Where are we going?" She was chipper, and the two men were certainly put off guard.

"I heard about this place called Lana's." Carlos said.

"Ooh, that's awesome, I love that place. Its shifter run, so everything will be yummy and the portions will be big enough to feed you two." She paused by the truck.

Derrick lifted her into the front seat and he went into the back. Carlos cranked up the truck and they were off. She kept up a steady stream of chatter which was so unlike her, he was struck mute. Carlos handed over the keys to the valet when they reached the restaurant, sliding his hand on her lower back. She greeted the hostess by name and they were quickly escorted to a secluded table towards the back. The lighting was dim enough to encourage intimacy. They slid into a booth, the three of them crowding into the middle. He spotted their security detail and relaxed. They were good at their job, blending into the restaurant without standing out.

After another look around at their surroundings he focused on their mate. "So, how was your day?"

She smiled. "I had an amazing day and am excited for our date."

Derrick's eyebrows winged up. "You mean this date we had to coerce you into?" Carlos chuckled on the other side of her. "I mean, no complaints, I'm just curious about the one eighty."

She leaned over and instead of answering, she gripped his chin and kissed him. And not a meek kiss, but one that had him wanting to put her up on the table and claw off the pants she wore. He gripped her waist, the temptation almost too much for him to resist.

She pulled back and smiled. "I've wanted to do that for a while now."

Derrick growled and leaned back in, delving his tongue in her mouth, needing the taste of her. She laughed and pulled back. She picked up a menu and started humming over food choices.

"It's been a while since I've been here, so I don't know what to try." One hand held the menu, her other hand slid back and forth up his leg.

He looked at Carlos stunned. His friend shrugged his shoulder and picked up a menu. The waitress brought bread over for them and took their drink orders. Carlos ordered tea, overly specifying that he didn't want sweet tea. Savi ordered a glass of wine, and water. While he ordered a beer.

"What do you have against sweet tea," she teased Carlos and handed her menu over to the waitress.

"It's nasty sugar water." Carlos grumbled.

She laughed and leaned over and smacked a kiss against his lips. "You don't know a good beverage, sir."

She exaggerated her accent and he grew hard. He found it sexy, and found her playful side endearing. They ordered and Savannah's eyes watched the woman until she was out of sight. Once that happened, she turned her attention to the Felix.

"Tell me about your day," she said, nibbling on bread.

They went over their day with her, and he loved it. Loved how natural it felt for them to be together. She fed them both bread as they talked, her fingers lingering on their lips, tracing their faces. Her eyes smoldered the whole time, rousing his panther.

"Something has changed." Carlos insisted.

"It has," she easily agreed, kissing the Alpha's cheek.

"Does this mean…" Derrick paused hopefully. If all the teasing was leading to where he thought, he was down.

"It means, I want to get to know the two of you, date, see how well we get along." She cupped Derrick's cheek.

And they did just that. Dinner went by quickly, conversation flowing between them easily. She kept up her teasing, her hands busy under the table while she nearly neglected her food. She touched them, nibbled kisses along any bit of exposed skin she could reach. Derrick's cock twitched as her hand gripped him, not for the first time.

"Enough," Carlos hissed, motioning for the check.

She giggled as the Felix shuffled them both from the booth and out to the valet to wait for their car.

Derrick stood behind Savannah, wallowing in her scent. "Come home with us." He whispered into her ear.

She shuddered and pulled his arms around her waist. "Yes."

He was surprised and he blinked, looking for something to say. Carlos got in the driver's side, and this time he put Savi in the back.

When he got in, he turned to his Carlos. "Our mate has agreed to come home with us."

"For a night cap," she chimed in from the back. "I'm not spending the night."

He groaned. For every step forward there was another step back.

Carlos gripped the steering wheel and begged his panther to have patience. He needed to get them all home safely if they were to get anything from their mate. He peeked in the rearview mirror and caught her profile as she stared at passing traffic. She took his breath away. She seemed to feel his gaze. She looked up and smiled. He turned his attention back to the road, but pressed his foot harder on the gas.

By the time he turned into the garage at their prowl house he was hard as stone, and his hands were shaking with need. Derrick helped her out of the truck and he kept a distance from them. If he touched her, they wouldn't make it upstairs. Her scent filled the elevator, lust and gardenias. He closed his eyes and took a deep breath. A snarl rumbled his chest.

"Problem, Felix?" Her voice was soft, taunting.

He turned his gaze to her, his panther pushing to the forefront. Her lust rose thicker, her chest heaving. He growled, his claws growing as he lost a little of his control. The ding of the elevator reaching their floor pulled him back.

Derrick held the door open and their mate rushed off the lift.

"I'm going to change, but will join you two in a moment." Derrick kissed her, lifting her to fit their mouths together. He put her down and she gripped his shirt.

"No fair, I have to stay in these clothes." She pouted.

Carlos nuzzled into her neck. "No you don't. I can take them off."

She released Derrick and turned into his chest. "Lead the way then."

Her husky voice was nearly his undoing. His hands shook as he unlocked the door. Once inside, he turned and lifted her against the front door. He had to kiss her. His panther was damn near ripping through his insides to get to its mate. She moaned into his mouth and he slid his hands down her sides.

He ran his hands down the front of her body. "Do you have any idea what this shirt has been doing to me all night?"

She arched her back, pushing her breast into his hands. "You like it?" She fluttered her eyes, teasing.

"Have you always been this playful?"

"A lot changes when you're not running from fate."

He frowned, not understanding that, and she didn't give him time to delve into the matter. She gripped him through his dress pants and he closed his eyes.

"I need to be inside you," he whispered.

"I'm not stopping you," she whispered back and his cock jerked in her hands.

He devoured her mouth and pushed her shirt further down her shoulders, it exposed her chest and the fact that she didn't wear a bra. He wanted to go to his knees.

"You're so sexy." He leaned down and pulled one of her nipples into his mouth, lavishing it with his tongue.

She arched her back and moaned.

"Legs around my waist." He ordered.

She did as he bade, her exhale rough when her center met his pulsing hard-on. He kissed her and carried her into his bedroom. He set her legs down just long enough to walk her back to his bed.

"Clothes off," he ordered, his voice rough with his panther.

"Rules first." She panted as she tossed her shirt to the side.

He halted, wary. "Rules?"

"No biting, not yet. I'm still not ready."

He growled. He was torn. He didn't have to bite her, but the way his panther was riding him, it would be a near thing. He seriously debated if he could abide by her rule. She stood there, awaiting his answer in a silky corset that cinched her waist, but left her breasts bare. Would he be able to control his power once he was inside her?

He would die trying.

"Deal." His hands shook as he worked to divest himself of his own clothing. "Clothes. Now."

He was impatient to get at Savannah, to feel her skin against his. She complied easily, a point that touched the alpha in him. He growled as she leaned over to drop her pants. Once done, he laid her out on the bed and feasted on the sight of her. He only had a few hours with her.

He planned to make the most of them.

Chapter 24

Carlos watched her like the hungry panther he was and it sent her body into heat. She watched his muscles flex as he pulled off his shirt and her mouth watered. He was truly beautiful.

"What about Derrick?"

Carlos kicked his pants off. "He'll catch up."

His eyes swept her body and instead of self-conscious it made her feel beautiful, desirable. The heat in his eyes could light a fire. He prowled to the bed, her body dipping as he kneeled at the edge of the mattress. He crawled over her and she shivered in anticipation.

He cupped her cheek, his gaze softening. "Do I need to stop?"

Her body called her all types of idiot for even having the gall to pause, much less stop. His cock brushed her thigh and she looked down. She swallowed hard at his size. Stopping?

Hell no.

"No." She whispered desperately, pulling him down into another kiss.

She had no reason to deny herself this with her mates. Though she didn't know if she was ready to be an alpha female, she knew she was ready to, at the very least, taste her mates. She'd fantasized about them for some time, and so far, her dreams paled in comparison.

Carlos trailed his hands across her abdomen, his soft touch contrasting the aggressive way his tongue battled with hers. Her power raised, with it, her skin sensitized. He pulled back from their kiss and gasped. He rubbed his face along hers and moaned.

"Your power." He whispered reverently. "Such a fucking turn on."

He gripped her chin and devoured her mouth. She lifted her hips, her center pulsing, flexing in emptiness. His hand trailed down and he swiped a finger between her wet folds.

"Need you." She panted, canting her hips when his finger dipped into her.

"You're so hot and ready for me."

He leaned over and opened the drawer of his bedside table. She grabbed the condom from him. He bent down and laved at her nipples. She cursed, unable to open the package, her hands were shaking so badly. She'd never felt need like what was melting her body.

His dark chuckle rumbled across her skin before he grabbed it from her and tore the package. She made quick work of sheathing his cock.

"Ready?" he whispered.

"Yes, please." She begged.

He lifted his body off hers and his head bent to watch that first slow slide into her. When he lifted his head, his eyes were glowing, his mouth slack in ecstasy. She rocked her hips to make him move. He kissed her again and pushed into her, over and over. She mewled as his deep strokes stretched her. He growled, pulled out and spun her around. She lifted her hips and he snarled.

"Oh, mate of mine." His hand came down, a light tap on her ass.

She hissed and he drove into her. This position made his strokes much deeper and she pushed back, wanting every inch.

She tensed at the knock on the door. Derrick walked in, in just jogging pants. Liquid flooded her core as he stalked in, his cock showing a daunting print through the pants.

She arched her back and Carlos hit a spot. "Right there." She panted.

Derrick sat next to her on the bed. His eyes were dark, flashing from gold to dark brown as he watched her. He leaned over and traced her neck with his hands.

"Do you have any idea how beautiful and amazing you look in the throes of your pleasure?" He whispered in her ear.

She moaned as his words gave her a thrill. She should be embarrassed but the fact that Derrick was whispering to her as Carlos pounded into her completely turned her on. She squeezed on Carlos, flexing her hips to drive him deeper.

Carlos hissed. "Shit."

She did it again, taking pleasure in his snarl, her womb tightening.

Derrick kissed the side of her neck. "What are you doing to our mate, kitten? You should see our Alpha's face."

He pulled her ear into his mouth. He reached under her body and fondled her breast, rolling the nipple between his fingers. She moaned in need, rolling her hips.

"Derrick." She whispered his name.

Derrick chuckled and grabbed her chin with his other hand, plunging his tongue in her mouth. She whimpered, sensations swamping her body. Carlos growled, his hips picking up speed. He adjusted her waist, changing the angle until his cock was rubbing against a spot deep within her.

She pulled from Derrick's mouth gasping her pleasure. "Yes."

Carlos ran his nails across her back and she whimpered.

"See that sound she makes, Derrick." Carlos fought for breath, slowed his thrust, but drove deeper.

Derrick pinched her nipple and before she could control it, she went careening into orgasm. Derrick groaned and leaned down biting into her neck, but not breaking the skin.

"Kitten, the look on your face is everything." He kissed her again. "Again," he whispered against her lips.

She shook her head. She couldn't possibly come again. Not so soon, not after the explosion that went off in her body.

Carlos adjusted his position, "you can give us another one, love."

"I can't," her breath left in a harsh exhalation as he hit that spot again

Derrick sucked on her neck. "One more time, kitten. I want to see the look on your face again."

She whimpered. She fought the urge to lift her chin and submit to Derrick. The compulsion to beg for their bite had her gritting her teeth.

"How does it feel, Felix?"

"Like a fucking dream, Beta. Just wait until you slide inside our mate. The way she grips you..."

Her body tightened and Carlos' word cut off as a snarl erupted from him.

Derrick kissed his way up to her ear. "I can't wait to feel you squeezing around me, kitten."

She moaned. His erotic words hiking up her arousal.

"Will you be ready for me?"

She nodded, unable to control the mewling sound leaving her throat.

Carlos growled. "That fucking sound, baby." He pounded into her, their skin slapping as more snarls rumbled his chest.

"Can you take the both of us? We'll ease you into it. Maybe the first time we'll take you this way. Carlos driving into you as you take me into your mouth." Derrick brought her attention back to him.

She licked her lips as she imagined it. Saw the picture so clearly. Her eyes darted to his crotch so close to her head. His hard-on pushed against his jogging pants. No doubt he was not small. She found that she wanted that very much, the erotic image his words painted.

"I'll coach you through how I want it, kitten. Whispering to you how to take me deeper into your mouth, down your throat. You'll take me right baby?" He traced her throat column.

She nodded eagerly. He kissed her, pushing his tongue down her throat mimicking what he wanted.

"I need to hear the words." He whispered against her lips.

"Yes" it came out breathless. "Yes I'll take you. I want you now." She squeezed down on Carlos, her body flexing on his shaft.

"Fuck yes!" Carlos shouted.

Derrick adjusted her body across his lap, his hand kneading her breast. "Not now, but soon," he promised.

Still, she opened her mouth over his bulge, gripping it with her lips, through his pants. He groaned and gave up easily, freeing his cock. She was using her hands to keep her body angled, but she used one to bring Derrick's shaft to her mouth.

She slid it down as far as she could take it and he hissed in pleasure. She licked around the head, sucking it into her mouth.

"Shit," Derrick whispered.

"'Come for me, baby," Carlos demanded, his strokes speeding.

"Come for him, kitten," Derrick whispered.

The intensity of her approaching orgasm scared her. She shook her head to fight it. Tingles started down her spine, her sex pulsed, squeezing around his cock and power danced along her skin. Carlos reached between them, his fingers pinching her clit and she exploded. She screamed, her eyes closing tight as stars dotted her vision. Derrick moaned, cursing, pulling from her mouth. Carlos shouted his pleasure. She collapsed on top of Derrick, with Carlos pinning her in his lap.

Carlos laughed and kissed her spine. "My God, you feel amazing."

He pulled out of her and Derrick pulled her further up into his lap, having her straddle him. She burrowed her face into his shoulder, hiding her face. She dragged her teeth across the column of Derrick's throat and he gave a throaty moan. Though she knew it was natural, she couldn't help feeling a little self-conscious.

Carlos watched her, his lust nowhere near sated. He pulled the condom from his length and Derrick longed for the day they wouldn't need the latex separating them from their mate. Carlos walked into the bathroom and Derrick focused his attention back to Savannah, and her wet center, currently resting on his still hard cock.

She was nibbling on his neck, and he was debating how far they would take her this night. Carlos came back into the room with wet a cloth. Derrick couldn't help but smile at the smug expression on the Alpha's face. He was shocked Carlos hadn't bitten their mate.

"No bite?" he asked, as Carlos turned their mate to clean her.

Carlos stared at her, the heat still in his eyes. Hell, it was burning down their connection.

"One of her rules." The Felix gently cleansed their mate's sex.

Derrick tugged on Savannah's ponytail. "Rules, huh?"

She hissed as he tugged again, bringing her into his chest. He released her hair and cupped her breast.

She moaned. "Rule. Just one. No biting."

She wiggled on his dick and he scraped his teeth down her neck. Why the fuck would Carlos agree to that?

"How set in stone is that rule?" He whispered in her ear.

"Very." She growled, her power raising the hair on his arms.

Carlos threw the wash cloth over his shoulder, and lifted their mate's legs. She threw her head back as Carlos' mouth covered her sex. He watched him devour her, nearly coming from her grinding her ass into his cock. Derrick's panther swiped at his insides, his need for her fogging his brain.

"Need you." He hissed.

Carlos pulled back and she turned. She straddled Derrick's legs and he pulled her over his cock where he needed her. Carlos passed him a condom and he'd never put one faster in his life.

Savannah reached down and guided him inside. He pushed his way into her pulsing channel and she moaned, her body reacting as if she'd not just had an explosive release. Derrick closed his eyes and hugged her to him, keeping her from moving for long moments while he reveled in his mate. Soon, though, her heat got to him and he lifted his hips.

"Ride me, sweetheart."

"With. Pleasure." Her hips canted, sucking him into her wet core.

His gripped her hips, lifting her on and off his cock, his back arching to push further into her. Carlos straddled his legs until he was flush with Savannah's back. She wrapped her arms around Carlos' neck, her mouth parted, her breath coming out in jagged pants.

She was worth every second they had to wait. The way her channel flexed around him. The heat of her skin against his. It was better than his wildest fantasy about his mate.

An explosive orgasm stole his breath, his teeth cutting into his lip as they grew. Carlos' arm was there, taking his bite as his panther ripped from his control. Savannah's eyes were closed, her face pinched in ecstasy so luckily she didn't notice. He snarled and pulled his teeth from his Carlos' arm, the blood of the alpha doing nothing to help calm his animal. If nothing, it raised the power between the three of them. He threw his head back and an aftershock of his orgasm rocked through him. Through the three of them. Savannah and Carlos gasped simultaneously and power saturated the room.

Gasping, Carlos collapsed on the bed next to him. "What the fuck was that?"

Savannah snuggled into his chest, her soft chuckle tickling his sensitive skin. "That was awesome."

He couldn't disagree. No biting tonight, he reminded himself as he wrapped his arms tighter around her. She didn't say anything about the morning.

Chapter 25

A total of six women had been attacked. The latest one happening last night. She had been attacked leaving her job, before the person who was to be her partner arrived to pick her up. Derrick growled and wiped the steam off the bathroom mirror. He'd left Callie's house just a little while ago. Her sister Mallory had screamed at him the whole time he was there.

Callie had been shaken, but had fought off her attacker, at least according to her. He didn't trust Callie, her sister Mallory, or their brother Ryan. Even after admonishment from the Felix, they were still talking about proposing peace between the prowls. He'd spent a better part of the morning questioning them. The three of them claimed not to know who the prowl was, or where they were located. Which was different from their claim that they'd heard from the other prowl's Felix. They were lying. He just needed to find out why. He sighed and dried off. He needed to be downstairs, updating Carlos. They also needed to go over the upcoming council meeting, and yet...

He was fucking tired, and cranky.

Even as he and Carlos trekked their territory late into the night, familiarizing themselves with the territory, the attackers had been a step ahead of them, as though they had inside information on their patrol routes. The prowl land was vast and the responsibility added tension to his already tightened shoulders. He sat on the edge of the bed and wished his mate was near. His panther was getting harder to control, especially since he'd gotten a taste of her last night.

He was sliding a pair of jeans up over his hips when his doorbell rang. He frowned and walked into the living room. He paused near his couch, a familiar smell hardening his body.

Savannah was at the door.

He took a hasty look around, snatching up clothes and stuffing them into the hallway closet. He rushed to the door and opened it.

She smiled at him and his chest tightened. Her hair was braided in cornrows, and she wore a pair of black jogging pants that were ripped at the knee and a cropped sweatshirt. The way the pants fit had him salivating slightly. Her eyes were as busy as his, traveling up the length of his body. She stopped to ogle his chest a moment.

She cleared her throat. "Are you going to invite me in? I come bearing gifts." She held up the cake dish she was holding, wafting it under his nose.

He hadn't even noticed she was carrying it. He stepped back. "Please, come in."

He stopped her as she passed him. He lifted her chin and kissed her. Her lips parted immediately and he drove his tongue into her mouth. She pulled back and smiled and walked into his apartment. The worries from his day shed as her power entered his space. His panther rolled in his body, her soothing magic dissipating some of the stress from his morning. He grabbed the dish she had and walked it into the kitchen. He came back to find her wandering the room.

She gave him a sheepish smile. "Sorry for not calling ahead. It was kind of spur of the moment."

He shrugged and closed the distance between them. "You're welcome in my apartment anytime. As a matter of point, I can't wait until the day we mate so we can move into the penthouse together."

"Carlos' apartment isn't the penthouse?"

"Nope. We're still waiting on it to be done. Plus, we're waiting on our mate to decorate it, so…" he leaned down and kissed away the stunned look on her face.

God, he couldn't get enough of kissing her. He wrapped his hands around her waist and pulled her closer. He lifted her to get a better angle on her mouth and wrapped her legs around his waist. He nearly lost it. He pushed his hard-on into her center and she whimpered and that sound was nearly his undoing as the memories from last night swamped him.

She pulled back breathing hard. "I didn't..."

He kissed her neck, pulling the skin into his mouth and biting down. She moaned and dropped her head back. He opened his mouth right over her throat under her chin, his teeth aching with the need to bite down and claim his mate.

"Derrick," she whispered.

"Yes, kitten."

"I came to talk to you."

He sighed and released her neck. "About what, babe?"

She didn't move her legs, so he walked them back to the sofa and sat with her on his lap.

"Let's talk then." He nibbled on her neck.

She tapped his shoulder. "I can't think when you do that."

"Fine." He pouted, giving one last lingering kiss to her lips. "I'm listening."

She traced his face. "I have no idea what to say. I'm nervous."

"What did you bring me?" He rubbed her back.

Her face lit. "Red velvet cake."

"Word?" He pretended to lift her. She laughed and locked her arms around his neck. He pecked her lips. "You left us last night."

She pushed out her lips and looked away. "Staying was not a good idea."

"And why not?"

"Eventually one of you would've bitten me." She whispered.

He sucked in a breath, his cock flexing. She was right. He wasn't sure that he could've fucked her and kept his panther from claiming her. Not after the amount of power that flowed between the three of them. He looked into her eyes, she lowered them after a moment, unable to hold his gaze. Their full mating would take care of that.

"While I generally know what a Tribond entails, as I've seen it before, I just don't know the details. What would that mean for you, as a third? I always wondered how Grandpa Harper felt, but I can't imagine asking him."

He sighed and ran his hand over her braids. "It means that you are mine as well as I am yours."

"So, like you wouldn't have any other women."

He smiled, the dimple in his cheek peeking out. "That's what you're worried about?"

She swatted his chest, "yes, I'm possessive and to me, it feels wrong that you both have to share me, when I'd blow a gasket if I had to share either of you with anyone else—"

He cut her off by taking her lips in a kiss that was possessive, aggressive and damn near blew his own head off. He growled and grabbed her waist, lifting and pushing her back down on the leather couch. He settled in between her legs and she raised her hips.

She loved the feel of him on top of her.

"There is nothing about our mating that is wrong," he said breathing hard as he broke their kiss. He nipped her lip with a hard bite. "You are a part of my soul, kitten. My animal wouldn't allow another woman anywhere near us. Do you understand?"

She nodded quickly, a little scared, a lot turned on. He lifted her back into his lap.

"Tribonds are extremely rare, but you have more than one in the prowl, you should know how it works."

"I left the prowl before I was old enough to know about these types of things. Besides, no way could I be this lucky, Derrick," she said softly.

"Kitten," he whispered and kissed her tenderly.

"Ok." she said.

"Ok, you're ready to seal this mating?"

She laughed and wiped a tear from her eye. "No, ok to understanding."

He kissed her forehead. "Is that why you brought me cake? To butter me up for this conversation."

"Yes, I thought I'd soften the blow with something sweet. It's hard showing my jealous side."

"Be jealous all you want, it makes my animal very secure."

She smiled at him. "You have some place to be today?"

He nibbled on her neck. "Some prowl stuff a little later in the afternoon, but I'd love to have some time with you."

She lowered her head and nuzzled into his neck. "Perfect. Now we can get to know each other."

"You never answered us last night. What's changed?"

She sighed and moved from his lap. He grabbed her legs and put them across his own, running his hands along her calves.

"I talked to the Seer yesterday."

"And?"

"When I was ten, my aunt Toni told me that if a latent became Fela, it would tear the prowl apart. But specifically, that if I ever dated an alpha shifter, it would bring our prowl down."

He growled. "Did you tell anyone?"

"No. I ignored her and kept going to meetings. Which…got harder." She was fighting every prowl gathering. Every gathering, they had kept coming after her for being latent.

"Why did you eventually stop?"

She looked away, not even wanting to say her fears aloud. "She reiterated that I stay away from alphas, but added that my latency would make the prowl sterile. I didn't want to risk it."

Even after her talk with Joelle it still hurt. He cursed, and gathered her back into his lap.

"Joelle cleared it up?" He asked softly.

"Well, she told me there would be kids in the prowl. And that my mates had no plans to give up on me." She cupped his face.

"Fucking right. I'm good at wearing people down, just ask Carlos."

She laughed. "How did the two of you meet?"

He trailed kisses along her neck, using his fingers to trail across her stomach. "We were in the same Rangers unit. Nearly all of our prowl is from that unit."

"You two are close, I mean you obviously have to be for our Tribond to work." She moaned as he licked across her pulse.

"Very. We've been together nearly fifteen years, he's like a brother to me." He murmured.

She had other questions to ask him. Other things she wanted to know, but he'd slid his hand down the front of her pants. He drew little circles on the top of her mound and she desperately wanted his fingers lower.

"Anything else you want to know?" He whispered against the skin of her collarbone.

"How long are you going to tease me?" She panted.

"Same rules from last night?" He let a single claw grow, using it to rip the crotch of her pants.

Did that make her wetter?

Yes. Yes it did.

"I'm not ready to be Fela yet." She arched as he ripped through her sweatshirt and exposed her bra.

She moved her hands from around his neck and unsnapped her bra with impatient hands. She worked on the front of his jeans, unzipping them. He hissed as she freed his cock.

"Need." She whispered.

"Condoms are in the room." He lifted her and stood. He tripped as she pumped his shaft. "Fuck, babe, give me like, a second."

She licked up his neck and his chest rumbled against hers. He reached the bedroom and plopped her down on a dresser. He was rummaging in the drawer with one hand, using the other to cut through the fabric on her pants.

"Hurry."

He ripped through the package with his teeth and she snatched it from him. He closed his eyes as she rolled it over his cock.

"Now, where were we?"

She pulled his head down into a kiss, squirming in anticipation. He pulled her to the edge of the dresser and positioned his hard length right at the center of her wet entrance. She used her hand and guided him inside. She threw her head back as he thrust through her tight sheath.

"Shit, Savi." He whispered against her throat.

His hips started moving, his strokes deep as he kissed his way down her chest. Heat moved through her body, her power raising and filling the room. His panther stroked across the front of her body in response.

He looked up in surprise, his eyes amber, and his power surrounding them. "Behave before you bring him out, my mate."

His voice was deep, and while she knew what he meant, with every stroke of his cock inside her, her power escaped her control. He growled and picked up speed, his claws scraping her skin as he lost control. She gripped his ass and urged him on, wanting, no needing him to hit...

Shit, right there.

She arched her back as he pounded into her, hitting that spot with every stroke.

"Coming." She whispered.

He kissed her, swallowing her cry as she crashed over the edge. He lifted her, and turned towards the bed, grinding her hips against him, prolonging her orgasm, she didn't complain. He put her on the edge of the bed, and pushed in to the hilt.

"One."

One? How many did he expect to wring out of her? He started stroking her again, moving his hips in a circular motion that made her see stars. She decided that she didn't care how many, so long as he kept up his rhythm.

Chapter 26

Derrick worked to get his heartbeat back under control. His mate was sprawled against his chest, her breathing coming out in hard pants. He gripped her ass, loving the feel of it in his hands.

"You cannot possibly be ready to go again." She murmured against his skin.

"Doesn't mean I can't enjoy having your body on mine."

She sighed, the happy sound sinking into his heart.

"I barely know anything about you," she said after a few moments. She kissed his shoulder. "Do you have any siblings? Where are you from?"

He stiffened, the faces of his family speeding across his mind. Their faces grew fuzzier with each passing year and he mourned every piece of them that he lost.

"Derrick." Savannah whispered and cupped his face. "What's wrong?"

He shook his head. "I had a little sister."

"Had?" Her brows furrowed.

He cleared his throat. "She and my parents were murdered."

"Oh no. Derrick, I'm so sorry."

"It's..." he swallowed the polite lie he was used to muttering. It wasn't alright, but after so long, he could finally think about them without his chest constricting.

"What happened?"

He rubbed a hand down her back. "I don't know what happened. I came home from boot camp and found them."

"Oh, Derrick," she whispered.

It was the worst thing he'd ever seen in his life and no amount of war zones had wiped the image. He shook his head. He didn't want to put the image of his dead family into her head.

"They were murdered while they were in panther form. We were a small prowl, maybe fifteen or so, including the children." His throat worked.

Savannah made a sympathetic sound and hugged him tighter.

"I'm from a small town in Indiana. I wanted out of that place in the worst way, so I joined the army. I didn't realize I was leaving my family unprotected."

"What do you think you could've done, babe?" She said softly.

"I don't know, love, but it doesn't stop the what ifs."

She nodded.

"I was barely getting through my days until I met Carlos. When I say I saw my future with him, I mean that literally. I saw him and me together with our mate. The moment I laid eyes on you, I knew you were it."

She kissed him, a tear sliding down her cheek.

"Does that bother you, that I had seers in my family?" He searched her face for any signs that she was uncomfortable."

She shook her head and cupped his face. "I know you would never hurt me, Derrick."

He growled and took her mouth in a possessive kiss. She arched her back and moaned. He broke from their kiss and rubbed his head against her neck, marking her with his scent.

"My grandmother used to always tell me that I would have twice the love of anyone in our prowl. I never knew what she meant until I met Carlos." He murmured against her skin.

She turned her head to face him. "I feel a little guilty without Carlos here."

His phone rang and he stretched to get it from the bedside table without dislodging her. It was Carlos. "Speak of the devil."

She tensed and her nervousness transferred across their bond. He put the call on speaker to reassure her.

"What are you doing?" Carlos' voice was gruff.

He angled his head to nip her lip. "Thinking of how to convince our mate to stay in bed without feeling guilty."

Carlos laughed. "Well, I'm a little jealous that I'm dealing with prowl business and you're in bed with Savannah."

"She's naked too," Derrick said.

She swatted his arm, her face reddening.

Carlos groaned, "I can be up there in like an hour, can you keep her naked that long?"

"No," she answered, rolling off him and burying her head in a pillow.

They both laughed. "I'll work on that until you get here." Derrick ended the call on Carlos' laugh.

"I'm hungry." She announced and got out of bed. She grabbed a t-shirt hanging over a chair in his bedroom and smelled it. "So good," she moaned and put it on.

"Have mercy," he whispered as she walked away, the shirt lifting and showing off her ass.

He would most certainly try and keep their mate naked until Carlos could make it upstairs.

****

Carlos cursed and deleted the last two paragraphs in his email proposal. Between the messes with the prowl, he still had a business to run and new clients to cultivate. Except…

Now all he could think about was his mate upstairs, naked with his Beta. God, he wanted to join them. He adjusted the bulge in his trousers and tried to concentrate again. He glanced at the time. He could finish what he was doing and go up before his next conference call.

His desk phone beeped a moment before his assistant spoke. "There is an enforcer here to see you."

He growled in frustration. He'd never get any work done and worse, he wouldn't get to have afternoon sex with Savannah.

"Fine." He barked into the phone.

Brielle strolled in, a pair of fitted jeans, torn at the knee and a blue button down, hastily tucked into the front of her pants. She had the sleeves rolled up and carried a suit jacket in her right hand, he assumed to cover the knife holster she wore on the side of her belt. He wondered where else she hid weapons.

Her panther moved through her body in his presence, the cat sending a flare of power in greeting. Her power was stronger than when they last saw each other. He felt a small amount of pride for that, because as a whole, the prowl's power was rising. He couldn't imagine how it would rise once their Tribond was completed.

"What can I help you with, Brielle?" He waved her into one of the chairs in front of his desk.

She pulled her hair up into a bun as she sat. Her hand was covered in scars and nicks, no doubt from the many fights and challenges she had to go through to get to her position in the hierarchy.

Brielle crossed her legs. "Got a report and I can't find the Beta."

He snorted. "He's otherwise occupied. What do you have?" He closed the screens he was working on.

"There is a lot of buzz in the surrounding prowls about you. They don't know it's you specifically, but they understand that there is a new power in town. I put a few different stories about you out to people I know will spread it."

He sat back impressed. "To what result?"

She leaned forward and set her elbows on her knees. "Well, for one, we want it known that we have a new Felix. A young one. That will automatically put off some of the prowls sniffing around to take territory from us. For two, it will bring any who would want to renew their alliance with us forward in a rush to solidify our truces."

He smiled, very pleased with his new enforcer.

"What?" She asked.

He shook his head, "nothing, I just realized why your grandfather never seemed pressed about our negotiations. Between you and your cousins, he had all the time in the world to find a Felix who would fit this prowl."

"Are you surprised a bunch of women could handle it?"

He snorted. "Have you met my sisters?"

She smiled.

"In most cultures, a panther's spirit is female. Meeting and blending with this prowl, it fits."

She inclined her head. "I suspect before the next council meetings you should be getting an 'outreach' of new friends wanting to make your acquaintance."

"Who does council meetings, you or Brianne?"

"Brianne. She has way more patience than I."

He grunted. "What are you doing today?"

"Working."

He hummed. "For who?" All the panthers in his prowl worked for the prowl in one capacity or another. They rarely sought out jobs in the human world. He had to get used to the way the Tampa prowl operated.

"I'm a nurse at a shifter hospital near here, I'm on nights this week."

He picked up the phone, "can you get your sister on the phone? I need a meeting with her, and Joelle, I think."

She nodded.

"I'll call the Beta and Simon and we will flush out what to do before our new friends start calling."

She looked, pleased, surprised.

"What? You thought I was going to be a sexist pig?"

"Kind of. Most cats in this area are." She laughed.

He smiled, "Brielle, you're now my fourth in rank, anything that affects the security of this prowl you will know. Your grandfathers relied on your counsel, it will be no different with me."

She nodded.

Derrick finally answered the phone and from his breathlessness, he was still busy with their mate.

He growled. "I'm officially jealous."

Derrick laughed. "What is it?"

"I need you down here for a meeting."

"Now?" Now the Beta sounded frustrated.

Carlos snickered, knowing it was petty. "Kiss our mate and come down. It's about our council appearance."

Derrick growled. "Ok, but like thirty minutes."

"Now, Beta."

He hung up and called Simon and then at the last minute thought about his brother in law. He used Theo in every negotiation he'd ever done for their prowl, he wanted him to be his representative in council meetings. Since Theo and Laura were his in-house council, he knew they would be in the building at least.

He turned back to Brielle once all the calls were made. "Any word on the prowl member attacked last night?"

"Another thing we'll need to have our story straight on before we go to the council."

He nodded in agreement. They definitely could not go into his very first council meeting with the threat to his prowl members hanging over their head.

"So far, she didn't see anything. But, she managed to fight them off herself. By the time back up arrived they were long gone."

He hummed. It matched the report Derrick had given him this morning. "We'll brainstorm when the others get here.

Derrick strolled into the near full office twenty minutes later, smelling of their mate and Carlos closed his eyes and gripped the arms of his chair. He wanted to go back upstairs to Savannah. Derrick wiggled his eyebrows at him and he shot him a bird and laughed.

Derrick saw Brielle and Brianne as well as the young seer. "Ladies." A chagrined look on his face since they'd beat him there.

Brianne raised her chin. "Are you surprised to see us here?"

He frowned, "no, Felix said we were meeting about our council appearance, don't you handle council matters?"

She looked perplexed. "Well, yes. Yes, I..."

Carlos laughed. "She and her sister expected us to be pigs."

She adjusted her skirt and scoffed. "In my defense, and you'll soon see, I deal with a group of pigs once a month in council meetings. If grandfather wasn't with me, I don't think anything for our prowl would've gotten done."

Derrick shrugged. "I assume they haven't seen you fight."

Brielle snickered. "I told her she should slap them around a little bit, I'm sure it would change their attitudes."

Brianne rolled her eyes. "And that's why I'm stuck doing it."

"That and you're a PR rep."

Theo sauntered in and waved. "Hey ladies…Brielle."

Brielle stuck her tongue out at him and Theo laughed. He assumed it was some sort of inside joke so he sat on the sofa next to Joelle.

She smiled at him. "I take it things are going well."

He laughed and waggled his eyebrows. "Thank you for what you did for our mate. She's a lot more…amenable to our Tribond now."

"I bet," she said smiling.

Once everyone was in the room they started the meeting. The council meeting was coming up and they needed to make sure they presented a united front.

"We need to get a firm grip on the way this first meeting goes for us. We need to control the narrative early on." Brianne pulled out a tablet. "Beta, for this first meeting you will need to attend for a show of force."

"All of us in the room, will attend." Carlos leaned back in his chair.

Joelle started with surprise. "Me?"

"Yes, I don't know what your duties were with Felix Jeremiah, but in the army, everyone who could be of use, was used. I want insight on everyone in the room and you can provide that faster than Derrick usually can. He gets little snatches of stuff, but having you there will help."

Theo spoke up. "That's a big show of force."

Brianne agreed. "But in this one instance, we can use your ignorance of the process to our advantage. They don't know anything about you. You're not from around here, and it can't be helped if you don't know how the council is run."

"You'll take that hit though, Brianne." Theo said.

She nodded. "They think I'm female and therefore dumb. I can afford it."

"She'll take the hit how?" Derrick asked.

"They'll probably scold her for not giving her new alpha protocol." Theo said.

He trusted Theo to know what he was talking about. His friend was smart, cunning. There was a reason he handled negotiations for the prowl.

"There are some who will see it for what it is," Brianne warned.

"This will also be the first time you're facing your father's prowl." Derrick said gently.

He'd just talked to Samella himself yesterday. Carlos' mother had claimed Derrick as her own, calling him to nag as she did her other children. She wanted to hear all about Savannah, having heard from everyone but her sons about them meeting their mate. He'd taken her fussing and filled her in on their progress with the mating. She'd exacted his promise to protect Carlos from anything Yasim would throw their way. Even after so many years, Samella didn't trust her ex-mate.

"So the show will be two fold. It will show how strong we are under you," Brielle spoke up, pulling him from his thoughts.

"And my little play of ignorance will make it seem as though I'm an inexperienced alpha, and amenable." Carlos shrugged.

Brielle narrowed her eyes, her mind working. "I think once he realizes it's you, he's likely to want to treat our territory as an extension of his own."

They all nodded.

"He only has one council rep, a weasel named Joaquin. He will more than likely be tasked with finding out your weak spots. He's very good at it, that and exploiting those weaknesses. He'll be more likely to slip up if he thinks you don't quite have your footing." Brianne made more notes on her tablet.

"How? Wouldn't he start acting bolder, attacking more?" Joelle asked.

"What do we know so far about these attacks?" Carlos rubbed a hand down his face.

Simon sighed. "We've followed their trail south. Each time, they headed south, but I'm not inclined to act without knowing the layout of the prowls here. The council meeting will be a good place to get insight."

Theo rubbed his hands, "this already sounds fun."

Derrick laughed.

"Theo, don't ham it up in this meeting." Carlos warned.

"I don't think we should bring up the attacks this meeting." Brianne brought them back to their point. "I think this is where Joelle could help. Whoever is doing it, won't miss an opportunity to taunt us with it."

Joelle sat straighter. "I can read malice for sure."

"Do we go in with introductions?" Theo asked.

Brianne scribbled on her tablet. "Absolutely not. The Felix and Beta yes, Theo because I assume you're taking over for grandfather and going with me to meetings, right?"

He nodded.

"So, everyone else, as far as they need be concerned, is muscle."

Joelle choked, "I don't look like muscle."

"Which will further enhance the mystique around our prowl. Who are you that you are so important to show up to a council meeting." Brianne waved away the Seer's concern.

"And if someone asks?" Derrick inquired.

She scribbled again and looked up at him, blinking. He thought he'd confused her so he repeated the question.

She smiled, "no. That's my answer and exactly how I plan to look if anyone asks me anything outside of what we're willing to answer."

Derrick smiled, impressed. "You're good."

"I am," she agreed. "On to the next point. Do we think it's Yasim's prowl attacking our women?" She looked to Joelle and then Simon.

Joelle closed her eyes and breathed deep. "He's the only one I see with a motive at the moment." She bit her lip. "I think the Felix is right by having me go to the meeting. It will help see the other players."

She nodded and made another note. "Simon?"

Brielle spoke up. "Simon and I have traced the scents as far as we could off our territory without causing an alarm. We haven't caught anyone, but all roads seem to lead south as he said."

Simon ran a frustrated hand over his face. "That's not to say a smaller prowl south of us is not making a play on a newly transitioned prowl."

Brianne scoffed and Brielle chuckled. "Trust me when I say, my cousins and I have a reputation, smaller prowls know good and well not to mess with us."

Brianne nodded. "So since we don't know for certain, we treat Yasim's rep like any other. We present a strong prowl, one still as close knit and even more deadly than before."

Carlos nodded. "I like it. We've doubled our enforcers by blending the prowls, but, there is a lot of territory to cover here, I don't want to stir unnecessary trouble."

"The meetings in general are to solve territory disputes and mediating scuffles between prowls, I want no hint from us that we have either." Brianne said sternly.

"This will make whoever attacking our women antsy." Simon commented.

"Bingo." Brianne touched her nose.

"How can we get your position more respect?" Derrick asked. He liked the way Brianne worked and he couldn't imagine her having to fight every meeting to be heard.

She looked up surprised. "I..."

Theo nodded "That's a good point."

Derrick shrugged at her shock. "Even allowing them to undermine you in meetings is in a way undermining our alpha. I want to start as we mean to go on."

She recovered quickly. "Well, grandfather was of the mind that if we let them underestimate us, it hurt more when we slapped them down."

Derrick scoffed. "No disrespect to your grandfather, but I think the best way to show how different Carlos is, will be to show that we won't have our council rep disrespected."

She pursed her lips and pushed her hair behind her ear. "Well, I think it will have to come from you directly, Felix."

Theo agreed. "If you talk as though she is the authority on you and our prowl, they'll have no choice but to treat her that way."

Brianne snorted. "Trust me, they'll have a choice, but it will go a long way."

That settled, they continued to plan out the rest of the council meeting, hammering out details.

Chapter 27

Carlos stared up at the unassuming brick building that was the current location for the panther council meeting. Brianne told him it rotated every month. It was his first council meeting...ever. Up until the day he'd merged his prowl with the Tampa one, theirs had been too small for representation at the Tri-City's council. There had been twenty of them, small by anyone's standards and with no territory of their own. Their lack of representation had made it easy for the tri-city alphas to run them out of town.

Not now.

Now, they had both territory and the manpower to claim a place on the Florida panther council. And not just that, Brianne had informed them that they were also on the high council. That council consisted of every species of shifter in Florida. Pride tightened his chest, that and a smidge of panic. It was a huge responsibility, one he wasn't all too sure he was ready for. He adjusted the cable knit sweater he wore, cursing Florida's seemingly year round heat. He ran a hand down the front of his black slacks, knocking off imagined dust.

"Stop it, you're more than prepared for this." Derrick stood in front of him, blocking his view.

He nodded at his best friend, adjusted the heavy gold watch on his arm and took a deep breath. He let his claws grow on his hands until they were fine points. His panther bucked for more control, but he quashed the animal. Subtle would be better for this first meeting.

"Remember, start as we mean to go on." Derrick whispered.

Brianne's sports car pulled up in the space next to them. She got out, she wore a pair of skinny navy blue slacks and a stark white button down, tucked into her trim waist. Her face all business. "Are we ready?"

They all filed in behind her and entered the building. Brianne waved to the receptionist and they entered a private elevator, hidden off to the side of the lobby. They were quiet, tension riding down the prowl link. Some he knew came from him. He suddenly wished for the calming touch of his mate. Though they'd talked last night, he hadn't had the chance to see her. She claimed work, and while disgruntled, he couldn't argue.

The elevator stopped on the fourth floor. There was a short hallway that led to double doors. Brianne opened both doors to let them in. The place was cavernous...and full. Carlos looked at Brianne and she raised an eyebrow but shook her head. Which meant it was not normal to have so many in attendance. They approached the large oak table in the center of the floor. They took the seats left in the middle of the table. Brianne and Theo sat first, with Carlos settling in the seat in the middle of them. The rest of his group lined up behind them, crowded among the other panthers.

His panther was riled, the alpha power in the room provoking it. He settled back in the chair and crossed his ankle over his knee. He'd been prepared for the shock to his senses, so he breathed deep and sent calming waves down the prowl link. The crew behind him visibly relaxed, the ease of their poses all the more intimidating in contradiction to the tense panthers surrounding them.

Brianne shot him a smile and pulled her tablet out of her purse. She greeted the council. "Gentlemen, I hadn't realized every alpha would be here." Undeterred by the silence, she pulled out her glasses and perched them on her nose. "If I may introduce the new Felix of the West Florida prowl, Carlos Ayala, and our Beta, Derrick Lincoln. Also, along with myself, Theo

Santiago will be our council rep." She introduced him to the neighboring Alphas, explaining their territories. Carlos met the eye of every alpha sitting, showing no sign of nervousness.

Brianne finished her introduction and settled back into her seat. "We're ready to begin the meeting when you are."

His gaze had skimmed over his biological father, but he didn't linger. He studied the alphas, and the panthers they brought with them, searching for any smug faces. He saw curiosity, from the alphas, but the enforcers around the room all stood at the ready, their bored faces belying their alert postures.

"We weren't aware your grandfather was looking for a new Felix." Someone at the table commented, drawing his attention. "Or did this one sneak into town and take over a prowl.

Brianne gave them a scathing look. "Our prowl's business is ours and no others."

Yasim's eyes narrowed. "You are Samella's?"

Carlos inclined his head in agreement.

Yasim's inhaled a long moment, taking in his scent. "How old are you?"

"Does it matter?" He asked almost bored like.

"There is a familial bond between this one and the Miami prowl." One of the other alphas snarled. "What's to stop you from consolidating your power, and taking more territory?"

Carlos kept his body language loose. "Yasim means nothing to me."

Shocked silence met his statement, and the representatives around the table shuffled in discomfort.

Yasim growled, "You are the son she took from me."

Carlos laughed. "Quite the revisionist history, Yasim. Everyone else tells the story different. My sister was ten at the time, but I trust her recollection of events more than yours. Either way, it doesn't matter. My territory is mine and mine alone. We ain't got shit to do with you or yours."

Yasim stood and slapped his hands on the table. Everyone in the room tensed. "You are my family—"

"And what I said still stands. You are no more my father than the panther that sits beside you. You have no claim to anything of mine." Carlos didn't stand, didn't raise his voice, just flexed his panther and his power.

The gazes in the room bounced between the two men.

"You think a new prowl has a chance against me?"

Brianne pushed her glasses up on her face. "Are you declaring war against a prowl who's done nothing to you…in front of the whole council? Is that what we're doing today?" Her voice was sharp, a verbal slap down that made every liaison wince.

Clearly she was more respected than she thought. Hot damn, he loved the women in this prowl. Yasim tensed, his rep stood and whispered in his ear. Yasim's eyes glanced over the rest of the room before he sat.

"Now," Brianne shuffled some pages. "I'll go over the minutes from our last meeting."

"What happened to your grandfather?" The panther at the head of the table spoke.

"He's enjoying retirement with his mates." She answered serenely. If not for his connection with the woman, he'd not know how irritated she was.

"You're allowing a woman to continue to represent your prowl?" Another alpha growled.

Instead of answering, Carlos looked to Brianne. "Is that all you needed from me?"

"It is Alpha, I'll keep you advised if anything else needs your attention." Surprise and pleasure bloomed in Brianne's eyes as he stood.

He inclined his head and cleared the room of everyone except his reps. There was stunned silence, as they walked out. The room exploded with noise when the door closed. He growled and started to go back in.

Derrick stopped him. "She will handle it. You'll undermine her if you go back in."

"What do you think of Yasim?" He asked his Beta as they waited on the elevator.

"I think he's poison. He looked genuinely surprised to see you, though."

His jaw worked while he fought to calm himself. Derrick was right, his father looked as shocked as the rest of the alphas at the table.

"Perhaps it means he's not the one." Simon said softly as they loaded into the elevator.

"We'll talk in the car." He growled.

They were silent all the way down. When the elevator doors opened, the humans who worked for the shifters looked up, gaping as they moved through the lobby. Their power moved everyone in their path. Once outside, Carlos whistled and put his finger up, winding it in a circle to gather the guards he'd left surrounding the building. They gathered at the SUVs they drove to the meeting.

Brielle smiled at him once they got to the car. "That was badass."

He looked back to the building. "I know you said the smaller prowls wouldn't try us, but put feelers out. I didn't see anything in there that led me to believe any of those prowls would touch us."

"I'm inclined to agree," Joelle said quietly.

Brielle nodded. "No problem, Felix."

They all loaded in their cars to leave. Carlos gave one last lingering look to the building. He'd felt nothing in the face of Yasim. He made a mental note to call his mother and reassure her.

"Did you feel anything, Joelle?" He asked as he started the car.

She leaned forward in her seat. "Honestly, Yasim was very shocked, their prowl link is…not exactly healthy, so it's hard to get a good read."

"Anything from the others?"

She sighed. "Ambition. A lot of it. Pride, greed, machinations that were spinning a hundred miles an hour, but nothing exactly targeting us."

Derrick hummed next to him. "But, as you said, the smaller prowls are not a part of the council. Someone searching for a spot there could want to go through us to do it."

He nodded. That was true enough. "Let's get with Brianne and set up meetings with the smaller prowls. We can get to know them, feel them out."

"That's a great idea." Derrick pulled out his phone and was typing away.

He pulled out from the parking lot. Not bad for his first prowl meeting, but he was no closer to finding out who was attacking their women.

Chapter 28

Savannah growled and slapped her hand against the steering wheel as she hit another red light. She was late. She hated being late. She sighed and looked down at the sensible slacks and button down shirt she was wearing. There was nothing sexy about what she wore, it certainly wasn't date clothes. But, her client run-through had taken longer than it was supposed to.

The builders had gone over the model home she'd staged with a fine tooth comb. They wanted to move the luxury condos fast and every detail counted. It had put her terribly behind schedule. The time she'd allotted to go home and change was gone.

She floored it as the light turned green. She'd told Carlos and Derrick she'd meet them at the theater a half hour ago. She pulled into the parking lot a little faster than was prudent, wincing.

She adjusted her makeup in the mirror and sighed. It was the best she could do with what she had. She got out of the car and rushed across the parking lot. The hair on the back of her neck stood up and she paused, glancing quickly over her shoulder. She didn't see anything, but the night had gone unusually silent.

She jumped at the sound of the theater door popping open. Patrons leaving the building broke the eerie silence as they spilled outside. She shook away the discomfort and rushed to the ticket counter. Derrick was there waiting for her.

"I'm so sorry." She panted, tiptoeing to kiss his cheek.

He rubbed his cheek against hers. "I understand, babe. Come, let's get inside." He looked behind her and narrowed his eyes before guiding her into the theater.

He gave the ticket agent their tickets and they walked towards the back. She frowned as she entered an empty room. Previews were playing, and in the dim light she spotted Carlos towards the back of the theater.

"What movie are we seeing?" Had to be an old movie, there was no one else there.

He named a newer movie and her eyes widened. He smiled. "We bought all the tickets so we'd have the place to ourselves."

"We could've just watched a movie at home if that's—"

He kissed her and cut her off. "Sit, darling."

She shook her head, but marched up the stairs toward Carlos. He stood and pulled her into his arms. She sighed, snuggling into his chest. It felt amazing after the day she'd had.

He pulled back and kissed her forehead. "How was your day?"

She groaned and waved away his question. She didn't want to get into it. "Is there food?"

He smiled and helped her into a seat. He lifted the arms and settled on one side of her while Derrick settled on the other side.

He whistled and one of his enforcers brought over a tray of movie food. Chicken fingers, fries, popcorn, soda, and candy. She clapped and made a happy squeal. Lunch had been many hours ago. They sat close enough to comfortably eat, passing snacks between the three of them as the movie played. Though, there was a lot more than eating happening. Her shirt was unbuttoned to her belly button, as both her mates 'dropped' candy and had to of course root around for it. The top of her breasts were sticky, and she was damn near panting. Derrick and Carlos took turn feeding her, their eyes glowing every time she nipped their fingertips. She applauded their restraint. Done eating, Carlos moved the tray to end of the aisle and came back.

Derrick pulled her legs into his lap and pulled off her shoes. She closed her eyes as he started massaging her feet. She sighed in bliss. Carlos sat and pulled her into the crook of his arm. He leaned over her neck, his teeth grazing her skin. Derrick moved up, kissing her, licking at the seam of her lips.

"I thought you wanted to watch a movie." She whispered, as moisture flooded her center.

"I don't remember saying that." Derrick whispered.

"Then why did we come to the movies?"

"Because, publicly claiming you is very much a fantasy of mine." Carlos growled into her ear.

"What?" She reared back, surprised, and turned on.

A hand moved down her leg, and she would've been hard pressed to say which one of their hands it was.

"I can smell how turned on you are right now, kitten." Derrick growled.

Carlos whispered in her ear. "I want to taste you."

Both men were driving her crazy, their mouths and hands everywhere. Until Carlos stiffened. A short whistle sounded in the theater. He raised his head and turned towards the exit. The light from the screen, caught his eye just right, reflecting off the pupil like a cat in the wild. Simon was standing there, and he inclined his head. Carlos shuffled her to stand, fixing her clothes.

"Let's go. Now. Now, *amor*." He shuffled her out of the theater quickly, Simon and two other enforcers falling in line behind them.

Simon stepped up to him, talking quietly as they moved through the lobby. Carlos snarled, the sound turning heads.

"I'll take her car, Beta." He announced when he and Simon had finished talking.

Derrick broke off from them once they were outside and went where she supposed they parked. Carlos reached his hand out for her keys and she gave them to him, a little afraid and confused as to what was happening. He hit the key fob, unlocking the car before they reached it. He cursed when he sat in her front seat, adjusting it to fit his big frame. He pulled out of the parking lot and headed towards her house.

"You're taking me home?" She looked around in surprise once she recognized the route to her neighborhood.

"I would prefer you go to the prowl house, but I know how you are with Jamie."

She was happy he respected her wishes with regard to her son, but disappointed their night had ended so abruptly. He drove her home, his gaze darting to the mirrors.

"What's happened?"

"Unknown cats in the area. Circling the parking lot."

She frowned, and thought of the eerie feeling she'd had when she first arrived at the movies. "What were they looking for, you think? There are always rogues that pass through town."

"These were not rogues. They were from the same pack."

She bit her lip. "Who were they?"

"I'll find out soon enough, *amor*." He murmured.

She left him to concentrate on driving. He pulled into her driveway minutes later. "Will Jamie and I be safe here?"

He walked around the car and helped her out. He guided her to the front door with his hand on the small of her back. He leaned her against it, his gaze tracing her face.

"To be honest, Savi, though I have someone here watching your house, I want you in my building, under our protection. But, I'm working to respect your decisions."

She smiled and wrapped her arms around his neck. He pulled her closer into his body.

"We'll have to talk about security soon though, love. You're alpha female and we're currently on high alert."

She nodded, her stomach pitching in nervousness. "Will they have to follow me around?"

He didn't answer, simply reaching down and nibbling at her lips. "We'll discuss it later."

She kissed him, knowing he was too preoccupied for her to push him for answers. "Goodnight then?"

"Who did you get to babysit?" He asked suddenly lifting his head and sniffing the air.

"My cousin, Naomi."

He sniffed the air again, his brows bunched in confusion.

"Is there a problem?" She moved her head to catch his eye.

"I'm sorry, there is something…" He shook his head. "Call me if at any point you feel unsafe."

"I will." She promised.

He kissed her, taking possession of her mouth before leaving. She went inside, but watched from the window next to her door. Two cats moved from the shadows and followed Carlos. Derrick pulled up and the men shifted from their panther form and talked to them both, naked as the day they were born. It was too dark for her to see anything, and she was too preoccupied to care. Carlos was still in the yard, and yet, she felt bereft at his absence at her side.

She sighed and released the curtain. Naomi walked up next to her.

"Still juggling?" Her cousin asked quietly.

"It's dumb, Nay. I know it is, but I'm so scared to screw this up."

Without even looking outside, she knew when her mates finally left her street. Her heart clenched and loneliness crashed down on her. What was her indecision costing them?

***

Carlos wiped a hand down his face and hung up the phone. He spun in his desk chair and looked out to the dark street below. False alarm. The cats that had been at the movie theater were passing through. And after the scare his enforcers had given them, would not be making the same mistake twice. It was customary for any group of shifters going through claimed territory to make their movements known to the local alpha. Those cats had not done so.

Tonight was the first time the two prowls had worked together without too much static. The enforcers from the Tampa prowl were trying to guide his enforcers but it was slow going. They were not working together as seamlessly as he'd wanted. The ladies in the Tampa prowl were pushing back on the Jersey prowl's army training, and his men were unused to breaking protocol to hunt and fight the ways in which the Tampa prowl were accustomed. He needed to find a way for the prowl to merge their methods.

His panther swiped at his insides, fur growing along his arms and receding as he and animal fought. Had he not been with Savannah, he would've chased the trespassers down himself. Just for the release of his animal. He should've been in bed with his mates, instead he was in his office brooding.

He sighed and got up, leaving the office. He punched the button for the top floor, as he got into the elevator, entering his code. He didn't want to go back to his apartment. Not yet.

Silence wrapped around him as he stepped from the elevator into the penthouse. Fresh paint scented the space, along with saw dust and various other construction smells. They'd finally finished and now the place sat empty, waiting on Savannah to make it her own. Movement along the floor to ceiling windows caught his eye. His Beta shuffled, staring out into the skyline, then went still, nearly disappearing into the shadow.

He walked over to him. Derrick turned around and rubbed his cheek against Carlos' cheek.

"I know, Beta."

Derrick didn't have to say anything. He knew what his best friend wanted. His cat was equally restless with Savannah being out from under them.

"We promised her we'd take it slow," Derrick commented.

"You trying to convince me, or yourself?"

Derrick sighed. "I want our mate."

Carlos stood at the window next to him and shoved his hands into his pants pockets. "The bond is stronger, I don't understand why she's fighting it so hard."

"I know, I feel it. I don't know that I'll be able to sleep with her again without biting her." Derrick said quietly.

He chuckled, though the sound held no amusement. "We can only wait."

Derrick nodded. "I found out what the old seer told her."

He tensed.

"She told Savannah if she became Fela, the prowl would be sterile, and torn apart."

He hissed and whipped his head to his best friend. Anger tore through him and his claws exploded from his hands, ripping through his pants. "You're serious?"

"I talked to Joelle after our meeting the other day. She says it's not true, but it explains why Savannah's fighting us so hard."

"I would give up the prowl to have her. It means nothing without Savannah."

Derrick sighed. "I agree, Felix."

Carlos thought about the threat that ended their date early. "Who the fuck is attacking our prowl, Beta?"

"We've met with all the prowls surrounding us. Unless they're expert liars, they're not gunning for our territory. If anything, Brielle and Brianne were right. They are scared shitless of this prowl." Derrick crossed his arms over his chest.

Carlos shrugged, frustration burning his chest. His phone started ringing and he looked down. It was their mate. He tensed and glanced at Derrick. He put it on speaker phone.

"What's wrong?" His cat went on alert.

"Nothing, God, I'm sorry. I didn't mean to scare you." She rushed to reassure him.

Anticipation tightened his shoulders. "Did you need something, Savi?"

"My mates." She said softly.

He gripped the phone and looked into his Beta's eyes. Derrick's hands were clenched at his sides, his eyes flickering in the dim light as he battled his panther.

"I just left your house. What's changed?"

"I don't like being separated from you. As soon as you left, I just…I can't sleep," she whispered.

"You only have to say the word, *amor*." He rested his head on the glass of the window.

Derrick growled low, his cat flashing in his eyes. "Your mates are waiting, and ready."

She sighed. "Jamie and I are packed. I'll be over shortly then."

"For how long, Savi? I swear I'm trying to be patient, but sweetheart…" Derrick grabbed the phone.

"I don't…I can't upend my son, but we can try a few nights, move in slowly."

Carlos released the breath he was holding. He turned and stepped closer to Derrick, speaking into the phone. "So you're ready to mate with us?"

"I don't want to be without either of you." That wasn't quite an answer, but he didn't want to push her for fear she would change her mind.

"Then we'll be waiting." He ended the call and turned to look at Derrick.

His Beta was once again facing the window, his hands clenched at his side.

"She's coming to us, it will be enough for now." Derrick's voice was hoarse, his anticipation running up and down the mating bond.

Carlos looked around the large condo. There was no furniture yet. It had four bedrooms upstairs and a guest bedroom downstairs, along with two separate office spaces. The contractor they'd hired had done an amazing job. The walls were white, and not a single piece of furniture or even light fixture had been put in place. He wanted the place blank for their mate.

"Do you think she'll like the place?"

"It has more square footage than the house she's in." Derrick answered.

"That's not what I meant, and I'm almost positive our mate cares nothing about that kind of stuff."

Derrick chuckled. "So you're saying she's not going to be impressed by our money."

He snorted. He knew their mate made a great living at what she did, and money wouldn't sway her. Derrick's phone beeped and he looked down.

"She's in the garage. Let's go down and get our family."

They headed to the elevator.

Derrick was anxious. His cat moved through his body in a restless manner. He'd gone to the penthouse to think, to daydream about the day his family would be in it. Funny that his mate would come to them on this night. She waved as she got out of the car. Jamie stepped out, groggy, half sleep. Derrick happily lifted him and the cub gave a sleepy sigh, settling his head on Derrick's shoulder.

"Hi, Beta," he murmured.

His heart melted. He knew he would be a softy where their kids were concerned. Jamie wrapped his arms around his neck and legs around his stomach. He adjusted the cub to carry him easier and leaned down to kiss his mate, his heart full to overflow. He was going to get his family. Yes he'd seen the visions of it, but to have it come true, to be fully realized... He took a shuddering breath. Jamie's small hands rubbed his shoulder. That the kid was reassuring him choked him up.

Carlos grabbed their bags and they headed to Carlos' apartment. By the time they'd taken the elevator to the fourth floor, Jamie was sleep again. He took him and dropped him off into the top bunk in Marcella's room. He leaned down and kissed her forehead, happy he was finally keeping his promise to the little girl. He'd promised her, as she clutched him, devastated at the loss of her prowl, that he'd give her a family.

He understood that feeling of loss too well. He'd come back from basic training to find his family's prowl land littered with the dead bodies of his small prowl. All of them in panther form indicating that they'd more than likely been on a run when they were hunted and murdered.

He didn't bother calling the police, knowing that in their small town, nothing would be done. By himself, he buried each and every one of them, finding a few missing, knowing they probably adorned the mantle of some supremacist's fireplace as a trophy. Even now, more than a decade later it made him sick to his stomach. He shook away the haunting thoughts, gave one last look to the cubs and left the room.

When he reached the living room, Savi was standing in the middle, wringing her hands. "How will this work?"

Derrick pushed down on his cat. "Tonight, we sleep here, and in the morning, we'll show you our home."

"We won't live here?" She turned her gaze to Carlos.

The Felix shook his head. "The contractors are finished with the penthouse so it's ready for you to go through and make it ours."

"Ours?" She whispered.

Derrick walked up to her, pulling her into his chest. She sighed and wrapped her arms around his waist.

"You can't go into this with doubts, love." He told her softly, reminding himself of that as well.

She nodded, burrowing her head into his shirt. Carlos came up behind her and encircled his arms around them both. They stood like that for long moments, letting the bond between them soothe them all.

Chapter 29

Daydreaming, Savannah turned in a lazy circle in their new penthouse apartment. Three nights in the arms of her mates and she was acting like a teenager. She sighed and glanced back at the notes she'd taken. Her first tour of the place had her falling in love. She could envision their family here, growing, happy and no amount of doubt would wipe away the image. Anticipation for the project brought a smile to her face.

Carlos hadn't been kidding when he'd told her not a fixture had been put into place, all awaiting her input. It made her giddy and she felt…spoiled. It was a new feeling. She'd dropped the kids off at school this morning and had wandered the aisles at the paint store for an hour. She'd come back to the penthouse to take measurements. Now that she had them, she'd call the contractor and have them start the projects she envisioned. This afternoon she was visiting one of her favorite showrooms for furniture.

She looked down at her watch and winced. She needed to leave now to make her appointment on time. She rushed to the elevator. She moved back when it stopped on the ninth floor. A woman entered, took a deep inhale and frowned. Savi ignored her as the elevator started its descent. The woman sniffed again and blew out an exasperated breath.

"Are we having a problem?" Savannah didn't have time to start shit, but it wasn't in her to ignore someone so obviously seeking attention. Panthers responding to nothing less than directness.

"You're latent." The woman's gaze raked her body with disdain.

"Fifty points for you." Savannah crossed her arms over her chest.

The woman sniffed. "You really think you could be alpha female?" The bell dinged and the elevator doors opened.

Neither of the women moved.

"You reek of jealousy. Is it a position you fancied for yourself? Bless your heart." Savannah pushed past her and walked into the parking garage.

"You won't last past the first challenge." The woman called after her.

"I've been fighting my whole life, honey, bring it." Savannah gave the woman her back and marched over to where she'd parked her car when she arrived that morning.

She frowned as she didn't see it. Instead a luxury SUV was in its place. She walked over to the next row, still not seeing her car. A horn blew and the woman she'd dismissed sped past her, close enough to ruffle the long skirt she wore. Savannah suppressed her growl. She'd warned Carlos how the women in the prowl would react. It was one of the reasons she still refused their bite, despite their efforts to change her mind.

Taking another a lap around another row, she frowned and walked over to the guard station. "My car is missing."

He frowned. "Are you sure, Fela?"

"I'm not alpha yet," she murmured, looking around. "But yes, I'm sure. I parked it right where that SUV is."

"Did you try pressing your key fob? Maybe you forgot where you parked."

She pursed her lips, irritated that she hadn't thought of that. The encounter with the stupid woman had distracted her. She looked down at the key fob on her key chain and frowned deeper. It was not hers. The key chain was hers. Her son bought her key chains when he went on trips with his father and stepmother. Her favorite two were there dangling.

She pressed the key fob. "What?" She whispered as the SUV's lights blinked. "That's not my car."

"I can call the Felix." The guard offered.

"Don't bother." She narrowed her eyes. It wasn't a coincidence that the keys were attached to her key chain, especially since she'd used her car this morning. He must've changed it when he came up to the penthouse to see what she was doing.

The little sneak.

She stomped to the elevator, and tapped her feet impatiently as it went up two floors to his office. His assistant took a deep breath, her nostrils flaring, then smiled at her as she walked in.

"Is he in a meeting?" Savannah growled.

"No, Fela."

She sighed. "I'm not alpha yet." She said more to herself as she entered his office.

Having anyone call her Fela already made her nervous and the responsibility settled on her shoulders. She winced as the door nearly slammed into the wall as she pushed it open.

"Where is my car?" She asked him.

He raised an eyebrow and told the person on the other line that he would call them back. He waved her over to him. She crossed her arms and stood in the middle of the room.

"What's wrong?" He loosened the tie cinched around his neck.

"Patrice is missing, and the keys have been replaced on my keychain." She held them up, jingling them.

He stared into her eyes, his mouth turning up into a small smile. "Come here, babe." He cajoled, popping the first two buttons of his shirt loose.

She suppressed a shudder of longing as his eyes heated.

"No." She cleared her throat, mad at her own husky tone.

God, the man got to her. He licked his lips and she mirrored him, wanting very much to close the distance between them. She shook her head. *Back on track, Savannah.*

"My car?"

His lips lifted, flashing canines as he smiled and damn if her body didn't betray her, warming and loosening her muscles. He stood and stalked around his desk. He perched on the edge of it, mere feet from her and crooked his finger.

"Come, my Fela."

She took two steps before her brain caught up. She cursed. "I'm not alpha female yet."

The small steps she'd taken was enough to put her within arm's length of him. He grabbed the bottom of her jean jacket and tugged, pulling her between his legs. She let out a shuddering breath as he nuzzled into her neck, sliding her jacket over her shoulders and down her arms.

"Why are people all of a sudden calling me that? What's changed?"

He hummed in answer and swiped his tongue along her neck in the spot where he'd scratched her last night. Its rough texture dragged a moan from her. He chuckled, the dark sound dampening her panties. He scraped a canine across the front of her neck.

"You're not answering my questions, Carlos, which means you're hiding something."

He pinched her chin and brought her down for a kiss. His tongue swept into her mouth, taking possession of it. Her body softened and went pliant beneath his roaming hands. She clenched her fists, the car keys digging into her palm reminding her of why she'd come into his office. She pulled back from his kiss reluctantly.

"My car?"

He sighed, and licked at her bottom lip. "I bought you a new car."

She pushed at his shoulders. "You what? When? I've only been here three days. When did you have time?"

He tightened his grip on her back, his legs caging her in. "You needed a new car, you said you wanted a bigger one. I bought it the morning after I had to drive it." His voice was matter of fact, and that just teed her off.

"You didn't ask me! You don't replace my shit without asking me."

His hand gripped her ass, bunching the material of her skirt and a growl left his throat. "What have I told you about your tone when talking to me, my love?"

She tried in vain to push out of his arms. "Don't give me that alpha bullshit, Carlos. You took my car, and bought another one without any input from me, I have a right to be mad."

He grabbed her ponytail and tugged her head back, gripping the front of her throat between his teeth. Another warning growl echoed through the room. The speed of his movements had her heart racing, even as her body went pliant in his arms. It was like a switch thrown, his dominant action skyrocketing her body's arousal. Her nipples tightened, and her channel flexed, suddenly feeling empty. He lapped at his teeth marks. She sighed in pleasure. Her forehead met his, and she closed her eyes.

"We talked about this last night, baby. You're our mate. It's a compulsion to take care of you, to see to your needs."

She sighed, vaguely remembering them having the conversation in between orgasms. "I didn't need a new car."

He stroked her back, the heat of his hands burning through the thin tank top she wore, lulling her.

He snorted. "You most definitely did. Now you and the kids can ride comfortably and I won't have to squeeze into that tiny death machine you loved."

She growled. "It was mine, you had no right sell it without consulting me."

"I didn't sell it, love. It's in storage, but I should've told you, you're right."

She reared back in surprise.

He kissed her chin. "I'm sorry, Savannah. I have to remember, you're no docile woman to wait around and let a man take care of you. You come from a line of alphas. I will try and tame some of my more...dominant tendencies."

She narrowed her eyes, not quite believing the about face. "Promise?"

"You owe ten cents in the curse jar." He lifted her shirt and ignored her question.

"Ugh, not you too. It's bad enough when Jamie does it."

He pulled her shirt over her head and hissed, cupping her breasts. "Do you have any idea how beautiful you are?" His thumbs grazed her lace covered nipples.

Her head lolled back and her fingers dug into his shoulders.

"Are we done discussing your new car?" He licked a path across her chest, his mouth hovering over her breast, his warm breath brushing a nipple.

She moaned, perfectly aware her mate had avoided the promise. "Yes."

He laughed and lifted her, spinning around and laying her across his desk. "Now, I seem to remember the last time I warned you against speaking to me in the tone of voice you used when you walked in here."

She sucked her teeth. "You may want to get used to that." Especially since she suspected he would not curb his more domineering traits.

"Hmm," he scraped his teeth along her chest. "I like a challenge. What were the consequences?"

Her breath hitched and the scent of her arousal filled his office. "Something about splaying me across the nearest surface," was her breathless reply as she arched her body.

He sucked a nipple into his mouth and she lifted off the desk with a moan. He pulled back and turned her around, pushing her skirt up to her waist. Her ass was in the air, right where he wanted it. He gave one cheek a resounding tap. The sound echoing in the office. She gasped, and raised her ass higher. He pulled her lace panties down, and rubbed a hand across her exposed skin. He gripped her flesh, knowing he wouldn't be able to last long with her in this position. He tapped her ass again, entranced with the way it moved. She hissed, her back arching. He unzipped his pants, and gripped his cock, telling it, and himself that they wouldn't blow after the first stroke.

He cursed as he remembered where he was. "Condom?"

She scrambled for her purse and dug one out. She passed it back to him and resumed her position.

Lord have mercy.

He sheathed his length, and tapped her other cheek. She squirmed, her mewl of need tearing through his control. He gripped the head of his cock tightly.

"Be still." He ordered.

She looked over her shoulder and gyrated, a teasing smile tilting her full lips. He cursed and pulled her hips back into him, slamming home in one stroke.

"Fuck." His hips jerked, as the walls of her channel clenched around him.

He wouldn't last, not with her being defiant. She raised every possessive instinct him, the need to dominate her ripping away his control. She rolled her hips again, pulled forward, squeezing her muscles until she pushed him nearly out. She released and pushed back against him, sucking him back into her sex.

"Aren't I supposed to be getting punished?" She pushed her lips out in a pout.

He pulled out, slamming home again. She hissed and arched her back. "You're playing with fire, love."

"Just what I wanted to do today." She said, rotating her hips.

Lord help him, Savannah had to know what her challenging him would do. He couldn't control his panther. Not with the way her heated sheath clenched around his cock. He fucked her with hard strokes that showed Savannah his cat's dominance. She gasped, begging for more, her power rising and wrapping around him.

He growled, his power answering her call. He lifted her hips so he could reach her sex, needing to feel her come apart beneath him. She mewled when he pinched her clit. He stroked her deep, gritting his teeth to hold on. He would wait for her to come first even if it killed him.

Chapter 30

Derrick stepped off the elevator smiling. He spied his mate fixing her hair, looking dazed as she came out of Carlos' office. He chuckled, his erection filling out his pants. She nearly ran into his chest before she realized he was there. He grabbed her waist and smiled down at her. Carlos' scent covered her.

"What have you been doing, Savi?"

Her eyes widened, a little guilty flicker over her shoulder. "I had a discussion with Carlos over my car."

He wanted to laugh. He saw how well their discussion went. Her hair was falling out of her ponytail and her clothes were disheveled. Maybe he should admit his part in it, just to give him a chance to argue with her as well. He kissed her swollen lips, she moaned and melted into him. He loved the way she responded to him. She smelled of sex with their mate, and yet, her body went pliant in his arms.

"And?" He asked.

She blinked up at him, a drowsy, sated look that made him want to drag her into the elevator car he'd just vacated.

"I have a new car."

He smiled and traced her cheekbone with a thumb. "And do you like it?"

"I don't want you guys spoiling me, Derrick."

He loved that she called him by his name and not his title. "Just a little spoiling, baby," he murmured and nibbled on her bottom lip.

She gripped his forearms, but tiptoed, licking across his lips. He opened his mouth, and she plunged her tongue in. He sighed, reveling in the kiss. He lost track of time when she kissed him. She pulled back, the heat in her eyes pleasing him. He adjusted the jean jacket she wore, and twisted her skirt correctly to the front.

"You are our mate, it's our pleasure."

She looked him in the eye, the conflict between her independence and their need to care for her reflected on her face.

"I'm not your mate just yet."

He swallowed the snarl rumbling his chest. "Where are you headed?" he asked, changing the subject to avoid the argument his cat wanted him to launch into.

She could deny all she liked, she was theirs, and despite telling her they would give her a choice, she didn't really have one. Yeah, they hadn't marked her yet, but she was as good as theirs. In just the three days she'd been sleeping with them, their scent was damn near intermingled, so any shifter within a mile of her knew she was taken.

She sighed. "To take another shower, then I need to call and reschedule my appointment at the showroom. I want to look at stuff for the penthouse." She held up a hand. "Before you even say it, I don't need security."

He grunted and kissed her forehead. Yeah right they would let her drive around town without protection. "I want to go with you. Come get me when you're ready?"

She nodded and stepped around him. He turned to watch her walk away, he had to. The way her ass moved when she walked was pure poetry. He waved as the elevator doors closed and turned back. Carlos' assistant smirked at him, typing on her keyboard.

"Is he busy?"

She raised an eyebrow. Not anymore, her expression said. She'd been with Carlos for a few years, and nothing seemed to ruffle the woman. He gave her a little salute and walked into his co-mate's office. Carlos was leaning back in his chair, looking out at the traffic flowing below.

Derrick groaned. "The scent of our mate is permeating this office, I don't know how you plan on getting any more work done."

Carlos wiped his face and smiled. "I didn't think it was possible, Beta, the way I feel about that woman."

Derrick grunted. He knew exactly what the Felix was talking about. She was under his skin, his every thought belonged to her.

"I take it she was upset about the car?"

Carlos laughed. "A little bit."

"Well, we knew going in that our mate wouldn't just sit back and allow us to care for her." Derrick sat in the chair across from Carlos.

Carlos grunted. "Was there a reason you came to see me?"

"Nope. Just wanted to bask in Savannah's scent." Derrick licked his lips, tasting his mate's scent in the air. "I'm sure you had such a hard time convincing her to take the new car."

Carlos sighed, the sound content. "She's so stubborn. But, I enjoyed every minute of the debate." Carlos' smile was devilish, his obvious enjoyment in it written all over his face.

"She left your office in a daze, but I foresee you having this conversation again when the sexual haze wears off." He warned the Alpha.

Carlos laughed. "God, that woman is stubborn."

Derrick grunted. She was that. "I want her trained to fight from an enforcer. The longer we go without catching the bastards attacking our women, the more uneasy I become."

Carlos tapped his finger on his desk and considered it. "She would probably like it. I'm sure it will make her feel more secure, independent. Has she spotted Simon yet?"

He thought to the conversation he and Savi just had. "As far as she knows, she doesn't have security."

Carlos groaned. "While we're on the subject of security, we need to do something about the enforcers working better together."

He sighed. "It's on the agenda. The country cats have their own way of doing things."

"They've kept their territory and held their prowl together using those same methods." Carlos reminded him.

Derrick grunted but said nothing. He was well aware of the enforcers' struggle. While the hierarchy was settled, hunting for the panthers attacking their prowl was exposing a weak point. The Tampa enforcers were reluctant to hunt using the Jersey's prowl's methods and vice versa. With every attack and their subsequent escape, it was becoming more noticeable.

"Brielle is taking me out, showing me and Simon their hunting methods, hopefully between the three of us, we can come up with something that blends the two." He finally answered.

"I'll leave that to you. Now back to our mate. We can bring up her getting training tonight. Debate it with her." Carlos waggled his eyebrows.

Derrick laughed and stood. "I'm headed out with her to some showroom, I'll soften her up for the debate."

Carlos laughed and waved him out. He waved to the Carlos' assistant as he passed her desk again, headed to his office, down the hall. The more he thought on it, the more the idea of training Savannah cemented. It would help twofold. He knew Savannah would have issues being alpha female. Her latency would be a sticking point until she could prove to the women she could lead them. Teaching her to fight as an enforcer would train her for any challenges she'd face. As a bonus, it would prepare her for any type of attack. He would certainly feel better about her flitting around town if he knew she could defend herself. Now to convince their mate. He smiled, like Carlos, he looked forward to the debate.

***

Giggling greeted him as he exited the elevator on the penthouse level. Ella and Jamie were running in circles in the middle of what would be the living room as Savannah seemingly tuned them out. She was scribbling in a notebook, muttering to herself. He winced as Ella squealed and started chasing Jamie. They bounded towards the stairs.

"Hey." Savannah barked absently.

The two continued, ignoring her protest.

"No, you two." His voice stopped them on the bottom step. "No playing on the stairs."

"Boooo," they both yelled, but stepped away. They rushed him with hugs and he laughed, savoring their affection.

Would this be what he came home to each night? Carlos grunted as he let them tackle him to the floor. He pushed them off, and walked into another room to strip. He shifted into his panther and slunk into the living to surprise the kids. Ella and Jamie screamed and ran when they saw him. His panther chased them across the empty apartment. He batted them around, and tackled them both, licking their faces, and chuffing against their stomach. Their every laugh melted away his tension. Savannah stood over them a few minutes later, as they wrestled on the floor.

"And here I thought you being here would bring some semblance of quiet." She harrumphed.

The kids jumped up and ran again. He shifted back to human and pulled Savannah's leg. She fell onto his lap with a squeak. He kissed her. "I don't know why you thought that."

She swatted him and rolled off his lap, breathless with laughter. "You're ridiculous. Put on some clothes."

He smiled and her eyes misted over as she stared down at him. She cleared her throat and offered him one of the drop cloths strewn across the floor. The elevator dinged again and they both turned as Derrick exited the lift holding two giant sized pizzas.

"Pizzas!" Jamie yelled, jumping with an excited whoop.

"Dinner in the penthouse." The Beta announced.

The kids cheered, circling Derrick. Carlos wrapped the cloth around his waist and went to change. By the time he came back, there were more drop cloths on the floor, picnic style. It was perfect, and everything he hadn't realized he wanted. He talked with his mates, and their cubs, enjoying his new family. It didn't take long for the kids to get bored, so they packed up their trash and headed downstairs.

Savannah set up a movie for them and the adults headed to the kitchen for coffee. Carlos pulled her into his lap after she poured their cups.

"I wanted to talk to you about something." He watched her face.

"Is it about my car?"

Derrick snorted. Carlos hid a smile. He knew it was only a matter of time before she brought it back up.

"If you're serious about giving this a chance you're going to have to start attending prowl meetings."

She groaned and lay her head on his shoulder.

"It needs to happen soon, Savannah." Derrick gently admonished.

"The next meeting is tomorrow night?"

Carlos hummed in agreement.

"Are we ready for this, for the scrutiny that will come with it?" She grabbed his cheeks and looked him in the eye.

"I have nothing to hide, sweetheart." He whispered.

She turned and looked at Derrick. He crossed his arms over his chest. "The sooner they understand that we're not giving you up, the better."

She sighed and stood. She took her coffee cup and dumped the contents in the sink, turning on the water. He looked at his Beta. Derrick shrugged. They sat quiet while she washed the mug, and waited. The only noise in the apartment came from whatever movie the kids were watching.

She turned and nodded at them. "I'll attend tomorrow night."

Derrick stood and gathered her in his arms. Carlos sat back in his chair and sipped at his coffee while his mates whispered to each other.

"One other thing."

Savannah tensed in Derrick's arm before peeking around his back.

"We were thinking that with this threat, we'd like you to be trained by an enforcer."

She frowned and looked between them. "Seriously?"

Derrick nodded. "It would make us feel better to know you can defend yourself."

"What makes the two of you think I can't defend myself?" The hot sting of her anger whipped through the room.

Carlos didn't have an answer to that, so he stayed silent.

"We can talk about it later." Derrick said hastily.

She pushed out of his arms. "I'm putting the kids to bed."

Derrick raised his eyebrows as she left the kitchen. "What did we say?"

He shrugged.

Hours later as he stood under the water, he was still confused. Damned if he understood their mate. He came out of the shower and Savannah was sitting in the middle of the bed, her hair tied, and the spaghetti strap of her silk tank top sliding down her arm. His mouth watered.

She held up her hand. "We're still getting to know each other, so we're going to butt heads, I understand that. But, you don't know me well enough to know what's 'best for me', understand?"

What could he say to that?

Derrick came into the room, a towel around his waist. "What's up?"

Carlos crossed his arms over his chest. "Our mate was just telling me that I don't know enough about her to make decisions for her. Am I taking that right?"

She lifted her chin and looked at the both of them. "Right."

"Is this about what we said in the kitchen?" Derrick sat on the edge of the mattress.

She nodded. "Instead of asking me, the two of you made assumptions about what I did or didn't know. I dealt with that in my marriage, I'm not dealing with it again."

Carlos studied her, and realized how serious she was. He nodded. "That's fair. I'm sorry."

Her eyes widened in surprise. He walked to her, crawling on the bed until he'd pinned her. "I need you to quit looking surprised when I apologize. It makes me feel like an ass."

She wrapped her arms around his neck and pulled him down. "Deal."

Chapter 31

Nervousness traveled up and down the mating bond, and picking out the source between the three of them would be impossible. Derrick knew Savannah had to feel some amount of nervousness, but her face showed none of it. She mingled with her cousins, her demeanor serene, despite the looks she received.

He'd barely tasted his dinner, his body tense and alert. He didn't know exactly what to expect at the meeting, but so far, outside of curious glances, nothing had happened. That was not to say that there hadn't been talk. From the moment the three of them stepped into the clearing together, the whispers had commenced.

"What do you think?" Carlos sidled up next to him.

"I don't know. It feels off, but so far no one is bothering her."

Simon walked up to them. "Ryan hasn't made contact with anyone outside of our prowl."

Derrick cursed. "I thought it would be a good lead."

Carlos looked between the two of them. "How long have you been following him?"

"Beta gave me the order after Callie was attacked." Simon crossed his arms over his chest.

"It made no sense that she was able to fight off attackers with minor scrapes when the other women were beaten." Derrick wiped a hand over his face. "They are in contact with the other prowl and I want to know how."

Carlos grunted. "And why."

"No way do they think they can take over our prowl." Simon commented.

"What I don't understand is how they made contacts so quickly down here. They arrived scant weeks ago with the rest of us." Derrick glanced over to the two sisters. They were off alone, talking, their heads close together.

"That's a good point actually. Simon, how far did you investigate them when they applied to join the Jersey prowl?" Carlos asked the enforcer.

"I went back a few years. Nothing flagged with either of them."

"Run the three of them again, this time looking for connections in this area." Carlos ordered.

"Done." Simon nodded. "Now, if you two will excuse me, I'm going to grab something to eat."

"You think he'll find anything?" Derrick asked.

"I'm almost sure of it."

Derrick shook his head. He knew he should've booted those bitches.

No sooner than he'd spoken, murmurs raised around them. Callie and Mallory marched over to Savannah where she sat with her cousins eating. He put a hand out as Carlos moved to intercept them.

"She has to handle it herself if she's to earn her place." The thought of it pissed him off though.

"I want our kids out of here." Carlos said between clenched teeth.

"I agree." Derrick gave two short whistles and inclined his head towards the children.

A couple of the elders grabbed them up and left the clearing with them. The night went still as Callie and Mallory approached the table.

"It's your fault my sister was attacked." Mallory stood over Savannah.

Savannah flicked a bored look over her shoulder. "I don't know you, bitch, move along."

Savannah rolled her eyes and kept eating. She knew sooner or later she'd have to fight. It was inevitable. But last night, she couldn't argue Carlos' point. The prowl would never take their relationship seriously if she didn't start attending prowl meetings.

So.

Here she sat, with some woman staring daggers at her back.

"You don't deserve to be alpha female."

She recognized that voice. She narrowed her eyes and swiveled her head. The woman from the elevator was staring at her, her arms crossed.

"If you want, I can give you some of the attention you're seeking." Savi pushed back from the picnic table and stood.

A man rushed up to them and stepped between her and the woman. "Callie, let's not do this. Mallory, let's go." He grabbed the other woman's arm.

Mallory shook her arm free. "No. I want to challenge her."

"Let's do this then." Savi already had her hair in two braids, her face makeup free and no jewelry on anywhere. She came to the meeting prepared to fight.

Charlotte had taken one look at her when she'd arrived and glued herself to Savannah's side the whole night. Her cousin knew what was up. Charlotte had been at her side for every fight she'd fought when they were younger. Her cousin stood beside her now.

"You can't challenge her, she's not alpha female yet. She's a nobody." Her cousin Liz spat, butting into their conversation.

"Fuck off, Liz!" Charlotte hissed.

"She can catch a 'pre-alpha status' beat down as far as I'm concerned." Savannah stepped closer to Mallory. "What do you say, Mallory?"

"You can fight everyone in this clearing, and it still won't make you a good Fela, latent." Liz marched into their circle, walking directly to Savannah.

Savannah turned her attention to Liz, waiting until she got just close enough. As soon as Liz stepped within her reach, she struck. Liz's head whipped back as Savannah punched her in the nose.

"You were told to mind your place, now step back and shut up." Savannah didn't raise her voice.

Liz grabbed her nose and screeched. "You bitch."

Savannah stared Liz down until the other woman looked away. The heat from her mates seared her back as they gathered behind her. She didn't dare glance at them. After the conversation they'd had last night, she was almost afraid to see their doubt of her in their faces. If they intervened in any way, it would undermine her.

Brielle came up on them and shoved Liz back out of the way. "Liz is dumb, but she's right. Even if you challenge Savi, it won't be for the alpha position, as she doesn't yet have it."

"I don't care. She has no place here and she should know it." Mallory spat at her feet.

Brielle growled, but Savannah placed a hand on her cousin's arm. "Call the challenge, Brielle, I have no problem showing her *my* place."

Brielle looked behind Savannah. Carlos must've given her assent because she gave a long whistle and the clearing quieted and formed a circle.

"Remember what we taught you, little cousin." Brielle whispered before turning and moving to the center of the circle.

Savannah followed Brielle, working to calm her racing heart. She wasn't worried about the fight with Mallory. She and Brielle worked out together, her cousin having taught her to fight years ago when she had Jamie. Brielle understood her need to make a place for her son.

She rolled her shoulders to loosen the tension. She knew half of it came from her mates. The two of them paced the circle, their worry for her flowing down their bond. Brielle went over the rules of the challenge, reiterating that it wasn't for alpha female.

"Savannah even though you're latent—"

"I understand." She cut Brielle off.

"All the same, I'll go over the rules of challenge. The fight stops as soon as one of the fighters submits. Savannah is latent, but Mallory still has the option to call forth her panther. No maiming, no killing, understood?" Brielle looked to both challengers.

Both women nodded. Mallory gave her a cocky smirk. One Savannah returned. Mallory's smirk died as Brielle called the match to start.

The two women circled each other, their faces equally determined. Savannah's gait was relaxed as she moved, her body positioned to take an attack, no matter how Mallory struck. Carlos clenched his hands, wincing as his claws sliced into his palms. He kept his expression stoic, no sign of his inner turmoil.

They couldn't intervene, he knew that, and yet his body tensed as Mallory struck first, swiping at Savannah with her claws. His mate easily ducked, moving faster than he thought a latent could move. Mallory lost her footing as she reached again for Savannah. Dodging her to one side, Savannah turned and kicked the back of Mallory's knees as she passed. The female buckled, one knee hitting the ground. She quickly rebounded, standing and growling before leaping at Savannah.

The two women collided and he cringed at the sound, his panther slamming against his control. Savannah was ruthless, striking Mallory with quick fists to her face, and solar plexus. Savi's focused gazed reminded him of his arrogance in assuming she wouldn't know how to protect herself. Savannah had been right to call him on his shit.

His mate blocked a blow with her forearm, back slapping Mallory. Savi reached to punch her, but missed as Mallory spun and raked her claws across Savannah's back. The crowd gasped, and he snarled. Tension flowed between him and Derrick, until his shoulders were tight with it, and his breath came out in short, urgent pants. Their mate, her face determined, spun, showing no sign that she was hurting.

Mallory rushed to her, her fist extending, Savi grabbed the woman's arm, punching her in the midsection twice. Mallory back away breathing heavily. She growled and fur sprouted along her arms, her claws coming out. His panther calmed and Carlos took a wary step back, unsure how the cat would react if Mallory shifted.

Savannah smiled and wiped blood from her lip. She charged at Mallory, grabbed her shirt and landed several punches to her face and neck. Mallory grabbed Savannah's arm, digging her claws into Savannah's shoulder.

Carlos' breath hitched and he moved forward. Savannah stepped back and clutched her arm.

Derrick gripped his forearm. "She has it."

He growled, but paused. Savannah's pain pushed down their mate bond. He warred with the need to help their mate, knowing it was necessary for her to prove herself. If he intervened now, after the conversation they'd had last night, Savannah would never trust him. Not to mention how much harder it would be for her to retain the Alpha female position.

He stepped back and rolled his shoulders, giving their mate his trust.

Mallory grabbed Savannah's head and kneed her in the chin. Savannah fell back, landing in the dirt. Derrick growled next to him, but crossed his arms over his chest, the Beta's body language showing his confidence in Savannah.

Mallory jumped and tried to land on Savannah. His mate had her legs extended, kicking her in the chest, sending her backwards. Savi rolled to the side and stood, blood trailing down her face.

"Fuck," Derrick whispered.

Snarls went up around the circle when Mallory shifted and charged Savannah. Savi smiled, blood coming from her mouth and she widened her stance. Mallory jumped and at the last minute, Savannah moved out of her path, but stuck out her arm to clothespin the cat. She grabbed the panther around the neck, using her momentum to slam Mallory into the ground. Savannah fell with her, and twisted, elbowing the panther in the back of the head and wrapping her legs around the cat's neck until Mallory shifted back, choking. Savi stood, her steps wobbly and put her foot on Mallory's neck, using her other leg to kick her in the stomach.

He snarled, and pumped his fist. God damn, that woman was vicious. Her strength shocked and pleased him.

Savannah didn't let her up, instead leaning her weight on her neck. "Are we done?"

Mallory struggled, kicking her legs and waving arms to reach Savannah. She raked her nails across Savannah's calf. Savannah yelled out and stepped back. He cursed. Why would she let her up? No sooner than Mallory stood, Savannah reared back and kicked her in the chest. It sent the woman back two feet, near the jeering panthers watching.

"Are we done?" Savannah shouted over the cheering crowd.

Mallory struggled for breath, hunched into a fetal position. The female nodded her capitulation. They all turned as someone screeched. Savannah's head was pulled back as Callie snatched the bottom of her braids and kicked the back of Savi's leg. He moved to intervene, but his mate was quick. Though she'd buckled under the kick, Savannah reached over her shoulder and in quick judo move, tossed Callie, face first, into the dirt. Savannah lifted Callie by her hair and hauled her into a headlock. She punched the woman until her cousins managed to pull her back. Still, his mate struggled to get to Callie, her legs kicking as Brielle held her high. The rough edge of her anger seemed to ignite her power. Everyone in the circle shuffled as that power pushed down the prowl's link.

Shock blanketed him.

"Shit, if she's just now angry…" Derrick said in wonder.

It meant Savannah had been playing with Mallory. Damn, they owed their mate an apology. Last night she was right in that he'd assumed she didn't know how to fight. Every time she spoke of not being strong, he'd attributed it to physical strength. He had a lot to learn about his mate.

He watched the faces change of those who had doubted Savannah, saw the awe on their face in reaction to his mate's power. Hell, his own panther, already riled from the fight, jumped to the forefront. The circle closed around her, her cousins comforting her.

"Our Fela." He whispered.

"Fucking right." Derrick growled.

They pushed through the crowd to get to their mate. She turned and saw them, a smile lighting her face. She walked to them, a confidence in the sway of her hips that hadn't been there when they first arrived. The fight with Mallory had done something he and Derrick could not do in all their pep talks.

It proved to her that she could hold her position.

He would refrain from jumping on Ryan and his sisters for that alone.

He cupped her face. "How you feeling?"

She went up on her toes and kissed him. Power zipped down his back, little stings that aroused him. He ate at Savannah's mouth, his panther steps from claiming her in front of God and everyone in the circle.

Derrick hugged her from behind, burying his head in the crook of her neck. Their combined touch raised the power in the circle. His prowl whistled in reaction, stepping closer to the alpha Tribond. Hands reached forward to touch the three of them, each touch adding power until it swelled into the night.

He pulled from their kiss and threw his head back, and exhaled. The prowl link snapped into place, tighter, purer. If given a chance to describe it, he'd be at a loss for words. Pride, elation, and contentment filled him. They all basked in the power, until he felt his mate's trembles. Her exhaustion registered to him and he lifted her into his arms. She kissed him, but pushed out of his embrace.

"I have to walk out of the circle, Felix." She whispered.

He put her down and stepped back. She grabbed his hand and Derrick's. They walked from the circle and into the darkening night.

"Where are we going?" Derrick asked as they walked deeper into the woods.

"There's a guest cabin not too far ahead." She stumbled on something.

He growled and lifted her into his arms. "There's no one around."

She slid her arms around his neck and smiled. "I'm not arguing, Alpha."

Why her use of his title turned him on, he couldn't say, but it did. And so he walked faster, his need for her skyrocketing. He put her down at the door of the small cabin they encountered.

She pushed open the door and they followed her inside. The place was sparsely decorated, but comfortable. She didn't stop in the living room, instead leading them into a bathroom, a lot bigger than he'd imagined. The shower could easily fit the three of them. Seemed like his mate knew that, from the teasing smile she gave them.

He shook his head and released the last of the tension in his body. This woman was theirs, all theirs. Mallory was one of the stronger females in their prowl who had opposed his mating to Savannah, and Savi took her easily. Her cousins, at least the stronger ones, supported her, so he wouldn't have to worry about anyone else challenging her. The last of his worries about her being alpha female disappeared and he could see hers did as well.

Watching her fight had stirred his animal instincts. Base desire hardened his body until he thought he would explode. She stripped out of her sweatshirt, and Derrick growled at the bruises blooming along her skin, with the healing cuts. He wondered how much the tank top she still wore hid. She slid her pants down her legs.

"It's not as bad as you think, babe." She went to Derrick and wrapped her arms around him. "Whatever power we raised in the circle went a long way to healing most of the bruises."

"I still don't like it." Derrick grumbled, kissing her.

Carlos removed his clothes as he watched them kiss. He started the water, making sure it was warm. Savannah turned and smiled at him, before slipping easily into his arms. He lifted her and smiled, resting her against the wall. She leaned back and lifted her tank top dragging off her sports bra with it. She shifted her hips back and forth making a show of it. He was entranced. Heat gathered in her eyes as she wormed her way out of her remaining clothes.

He purred as her beautiful breasts slipped from beneath her top. God the woman was luscious. How they got so lucky he would never know. Before her hands could fully escape her top, he sucked her nipple into his mouth. She moaned, tossing the top aside, holding his head to her chest. She was so sensual, his mate. Though she'd had doubts about being alpha female, she had never been shy once she'd been in their bed. Carlos hooked his hands under her supple ass and lifted her. Her legs gripped his waist, the heels of her feet pushing into his back.

He growled and walked them into the shower stall, his mate clutching at his shoulders. Hunger rose in him until he was dizzy. Gathering steam played against her skin, beading up and trickling down from her shoulders to her hips before dripping to the floor.

He nuzzled into her neck. "Do you still hurt anywhere, baby?" He ran his hands down the side of her body rolling his palms over her thighs, gently parting them.

She lifted her hips into him and moaned, "no, Alpha, but if you need to…you know... inspect my entire body, then I won't mind."

His hands slid up her back, holding her in place while he feasted on her breast. She twisted at her waist, offering the other nipple its turn. Hungrily Carlos took it, rolling it between his tongue and the roof of his mouth. He modified his hold on her, grabbing her hips and moving her until her moist center settled, scorching hot along his cock. Using her legs, she lifted, the heat of her sex sliding up and down on his shaft. He wanted inside her… now.

Derrick slipped into the stall closing the door behind him. Carlos turned, placing Savannah between the two of them. The Beta moved her hair, scraping his canines along the side of her neck. She arched her back and took full advantage, Carlos still suckling at her breast.

"There is nothing stopping us from making you ours." Derrick whispered.

"I'm ready," she panted, turning her head to kiss him, lifting her hands to wrap them around the Beta's head.

Carlos' panther leapt forward and his canines descended. Alpha power suffused him, and impatience rode him. He slid his hands down her body and parted the lips of her sex. She was hot, wet and ready for him. He adjusted her body until she was positioned right over his shaft.

"Now, sweetheart?" He choked out.

"Yes." She hissed as he slid inside, leaning forward to scrap her teeth against the skin of his neck.

He closed his eyes tightly, gritting his teeth. Her wet heat clutched at his shaft. Derrick held her body as Carlos stroked in and out of their mate, his hips moving frantically.

"Submit to me." He ordered.

His panther demanded it, no longer content to wait on their mate. She tossed her head back and moaned, grinding her hips into him. Derrick moved his hands slowly around her, reaching for her breasts. She gasped, the walls of her sex fluttering on Carlos' cock. She lifted her chin submitting to his Alpha panther and he thought his heart would leap from his chest. He loved her so much, loved how she understood him so well. There were times when he needed to say nothing and his mate provided. She spoiled him, put up with his temper and possessive animal with a humor that soothed and made him feel whole.

He leaned down, and gripped the front of her throat with his teeth. He breathed deep and trusted his panther to be careful. He gripped her throat tighter until just the tips of his canines pierced her skin. Power blasted into the bathroom as her blood hit his mouth. The bond they'd already made tightened, and her emotions bombarded him. He released her throat and lapped at the punctures as his panther rolled around his body in contentment. It rose and brushed against their bond, his mate gasping as power flowed between them.

"Don't come just yet, my love." Derrick whispered as he adjusted her.

Carlos pulled her into his chest, his strokes slowing as he savored their mating bond. His eyes met the Beta's and Derrick smiled,   anticipation   written   all   over   his   face.

Chapter 32

Derrick broke eye contact with the Felix and stared at the nape of his mate's neck. His panther moved through his body, ready for their mating bite. His teeth grew, the canines lowering past his top lip. He licked her skin, taking pleasure in her shudder.

"Trust me, mate?" His breath whispered across her neck.

She nodded, dropping her head onto Carlos' shoulder to give him more room. He stepped in closer to the heat of their bodies. Derrick reached up, taking a hold of the back of her head, pulling her hair into a fist. He leaned her head to the side and trailed a series of scorching kisses from her ear to her collar. Her hands reached back to firmly grab his shaft, stroking him forcefully. His knees nearly buckled as she tugged him from base to head. She worked her hands up and down his skin, the lubricant he'd put on prior to entering the shower making her hands slick. She paused at the base to reach her fingers down and teased his sack. She tugged at it before stroking back up his member.

He wanted to move his chest back to give her more room to work, but with every stroke of her hand, his need for her grew. His panther nearly shredded against his restraints to get at their mate, to put his mark on her. Beta power rose and melded with Carlos' Alpha power, searing his senses.

She released Derrick's cock and wrapped her arms around Carlos' neck, arching her back to show Derrick she was waiting for him. He gripped his length and prayed for patience. He guided it to the entrance of her ass and breathed deep.

"Push out when I push in, okay sweetheart?"

She moaned and wiggled her hips, but nodded. Derrick pushed into her entrance, his breath stalling as her tight walls gripped him. His hands grabbed her hips holding her in place as he pushed further, sliding his head all the way in. A new wash of energy flooded their bond as pleasure, pain, and passion ran over them. Her body responded to the power, heating and then relaxing into their embrace. He luxuriated in the feel of her gripping him as he filled her deeper. They all gasped as Derrick finally seated himself fully into her. His panther reared up, and his claws pushed out, forcing him to adjust his hold on Savannah.

She mewled and the sound did nothing for his control. His hips jerked, and need clawed his chest as he pulled away from her to settle into a more comfortable position. He grit his teeth as he reversed his motion, careful of how tight she was. Her head rolled as her hips swayed onto his cock, gently allowing him inside again. Once he was fully seated, he finally breathed. God, she was so warm and tight.

"Hurry, Beta." Carlos gritted his teeth.

Carlos shifted his feet and pushed them back up against a wall. Derrick followed his lead, not wanting to lose a shred of skin contact with Savannah. His back touched the icy stone wall but he barely felt it as they began to move in sync, pushing and pulling out of Savannah. Power filled the space of the shower stall, thicker than the steam that fogged the room.

He couldn't resist a few strokes, basking in the feel of her tight sheath. The three of them moaned in unison. The passionate sounds escaping her lips, pushed his panther further out of his control.

"Fuck, Derrick, quit playing and bite her." Carlos hissed.

Derrick chuckled and leaned into her, deeply breathing in her scent. He gripped the skin of her neck between his teeth, slowly allowing his teeth entrance. She moaned and power washed over the three of them, stronger than the tide that had washed over them in the clearing after her fight. He pulled his teeth out, but kept his grip on her neck, his panther relishing her submission.

He and Carlos took turns stroking in and out of her body, the heat climbing between them. Her walls quivered around his cock, signaling her oncoming release. He plunged into her body. Her muscles contracted, and he had to stop moving to keep himself from coming too soon.

Carlos growled and threw his head back. "Now, Savannah!"

She released a throaty chuckle, "yes, my mates," arching her back and taking Derrick deeper.

This woman was everything to him. That she laughed as they roughly took her, her nails scoring his skin, urging him on, showed him she was well his match in every way.

Derrick licked over his teeth marks as her body tensed and she gasped. He flexed his hips, and electricity ran up and down their link. Carlos held her face, ravaging her mouth. Savannah pulled back from the kiss and screamed her pleasure, her body moving frantically between them. Power poured over them all, mingled with fiery heat as his orgasm bowed his back.

Her nails dug into his arm and Carlos' shoulder, leaving a mark of her own on their skin as she bucked from the force of her orgasm. The three of them shook together as waves of their power and passion rolled them for what seemed like an eternity. His head swam with euphoria, the strength of the energy slowly gliding them back down to earth. Their hearts and breaths raced as they worked to regain control of their now sated bodies.

The thought that she'd taken down one of the stronger females in their prowl sent a new rush of arousal through him.

He already loved her, but knowing that she could take care of herself lifted a weight from him and inundated him with pride for his mate. Derrick stroked her hair, pulling her back into his chest for a kiss.

"Love you." She whispered, as their lips met.

He pulled out first, once Carlos supported her weight. The Felix slid her down his body until her feet touched the floor. Derrick turned into the water and soaped off his shaft, before turning to Savannah and pulling her into his arms. He kissed a trail up her body, lingering a bit at Carlos' mark. It was his turn to leave his mark on the front of her throat.

"Now?" Derrick was poised over her neck.

Carlos stared at Savannah, his eyes gold, his canines resting on his bottom lip, his gaze reverent as he licked down their mate's neck. The Felix growled a low rumbling sound that was all hunger. "Now."

They struck at the same time, biting down on their mate. Savannah screamed and his body shuddered, the taste of his mate coating his tongue. Her back bowed as their combined power filled the three of them. The hair on his arm stood on end, and electricity traveled up his spine until the top of his head buzzed and feelings from both his mates overwhelmed him. He pulled back and sucked on the bite before laving it with his tongue to close the mark.

"I love you, Savannah." He panted, his hips jerking with the need to bury himself in her body again.

Their eyes met and the connection between them deepened. His love for her burned his chest and the closeness he felt with Carlos filled him to overflow. They had their mate, finally, the dreams he'd had for so long were being fulfilled. He couldn't stop touching her. He skimmed his hands across her body, reveling in his mate's soft skin. She sighed, her happiness flooding him, along with the Alpha's. He could feel them all, their bond actively buzzing as it was finally sealed.

She slid her legs up against his, stroking him. She kissed first him, then Carlos.

"Is this how we really wanted to seal our bond?" Her smile reached from ear to ear as she stepped into the warm water.

"So long as you're ours." Carlos growled.

Derrick had to agree. He grabbed the soap on the shelf and soaped up his hands. He washed over her body, lingering at her sex. She closed her eyes. Carlos moved behind Savannah and plucked at her nipples, she gasped.

"Hold her up." He ordered the Felix.

Carlos easily lifted her and he kneeled on the tile, putting her legs over his shoulder. He growled, and buried his face between her legs. Her taste on his tongue was amazing, his favorite flavor and he ravenously partook. He devoured her, his tongue circling her clit, his teeth grazing the small bud. He inserted a finger, her walls quivered around it, signaling her oncoming release. Her nails dug into his shoulders, a moan cueing her orgasm.

Derrick slid her legs slowly to the floor, but Carlos gave her no time to recover, bending her forward on the Beta's shoulders and sliding into her sex to the hilt, giving her orgasm more fire. Derrick didn't know how long they played in the shower, but the water was long cold before they pulled their exhausted mate from the water.

**

An hour later, the three of them were cuddled into the only bed in the cabin. Unfortunately it was only queen sized…and a bit squeaky after the gymnastics they'd performed on it all through the night. Even after what they'd done in the shower, with mating magic thrumming through their veins, they'd become insatiable. Luckily for her, Derrick had called it, before falling asleep.

He was now snuggled into her back, his breathing deep, while the alpha cuddled against her front. Their bodies were intertwined, the blankets long kicked to the floor.

"Why didn't you say anything about being trained?" Carlos asked.

She snorted. "That's on y'all for assuming I wouldn't be able to protect myself."

Though she lay between them, her body sated, a part of her was a little hurt that they'd underestimated her. But, the very fact that they hadn't jumped in, even as Mallory's sister attacked her from behind let her know that they didn't anymore. She took comfort in that.

"You're right, I'm sorry and it won't happen again." Derrick reassured her in a sleepy voice.

The admission soothed her.

"You kicked her ass, babe." Carlos rubbed his head under chin, nuzzling her.

The fight with Mallory had brought back all the fights from her youth. With the added difference of Brielle's training helping her. She would be sure to send her cousins a gift basket. Between Brielle and Charlotte, fighting Mallory had been easier. Her cousins were dirty fighters, and she was happy for it. Mallory had counted on her panther to do the work, never expecting Savannah to be able to counter her moves. She hoped the challenge would stall others. She was serious when she said she didn't want to spend every prowl meeting fighting.

"You're now the Fela, how do you feel?" Carlos asked.

Her stomach pitched, nervousness invading her calm. Apprehension for her new position was something that wouldn't go away for a while. But, the power of their bond was zinging through her, giving her strength. She closed her eyes and all the sounds of the night filtered in through the walls of the cabin. Her connection to Carlos and Derrick brought with it, a connection to all the panthers in the prowl. She could feel them, feel their sense of wellbeing. It was scary, but reassuring at the same time.

She would need to get with her grandmother and learn more about what she needed to do as Alpha female. She wanted to do a good job, and really understand her new role.

Strangely missing from the cocktail of emotions, was panic. She smiled. "I think I can do it."

"I know you can do it." Derrick growled in her ear.

She sighed, enjoying the sensation of being sandwiched between them. She did miss Carlos' giant bed though. "Do we plan on spending the night in this uncomfortable bed, or can we go get our kids and go home?"

They both squeezed her tight before rolling out of the small bed. She watched their bodies, in awe of her luck. They were beautiful creatures, both different and sexy in their own way.

Derrick's cocky smile, as he caught her staring, stirred her power and heated her sex. God, she'd just had them both. She licked her lips and he growled, stalking back to the bed.

"Cut it out you two. I'm not fucking on that tiny bed again tonight." Carlos rolled his eyes and opened the drawers looking for clothes.

Derrick crawled over her on the bed. "I want you to have that same energy when we get home." He whispered against her lips.

"Bet." She licked his bottom lip.

Chapter 33

Life as Fela was proving to be different than what Savannah expected. It was nowhere near as harrowing as she'd built it up to be. Her grandmother was easing her into the role, and last month's prowl meeting hadn't erupted into spontaneous challenges. She would count it as a success. Brielle had come to her and suggested she work with Simon, her bodyguard on new techniques, so she spent a lot of time doing that.

Most weekends she trained with him and the rest of the enforcers, learning all they did to keep the prowl safe. It was eye-opening and gave her a new respect for her cousins. All of the enforcers were going through retraining, each learning from one another. It had been fascinating to witness.

She took a relieved breath as she stepped outside into the cold December air. A puff of smoke left her mouth at her irritated exhale. While life with her mates was settling into a pleasant rhythm, she was trying to adjust her work life to make room for a six foot four, redheaded Adonis who followed her everywhere.

Simon had been assigned as her personal security, and no amount of fussing with her mates was changing it. While Simon wasn't generally intrusive, he brought attention to him everywhere they went. She'd just come from a meeting with a building company and had to deal with half the women there drooling over him and the men pretending as though Simon was now in charge of her firm. Simon, as usual, uttered barely two words and yet every man in the room turned to him when it was time for a decision to be made.

She growled, the sound actually sounding animal since she was now mated. Though she was still latent, her powers had grown with the mating, and more traits of her non-existent panther manifested.

Simon sighed. "Fela. Are we going to have this argument again?"

"I didn't say anything."

"But you're agitated."

"Well, I just spent two hours having to pry professionals off your ass. 'Oh you were an Army Ranger.'" She mocked in a sing song voice.

He chuckled. "It's pretty cool, you have to admit."

She would not admit it, no matter how true it was. "Next time I have a meeting, I'm putting you in a sack."

He outright howled. "Now I'm too good looking?"

She eyed his tall frame next to her. His red hair was short on the sides, the shaggy top pushed back neatly from his forehead to reveal his angelic face. It was deceiving, she'd seen the way he fought at the prowl tournament. Nothing about the man was as innocent as his heavily lashed eyes and pale skin made him look.

He wore a pair of slim gray slacks, the material clinging to his muscular legs and a simple black sweater with the sleeves pushed up to his elbows. His Rangers' tattoo was displayed on his forearm. His whole look was understated, luxe and perfect for someone who was supposed to blend into the background. And yet…on Simon the whole thing projected power.

"Seriously Simon, you have hazel eyes, freckles and a sick body, the whole prowl ought to have to walk around in monks' robes. Not to mention all the…alpha-ness that enters a room with you. I'm surprised the builder didn't lay on the ground and expose his belly."

He snickered. "I'm going to tell your mates you find me hot."

She had to smile at that. They were nearing the parking garage when he stiffened and pulled her behind him. His demeanor changed within seconds. It wasn't hard to see the Army training in his body's alert posture. He pulled his phone from his pocket and lifted his head scenting the air. He tapped out a quick message before putting it away and signaling for her to follow him. They skirted the elevator they had taken to reach the ground floor and took the stairs.

"Unknown shifters, Fela, I need you to follow my instructions. Remember, we trained for this type of scenario."

"I remember." She took her keys and threaded them through her fingers like he'd taught her, and took the cap off her mace. She'd laughed and scoffed when Simon kept giving her kidnapping scenarios. Now?

Now she was making him a giant fucking chocolate cake when they got home.

"When we get to our floor, head down, fast track it to the truck, understood?" Simon ordered.

She bobbed her head and breathed deep to calm her racing heart. They walked the stairs until they reached the third floor where they were parked. He paused at the door, and turned back to look at her.

She held up her mace with shaky hands. "Ready."

He counted down from three on his fingers, and kicked open the door. A loud snarl sounded before a thud. She followed him through the door. There were three very large males waiting for them and they charged her and Simon simultaneously. A fourth one came up behind them, pulling at her briefcase. She shook out of it, dropping her keys in the process and kicked out at the male. Her forearm was on fire as she blocked a punched aimed at her face. She kicked out with her feet, hitting him in the midsection, and scraped her nails across his arms as he reached for her again.

He moved quickly, grabbing her hair and slinging her across the garage. Her heart thudded, fear stealing her breath as she landed hard, wrenching her knee. Another spike of adrenaline helped her force her body up. She swung on him, hitting him in the face. He staggered back a step, but recovered, and swung at her. She ducked and punched him twice in the kidney. He grunted and brought his elbow down on her shoulder.

"Fuck!" She hissed at the pain and stood, swinging.

He caught one fist and then the other as she swung again. "The stories are true then. You're strong for a latent."

She ignored his taunting, her only thought to leave the garage alive. She growled and kicked out at his stomach, he jumped back and tightened his grip on her fists. She clenched her teeth at the pain. She kicked again, this time aiming for his knee. He cursed and buckled, releasing her arms. Her elation was short lived as he swept her legs from under her.

She hit the concrete hard.

He lifted his leg to stomp her and she rolled, her heart hammering. She landed on her keys and she lifted to her knees to grab them and her mace, threading the keys through her fingers.

Her attacker growled and the wind left her in a hard whoosh as he kicked her in the ribs. She wheezed and fell flat. He rolled her over with his feet, and kneeled down over top of her.

"Unfortunately I can't have fun with you until our alpha does." His voice was raspy, his eyes glowing gold with his cat close to the surface.

No trace of humanity filled his determined gaze. If she didn't fight, at best he would kidnap her, at worst he'd kill her in the garage, all to strike at their prowl. She could not let that happen.

His hands loomed large as he reached down to choke her.

No, no, no.

She dropped the mace and swatted at his hands as he tried to grip her throat. She scraped her keys down his arms, using her nails to dig into his other arm. She twisted her body, praying he'd not get the chance to pin her. The acrid taste of panic filled her mouth, she feared what would happen if he did. He leaned his weight on her and smirked before licking up the side of her face.

She growled, frustrated anger burning through her. She brought her keys up and stabbed them into his cheek. He snarled and full on punched her in the face. Stunned, her ears ringing, she dropped the keys, blinking as black dots drifted across her vision. Her attacker stiffened and the faint sounds of tires squealing drifted to her.

He lifted his nose and inhaled. "They're here, I have her, let's go," he barked at the others.

She renewed her fight to get from under him, frantically grabbing for the mace she'd dropped. She nearly cried when she gripped the canister. She was tired, hurt, but if she could keep up just a little longer, their enforcers would be there. Her attacker grabbed her hair with one hand and dug his claws into her shoulders with the other, dragging her up to stand. She screamed and brought up her hand, aiming the mace spray towards his face, especially the spot where she'd keyed him.

She choked as some of the spray blew back into her face, the hot lash of pain making her breathless. He screamed and released her, she dropped to the ground, her eyes streaming.

Determination had her struggling to stand, but she did, and as soon as she got her feet under her, she took off running towards the sound of the approaching car. An SUV came barreling around the corner of the garage, and she sobbed in relief.

"You got lucky bitch, but next time you won't." He shouted behind her.

He dragged one of his fellow attackers off the ground and the one battling Simon grabbed another, supporting the male as they escaped. Simon dropped to the ground as he tried to chase them. He was bleeding from the back of his head, his half-shifted claws were bloody and his breathing jerky. She changed directions and rushed to him, her arm hanging limply at her side in pain, but before she could get to him, security from their prowl grabbed him up. They got in her face to check on her and she pushed them off with her good arm.

"No one touches me."

She would get Charlotte to get the scent. Their grandfather had always said Charlotte was the best tracker he'd ever seen.

"Fela," an enforcer pleaded, "let us help you."

She walked back to her briefcase and picked it up, using her good hand to shuffle in the contents. Limping to her SUV, she growled at anyone coming near here. No one would touch her until Charlotte got that scent.

One of the enforcers from Carlos' old prowl walked up to her with his hands raised. "At least let me drive, Fela. Simon is too hurt to drive." She nodded and handed him her key.

She looked around and saw as they loaded Simon into the large SUV they'd driven. The enforcers, except the one driving her, piled in the other truck. Before he pulled off, the driver murmured into a cell phone and passed it back to her. She knew who it was, knew they would be frantic.

"I'm okay," was the first thing she said. She hissed as the enforcer took a corner fast. "I'll be home shortly. I'm going to call Charlotte and have her meet me at the apartment."

"Whatever you need, baby." Derrick soothed.

Their worry coated their link, wrapping her in their concern. She sent as much reassurance as she was able through her pain.

"Save your energy sweetheart, don't use it to placate your mates. We'll have a healer waiting on you as well." Carlos' voice was barely over a rumble. His anger and worry was clear to discern. "Can you tell me what happened?"

"We were ambushed. Simon and I took the stairs up to the parking garage and as we came out of the stairwell they rushed us. There were four of them." Her breath hitched as she realized how close she'd been to getting kidnapped. She'd never complain about Simon ever again. His being there had surely saved her life.

"The rest can wait, sweetheart."

She nodded and ended the call. She called her cousin and Charlotte picked it up quickly.

"Char, are you at work?" Her voice broke.

"What happened?" Charlotte must've sensed the urgency.

"Someone attacked me and I want you to find them. Granddad said you were the best."

"Are you home, are you okay? Never mind, don't answer. I'll meet you there in ten." Charlotte ended the call, needing nothing but her cousin's request to come.

They drove the rest of the way in silence. Her body shook with left over adrenaline. Her vision was dimming around the edges, and blood was soaking her shirt at the shoulder. When they got to the complex she limped to the elevator. She stabbed in the code for the top floor.

"No, no extra scents," she whispered as the security tried to surround her.

She pressed the button, closing the door on them. When she got to the penthouse floor Carlos and Derrick paced the hallway in front of the elevator. They rushed at her.

"No, no, no." She backed away from them. They stopped, stunned, but kept their distance.

"Let me hold you, kitten," Derrick whispered.

Her knees buckled with the need to run to them both. To feel their arms around her, but the more scents Charlotte had to decipher the harder it would be.

"I need Char first, Derrick, please." Her voice broke but she refused to let tears fall.

Carlos' security team surrounded the penthouse, standing in front of the windows their faces solemn. Rage glittered in their eyes. Some of them were half shifted in their anger, their claws unleashed, fur rippling down their arm.

She'd wrenched her knee when she hit the concrete and it was throbbing like a bitch. She wanted to lay down, she wanted to have her mates surround her, but she stood in the middle of the apartment not touching anything. The wound at her shoulder was no longer bleeding, she wasn't sure if she should be worried about that or not, but she was thankful it was no longer numb.

Char rushed in, no longer than thirty seconds later and as soon as she got a look at Savannah, she growled. Her cousin wore a pair of black leather pants, a white silk tank top and a thin black trench coat with the sleeves pushed up to her elbows. Savannah looked down at her dirty blazer and ripped skirt, she had to look a mess. Her face was throbbing, and her arms burned from the scratches and scrapes she had. Char didn't rush her, instead she held up her hands and approached slowly.

"Is there a healer coming?" She asked Savannah's mates.

Derrick nodded.

"Alright, Vanna, I need to get their scent, okay?" Charlotte kept her voice quiet, approaching as one would a dangerous, wounded animal.

Savannah nodded. "I didn't let anyone else touch me," she whispered. "His scent should be the only one on me."

Derrick and Carlos both snarled, growls rumbled around the room as the security team expressed their anger.

"Good girl." Charlotte whispered. "Show me where he's touched you."

She swept her hands down the front of body, "he laid on top of me." She whispered.

The growl Carlos released raised the hair on her neck. She knew her mate was going crazy. He struggled to reign in his cat, his emotions broadcasting loudly through their bond and down the prowl link, riling his enforcers more.

"He licked my face," she told Charlotte, tensing as the room went deadly quiet, throbbing rage filling the space.

"That's enough, Fela," Charlotte's voice was a deep growl as she fought her own panther. Claws exploded from her hands, fur sprouting along the exposed skin of her lower arms, before it receded. "Which side, Savi?"

She pointed at the left side of her face. Charlotte leaned in closer. Savannah fought to keep her body still, fought to keep her trembling to a minimum as Charlotte inhaled the skin of her cheek.

Char let out a low, furious snarl and she jerked, flinching at a sound she'd never heard her cousin make.

Carlos growled again.

Charlotte turned to her mates. "I have the scent, Felix. He won't get away."

Further surprising her, Char leaned over and nuzzled underneath Savannah's chin, submitting to her and it brought tears to Savi's eyes. She loved her cousin as a sister, and the respect she was showing made her heart swell.

"I'll find him for you, Vanna," Charlotte whispered.

A righteous anger overwhelmed Savannah making her body tremble harder. "When you do, bring him back here, I don't want him able to stand before any council. Make him hurt, Char."

Charlotte nuzzled her face, "I swear it, cousin." She nodded at Derrick and Carlos and turned, her coat billowing behind her as she left the room.

Carlos whistled and three of the enforcers in the room followed Charlotte out.

Savannah turned and faced her mates fully for the first time, and staggered at the anger on their faces. Their eyes were completely amber, the slit in the middle narrowing and widening as they battled their cats. She nodded and they both rushed her. Carlos growled and gathered her in his arms. The three of them stood together, their breaths mingling as they reassured each other.

"Leave." Carlos ordered.

His remaining enforcers jumped to obey him. Each of them stroked a hand across her head, reassuring her in their own way as they left. Her body trembled and once the elevator doors closed, her knees gave out. Carlos lifted her before she could fall.

"Take her, I'll make sure the healer gets here." Derrick kissed her lips softly before he too was gone.

Chapter 34

Carlos tightened his grip on her, burying his head in her hair. "Never scare me like that again."

He took her mouth in an aggressive kiss that should have her scared but instead, heat rushed through her body and the need for her mate overrode everything. In the back of her mind she was sure it was Carlos and Derrick's need flooding their link, and making her desperate to have him, but she didn't care.

She needed the reassurance just as much as he did. He carried her to their bedroom, his mouth over the wound on her shoulder licking at it. With every lick of his tongue a spiral of heat warmed her until, slowly the numbness disappeared. A knock on the door brought the healer.

Carlos sat on the edge of the bed with her in his lap. The healer looked her over, touching the smaller scratches and wounds, infusing his power. She felt the warmth of his magic as he healed the deep claw marks on her shoulder.

"Enough," she gasped.

Her mates' need flooded their connection and the heat from the healer added to the maelstrom going on in her body. Carlos nodded the healer from the room.

"What's wrong, *amor*?"

"Need," she choked out, her back arching as the healing magic combined with the magic from her mates.

He lifted her, and she struggled to wrap her legs around his waist. He released his claws, tearing her skirt into strips. He backed her into a wall, and though he moved fast, he was gentle. Her back barely touched the wall. He let her up for air only to lean down and suck the skin of her neck into his mouth. He worried that spot, raked his teeth over his mark already there and entered her in one hard stroke.

She gasped at how good it felt and threw her head back as ecstasy whipped through her blood. He pulled her mouth down and devoured her, his tongue mimicking the motion of his hips. He released her mouth and licked over her shoulder again. Soothing heat warmed her from the inside, burning through the wound on her shoulder. There was nothing more healing than sex magic. And with the way her mate did it, more so. She crashed over the edge with a hoarse cry, him right behind her. He gentled his hands, and murmured how much he loved her. Apologizing to her for taking her so hard.

She brushed his curly hair back from his face, the length of it longer than when she'd met him. She liked the way it softened his face. She traced the savage planes of his features. She loved him so much and let him know with her eyes. Carlos licked over the bruises on her face, the healing saliva on his tongue soothing the throbbing pains. He leaned over her shoulder again, licking at the claw marks made by the other shifter. They were closed, the healer's magic remarkable, another side effect of the Tribond.

He growled, his anger again moving down their link. Despite that, he ran a gentle hand over her hair.

"I was so worried." He murmured.

Derrick entered the room. He put his forehead against Carlos' and nuzzled him, offering Carlos comfort.

"Give me our baby." He held out his arms and exhausted, Savi happily cuddled into his chest.

Derrick was gentle as he carried her into their bathroom. He sat her on the vanity, next to the bathroom sink she'd claimed as hers, making him and Carlos share the other. She shuddered when the skin of her legs hit the cold marble. Snarls rumbled his chest unbidden as he thought about what their mate went through. It had taken everything in them not to rush out the door when Simon had alerted them. There were enforcers closer to her who could get there faster. He'd damn near had to hold the Felix down.

He kissed her lips, running his hands across her skin. He licked at the wounds on her face, though he could tell by Carlos' scent that he'd already attended to them. He moved down to the scratches all over her arms, illuminated in stark detail by the recessed lighting above them. Her exhaustion loomed through their connection, along with her residual fear and it ate him.

He scanned her body, but didn't see or feel any major injuries. The healer had more than likely taken care of them, but he needed to reassure his panther. He pulled the tattered clothes from her body, smiling as he unsnapped what was left of her skirt. He knew the impatience Carlos felt. It rode him now, urging him to mark their mate again. He nuzzled at her shoulder, wishing he could reach the nurturing mark on the back of her neck.

Marking her with his scent to calm the cat, he rubbed his cheek against the top of her head. His panther was going crazy, battering against his body urging for the same primal claiming Carlos had reasserted on their mate. He walked over to the bathtub intending to make her soak as per the healer's instructions.

She shook her head. "No bath, I want a shower."

He moved to the other side of the bathroom, over to the enclosed tile shower and started the water, testing it to make sure it was warm enough.

"Hot," she whispered. "I want it hot."

"Baby." He sighed. He went to her and lifted her from the sink.

"I can feel your cat. Take what you need, Beta." Her voice was slurred with exhaustion.

"You can barely stand, Savi, my cat will wait."

He cringed a bit at the thought. It would be a hard battle, but once he got her to lay down and rest he would go out back and let his cat run. That should settle them both. He guided her into the shower but she stumbled. He pulled her into his chest, entering the enclosed glass with her.

He hissed as the hot water pelted his back and plastered his shirt to him. Savi bit on his neck, her tongue tracing over it and Derrick realized he'd been set up. His mate lifted on her toes and pulled his mouth down for a kiss. A kiss that showed him that she needed his reassurance as much as he needed hers.

Her fingers made quick work of the button and zipper on his jeans, her impatient hands pushing down the wet denim. He separated from her mouth long enough to pull his sopping dress shirt from his body.

"I need you." her urgent whisper shot heat straight to his cock.

He lifted her, wrapping her legs around his waist and gently backed her into the tile. Her mewl of pleasure pulled at his control. His first slide into her made him hiss in pleasure, it was his favorite part. She wouldn't allow him to go slow. No, his mate rolled her hips, driving him deeper.

"Allow me control, Savi," he begged.

He grabbed her ass, intending to halt the motion of her hips, instead lifting her body and slamming it down on his cock. God, she felt amazing. Wet and pulsing around him, he was helpless. Her moans spurred him on. He tried once more to gentle his strokes. He pulled out of her, chuckling as she growled at him.

"Savage little thing aren't you," his voice was husky with lust.

Turning her around to face the tile, he thrust back into her. He kissed his mark, biting down, reclaiming his mate. His cat stretched in satisfaction, now that that primal need was taken care of. The red haze that descended when he found out his mate was hurt, cleared. He sighed in pleasure and turned her again, kissing away her complaints.

He gazed at Savi, beautiful with her head thrown back in lust and thanked the gods that she was safe. He slowed his strokes, deepening them until he felt the approaching orgasm tingling the base of his spine. She pulsed around his shaft, a sure sign that she was moments from it herself. He quickened his strokes again, swallowing her scream as they both went over the edge. Her body slumped.

"I love you," she murmured.

He brushed her hair back from her face and turned her into the warm water. She made only a token huff of protest as he pulled out of her and slid her down his body to her feet. Satiated, his cat was content. With gentle hands he washed her body, even her hair, getting rid of any foreign scents on her. He smiled about her hair. It now sprung around her head in a puffy halo. She was going to fuss about him washing away her blowout. In the couple months they'd been living together, he'd learned a lot about his mate's grooming habits, most importantly how seriously she took her hair.

He washed her arms, staring at her bruised knuckles. Her hands had been covered with blood when she arrived, not her own from the scent. He growled in approval, she had defended herself, the evidence of it was all over her body.

When he was done. He shut off the water. Careful of the now healing scrapes and scratches on her body, he toweled her off. He smiled as her weight on him got heavier as she gave in to fatigue. He sat her again on the vanity, wrapping a towel around his waist. He walked into the closet they had in the bathroom and pulled on a new pair of jeans and t-shirt for himself. He grabbed her favorite sleep shirt from her drawer. By the time he came back she was leaning against the wall. Her eyes were closed, her breathing deep and even. He pulled her giant sleep shirt over her head. He hated the ratty tee but he knew she put it on when she felt down, or sick.

Drying her hair would be out of the question. He rooted around underneath the sink for that cream he'd seen her use in her and Ella's hair. Finding it, he slathered a couple handfuls of the cookie smelling concoction into her hair, and called it done. He grabbed another towel from the bathroom pantry and wrapped it around her hair to keep the pillows from getting too wet.

He carried her into their bedroom, laying her down, pulling their blanket over her.

"Check on Simon, please." She murmured, settling deeper into the bed.

"I'll do that now, sweetheart." He kissed her forehead.

She turned on her side and he stared at her sleeping form a few moments, thanking every deity he knew that she was home safe. He leaned down, kissed her forehead and left her sleeping. One of her cousins hovered anxiously at the door, waiting to go in. Even though Savannah had already seen a healer, their grandparents wanted reassurance that Savi was fine, so they sent Samantha. He waved the female in and caught sight of Simon near their bedroom door standing, healing bruises coloring his face.

"How the hell are you still standing?" Derrick knew that the male had fought hard for his mate. "Did you get a healer to look you over?"

Simon nodded, his jaw flexing, anger keeping the enforcer on edge. His stance was stiff, his eyes hazy as he stared into space.

Derrick sighed. "You're supposed to be resting, aren't you?"

Simon shrugged. "She healed my ribs and my head. The rest will heal in a matter of hours. I wanted to check on the Fela." The enforcer's words were slightly slurred, and he swayed a moment.

Derrick grabbed the back of Simon's neck and nuzzled his cheek. "You did fine, Simon. She's alive and well."

He smelled Carlos' scent on the male and knew the Felix had probably already reassured Simon, but as Beta, Derrick let him know that he was not upset with him.

"They ambushed us." Simon's jaw clenched and rage danced in his eyes.

"Do you think I think otherwise? I have seen the two of you in the training room, I don't doubt that they left in a lot worse condition than when they arrived."

Simon nodded. "I gave my report to Felix."

"Fine." He gripped the male's shoulder. "Rest Simon, you know the Fela, she'll be up in a few hours getting into more trouble."

A small twitch on his face was the only acknowledgement Derrick got. He dragged a chair from the kid's room, into their bedroom and set it against the wall. He pointed until Simon dropped into it.

"You can see with your own eyes that she's okay and rest at the same time. I'm sending another enforcer in here to keep watch over you both until you're one hundred percent."

He held up his hand as Simon opened his mouth to argue.

"Do not move from this chair unless it's to go home and rest." Derrick left him to go find his other mate before he tore up the city looking for those bastards.

Chapter 35

He found him downstairs in his office pacing, snarls reverberating throughout the room. Their enforcers had steely eyes, each responding to the Felix's anger. Men and women both, lined against the wall, awaiting their Alpha's orders. The explosive fury their alpha felt was being pushed down the prowl link and every panther within it was probably feeling edgy and unsettled.

Derrick nodded his head towards the door and cleared the room. He needed to calm his co-mate down and relieve some of the tension in the prowl's link. He walked up to Carlos and stopped him with a hand on his chest.

"She's fine, Alpha."

He addressed him as such because it would be the only way to get to Carlos' cat while he was this agitated.

Carlos growled and grabbed the back of Derrick's neck. "Do not placate me, Beta. I want him dead!"

"As do I, Felix."

"But?"

"No buts. We have every right to our rage."

Their foreheads touched and held, their cats reaching for each other and calming the other down. With every breath they took together, the anger lightened. He saw Carlos fight to keep his cat under control. Felt his panther's touch against his own, the anger in the animal abating each time Derrick's cat reached out.

There was a knock on the door and before they could answer, another cousin rushed in. Naomi's face was streaked with tears. He'd only seen her in the short times he'd visited

Savi, so he didn't know her well. The last time he'd seen her, though, she didn't have this power that preceded her entrance into the room. He realized the last time he'd seen her was before they'd sealed their mating. Their grandparents' words about her coming into power after Savannah ran through his mind. He inhaled, wondering at the difference in her.

"They won't let me see her, is she okay?" Naomi touched Carlos arm, and a flare of power rippled down the prowl link.

He raised his brows, but Carlos lowered his. The Felix reached for the female, his eyes narrowed. She went into his arms and uncharacteristically Carlos brought her closer. Their foreheads touched and through his link with Carlos, he felt the Felix bring in the female. Soon, a huge pressure released on the prowl link and he braced himself on the desk. A sense of calm, and wellbeing flowed down the prowl link.

"What was that?" she whispered.

Carlos pulled his head back and kissed Naomi's forehead. "Welcome. Your power is amazing, but I wanted to be mad."

She smiled, through her tears and he reached on Carlos' desk and gave her a box of tissues.

"What was that?" She asked again.

"I've heard of Zeta powers but I'd never experienced it. I'm sorry, I should've asked your permission before I joined you to our prowl. But instinct overrode my manners."

She shook her head, "that's okay. I've been out of town, or I would've have come by to talk to you. Joelle…" She cleared her throat and shook her head.

"Who are you?" Carlos asked, guiding her to the chair in front of his desk.

"Oh, sorry," she held out her hand, "I'm Naomi, Savannah's cousin."

"Charlotte is your sister, right?" He asked.

"Yes, Savi called her and she called me and it took me forever to get from the airport and then when I went upstairs they wouldn't let me see her." She hiccupped.

Derrick nodded and pulled out his phone. He texted the enforcer he had on the door. He waved the phone. "Fixed it. She's sleeping now, but you can go up and see her, I'm sure you will feel better once you do. I didn't mean for him to keep family away, but with the Felix on edge as he was, I imagine he took the order a little more serious than normal."

"Thank you," Naomi breathed out and rushed to the door. She turned around, "Felix, can we speak later, once I've checked on Savi?"

"Of course." Carlos murmured.

He waited until Naomi left the room before going around his desk to sit. He leaned back in his chair and took a deep breath. He was stunned and working to process what had just happened. Most of it was instinct, and out of his control. Something about Naomi had called to him immediately, his power reacting differently than it did with his mate. He'd heard Savannah talking about Naomi, and talking to her cousin frequently on the phone, he hadn't met her until today.

Derrick looked at the door again before turning back to him. "That was…"

"We have a prowl Zeta. Can you believe it?"

Derrick sat in the chair Naomi vacated. "Zetas are only drawn to settled prowls, she's family, why wouldn't she have been in the prowl prior to us?"

"Remember Elder Jeremiah said Savannah had to come into her power first."

Derrick nodded.

Carlos growled and clapped his hands together. "I want this guy found."

His Beta sighed. "Has Charlotte left yet?

"With six enforcers. Her cousins are livid, and were ready to ride before I gave the order. I had to hold a good portion of them back. It wasn't pretty. " He wiped a tired hand over his face. "Let's hope your new training pays off this time. I don't know what I'd do if they came back empty handed."

"Maybe we should send the kids to the country. It's more isolated, easier to protect." Derrick suggested.

His panther protested immediately. "I don't want our family separated."

No way did he want their kids away from him when so much was going on. He'd been lulled by the months of silence and he blamed himself. He wouldn't say that they'd become lax, but he certainly hadn't really expected them to go after his mate. It was a declaration of war. One he planned to answer.

Where rage had previously danced along his nerve endings, calm settled. A Zeta. He still wanted to kill something, but his thoughts were no longer clouded with hate. Derrick watched him carefully, his Beta's mere presence calming his animal marginally. He knew until the bastard who touched his wife was in front of him, he still wouldn't be placated.

"Is she resting?" Carlos asked, wincing a little at how rough he was with their mate.

She'd accepted him, giving back as aggressive as he'd given her. There was nothing but love in her eyes when she cupped his cheek. To think, she used to worry she wasn't strong enough for them. He worshipped Savannah. She was perfect for him and someone would pay for touching her.

Derrick cut into his thoughts. "She's asleep in that ugly shirt she loves so much."

"I'll kill him," Carlos whispered. "If it's Yasim, he's dead."

Derrick stretched out his feet and crossed his ankles on Carlos' desktop. "Do I need to go over the problems that would bring to our prowl? Besides the shit time we'd have managing that much territory."

Carlos wiped a hand over his face cursing Derrick for making so much sense. Even as he said it, he knew killing his father was a bad idea. He would find another way to punish the bastard. One council approved, especially since the male who put his hands on their mate would not live to see the end of this day.

As though reading his mind, Derrick chuckled. "Yes, let's keep the broken laws to a minimum. It will give Theo and Brianne an easier time during council meetings."

His panther calmed a little more at his co-mate's laugh. His remaining anger simmering lower.

"Our mate did well today," Pride filled him.

"Of course she did. Brielle did an amazing job training her, and Simon's sparring prepared her for this very scenario."

Carlos sighed. "She won't accept more guards?"

Derrick grunted.

"Yeah I didn't think so."

He had maybe two days to keep her near him before she bucked his extra security measures. Hopefully he would have his cat's possessiveness under control by then.

***

Carlos hung up the phone with his mother with a sigh. Samella had called, panicked about the attacks. He'd purposely stalled in telling her, knowing how his mother was. But, his sisters had beat him to it. She was the last call, in a long line of calls he'd had to make as he waited to hear back about Savannah's attackers.

Someone had leaked word to the Panther council about the attack and they wanted reassurance that it would be handled within their parameters. He'd come dangerously close to tell them to go fuck themselves, but with Theo looking over his shoulder, he'd assured them that his prowl would, of course, handle it correctly.

He looked up as the door to his office slammed open. Charlotte strolled in, her white shirt dirty and ripped, her face and arms slightly bruised and scratched, but her expression, exultant.

"I've found them all, Felix."

Carlos glanced at the clock. It had only been two hours. Pride for his young enforcer bloomed. He growled and rounded his desk to stand in front of her. He rubbed his chin over the top of Charlotte's hair. He bent his head and held his forehead on hers, pushing his pride and reassurance to her.

She breathed deep and rubbed her head under his chin. She straightened, a smile covering her pretty face. "We put them all in separate rooms in the basement and left the enforcers you sent with me, to watch them."

"Great job, Charlotte." He turned her body and marched her from his office, eager to get to the basement. "Let's go see what they have to say."

His panther circled his body in anticipation as they rode the elevator to the basement. He texted Derrick on the way down. His Beta met them as the doors opened.

Carlos' eyes widened. "What, did you fly down the stairs?"

Derrick showed him his canines. "I'm ready." He grabbed the back of Charlotte's neck and rubbed his cheek against the top of her head. "Great job, Charlotte."

"Thank you, Beta."

"Which room has the one who touched our mate?" Carlos' voice was deep, his panther riding him close.

She pointed to the last room and they followed her to the door. She stood back allowing them to enter first. Carlos walked in, his power jacked and straining against his control. The three enforcers standing around the prisoner exposed their necks. He smiled, their immediate submission pleasing his cat.

Their prisoner was chained to a metal chair. Charlotte had made good on her promise to her cousin, the cat was seriously worked over. But then, Carlos had no doubt her cousin would want revenge for what happened to Savannah. One of the male's eyes was swollen shut, his lip busted, and healing bruises covered his face and neck. Though healing, a gouge on his cheek was still crusted over, which meant it was old enough to be from his mate.

Carlos growled in grim satisfaction.

The male spit blood on the floor, "I'm not saying shit until I see the council."

"Council." Carlos laughed. "As far as the council is concerned we're still searching for the people who attacked our mate, right Beta?"

Derrick crossed his arms over his chest. "I'll be properly distressed tomorrow when I let them know we haven't been able to find them. 'A whole twelve hours later and we have no clue as to who attacked our Fela.'"

The enforcers around the room growled at the reminder.

"Surely he's made it back to his own territory by now?" Carlos said casually. "Perhaps when we're done, we'll leave your body back on your land, maybe they'll think your Alpha punished you for your failure."

"No, our scent would be all over him," Derrick said.

"Good point." Carlos rubbed his chin. "We'll just burn the remains. What do you think, Charlotte, will that get rid of the scent?"

"It would indeed, Felix. And if it doesn't, my granddaddies taught us a few ways to dispose of a body."

"Excellent," he turned to one of his enforcers. "Go burn the bodies of the others. Not to ash, just enough to burn off our scent and drop them at the edge of our border."

The male in the chair squirmed, looking uncomfortable for the first time as one of the enforcers left the room to seemingly do his bidding.

"My Alpha will strike back." The male threatened.

Carlos lifted his lip, his canines dropping. "Will he? Good, we're looking forward to it."

Some of the cockiness leeched from the male's eyes. "You're a new prowl, no match for us."

"And yet, here you and your friends are, caught within a few hours of attacking our mate. And how did that go by the way?" Derrick asked.

Carlos leaned over him, his voice lowering, "if three of you can't handle one alpha female and her guard, why the fuck do you think we'd be scared of anyone in your prowl?"

The snarls around the room showed the pride in their Fela. That pride traveled down the prowl link, gaining strength as it flowed down the hierarchy. The door opened and another alpha power entered. He didn't bother pretending to be surprised. He knew the males would not sit at home idly.

"I see we're a little late to the party." Harper said casually, posting up against the wall at the door.

Jeremiah stepped closer to the cat. "I see tales of my granddaughters' handiwork were not exaggerated."

Carlos smiled.

"The old alpha lives, and you think you're a match for our Felix. What kind of pussy leaves the old Felix to live?" The male taunted.

Carlos and Jeremiah both laughed.

"Seems we overestimated their intellect, Felix." Jeremiah said shaking his head. "Have you figured out how to remove our scent when we're done?"

"Just discussing that in fact. Charlotte said you had some interesting techniques," Carlos said casually.

"We do indeed." Jeremiah pushed his hands into the pocket of his worn jeans. "On your mark, Felix."

The panther's eyes widened, true fear coloring his scent for the first time. Carlos figured he thought they'd been bluffing. He fully planned for the cat to be dead before the night ended. He would send a message to his father or anyone coming up behind him. No one would fuck with their prowl and live to tell about it.

Chapter 36

Three hours.

Three hours they'd questioned the male and still his story hadn't changed. Someone in their prowl was selling out their secrets. They'd skirted the thin line between torture and interrogation, but Derrick wanted to know who was attacking their prowl, and he'd reached the point where he didn't care how they got the information.

Every time he closed his eyes, he saw Savannah's bloodied clothes. And every time he inhaled the male's scent, knowing it had covered their mate when she got home, fury blinded him. So, yeah, fuck that guy. Whatever he needed to do to get the information, Derrick would do.

They'd cleared the enforcers out an hour ago, and now sent them back in to keep watch over the male until they could question him again. Stopping Carlos from killing him had been a near thing a few times during the questioning. The Alpha's panther wouldn't have been satisfied with anything less than the male's death.

His panther agreed wholeheartedly.

But, they still needed information from him. Carlos walked from the room, stunned. They had been shocked to find out that it wasn't Yasim attacking their prowl. The Felix who had sent the men, had chosen well. Nothing had persuaded the male to give up the name of his Alpha. While they didn't know who it was, they did know who it wasn't. The whole time he'd been prepared to kill Carlos' father for coming after their mate and turned out it wasn't Yasim at all.

"Do you believe him about having traitors in the prowl?" he asked.

Carlos frowned as he considered the question. Derrick had to admire how the Felix pulled the anger back from the prowl link. Having a Zeta seemed to already be working.

"He has to, no way had they got information on our safe houses without someone inside."

"He still wouldn't give any information on his Alpha, he was almost taunting us." Harper commented.

"Give him a few more hours under our care and I don't doubt we'll get answers." Derrick promised. He would make sure of it.

"He smelled familiar to me." Jeremiah said softly.

"In what way?" Carlos asked.

Jeremiah looked back towards the door. "Family."

They all frowned in surprise.

"He smells like family?" Harper asked sharply.

Jeremiah shook his head. "Not him per se, but he's been around our family long enough to carry some of the scent. Perhaps his alpha."

"What do you want to do about the traitors?" Derrick asked Carlos.

"Put the old prowl enforcers on it."

Derrick reared back in surprise.

Carlos hummed. "They know the old prowl better than we do, and they will be more objective about the panthers we've brought here."

"It's not a bad plan. If what Elder Jeremiah says is true, they'd also recognize the familial scent." Derrick conceded. "What do you want me to do with the others?"

"Take them before the council. Once their alpha gets word that they are in council custody, perhaps he or she will wonder about this one." Carlos answered.

"So you believe him when he says it's not Yasim?"

"Yes. No way would Yasim have enough influence with this prowl to have spies. We'll break him eventually and get his alpha's name." Carlos growled.

"And then?"

"Then as I bluffed earlier, we'll drop his body off to the south, directly off our land. Some where they won't miss it. It will serve as a warning. We're willing to play by the rules, up to a certain point."

Derrick growled, loving the plan. "Done." He would take a break, and allow the prisoner's injuries to heal just enough before he began another round of questioning.

***

The house was quiet by the time Carlos made it upstairs. He'd looked in on the kids before taking a shower and washing the stench of what he'd done off his body. He now sat in his home office, waiting on the call that everything had been completed. They'd finally gotten a name. Now all they had to do was find them. He'd been grateful for Jeremiah's guidance. The old Felix' presence had calmed him and lent him strength. There had been no judgements or even advice, just his strong, quiet presence.

He sat up in his chair as the scent of his mate wafted into the room. He turned to greet her, his heart lifting at her presence. She looked rested, the bruises along her face, faded, the purplish hue nearly indiscernible. She'd braided her hair into a braid that went around the crown of her head, making her look years younger than she was. She wore a nightgown, the silky fabric flowing around her body.

He inclined his head and she took measured steps around his desk, sliding into his lap. He breathed in her scent, hugging her tight.

"How are you feeling?"

She burrowed into his neck. "Sore, but better."

He withheld his growl. She lifted her head and kissed him, her tongue licking at his lips gently. He parted his lips and Savannah delved her tongue in his mouth, her kiss ravenous and eager. He adjusted her, moving her body so she straddled his lap and chair. Much better. He held her head in place while he plundered her mouth.

She pulled back from their kiss and put her forehead against his while she caught her breath.

She sighed after a moment of silence. "Has he been found?"

He studied her face, unsure how much to tell her. "He has."

Her eyes lit, anger washing over her face. "What's being done to him?"

He stayed quiet, rubbing his hand down her back.

"Tortured?"

He said nothing, watching her eyes go through emotions ranging from her anger, a little fear and trepidation.

"Yes." He finally answered.

A satisfied gleam entered her eyes. "What will the council say?"

"He will not see the council."

"How will you avoid him going to the council?"

He weighed his next words.

"I can take it, my love." She cupped his cheeks. "I want… no, I need to know."

"He's not in a position to tell anyone, anything, much less the council."

She sucked in a breath. "You mean…"she turned her head and looked away.

He waited her out.

Her heartbeat raced and then settled. "That's that then. What about the others?"

"We're turning them over to the council for questioning, of course, we were unable to find the last coward."

She hummed. "And they bought it?"

"It should take more than that for them to question us about something they can't prove."

"Unseemly for them to pick on a new prowl. Smart to use that while we have it at our advantage, we'll only be a new prowl for so long."

Deep respect for his mate blossomed. She understood much more than they gave her credit for. She fell into the role of alpha female like she was born to it...which, he supposed she was.

"Quite," he agreed.

"And your dad, what do you imagine his next move will be?"

He sighed, "That, my mate, has a bit of a twist to it."

"What happened?"

"Yasim isn't the one behind the attacks. A Felix named Alexander is."

"I don't know that name. So this prowl has been setting it up to look like Yasim?" She bunched her brows.

He shrugged. The name was all they'd been able to get from the enforcers they'd caught. No other information had been forthcoming. They had nothing regarding the alpha's motive for targeting their prowl. Nothing about the Seer's predictions were helping.

"Your grandfather said he smelled a familial connection."

Her eyes widened. "Family?"

He nodded.

"What the hell is going on?"

He sighed. "I'll find out before too long. I want guards on you all."

"I don't think he's desperate enough to go after our children."

"Neither do I, but just in case."

"Of course," she readily agreed. "Put as many guards on the children as you deem. I won't argue with that. Should we send them out to the old prowl land?"

"I'd rather not have the children too far from us." He grabbed her chin and brought her eyes to his. "And you, my love, will you allow extra security."

She sighed and darted her eyes away. She wrapped her arms around his neck and snuggled in tighter. "For a little while." Her voice was muffled, her reluctance clear. She leaned back from his neck. "I don't want to be the distraction that causes us to lose what you've worked hard for."

His heart swelled and he couldn't help but take her lips in a scorching kiss. "I love you," he whispered fiercely.

"Of that I have no doubts," her whisper brushed his lips.

Chapter 37

Savannah checked her watch for the third time and sighed. She was on edge, her power flaring out of her control. It had been that way all day. She looked around her old house and sighed. She and Jamie had made some good memories in the house. Perhaps nostalgia had her on edge and apprehensive.

She was supposed to be meeting her ex-husband here, but he was late, as usual. She'd tried to combine all her chores into one today, so she'd asked Greg to meet her at her house while she prepped it for the open house happening tomorrow. She would miss the place, but she loved their penthouse. She was still working on it, indecisive about some of the wall colors and furniture. She smiled wistfully. Her mates were probably sick and tired of her decorating, but she wanted it just right. They'd been in the penthouse for weeks and she was finally finished with the living room.

She sighed when the doorbell rang. Savi opened the door and Greg came in, kissing her on the cheek in greeting. Fastidious, his suit was custom made, and fit to his trim body, not a wrinkle to be found.

"Sorry, I'm late. I had some work."

"You always have work," she said, walking into the kitchen.

She handed him a mug of coffee.

He sipped quietly a moment before raising an eyebrow. "So, two mates."

Getting right to it then. "Yes, I'm in a Tribond."

"Like your grandparents?"

She nodded.

He hummed.

"What?"

"Nothing, maybe that's why we didn't work."

She snorted. "You cheated, that's why we didn't work."

He tilted his head and smiled sheepishly. "How will having two mates work?"

She raised an eyebrow. "In what way?"

"Well, does jealousy not play a part in a relationship like that?"

"Now you're in my business," she pointed her pen at him and ignored his question.

He shrugged, not at all embarrassed. "Explain to me the extra security. Jamie's explanation was vague at best." He put his mug down and clasped his hands together on the table.

She sighed and leaned back against the sink. "My mate is the new Felix, so our son will have security when he's out from under the prowl. There's also the matter of people being attacked in our prowl."

"How are you, speaking of that?"

She waved away his concern. "I'm fine."

He watched her quietly. "You're certainly different."

"What does that mean?"

His gaze seemed to catalogue her appearance. She fought the need to adjust the oversize sweater dress she wore under his scrutiny.

"I don't know. You're glowing and you seem…settled maybe, certainly more intimidating than you used to be."

"I've never been meek."

He snorted. "I definitely would never call you that, Vanna. But now you exude confidence, it's sexy."

"Right," She rolled her eyes and changed the subject. "So, I'll need all the details for when you travel."

"No problem."

She studied him. "You don't have an issue with this?"

He waved his hands around. "We may have had a rocky start with the co-parenting, but I trust you and don't judge me, but having a child full time is exhausting, as I'm sure you know. Being a weekend dad seems to work better for me. I'm okay with doing whatever it takes to make this work and keep Jamie safe."

She didn't say anything, couldn't say anything because whatever she said would be rude. Instead, she decided to move on to the next item on the list. She grabbed her notebook next to her. She had everything she and Greg needed to discuss with regards to their son.

She scratched off 'security talk'. "We need to talk about his panther."

"So he's definitely a shifter?"

"For sure."

He rubbed a hand across his short cropped hair. "What does that mean exactly?"

"He's strong, so he'll probably go through puberty sooner than he should. Outbursts, temper issues, restlessness is what Carlos tells me to expect."

"Carlos is the new Felix, your mate?"

She nodded.

"Well, I'll concede to his expertise on it."

She checked it off the list. "Christmas break is coming up. Do you want him for the whole week?"

He shook his head. "I can't take that week off. I'll take him an extra week in the summer and if your new mates don't mind, I'll do like I always do and show up Christmas morning."

Another check and a note about the extra week. "That will work. He'll need to go to camp this coming summer to prepare him for the shift."

"That's fine with me, email me the dates so I can plan our trip around it."

"Where are you guys going this year? Jamie said he had a blast in Greece."

"Portugal."

"Nice."

"Do you know, even on summer vacation, your son wakes up early?" He sighed. "Why does he wake up so early?"

She gave him a droll look. "What time did you wake up this morning?"

He chuckled. "Touché."

Her phone rang, breaking into their conversation. It was the principal of Jamie's school. She gripped the edge of the counter as the woman spoke, some of it not registering.

Greg came around the counter and put a hand on her shoulder. "What's wrong?"

She looked up at him, dazed, her lips numb as she tried to push out the words.

"Someone took Jamie from the school."

***

Carlos stood next to the truck and took a deep breath. His hands shook as he wiped over his face. He couldn't enter the school in his current state. His mate and sister both needed him calm. Derrick came around the front of the truck and touched his forehead to Carlos'.

"Reign it in, Alpha. We'll get them back." Derrick whispered.

Carlos cleared his throat and wrestled back his panther. "Any luck finding the prowl?"

"None yet. You think they're behind this?" Derrick pulled back, his own battle waging with his panther.

"Who else but them?" He sighed. "Let's go."

They marched to the school, four enforcers behind them. Theo was waiting in the front office for them when they arrived. His brother-in-law looked a lot more disheveled than he normally did. His tie was loose at his throat, and his hair was sticking up in places where he'd pulled at it. Theo spoke with the front desk clerk and cleared them to go through to the principal's office. His mate was in the small office, her and his sister Laura embraced, tears dried on their face.

He pulled them both to their feet and him and Derrick enveloped them, surrounding them with their power. The women shuddered, their fear riling his panther. Not only was his son missing, but also his nephew. He was furious, a helpless frustration burning his chest.

"We'll get them back, I swear it." He promised them.

The principal cleared her throat. Carlos spared her a glance, long enough to note her feline features, but she wasn't a panther.

"I have video queued up for you, Felix Ayala." She told him.

He nodded and released his sister and mate.

"They were on the playground with their class when four panthers climbed over the wall and snatched them." The principal explained.

"The teacher?" Derrick asked.

She sighed. And nodded to a person behind them. A meek woman entered the office, her fear not helping the situation. She explained to them in a quiet voice what happened. Derrick growled which caused her to freeze, her eyes wide.

"This school was supposed to be safe for shifters. You're saying people can just scale the wall and help themselves?" A male asked in a low, lethal voice.

Carlos turned his attention to the man, his features the adult version of Jamie's. So that was Greg. Savannah put an arm on the male's shoulder and Carlos clenched his hands to keep from reacting. Greg was Jamie's father, he had to remember he would be as concerned as the rest of them.

"Nothing like this has ever happened here before. There is a treaty in place. Children from all packs and prowls go here, no one is supposed to violate the sanctity of that." The principal hastily explained.

Greg stood and walked from the office. Savannah went after him.

"Let's see the surveillance, please." Carlos wanted to be out looking for his son, he didn't want to be in this cramped office.

"Of course."

They all turned to the monitor on the wall. The picture was crystal clear, indicating that the surveillance system in place was top notch. They watched as the children played. The principal fast-forwarded until the moment two panthers, in animal form, jumped across the high brick wall surrounding the yard. Kids scattered, as two others came over the fence behind them. The four of them headed straight for Jamie. They shifted into human form and made to grab him. Jamie fought, his nephew Ross joining in to help. Both boys were eventually overwhelmed and hauled over the intruder's shoulders.

The teacher was trampled by students running to her for help. She didn't even have a chance to help the boys. Carlos cursed.

"Thank you. I want my daughter, now." He ordered the principal.

Derrick turned to Theo. "Get Yasmeen here, I want her kids out as well until we catch these bastards. Matter of fact, I don't want any of the prowl kids here while this is going on."

The principle nodded and Theo pulled out his phone.

"Let's go." He said to Derrick and left the office.

Savannah was in the hall, calming down Greg. He held out his hand and she took it immediately.

They waited in silence until his daughter's curly ponytail came swinging down the hall. Relief weakened his knees and he dropped to the floor to catch Ella as she ran to him.

"Papa, are Jamie and I leaving early?" Her face was bright with expectation.

Savannah turned her back, and Derrick was there to comfort her. Ella looked behind him and her smile fell.

"We had a lock-down drill earlier today, did something really happen?" She whispered. The light left her eyes.

Savannah rushed to her and dropped to her knees. "Everything is fine, sweetheart. Jamie is away for now, but he'll be home soon."

"Did someone take him, papa?" Ella's lip trembled.

Carlos lifted her into his arms. "Let's go home, bunny. Jamie will be safe, I promise you."

He grabbed Savannah's hand and walked towards the exit.

"Greg, we can plan at the house." Savannah waved for Jamie's father to follow them.

"We need to call the police." Greg insisted.

"No." Savannah barked. "I'm not waiting on the police. My mates will find them faster."

His panther preened under her praise. "She's right. We'll coordinate from the prowl house."

Greg nodded and followed them out.

Just outside of the school doors, Carlos passed Ella to Simon and the enforcer took her swiftly to their truck. Carlos pulled his mate aside and studied her face.

"How we doing, Savi?" He asked quietly.

"I want my baby back, Carlos."

The tears in her voice shredded through him. He kissed her forehead and pulled her into a hug. One he needed more than she did.

He whistled and his enforcers fell in line behind them. They sped to the prowl building, him on the phone the whole time while Derrick drove. He planned to have their son back before the day ended.

Chapter 38

Her head was pounding. Fear, anger and helplessness swirled in her belly until she was nauseous. Her son had only been missing for two hours and yet it felt like a year had passed. She sat, clutching her sister in law, watching all the activity around them. Laura hadn't said a word since they'd arrived at the school. She well understood the woman's shock.

"They'll find them, I know it." Laura whispered.

Savannah didn't answer, the reassurance seemed more for Laura than for her. She rubbed Laura's back. Carlos was barking orders in the phone. He had been since they left the school. People were coming in and out of the penthouse and she felt like she should be doing something to help, she just didn't know what…so she stared into nothing. Ella was currently with her Aunt Yasmeen downstairs and she had nothing to do.

She took a deep breath and fought to shake off some of the fear currently drowning her. She was first and foremost a Watson. And Watsons were nothing if not stubborn. She would not freeze while her son was out there with God knows who. She did what she normally did when she needed help. She called her cousins. Charlotte answered on the first ring.

"We're almost there, Savi. I just heard."

A shudder of relief shook her body. "Thank you." She hung up and stood.

She walked over to her mate. She pulled the phone from him. "Charlotte is the only one of your enforcers who's gotten close to finding this prowl. She's on her way."

Carlos watched, or rather to say his panther did. It stared from her mate's eyes, watchful, ready for vengeance. She rubbed her head under his chin and a rumble shook his chest.

The elevator dinged and her grandparents marched into their living room.

"What's this I hear about Antoinette?" Jeremiah demanded.

Her heart clenched, and her hands trembled as she stepped back from her mate. "What's he talking about?"

Carlos rubbed a hand down his face. "I was going to tell you."

"Well tell me now!" She took another step back.

Derrick came up behind her and rested his hands on her shoulders. She shook off his touch.

"Savi, we literally just found out last night." Carlos told.

"So it's true then. Antoinette is behind the attacks on our prowl?" Jeremiah asked.

"No." She gasped.

Her aunt's prophecies spiraled through her mind. Every prediction about her costing the prowl, playing in detail. She was the cause of this. Because she was stubborn, her son had been taken. She should've listened, heeded the warnings.

But temptation had been too much.

"Don't, Savi." Derrick reached for her.

She back away. "It's my fault."

"No, that's not…" Carlos growled as his phone rang.

The elevator dinged again, this time Charlotte and Naomi came in. She looked at her cousins and shook her head.

"It's still going to come true." She whispered.

Naomi rushed to her side and enfolded her. Tears escaped, streaming down her face as the consequences of her actions flooded her.

"He's gone and everything that bitch said is going to come true." She sobbed onto Naomi's shoulder.

Naomi said nothing, simply guided her upstairs and into the bedroom she shared with her mates. She stopped at the door. Their combined scents dominated her senses, something she'd taken comfort in just that morning before she left. Now? Now it was a slap in the face, a reminder of what she'd chosen over her son's safety. Naomi pushed her further inside before shutting the door, allowing them privacy.

"Nothing will happen to Jamie, Savi. They won't let it." Naomi brushed a hand over her hair.

"It doesn't matter, because when this is all done, I will lose them." Her knees weakened and she buckled.

Naomi caught her. She always did, and always had. When there was no one, there was always Naomi and Charlotte. A wave of calming energy entered her body and she shuddered under its power. She looked up at her cousin with wide eyes.

"Is that you?"

Naomi nodded.

"It's over, Nay."

"You would give them up?" Naomi whispered.

"I'll do anything to keep Jamie safe."

"She wins if you give up, Savi."

"She has my son, she's won already. Do you think the prowl will want me as Fela with this threat hanging over their children?" She turned her back on her cousin.

"Then end the threat." Naomi clenched her fist. "Find her and end her."

Rage suffused her, her power filling the room. Naomi was right in at least that. She would find Antoinette and she would end her. But if one part of her prophecy came true, could she risk staying Fela if the rest was a possibility?

She wiped the tears from her face. She would think about that only after she got her son back safely. She had to push everything else aside. She went into the bathroom and washed her face. Naomi gave her a critical once over when she came out.

"I'm ready."

Naomi nodded and they went back into the living room. Charlotte was standing over the kitchen table with her grandfathers and mates hovering over a tablet. She walked closer. Derrick pulled her into his side with one arm and kissed the top of her head.

"So I found them here in this area. It's just a few miles off our territory and as far as I know, no one owns that territory." Charlotte used her fingers to zoom in on the tablet.

"Uh-uh, someone does own that territory. It's a small prowl, an older one, they met with grandfather years ago." Brielle corrected.

"There were no scent markers on that land, and we went in pretty far to get them. They were holed up on an abandoned farm." Charlotte told them.

Carlos looked to Brianne. "Did you try and contact the alpha from that area when we were meeting with the other prowls?"

Brianne nodded. "Charlotte's right. No one was on that territory."

Brielle hummed and studied it more. "You think they moved?"

"Or were wiped out." Carlos said grimly.

"Why take the land and not mark it?" Derrick puzzled.

"That close to our land, they knew we'd recognize the scent." Jeremiah sighed.

Savannah stiffened at his side and his panther went alert. He pulled her closer and rubbed his chin in her hair, hoping to calm the riotous feelings flooding their mating bond. He couldn't decipher the different emotions, not with Carlos' anger so dominant. He was worried for Jamie and Ian both, but stayed calm and fought to keep some semblance of control over his emotions. Last thing he wanted was to add to Savannah's stress.

He wanted to pause, and pull her aside and check in with her. Something was off. He knew them keeping Antoinette's involvement a secret from her was a risk. His gaze went back to the map on the kitchen table. It was a tiny territory, was the prowl that inhabited wiped out as a part of someone's plot against them? It brought home the reason he'd wanted to build such a big prowl. The smaller ones were always at the mercy of territorial disputes.

"Do you think we should start at that farm and track the scent from there?" Carlos asked, cutting into his musings.

"It's what I would do, Felix. It's the last place we found them and they were holed up there. So I would bet it's one of their safe houses." Charlotte straightened and put her hands on her hips.

Carlos looked up at him with a raised eyebrow. "We could send Charlotte and another enforcer ahead of us, go in stealth."

"Are you willing to take the risk, Charlotte?" He turned to the young enforcer.

He pushed aside his feelings to get into Beta mode. It was the only thing he could do to keep his fear and the weight of his memories from crushing his mates in the mating bond. He needed his focus on the cubs and getting them back safely. He rolled his shoulders as he waited on Charlotte's answer.

"Yes."

"I'll go with her." Brielle announced.

"Call us as soon as you find them. We'll plan our attack once we know where they are." Carlos closed the tablet.

"We're going full attack?" Brianne asked.

Derrick's panther rumbled, his chest vibrating. "Can you handle the fall out we'll get from it?"

Brianne nodded. "Fuck the council."

Chapter 39

Dusk was steadily darkening the day, making everyone in the penthouse more anxious as each minute went by. His mate whimpered and paced back to the window. She'd steadily withdrew into herself using no more than one or two words to answer his questions. He was worried about the missing cubs, yes, but Savannah's silence scared him on a whole different level.

An hour ago, Simon had come in and told them that he'd dug into Ryan's past and found a tentative familial connection to a prowl in the area. A small prowl, one that even Jeremiah had a hard time placing. They'd sent another wave of enforcers there and re-routed Charlotte and Brielle. He gave Charlotte credit though, because she was only a few miles away, having traced the scent damn near to the location.

Carlos' phone rang and vibrated across the dining room table. He picked it up and everyone held their breath.

"We found them, Alpha." Charlotte's voice was barely a whisper.

Carlos looked at him with grim satisfaction. "What do we have?"

Charlotte went through her report, giving them coordinates to where she and Brielle waited and watched the small prowl.

"Any sign of the boys, Char?" Savannah asked.

"I haven't seen them with my eyes, Savi, but there are six enforcers guarding this house, and that's a lot considering the size of their prowl." Charlotte answered.

Savannah covered her mouth and turned her back to them. Carlos handed him the phone and went to soothe their mate. He had Charlotte walk them through how she approached the land. He would direct the enforcers he brought with him to follow the same path. It took them only twenty minutes to coordinate. He hung up with her and called the enforcers closer.

He and Simon pulled together a plan of attack, gearing up as they spoke. They were getting ready to leave when he noticed his mate walking with them. Carlos put a hand on her shoulder.

"I'm going." She lifted her chin.

"Savi, it could be dangerous." Derrick pleaded.

Laura walked over and put her hands on Savannah's shoulders. "I'm going with the Fela."

Theo growled, but said nothing.

Carlos sighed. "You'll follow instructions."

Both women nodded. He stared at his co-mate. Carlos shrugged and he swallowed his own growl. It would take more time to argue so he said nothing, simply following the Alpha to the elevator. He wanted their son back and splitting his attention was dangerous, but, he'd trust his mate. She wouldn't do anything to endanger herself, or Jamie. They took fifteen enforcers with them. According to Charlotte, the kidnappers only had twenty members in the whole prowl. What made them think they could take on a prowl the size of theirs? He didn't care, they would pay for the mistake. What would happen to the small prowl, to the innocent members? He squashed some guilt at the thought.

They piled into two vans, tense silence blanketing the vehicle while they rode. Soon they pulled off the road, into a dark forest. They killed the lights the moment the left the highway, slowing to a stop once the forest became too dense. He spotted the marker Brielle said she used to signal where they'd entered the prowl's territory.

They filed out of the car and Carlos stood, holding his hand up for silence. He gave a quiet whistle that was returned a moment before Brielle came out of the shadows.

She inclined her head and the enforcers in her unit filed in formation. Carlos led one flank while Derrick led a third one. Savannah looked back at him put her hand over her heart. Derrick nodded, understanding her message. He prayed Carlos kept their mate safe, but put it out of his head as he lead his team towards the east to approach the property from another direction.

Carlos kept a tight grip on his panther, his footsteps silent through the brush as he let him out just enough to move unseen through the forest. His mate was surprisingly quiet at his back and he could only be thankful. She followed him closely, not saying a word as they moved through the forest approaching the house where they were holding their cubs. A lake sat to the west side of the property where the house faced. The exterior of the house was worn, a mix of grime and algae covering most of the windows. The back door and a garage on the north side of the house were potential escape paths, Carlos signaled for half of his team to approach cautiously.

The south east edge of the property was fenced off with a hedge wall along the neighboring land that Brielle's unit was using it for covering as they awaited Carlos' signal. Derrick's power pushed through the bond link indicating that all the units were in place and ready to move.

He held up his fist and everyone behind him paused. He pointed the enforcers into their respective positions and they melted into the shadows, moving into place. He pointed to the ground and his mate nodded, kneeling next to him.

Her fear was moving down their mating bond, but no trace of it showed on her face or in her manner. They watched quietly as the other prowl's enforcers circled the house, and some the yard. Two lean young men walked with weapons out, monitoring the clearing around them. They were alert, he had to give them that. They didn't know what was coming, and that would prove a fatal mistake for them. He heard two short whistles and he answered back. As one, his prowl moved out of the woods and attacked. He ached to join the fight, but no way was he leaving his mate unprotected.

As synchronized units, the teams moved to block the obvious escape paths as they approached the house. Brielle's team stalked in silently behind the kidnapper's patrol group, just passing the covered area into the moonlight of the clearing. Derrick's anxiety ramped slightly as the sounds of a scuffle off to the left of them sounded.

Quick footsteps sounded behind him and before he could tell his mate to duck she was rolling out of the way. A panther jumped at him, claws out, raking at the spot where Carlos' head had only been moments before. Swiftly rolling away from Savannah and his attacker, he reached into his boot strap and pulled a heavy blade, crouching into a ball as the attacking panther landed and turned to continue its assault. The massive cat reared back and pounced. This time its eyes on Savannah, reaching to slash at her. Carlos standing ready, grabbed it by the throat mid-flight, fury strengthening him as he turned the cat mid-air and slammed it to the ground. He stomped, but the cat rolled out of the way, coming back up to its feet. He dove at Carlos again, his mouth open. Carlos ducked, and the panther sailed over him. He turned and grabbed the back of its scruff and wrestled with the panther for long moments as it tried to escape. He tightened his grip and twisted, breaking the panther's neck, tossing it to the side.

"I have what you came for, Alpha." A voice called out into the now silent night.

Savannah gasped. "No."

Carlos looked away from the dead panther and saw why Savannah had frozen in fear. The small prowl's Alpha had both cubs standing next to him, his claws at their throats. She moved to rush forward and he caught her around the waist.

"Not yet, baby. Just a moment, let our enforcers get in place."

She was trembling, her sobs quiet, but still shaking her body. Simon sidled up behind them, taking his place as Savi's bodyguard and Carlos stepped from his mate.

"I got this." He held her eyes until she nodded.

He stepped from the forest into the yard. "You have my attention, Alexander, though it may not bring you what you've been looking for."

If the male was surprised Carlos knew his name, he didn't show it. "I want the Watson prowl, and all the land that comes with it. It's rightfully mine and I will take it back, as it was taken from my family."

The Alpha was arrogant, much more than he should've been seeing as how half his prowl was dead on the ground around them. Carlos' eyes flickered to the rooftop behind Alexander, relaxing as his Beta took up position.

"Cowardly and dumb. How long did you think you'd be able to hold my prowl?" Carlos kept his eye on the Alpha's claws so close to Jamie and Ross' neck.

He thought back to Joelle's prophecy, and the doubt he'd had. Everything that they'd attributed to Yasim, could've applied to Alexander. In every way, what she had predicted had come true. Who then, was feeding into his paranoia?

"Alexander will have no problem holding Tampa with my guidance." A woman walked from the house.

He knew who she was immediately. Her scent and features put her in the Watson family. Ryan walked out behind her, his head down in a submissive position.

"No." Savannah shouted and rushed from the woods, Simon on her heels.

He held in his growl. "Antoinette, I presume?"

She nodded gleefully. "I'm sorry you won't get to enjoy your territory. But don't worry. Ryan here has kept us apprised of everything happening. Our takeover will be seamless."

Carlos narrowed his eyes on the traitor. He debated the male's life as he stood at Antoinette's side with his head down. Could he allow Ryan to live, would it set a bad example?

"I'm curious, Ryan. What did they promise you that would make you give up the safety of our prowl?" Carlos' voice was a deep rumble as his panther struggled to end the male where he stood.

"Alexander promised to mate with my sister and make her Alpha female." Ryan said softly. He was a submissive, and always had been.

It didn't surprise Carlos that the male bargained on behalf of his sisters. But…

"Did they know?"

Ryan raised his head, regret, fear swirling in his eyes. "I wanted to prove to them that I could provide."

Carlos would've felt bad for him, if Ryan's terrible decisions didn't put his cub's life in the hand of a cowardly Alpha. Carlos turned his gaze to his stepson and nephew, using the prowl link to push reassurance to them. Both boys relaxed, their tear stained faces, clearing. Suddenly a series of whistles came from the darkness around the home. He kept the boys trapped in his gaze to keep their panic down. Two of Alexander's enforcers were pushed into the moonlight, landing in a thud, unconscious. Brielle and her team, in cat form, stalked behind them from the trees, slinking into view.

More of Carlos' enforcers came out of the brush, in both human and panther form, the power of their prowl filling the clearing. Antoinette's face registered the change of tide and she inched away.

Carlos gave a small nod and Derrick sprang from the top of the house, landing on Alexander's back. The force of it pushed the kids forward. Carlos raced and grabbed them, before they hit the ground, passing them back to his mate. Derrick's panther shredded Alexander's back. Alexander growled and shifted, angling his body around. Derrick's panther was relentless, he didn't pause in his assault. Alexander gave a gurgling cry a moment later, falling to the ground. Derrick stood behind his lifeless body, his claws bloody from slitting the Alpha's throat.

Carlos flickered a glance at the fallen alpha, then back to Antoinette. "You were saying?"

Her face registered shock right before two of his enforcers forced her to the ground. He stooped while they forced her face into the grass.

"I would love to kill you, but I'm new here and have already broken enough rules this evening. So, here's what's going to happen. We're going to deliver you to the council for punishment."

Antoinette struggled, but the enforcers held her down. Fear finally settling on her face, she struggled to look as a final bundle of her protectors hit the ground behind her, coming out the front door of the house. Theo sauntered out of the doorway, anger lighting his eyes, signs of his battle all over his bloodied and torn clothes. Carlos smiled, knowing no further threats would be coming out after his brother-in-law.

***

Savi did the hardest thing she'd had to do ever. She gave her son over to her cousin to keep safe. She was going back. She was going to kill her aunt. The moment she saw the glee with which her aunt made her announcement while that bastard's hands were around son's neck, she'd decided.

She marched back to the yard, her eyes focused on Antoinette. Her aunt looked up as she entered the clearing, calculation lighting her eyes.

"Oh you've ascended to alpha female. How selfish. You'll take your whole prowl down and for what?" Her aunt spat in her direction.

"I know about your lies, you don't even have power."

"But I collect powerful things, little girl. If you think taking me to see the council will avert your fate, you're even stupider than I thought."

"You don't know what you're talking about."

"I know what I know, and I know a latent alpha female will breed only weaklings."

"That's enough, take her out of here." Carlos ordered.

"No, let her go." Savannah whispered. She was going to kill her. She couldn't allow Antoinette to hang over their heads the rest of her life.

Antoinette gave an evil smirk, "so sure of herself. You think you can take me." She laughed.

"I'll accept nothing less than your death." Savannah promised.

Carlos nodded, and Derrick rushed to her. "You don't need to do this, Savannah."

Carlos grabbed Derrick's arm and pulled him to the side. "I think she does."

Savannah reached over to Charlotte and pulled her cousin's hunting knife out. "Let her go."

Antoinette scoffed. "Your funeral."

Her aunt immediately shifted, her fur and claws flowing quicksilver over her body. Age had not slowed her, Antoinette's panther was strong and agile as she moved.

She leapt and Savannah braced for her impact. She did what Brielle had taught her, holding her knife out right where Antoinette's throat would be. Her angle was off and she was slammed into the ground by Antoinette's heavy panther. Her shoulder hit the ground and she lost hold of the knife. Anger left no room for panic or fear. She put her feet to her aunt's chest just as Antoinette snapped her jaws an inch from her face. Heart thumping, Savannah used her legs to keep the animal off her. She screamed when her aunt's claws found its mark, slicing into her stomach. At the same time her fingers clutched the knife. She brought it up and buried it in Antoinette's neck.

Antoinette struggled, her claws gouging across Savannah's stomach again before she could roll from beneath her. She left the knife imbedded in her throat.

Antoinette shifted, her eyes wide in surprise.

Savannah leaned over her, clutching her stomach. "Oh, you thought I would fight fair?" She pulled the knife from Antoinette's throat and tossed it to the ground. "You'll never hurt my family again."

She walked back to her mates, wincing with every step. "I'm ready to go."

Carlos growled, and nuzzled under her chin. Derrick did the same and the enforcers with them took turns nuzzling against their Fela.

Derrick watched with pride, his panther deeply satisfied with its mate. He blew out three short whistles and his enforcers started cleaning up the area. The old pride members led the charge, showing the city panthers how they handled business in the south. If there was anything he'd learned about pulling together this blended prowl, was how to use the best qualities from each of them. They left the remaining panthers in Alexander's prowl, tied together. Their alpha was dead, along with any enforcers who'd stood in their way in the quest to get to Antoinette. He trusted his enforcers to take care of it all.

They marched back to the vans, quickly, no need for stealth this time. First, he pulled his mate aside.

"How bad is it?" He whispered.

"I'll definitely need to see a healer." She grimaced.

He darted an eye to enforcers around them. Carlos noticed and sent them ahead. Derrick kneeled at her side and pulled up her ripped shirt. He hissed, but swallowed his worry. His panther surged forward, power filling him, her power rising to meet it. He sighed in relief knowing that power would help him heal his mate. He licked across the skin, his saliva helping along her healing. Savannah's eyes closed, and she threw her head back. She moaned as Derrick continued, heat flowing down their mating bond.

"Enough, babe," she whispered.

Derrick stood and pulled her into his chest. "It's not healed all the way, but it will hold."

Carlos nodded. "Then let's go."

Everyone was loaded into the vans waiting for them. He looked at Theo who clutched his son and mate tight. He knew they would have to answer before the council for what they had done, but he couldn't find it in him to care at the moment. He guided his mate to the van where their cub was resting in his cousin's arms. Savannah pulled Jamie to her, tears streaming down her face. Her pain flooded their connection. He took their cub and cuddled him close, using his power to reassure him. Jamie rubbed his head under his chin, his thin arms clutching his neck tight.

He chuffed against the boy's neck, "You're okay."

Jamie gave him one final rubbed and turned and held his hands out to Carlos. The Felix cuddled the boy tight, murmuring to him. Alpha power filled the van and their mate shuddered next to him. He leaned over and kissed her temple.

Carlos passed Jamie back to his mother. He and Felix shared a look. He knew they would possibly get some sort of sanction for what they'd done. He would've done anything to make sure their cubs returned safely. Nothing the council could do or say would make him regret what they'd done this night.

Chapter 40

Savannah sat on the floor of Jamie's bedroom hours later, watching both children sleep. Ella had begged to sleep in her brother's room. They slept now cuddled with each other, held tight even in sleep.

She was numb. She'd kept up appearances as her family filtered in to see for themselves that the kids were safe. She'd held it together up until the point Greg and his wife had finally left with promises to check on their son in the morning. A warm shower had not helped thaw her feelings, nor had the pep talk from Charlotte and Naomi before they left.

Her son was home safe and that's all that mattered, but…she knew what needed to happen. It weighed on her, the decision. Toni was dead, she wouldn't cause them any more trouble, and yet, her words rang in Savannah's ear.

Toni said she knew what she knew. Savannah's latency would weaken the prowl, no matter her determination not to. She looked up at the quiet knock.

Derrick stood there, his arms crossed over his bare chest. "They're sleeping, babe, come rest. The healer ordered you to sleep, hours ago."

She wrapped her arms around her knees, hiding her wince as the skin of her stomach pulled. She looked back at the children. Would she be able to sleep? She doubted it. Seeing Jamie with the Alpha's claw at his throat would haunt her the rest of her life. She'd caused that. Derrick sighed and joined her on the floor. She avoided his gaze. He always saw too much. With Carlos, even if he knew something was wrong, he let her come to him. Not so with the Beta.

He wouldn't let her hide.

She couldn't go to him. Taking comfort in his arms would make what she had to do so much harder. If she left the children's room, she'd have to talk to her mates and let them know the decision she'd made. She stared at Ella. The little girl was as much a part of her as Jamie. Being her mother was something she was looking forward to. Tears escaped and she turned her head.

Sobs shook her shoulders and Derrick said nothing, simply put his hand on her back. The warmth of it nearly broke through the numbness. Derrick scooped her up, and pulled her into his lap. He still didn't say anything, and she couldn't talk through the tears. She watched the children sleep, her body trembling. She didn't know how long she cried, but soon exhaustion won.

Derrick held his mate, finally breathing once her body went slack with sleep. Something was wrong. She was pulling from them, he felt it, and his panther felt it. He just didn't know what to do about it, so he held her. He wondered if killing Antoinette had bothered her, but when he thought on it, she'd been pulling away from the moment she learned who'd been attacking the prowl.

Savannah told him what her aunt had told her so long ago. He compared that to what Antoinette said tonight. Savannah couldn't possibly think she wasn't strong enough to be the alpha female. She'd proved that and more when she killed the old Seer. The enforcers there had given their submission to her, surely she understood her place in the prowl was secure.

He thought about the carnage they'd left behind this night. A part of him felt guilt. He thought about his family's prowl and how easily they'd been wiped out. He knew how it felt to be in a small prowl. Carlos showed up in the doorway with a blanket and pillows.

"It's not the same, Beta." It was if Carlos read his mind.

"I can't help—"

"Your prowl was minding their business, Ella's as well. You had no control over racists destroying your prowls. These panthers came after *us*." Carlos' voice was raspy. He kneeled next to Derrick and touched their foreheads together. "They came after our family, Derrick, I'm not about to let you feel guilt for protecting what's ours."

He took a deep breath and took in the soothing energy from his Alpha. Carlos kissed Savannah's cheek in his lap, and stood. Derrick clutched their mate tighter, he was loathe to put her down. Carlos spread out multiple blankets and they settled on the floor of the children's room with their mate between them.

Sometime in the middle of the night, he'd carried their mate to bed. The next morning he leaned his head on his bent arm and watched her sleep. He sighed. Her body stiffened and the pulse at her neck sped.

"Jamie!" She sat up, breathing hard and fast.

He gripped her shoulder and sat up. "He's safe, babe," he whispered and pulled her back into his arms.

He kissed her neck, and murmured to her until her heart beat slowed and awareness slowly crept into her eyes. She looked at him, really seeing him and blinked.

"He's safe, love." He repeated and cocked his head. "From the sound of it, they're making breakfast."

She swallowed and nodded.

"Come."

He rolled from the other side of the bed and grabbed a robe and held it out to her. She rushed from beneath the blankets and turned her back to him, throwing her arms into the robe. She beat him out of the room, pausing at the top of the stairs. He watched her, leaned against the doorway of their room.

Jamie and Ella were sitting at the kitchen counter eating waffles. Carlos looked up and smiled. He inclined his head, beckoning their mate. She held up a finger and turned back towards their bedroom. She leaned into Derrick's chest and he encircled her in his arms. Her shoulders shook and tears wet his t-shirt.

"Everything will be fine, love." He whispered.

She nodded, but her tears didn't stop. He pulled her back into their room and sat on the edge of the bed with her in his lap. She shuddered after a few moments.

"Ready to go downstairs?"

She sighed. "Let me wash my face first."

He released her and stood to change his shirt. He looked up as alpha power preceded Carlos.

"What is it?" Derrick asked.

Carlos waved the phone his face grim. "Emergency council meeting."

He growled and Savannah rushed out of the bathroom.

"Now?"

Carlos nodded.

Savannah's eyes widened and narrowed. "I'm coming with you, but I need to make a phone call first."

Chapter 41

Carlos stood in the middle of the room, the alphas on the Florida council all staring in judgement. He clenched his hands, fighting down his panther. He was pissed, and not really having the stores of patience he normally would.

He'd spent the night consoling his mates, helping them fight through nightmares and to say he was on edge was an understatement. He'd left Savannah in the car, talking rapidly to someone on her cellphone and his Beta stood beside him, Derrick's anger a hot lash at Carlos' side. His best friend snarled under breath.

Brianne stood in front of them along with Theo, speaking for their prowl. His liaisons were good, their argument for their decisions sound. But, he had a feeling Yasim had a lot more friends on the council than he did, so they would make sure his prowl suffered.

"They didn't even know that prowl existed two weeks ago, now their affronted on their behalf." Derrick growled.

Theo turned and shot them a look. Derrick clamped his mouth shut.

"A debt is owed to the remaining prowl members. You killed their alpha, along with a lot of their stronger enforcers. They'll be helpless until they can regroup." The East coast Alpha stated.

"And I'm sure you lot don't plan on divvying up their little bit of territory amongst yourself." Carlos growled.

"Well…" they huffed.

Yasim waved away his words. "It's our duty to take care of the disbanded prowl. Recompense is owed."

The doors opened and his panther leapt in joy as his mate stormed into the room.

"They're lucky we didn't burn their shit to the ground." Savannah declared.

Behind his mate were alphas from other species, their powers filling the already testosterone laden room. Bear, wolves, and he inhaled…lions. They entered and with them, their power. They all nodded at Carlos, a wary, but respectful greeting.

"We will be intervening on behalf of the Tampa prowl." The bear announced.

Brianne stepped back to Carlos. "The high council." she whispered.

One panther stood from his chair. "You can't do that."

"We are doing that," the wolf alpha lazily sauntered to an empty chair and slouched into it.

The bear sat as well. "Where are we in the proceedings?"

Awe filled him at Savannah's feat. So that's what she was doing on the phone.

She gave them both a pleading look for understanding, but walked past them. "If you reward this prowl with even a tiny square footage of our territory then it will embolden the next prowl."

"You should pay for what you did. And no amount of smooth talking from that one should get you out of it." Yasim pointed at Brianne.

"They should pay for breaking the sanctity of our children's school. Do you want the next hungry prowl to use your child in a bid for your land?" Savannah asked.

A few of the Alphas shuffled uncomfortably. Carlos watched his mate in pride and hunger.

"Our children also go to that school, and I'm to understand that the prowl in question went onto school grounds and kidnapped the alpha's child?" The bear asked.

"It's not even his child," Yasim spoke up.

Carlos growled, his panther riled. "That's the last time you speak about my son."

The wolf smirked.

The bear slammed his hand on the table. "That prowl violated the safety of the school, a school I will remind you that has been declared off limits and one where all of our children go. As far as I'm concerned, the Tampa prowl set a stunning example of what happens when our children are fucked with."

The wolf, smiled, his canines low. "I vote for no punishment."

A panther alpha snarled. "This council has decided."

"And this council will overrule it. We're not willing to let our children's school become a battle ground. A truce was laid out, that school and our children were to be off limits." The bear's power flexed, accompanying his statement.

Yasim scoffed. "They can't take out an entire prowl, that's a precedent that shouldn't be set."

Savannah opened her mouth, but Brianne squeezed her hand and spoke up. "We didn't 'take out' an entire prowl. We went in to get our cubs, they fought and unfortunately there were casualties. The ones who kidnapped our cubs were punished."

"It's not your place to punish." Yasim sneered.

Brianne stood taller. "It's my Fela's place to do anything she felt right for the safety and well-being of our prowl."

Derrick's gaze didn't leave their mate. His eyes devoured her, his panther damn near purring in his subconscious. The alphas around the room argued back and forth about punishment but he only had eyes for Savannah. She'd walked into the room, her Fela power around her like a mantle. In that moment he let go of any lingering doubts he had. He finally had the family he craved, and a strong prowl in which to protect them.

"Who gives a fuck what the high council has to say on this?" Yasim's voice cut into his thoughts.

The whole of the high council turned as one to face Yasim.

"You wanna repeat that," the lion said, his voice bringing power into the room.

Carlos raised his hand. "Gentlemen, let's not get into a power match. My prowl will not pay a cent of recompense for what was done. As my mate said, allowing them to get away with stealing our children sets a dangerous precedent."

Derrick held his hand out and his mate grabbed it hastily. The touch of her skin against his soothed him. He closed his eyes.

"I don't regret a second of it," Savannah stepped forward, clutching his hand tight. "They deserved to die. Now the next person who even thinks of threatening our children will think twice." She looked directly to Yasim.

"The high council agrees. This meeting is adjourned." The bear announced and the high council stood as one and walked out.

Carlos waited until the door closed. He grabbed Savannah's other hand. "We may be a new prowl, but I promise you, don't wanna keep trying us."

He turned with that threat and they all walked out. Savannah's feet moved fast as she struggled to keep up with the Felix's long stride.

"That was close," Savannah whispered as they took the elevator down.

Carlos merely grunted. Derrick waited until they were in the parking lot before he turned to face his mate.

He cupped her cheek. "Why do you have contacts on the high council?"

She grabbed his wrist and kissed it. "You'd be surprised what kind of contacts I have."

"Not here," Carlos growled, obviously still peeved about the proceedings.

Derrick helped Savannah into the back seat and they took off for home.

The ride was quiet but the tension and energy was heavy in the car. By the time they got to the prowl house, Derrick's hands were shaking with impatience, his panther shredding his insides to come out. He took a shaky breath. As soon as the elevator doors closed, he was shedding his clothes. Savannah squealed and backed against the wall.

"Don't run, mate. Clothes. Off. Now." Derrick unsnapped his pants and stalked to their mate. He had just enough to control to keep his claws sheathed.

Carlos growled and crossed his arms over his chest, leaning against the wall across from them.

"We're doing this here?" She was breathless.

"Hit the button, Alpha." Derrick ordered.

"With pleasure." Carlos slapped the emergency stop on the elevator.

Savi squealed again as it jerked to a halt.

"Clothes, mate." Carlos growled.

She stripped quickly, and with every article of clothing she threw off, Derrick's panther slammed against his subconscious. She gave him a coy look from beneath her lowered lashes and he squeezed his cock to keep from releasing. He growled, long and low, and Savannah's nipples beaded.

"Fuck yeah," Carlos whispered.

Derrick leaned over their mate, dragging his gaze over her body. "Do you have any idea how hot it is watching you throw your weight around?"

She shook her head, her chest heaving as she panted. The scent of her arousal scented the elevator car. Felix's phone rang.

"We're fine," was all Carlos said before ending the call and shoving the phone back into his pocket.

Savannah went up on her toes and kissed Derrick, her tongue spearing into his mouth. He lifted her and fit his cock right at her entrance.

"Yes?" He dragged his tongue across their mating mark.

"Please," she panted.

Derrick entered her in one stroke, hissing as she clenched around his length. God, the feel of her. Savannah threw her head back and moaned. He trailed kisses down the front of her body, raking his canines against her skin. He braced them against the wall and he drove into her, gripping her thighs. He ground against her clit with his every stroke, swallowing Savannah's gasps. Her power rose up, and his panther reacted. His teeth grew in his mouth, fur rippling up and down his arm. He moved his hips faster needing more.

Savannah arched her back, her nails digging into his shoulder. His Beta power brushed against her power and she mewled, her sex flexing, tightening around his cock. Their movements were frantic, their kisses rougher as he deepened his strokes.

"Harder." She whispered.

He snarled, all too happy to oblige his mate. His chest rumbled as she bit the side of his neck. Their power danced in the space between them, and he lost it. Savannah threw back her head and he gripped her throat between his teeth. The orgasm that rocked through him stole his breath and sent electric shocks across his skin. His mate screamed and her sex locked on him, weakening his knees.

"Shit, shit, shit," He panted, pumping into her, prolonging their orgasm.

His legs buckled and the two of them tumbled to the floor. Savannah laughed, trailing kisses across his face.

"You're going to kill me." He gulped in air, his heart thundering.

Carlos chuckled next to them, holding out his hand. Derrick gently pulled out of Savannah and pushed her up into his co-mate's arms. Carlos cradled her against his chest, and kissed her. She wrapped her arms around the Alpha's neck and Derrick watched from the floor.

"My turn," Carlos whispered.

"In the bed if you please." Savannah nibbled against his lips.

Derrick snorted.

Carlos hit the button to restart the elevator. "Fine."

***

The next evening was life back to normal, or what they could call normal. Savannah sighed in happiness. She sipped her tea, standing at the stove. Dinner was scenting the air, and everything she held dear in her world surrounded her. Derrick was at the kitchen table frowning over 'new math' as he helped the kids with homework and Carlos had his own work spread on the other side of the table.

She would do anything to preserve the scene, to keep those close to her safe. Two days ago she'd given serious thought to running away. To leaving the prowl again, all in the slim chance that her aunt's prophecy would come true. But yesterday, seeing Carlos take care of her son, watching Jamie interact with Ella, made her realize how foolish it would've been.

And pointless.

There was no way she could stay away from Carlos and Derrick. Her body was deliciously sore in all the right places. Her mates had put their mark on every part of her body, renewing their claim. She was lucky and she wouldn't take it for granted again.

Heaven forbid the next person to mess with their family. Everyone turned to her as her power rose, filling the kitchen. Derrick purred, and Carlos growled.

"What in the world were you thinking of, just now?" Derrick arched a brow.

She smiled and shrugged. "I'm thinking sage for the walls."

Carlos stood and walked to her, his arms banding around her waist. "Paint color, that's what you're thinking about?"

His power reached out and surrounded her, his panther flexing against her own power. It did delicious things to her body. She set her tea cup down and kissed him.

"You don't like sage?" She teased.

"I don't care what color you paint the walls, love." He murmured against her lips.

"I want blue for my bedroom," Jamie called out.

"Oh, can I do purple?" Ella asked.

Carlos grinned at her, and happiness, a soul deep happiness settled over Savannah. She thought about how far she'd come. She'd nearly given them up. She would never be that stupid again.

Epilogue

Savannah walked through the prowl gathering, a baby belonging to her cousin on her hip. It was a full gathering, with close to ninety panthers in attendance. They were celebrating both Christmas and the return of their cubs, and the fact that they'd gotten rid of the threat. She worried that the panther council could still come back and punish them in some way for the way they'd handled the other prowl, but she put it aside. They would deal with whatever the council tried to throw at them.

Smoke was churning from the grills, despite how cold it was outside. The smell of cooking meats and vegetables made her stomach grumble. She needed to eat, but she was content to wander the meeting area and soak up the vibe of those gathered. Her connection to Derrick and Carlos deepened each day, and with it, her connection to the prowl.

"It's good, right?" Naomi's quiet voice washed over her.

"It is, Nay." She whispered, letting her cousin's voice calm her further.

It had only been a couple weeks since Naomi had been added to the prowl's link, but in that time, her Zeta power had done as Joelle predicted and stabilized the prowl. A sense of contentment pervaded the link.

"Did you imagine we would be in the prowl again?" Naomi reached out and grabbed the baby from her, and cooed at the cute little girl.

"No, but I'm so glad we have. I feel whole." She looked around at the prowl.

Her grandfathers were manning the grill, there were kids running around screaming and playing and her mates were…

She narrowed her eyes. Where were they?

Naomi chuckled. "I was instructed to come get the baby, and tell you to meet them at grandma's."

Her heartbeat picked up and she smiled. She had a feeling she knew what they wanted. She waved at her cousin and rushed towards her grandparents' home.

***

He watched her from within his panther. He moved stealthily through the brush surrounding the house, keeping his body low to the ground. He chuffed a signal to the Alpha hunting with him.

They weren't hunting rabbit, no, their prey was of the human variety. She stood on the porch of her grandparents, her tight jeans showing him miles of legs. They moved closer to the porch, hidden in the bushes. Her body tensed, her senses alerting her to the fact that she was hunted.

She stretched her arms, and rolled her neck, the skin of her stomach peeking from the bottom of her sweater. He swallowed a growl, and moved, knowing he'd be rewarded for his patience. She preened, her steps seductive as she moved to the edge of the porch. Her hips swayed as she descended the wooden steps.

A growl escaped the Alpha, and her lips turned up into a knowing smile. His heartbeat picked up its rhythm, excited that their mate would play with them. Adrenaline spiked and his panther became anxious, its steps quicker through the brush. She walked slowly to the edge of the bushes. He tracked the direction she would run and moved to intercept. She smiled again, the devilish tilt to her mouth making him hungry. In that one moment of distraction, she took off in the opposite direction.

Carlos shot off after her, his panther damn near euphoric. Savannah grew up in these woods so she knew them well and gave them a hell of a chase. He whistled and Derrick cut to the left of him to cut their mate off. He ruffled the foliage purposefully letting her know they were gaining on her. She laughed and picked up her speed. He moved in closer, brushing across her legs before disappearing again into the brush. Derrick herded her to the left and she sprinted in that direction. He knew where his co mate was guiding her.

Soon, the cabin where they'd sealed their bond came into focus. She jumped on the porch and squealed when he jumped after her. She raced in and made it to the bedroom before Derrick clipped her legs and she ended up on the bed, splayed, her sides shaking in laughter. He shifted and growled. Her laughter stopped, and her smiled turned wicked. She crawled backwards on the bed until she reached the headboard.

He knelt on the bed and crawled on top of her. "I've decided that I like chasing you."

Derrick lifted her upper body and slid under her. "I agree, I like chasing Savannah," he murmured and licked a line up their mate's neck.

"Now that you've caught me, what do you plan to do with me?"

Carlos gave her a smile that had her eyes widening, along with her legs. Her arousal scented the small cabin and he purred. He'd show her rather than tell.

About the Author

I am a full time photographer, and a mom of two. I've been writing my whole life, and after the birth of my first kid, I decided I couldn't very well bring up a fearless human without first trying the things that scared me. So, I wrote my first book, and then subsequently more.

I try to write stories I love to read: love stories that feature brown girls like me. Some of my stories feature gods and goddesses, and creatures I derived from old, African folk tales remixed and thrust into a modern world. Visit my website, www.driaandersen.com for more information on my other novels.

Other titles by Dria Andersen

Destiny Series

A Destiny Awakened

A Destiny Revealed

Haven Series

Haven

Soul Bonded